A Paula S

Susan Calder

TouchWood
Editions

TouchWood Editions
www.touchwoodeditions.com

Library and Archives Canada Cataloguing in Publication
Calder, Susan, 1951–
Deadly fall / Susan Calder.

Print format: ISBN 978-1-926741-18-5 (bound).—ISBN 978-1-926741-19-2 (pbk.)
Electronic monograph in PDF format: ISBN 978-1-926741-36-9
Electronic monograph in HTML format: ISBN 978-1-926741-37-6

I. Title.

PS8605.A4568D43 2011   C813'.6   C2010-906340-6

Editor: Frances Thorsen
Proofreader: Lenore Hietkamp
Design and cover illustration: Pete Kohut
Leaf texture: Irina14, stock.xchng
Author photo: Leap Frog Photography

We gratefully acknowledge the financial support for our publishing activities
from the Government of Canada through the Canada Book Fund, Canada
Council for the Arts, and the province of British Columbia through the
British Columbia Arts Council and the Book Publishing Tax Credit.

The interior pages of this book have been printed on 100% post-consumer
recycled paper, processed chlorine free, and printed with vegetable-based inks.

1 2 3 4 5 14 13 12 11

PRINTED IN CANADA

To Will, Dan, and Matt, with love.

Chapter One

Yellow tape cordoned off the entrance to the Elbow River trail. Behind it, a policeman stood guard. He talked to the spectators crowding the sidewalk. Paula stopped at the railway crossing and lowered her passenger side window. She strained to hear the conversation above the freight train's roar. "Body . . . morning . . ."

With a clang, the railway barriers lifted. Her car bumped over the tracks. A crime scene van was parked in front of the entrance to the second pathway, also barricaded with tape. Men in coveralls squatted to search the grass.

She rested her elbow on the car's window frame. A warm breeze licked her skin. Steering away from the sun, she drove down 8th Street. Two turns brought her to her side street of clapboard and stucco bungalows set into tiny front yards. She parked in front of her neighbor's pickup truck. She should clear the junk from her garage before snow arrived. In Calgary that could be next week.

Her neighbor, Walter, rocked on his porch, enjoying a pre-dinner smoke. He would want to chat. All she wanted to do was strip off her business clothes, eat dinner, and go for a walk. She grabbed her sweater, purse, and take-out salad from the passenger's seat. No laptop or briefcase tonight. She had left them at work so she wouldn't be tempted to review any claims.

"You're home," Walter called from the porch. "The wife and I noticed your car was gone overnight."

She squeezed between her trunk's bumper and his pickup. Nosey neighbors were another reason to clean out the garage, so she could come home by the back lane.

Walter dropped his cigarette butt over the railing. "I put your newspaper behind the screen door so burglars wouldn't know you were away."

"Thanks." She rested her hand on her iron gate. If she asked him about the police tape at the trail entrance, it would give him an opening to talk.

He made his way down his steps, holding onto the railing. "What do you think of all the excitement?"

She glanced west, toward the Elbow River. "You mean over by the railroad bridge? What's going on?"

"It's been on the radio all day. I heard it first thing when I got up." He stopped in the middle of his yard, squinted at her, took a deep breath, and said, "A woman was shot."

"What?"

"Killed."

"When?"

"On the river path, a few feet this side of the bridge." He scratched his whisker stubble. "A man riding his bicycle to work found her. The wife and I walked over. Cops were everywhere, taking pictures."

"Good God. Is it related to that killing a few weeks ago?" The body of a prostitute had been discovered farther down the trail; much farther down.

"At first, the wife and I were scared the woman was you, since you didn't come home last night. The radio said she looked to be about your age, early forties."

She was fifty-two. Trust him to fish for personal information.

"At the scene, we heard a man say the victim had long, blond hair and the wife said, 'That can't be Paula, her hair is short and dark.'" He checked his watch. "The news'll be on in twenty minutes. They'll have more details."

"I better get in, so I don't miss it."

Walter looked at her take-out bag. "What's cooking?"

"Greek salad." Olive oil seeped through the paper. She held it away from her silk shirt.

"You call that dinner?" he said. "Careful locking up, in case there's a mass murderer on the loose."

"They think it's related, then?" She shuddered. "A serial killing?"

"Feeling sorry you moved here?" He grinned. "You could ask your boyfriend to bunk in with you."

Asshole. She opened her gate and crunched over fallen leaves. Walter's presence next door and airplanes flying overhead were her only regrets about her choice of neighborhood. She hoped the murder wouldn't change that view. During her month of living here, she had enjoyed Ramsay's urban character, even the street people who slept in abandoned lots and prowled her back lane for bottles and cans. She left them her empties beside the garage. As for inviting Hayden to "bunk in," they were far from ready for that.

She collected the letters and flyers from her mailbox and opened the screen door. The newspaper tumbled out. "Hostage escapes Iraqi beheading," the headline read. The local murder would have been discovered after the paper went to press.

Inside, she kicked off her high heels, sniffing the fresh paint smell, and plunked her salad on the ottoman tray. She flicked the remote control to the channel that featured local news at six o'clock, after *Entertainment Report.*

She brushed her bangs back from her sweaty brow. Sun poured through the living room windows. Dust hovered in the beams of light. The house had been closed up for over a day. Should she open the windows with a murderer on the loose? Screw Walter and his attempts to rattle her. The streets were safe, and she wasn't stupid enough to walk on the trail at night. She cranked open a window, inhaled the scent of dry leaves, and padded across the hardwood to the kitchen. The answering machine flashed five messages. She pressed the play button.

Hi Paula, it's Callie—She forwarded through her friend's old message and then played two blank ones. They were probably from telemarketers. The fourth caller was her ex-husband. *Hey, it's Gary. I heard about the murder in your new neighborhood. I hope it hasn't shaken you up. If you feel like it, give me a shout. Talk to you later.* Hayden's voice followed. *If I work tomorrow night, I'll be free Saturday. Are you up for tennis?*

She deleted the blank messages as well as Gary's. "Talk to you later" was his habitual signoff. He didn't expect her to return the call and phoning his house was useless. His girlfriend always answered, said Gary was busy, and rarely passed along the message.

She left Hayden's and Callie's messages on the machine as reminders to return the calls. She should have phoned Callie days ago, but had been occupied with Hayden, work, and enjoying this burst of summer-like weather, all of which were more appealing than listening to Callie prattle about her perfect life.

In her bedroom, she placed her shirt on the dresser to be hand-washed, peeled off her bra, and slid down her nylons and skirt. Her skin breathing freely, she put on shorts and a T-shirt and opened the windows. Low-hanging sunlight splashed her poplar tree. Its leaves fluttered emerald, gold, and sienna against a clear, blue sky.

Callie's perfect life. It was petty to resent it, when her life was going reasonably well. Her job adjusting insurance claims paid for her needs and wants and she enjoyed the challenge of negotiating with claimants, at times. Her daughters were independent and content, even if the eldest was living with a jerk and squandering her talents working as a barmaid. Like Callie, Paula had a new romance. She wondered if it was going somewhere, or not? That was a topic to discuss when she met Callie for lunch. And Callie must have a lot to tell her, since Callie had been too busy this summer to return any phone messages. They hadn't talked since April, after Paula had slept with Hayden for the first time. Paula had described the event as less than stellar and Callie replied, "The important thing, kid, is that after five post-Gary years, you got yourself laid."

Paula smiled, missing their conversations. She would definitely call tonight.

"Martha Stewart," a TV voice blared through the bedroom wall. "Household guru . . . prison . . . lying."

The clock radio indicated enough time before the news to get a drink. Paula hurried to the kitchen, uncorked the bottle and filled a glass with red wine—good for her aging heart. She carried the glass to the living room and settled on the sofa. A commercial followed the Martha Stewart story. She removed the lid of the take-out bowl, mixed the olive oil into the greens, cucumbers, tomatoes, black olives and feta cheese, and scanned her wall unit full of DVDs and videos. If there was time tonight, she would treat herself to a movie, popcorn, and a second glass of wine, doubly good for the heart. She speared a tomato wedge.

Two news anchors appeared on the screen. Behind them, sunlight bounced off the Calgary skyline with its landmark tower.

The male anchor spoke. "A woman was murdered early this morning on the Elbow River pathway. The hostage drama in Iraq ends happily . . ." An airplane roared overhead. ". . . what to do with the government of Alberta's two billion dollar surplus."

The camera zoomed in on the female anchor. "Tonight's top story: A Calgary woman was shot to death on the Elbow River Pathway. A morning bicycle commuter discovered the body near the Canadian Pacific Railway Bridge in the inner city Ramsay neighborhood. Police estimate the time of death to be between 3:00 and 7:00 AM. Fiona Terry is at the site."

A breeze ruffling her hair, Fiona spoke into a microphone. Behind her, people milled in front of the taped-off trail entrance. The auto body shop and pathway sign framed the scene. While Paula nibbled a feta-smeared olive, Fiona repeated the news capsule and added, "Police have now identified the woman as Calandra Moss. Moss is the wife of prominent architect Sam Moss."

Paula stopped chewing. Her fork dropped to the bowl.

Chapter Two

Morning light illuminated the crabapple tree outside her kitchen window. Paula gulped coffee, hoping the caffeine would jumpstart her into motion. She hadn't slept more than an hour last night. Every time she closed her eyes, she pictured gawking spectators, policemen, and news anchors telling her Callie was dead. She had finally drifted off, to be awakened by a hang-up phone call, her first one since moving to this house. Strange it should happen today.

Were the spectators and police still at the murder site? Did yellow tape still seal off the trail? She would check on her way to work. If she had driven to the office from her home yesterday, rather than from Hayden's, she would have seen commotion by the trail. Would she have stopped and learned about Callie earlier? She drove by that spot daily and must have walked the Elbow pathway a dozen times.

She refreshed her mug, smoothed the newspaper on the table and stared at the front page. "Woman murdered in Ramsay." Below the headline was a large color photo of the crime scene unit scouring the site. Within the article was a wallet-sized portrait of Callie smiling straight at the camera looking happy and closer to thirty-two than fifty-two years old, the way she had looked for the past twenty years. Last October, they met for lunch. Callie had spent the morning shopping for a vacation to Hawaii, where she was going to marry her new love, Sam. During dessert, she took out the bikini she had bought. Paula joked about its skimpiness, saying she hadn't worn an outfit like that since her twenties. Callie was still slim enough to pull it off. She had held up the bra top. The orange and yellow sunset pattern heightened the brown tones of her eyes and hair. She had said, "Won't this suit look awesome with a tropical tan?"

In the newspaper portrait, Callie's frizzy hair looked blond. Was that a fault in the print or had she lightened it this past year?

Paula removed her reading glasses to get a clearer view of the sunrise outside. The thermometer on the garage said forty-six degrees Fahrenheit. It would shoot up to sixty-eight this afternoon.

She got a yogurt for breakfast. The answering machine showed "01" message remaining. Thank God she hadn't replaced the ancient pre-digital contraption, so she could save the tape of Callie's voice. Like her friend's appearance, the voice was youthful. For the dozenth time since the news report, she pressed "play" to hear the rapid, high-pitched tones. *Hi Paula, it's Callie. Long time since we've had lunch. Are you free this week? I want to hear all about your move to Ramsay. There are some new restaurants near there that might be fun to try. Give me a call tomorrow.* The voice existed no more.

Callie had jogged the Elbow River pathway that led to Paula's house. The route snaked from the home she had purchased with Sam, whom Paula had never met. During the past two years, Callie had arranged several dinners that were canceled because something came up at Sam's work. He was an architect who had left for the States in the mid 1980s. Ten years ago, he returned to Calgary and resumed his friendship with Callie's first husband, Kenneth. Eight years later, love happened between Callie and him. Callie had been vague about the details.

How did Kenneth feel about his wife running off with his old pal? Callie had said, "You know how Kenneth is. He doesn't reveal much." Right now, Kenneth would be feeling broken or numb. And Callie's children must be in shock. Her son lived in Vancouver, but, no doubt, would come home. Her daughter, Skye, shared an apartment with theater friends in Calgary.

Paula dug her spoon into the yogurt and stirred in the apricot chunks. She wasn't up to food, or anything else today. Last night, when she called Hayden, he had advised her to throw herself into work to take her mind off the murder. She couldn't bring herself to do that and rescheduled her afternoon and evening meetings to next week. One benefit of her insurance adjusting job was being in control of her time. Hayden had also offered to come over and spend the night, but in a voice so tired, she insisted she was fine. He never slept well when he was with her, so last night he needed to catch up on his rest. The ring of the telephone startled her.

"Mom?" Leah said.

The wall clock showed seven thirty-five. Her daughter never called at this hour. Paula's stomach tightened. She couldn't take more bad news. "You're up early."

"I haven't been to bed. When I got home from work, I got to talking with Jarrett and some friends he had over. Mom, there was a murder yesterday, near where you live."

"I know. I—"

"It was Callie Moss."

"Yes."

"Why didn't you call me? I can't believe it."

"Me neither." Paula leaned against the telephone stand. Last night, she hadn't felt like talking to anyone except Hayden. "I'm surprised you remembered Callie's new surname."

"At the bar, people were discussing the murder, but I never connected her to you until this morning, when I heard her name on the radio. I recognized it because we went to that play Skye was in and we were talking about Callie's hotshot husband. Mom, this is horrible. You must feel awful."

"I don't think it's sunk in yet." Paula's legs wobbled and she slumped to a kitchen chair.

"I was thinking about that week I spent with Callie and Skye in Palm Springs," Leah said.

"I forgot you and Skye used to be good friends. I should have called you—"

"One night we all went out to see this grunge band," Leah said. "Callie got into it, singing along with the music. I mean, how many people her age got grunge?"

"Not many." Paula coiled her bathrobe sash around her fingers. A cigarette would taste so good. She hadn't craved one in years.

"Callie told us she was in a rock group when she was young."

"They were more like folk rock—"

"Does Dad know she was killed? When I talked to him yesterday, he didn't say anything."

"Your father left me a message. He heard about the murder. I don't know if—"

"I was thinking I'd give Skye a call later," Leah said.

"I'm sure she'd appreciate that."

"Didn't Callie live in Mount Royal?"

"She did when she was married to Kenneth. Last year, Callie bought a house in Riverdale with Sam. Why do you ask?"

"Both are a long way from Ramsay. What was she doing there?"

"Jogging, apparently. The Elbow path runs from Riverdale to Ramsay."

"Was she coming to see you?"

"At that hour in the morning? She knows me better than that." Callie's picture in the newspaper stared up at her: smiling, carefree, unaware of what was to come. "I've been wondering. It's possible she wanted to catch me before I left for work. A few days ago, Callie left a message suggesting we meet for lunch. She sounded casual, but what if she wanted to discuss something important? I didn't return her call. I meant to. I wish I had. There's no excuse." Her voice croaked.

Leah yawned. "I've gotta get to bed. Mom, I am sorry about Callie"

Paula massaged her throat. What if Leah was knifed tonight while working at the bar or walking home on a deserted street?

"Be careful," she said as they signed off. "I love you."

The line was silent. Her daughters weren't used to hearing endearments from her for no reason.

"Yeah," Leah said.

"Bye, honey." Paula set the phone in its cradle. It rang under her hand.

"Have you heard . . . ?" Anne, her fitness partner, said.

"About Callie?"

"I'm in shock."

"Me too."

"I found out this morning, from a woman at the center. I can't believe a whole day has gone by without my knowing it."

Anne's fitness center business consumed her life. She spent fourteen-hour days on the premises and got most of her news from the center's TVs.

"What time are you coming in today?" Anne said.

Paula's arms ached at the prospect of lifting weights. "I have a ton of work . . ."

"I can't believe it." Anne's voice quivered. "Callie was so full of life."

Anne was Callie's long-time friend, too. Callie had introduced them. Anne would be going through the same thing as Paula.

"I'll aim for mid-afternoon," Paula said.

"Two o'clock?"

"Three, at the latest."

"I'll keep those hours open." Anne said she had to leave to deal with the machine maintenance man.

Paula poured the remains from the coffee carafe into her mug. Outside, a squirrel nibbled a sour apple on the tree. Next spring, Paula would build a new deck or lay patio stones between the kitchen and tree. Grass seed would spruce up her backyard, which was mostly crabgrass and dirt. She put on her reading glasses. *The body . . . discovered . . . 7:00 AM.*

Moss was known locally for her charity work. She co-chaired the 1997 Fundraiser for Children with Cancer. Sam Moss is an internationally renowned architect. Her former husband, Kenneth Unsworth, president and CEO of Unsworth Oil Ltd., was twice honored as Calgary's entrepreneur of the year. She leaves a son, Cameron Unsworth, an award-winning graphic artist, and a daughter, Skye Ravenshaw, a Calgary actress and winner of this year's Betty award for supporting actress.

Family members reported that Moss was in the habit of going out alone for morning jogs. "We're both early risers," Sam Moss told police. "I work out most days in the basement before work. I assumed Callie was jogging through our neighborhood. It never occurred to me that she would run on the (Elbow River) pathway before dawn."

He wasn't surprised when his wife didn't return home for breakfast. "I saw no reason to worry about her being out at that hour. I've always considered Calgary to be a safe city." He didn't report her missing.

An autopsy will be performed today. Preliminary evidence shows no indication of struggle or sexual assault. Homicide police are investigating.

No sexual assault, thank God, but what was the motive? Robbery? You wouldn't expect a jogger to carry much cash.

Strange that the article mentioned Callie's old volunteer work and made no reference to her current pursuit of a masters degree in music. Yet it highlighted Sam's, Kenneth's, Cameron's, and Skye's achievements. Callie was more than the wife of two alpha men and the mother of alpha children.

Sam hadn't realized his wife was missing. The police must have shown up at his office with the dreadful news and taken him to the morgue to identify the body. It had probably fallen to him to contact Callie's children, her sister in Toronto, her brother in Montreal, any close friends, and possibly her ex-husband Kenneth.

Paula had to call Sam. The article said he was an early riser, but he might be sleeping late after a troubled night. First, she would shower and dress, then phone Gary at his office. Her ex would want to know that the murder victim was their friend.

She got Gary's voice mail. "Thanks for phoning last night," she said. "Yes, the murder has shaken me up. Call if you want to talk."

She tried Sam's house next. To her surprise, a woman answered.

"He's not in," the woman said. "Who's calling?" Callie's voice.

It was all a mistake. Another body had been falsely identified. Callie was alive. Don't be stupid.

"Is anyone there?" the young woman said.

"Skye? Is that you?"

"Uh huh."

"It . . . it's Paula. Paula Savard, your mother's friend."

"You and a hundred others."

"Pardon?"

"Now that she's dead, people are phoning non-stop, claiming they were her friends. Why weren't you there for her when she was alive?"

The answering machine's "01" message stared up at Paula. If she had returned that Monday call, she and Callie might have met for lunch and Callie might have told her . . . what?

"Skye, I'm so sorry about your mother," she said. "The last time I saw her was at your play. Congratulations, by the way, on the Betty award. I phoned Callie when I heard. She wasn't home. I left a—"

"Look, Paula, I can't chat with you now. We're up to our fucking ears in funeral arrangements."

Paula's stomach knotted. "Are you staying with Sam?"

"Why would I do that?" The voice was Callie's with an edge.

"I thought, maybe—"

"My aunt drags me over here to discuss funerals, and then Sam buggers off."

The knot tightened. "Will he be back soon?"

"He didn't say."

"I'll leave my number for him to call. Do you have a paper and pen?" Skye's aunt would be Callie's sister. Paula hadn't seen her in twenty years. The funeral might be too formal and pressured for a genuine talk. "Will there be a visitation?"

"We decided not to go through with that." Skye's voice drifted from the

11

phone. "Where the fuck do they keep pens around here?"

Paula looked out at the garage thermometer. It was already pushing toward sixty degrees.

"Never mind," she said. "I'll come over for a short visit. Will you be there this afternoon?"

"Not me."

"Will your aunt?"

"I don't imagine she's going anywhere."

"Sam?"

"Who knows about him?" There was a bite to the tone.

Clearly, Skye was not impressed with Sam's behavior. His "buggering off" was odd. Or it might not be. People expressed grief differently. Lashing out was typical of Skye, who had inherited her mother's voice and delicate features, but not her temperament. Skye and Callie had often clashed, but Callie had been proud of her daughter's spirit. It was natural that Skye would be upset by her mother's shocking death and annoyed by ghoulish public interest.

Paula had promised Anne she'd be at the fitness center this afternoon, but could postpone that to the evening. Meanwhile, she had to get to work.

Seated at her office desk, Paula skimmed the hit-and-run claim that had come in this morning. Damage along the vehicle's right side. Time of accident: 11:50 PM. Driver states it was too dark and happened too fast for him to identify that car that sideswiped him. Minor whiplash.

Paula phoned for the police report; she called an appraiser to inspect the vehicle at the garage and left a message on the claimant's voice mail to arrange a meeting. A junior adjuster could have handled that. She would talk to Nils, her boss, again and insist he hire the next good candidate who came along. It wasn't fair of him to saddle her with routine work, while he grabbed the fun claims for himself. Right now, Nils was at a construction site examining a building that had collapsed.

She moved on to the liability claim: a neighbor fell off the homeowner's roof. Neither the insured nor the claimant had returned her Tuesday call. *Shit.* A junior adjuster would have followed it up. Nils' fussiness was dragging the business down. The claimant sustained a concussion, broken arm, and bruised ribs. What was he doing on the roof? The file didn't say.

One story or two? The fall could have resulted in worse, so much worse. He was lucky.

Unlike Callie. She'd had no luck, at the end. Paula rapped her pen on the folder. From her bookshelf, Hayden and her daughters gazed from photographs. In Paula's favourite one, Leah's head leaned into Erin's, dark hair against fair, hazel eyes and blue. They were laughing, loving sisters, for the moment, despite their differences and frequent scraps. Paula had no sister. Callie was as close to a sister as she would get. Now Callie was gone. Forever. The end. Paula blinked and swallowed tears.

Chapter Three

The murder site looked benign. No marks marred the pavement or earth. Shrubs lined the ridge that dropped to the Elbow River. Their jade leaves glistened in the afternoon sun; limbs swayed in the warm breeze. Across the river gorge, the Saddledome's curved roof embraced the sky.

A pair of cyclists coasted down the slope. Paula stepped aside to let them pass. Last evening, she had walked to the blocked-off pathway entrance. The police refused to tell her anything. A spectator had heard the murder took place behind the auto body shop, which would have been closed when Callie died. A poplar grove obscured the view from a hilltop house, the only residence in the area. Witnesses to the murder were unlikely. The spectator didn't know if Callie had been shot in the chest or back. Had the killer crept up behind her? Had she heard footsteps getting closer and whirled around? Or had she jogged toward someone who appeared normal, like this couple walking down the slope, holding hands?

Paula nodded hello.

"Lovely afternoon," the gray-haired pair said.

A roller-blader wove between the three of them. The weather was drawing a good crowd for a Friday afternoon. On dreary days, this stretch of trail behind the Stampede grounds was deserted. What had Callie been thinking, jogging here alone in darkness?

Paula picked up her pace to get some exercise, even though she would get more later on the fitness center machines. She couldn't wait to hear Anne's take on the murder. Unlike her, Anne was acquainted with Sam, being his former girlfriend and mother of his son.

She passed some wildflowers sprouting by the trail. Why hadn't she thought to bring the family flowers? She detoured off the trail into Mission, a trendy neighborhood she had considered moving to until she discovered the price of its homes. Ramsay was a relative bargain and, according to her real estate agent, poised to take off. Artists and professionals were replacing aging working class residents, like her neighbor, Walter, whom she had managed to avoid today when she left the house.

At a florist shop, she bought a bouquet of lilies, roses, and spider mums in fall shades of orange, gold, burgundy, and brown. All the way to Riverdale, she inhaled their wistful scents. She arrived sweating from her power walk. What a dumb decision to wear a rayon blouse. A cotton T-shirt and shorts would have suited the weather, but the blouse and capris were more appropriate for a sympathy visit. Too bad she hadn't thrown a mirror and powder into her fanny pack. Her warm, damp forehead must be glowing. She patted her windblown hair, which could use a comb.

Large, solid trees lined the entry street into Riverdale, an enclave of old luxury homes. During the past year, she had driven by Callie's house when she was in the area adjusting claims. Once she had knocked on the door; no one was home. She had followed the progress of the exterior renovations: wood siding torn off and replaced with river stone, cracked driveway dug up and redone with patterned concrete, single garage morphed into a triple.

The two-story house didn't look large from the front, but it extended deep into the backyard bordering the Elbow River. The driveway curved around a garden that must have bloomed all summer. Now, a sapling dripped orange-red leaves onto a patch of haggard roses.

No cars were parked on the driveway or by the curb. She wouldn't be disturbing other visitors. Plantation blinds covered the front bow windows, blocking her view into the house. She rang the bell on the huge center door. It was opened by a teenager.

Blond hair fell over the girl's shoulders. Her tank top with spaghetti straps stopped several inches above her navel. This had to be the right house. Paula said she was looking for Sam Moss.

"He's in the basement," the girl said. "Do you want me to get him?"

"Is Dorothy . . . ?" What was Callie's sister's married name?

"Aunt Dorothy's out shopping."

Paula stepped back. "Isabelle?"

"Uh huh."

This was Callie's brother's daughter. Isabelle scratched her earlobe decorated with a half dozen earrings. An amber navel ring nestled in her flat waist. A scissor-kick skirt flared from her hips.

"Callie showed me pictures of you growing up," Paula said. "In the last ones, you were this little girl with wispy hair. Now, you must be, what? Seventeen, eighteen?"

"Twenty-one."

"You look young for your age." Like her Aunt Callie.

Tanned legs extended flamingo-like from Isabelle's skirt to her bare feet. Somehow, she combined slimness with curving hips and good-sized breasts. Nipples protruded into her shirt. She was braless and firm enough to carry it off.

"Is your father here?" Paula said.

"He went with my mother and Aunt Dorothy to look for a caterer." Footsteps sounded in the hall. Isabelle spun around. "Here's Sam."

He stopped beside Isabelle. Dark hair slicked back from his forehead.

"Sam," Isabelle said, "This is . . ."

"I'm Callie's friend—"

"Paula." Sam reached through the bouquet to shake her hand. His fingers got tangled in the flowers.

"These are for you."

He extricated the bouquet from her hand and asked Isabelle to put the flowers in water. Isabelle padded down the hall, skirt swaying.

"How did you know who I was?" Paula asked Sam.

"Callie has a picture of you and her upstairs, taken at a fancy restaurant. Your hair was longer, a bit straighter."

She tried to smooth it down. That would be the picture taken at Kenneth's and Callie's last anniversary dinner. She had seen pictures of Sam, too. He was shorter than she expected, around five-foot-six, an inch taller than her, she estimated while babbling platitudes: "I'm sorry about Callie. It was such a shock. I still can't believe it." Sam's hair, she realized, was wet. Had he come from the shower? His black polo shirt and cream chino pants were dressy enough for going out. Here she was sweating, with her hair all over the place.

"I'm glad we meet at last," she said. Was there no end to her inane comments? "Callie arranged a number of dinners. Something always came up with your work."

"I thought it came up with your work."

His upturned mouth lines and eye crinkles suggested he had a sense of humor, although dark circles under his eyes hinted at the recent strain. She liked his high cheekbones. Hair covered his lower arms. Despite his upper body stockiness, his waist was trim, presumably from the morning workouts he did while Callie jogged to her death. He dug his hand into his pants pocket and jangled his keys.

"Is this a bad time?" she said. "Skye said Callie's sister would probably be here."

"Were you talking to Skye?"

"Didn't she tell you?"

"No." He glanced at his watch. "I can spare a few minutes for Callie's best friend."

She hadn't been such a best friend lately. Above them, a chandelier dangled from the twenty foot ceiling. The mahogany staircase rose straight to the second-floor landing, which was bordered by a railing. Isabelle loped down the hall from the kitchen.

"I gather you and Callie grew up together in Montreal," Sam said.

"She knows my father and Aunt Dorothy," Isabelle said. "Where are you going, Sam?"

"To meet friends for dinner."

"It's only three o'clock."

"Don't you have to get to work? In fact, shouldn't you have left an hour ago?"

"I quit."

Sam's eyebrows rose. "Since when?"

Isabelle touched the bead of her navel ring. "Last night. I asked the manager for time off, on account of my aunt being killed. He said I could have a half day for the funeral and that was it."

"We can talk about it later," Sam said.

"He's a retard," Isabelle continued. "He didn't give a shit that I'm in mourning. I told him, 'fuck you' and split. He better pay me for the time I worked."

To avoid appearing like an eavesdropper, Paula studied the living room that was framed by an arch. A white love seat and two chairs grouped in front of a fireplace, above which hung a painting of a beach café. An oriental carpet accented the oak floor and cranberry walls. She glimpsed the corner of a grand piano.

Isabelle tapped her bare foot. "I was hoping you'd be here for supper, Sam. Daddy will go ballistic when he finds out I quit."

"He doesn't know?" Sam said.

17

"I might tell him tomorrow."

"I'll be glad to miss that conversation." Sam looked at Paula. "Sorry about the interruption. When did you move to Calgary? Callie didn't—"

"I don't need that crappy job," Isabelle said. "It was even shittier than the one at the pizza place."

"I won't keep you any longer," Paula told Sam.

"We'll have you to dinner another time," he said, "when this is over."

"You can show me all you've done with the house."

"We haven't done much this past month. When were you last here?"

"This is my first time. Callie said you didn't want visitors until all the renovations were finished."

"We'd never have any company if we waited that long."

Isabelle touched Sam's arm. "Can I take Callie's car this afternoon?"

"What for?" he said.

"To look for work." Isabelle's hand lingered on his skin.

Sam didn't flinch. Nor did he shake the hand off.

His eyes crinkled. "I thought you were in mourning."

Isabelle's fingers drifted from his arm. His shadowed eyes aside, Sam seemed too glib or relaxed or something for a man whose wife was murdered yesterday.

"I really must leave," Paula said.

Sam and Isabelle didn't argue. They followed her onto the porch.

"Where did you park?" Sam squinted at the street.

"I walked along—" She stopped herself from saying "the Elbow path."

Sunlight glanced off Sam's wedding ring. His hair was fluffing and drying to a blend of black and gray.

"Can I give you a lift somewhere?" he asked.

"Thanks, no." Although it would be nice to avoid the trek home.

"So, can I borrow Callie's car?" Isabelle edged toward Sam.

He didn't step back. "No one else is driving it," he said. "But this time you're paying for any parking tickets."

Isabelle darted into the house. Sam raised his eyebrows at Paula. Was this to show exasperation? They headed down the driveway.

"I guess I'll see you at the funeral," she said. "When is it?"

"Monday. I'd have preferred later, but Callie's sister has to leave the next day." He pressed the code for the automatic garage door. "Sorry I have to cut out like this. I've got these friends waiting."

Since she had already delayed him, she didn't say she had changed her mind about his offer of the drive. His red car cruised past as she walked down the shaded Riverdale street to the trail. Evidently, Isabelle had been living with Callie and Sam long enough to find and lose two jobs. It seemed she intended to remain alone in the house with Sam, who didn't appear to object. Nor did he object to her touching his arm. When he had said "we" would have her to dinner, did he mean him and Isabelle?

Had Callie lied about Sam's not wanting visitors during the renovation? And what about those get-togethers, allegedly canceled because of Sam's work? Had Callie purposely kept her away from Sam and the house? Why? So she wouldn't see what was going on? Or was Sam the one who lied? Interesting that he had remembered seeing her in the photograph.

Her legs ached as she rounded the Stampede grounds. It was possible neither one had lied. It might be miscommunication. Sam and Isabelle might be types who touch everyone naturally. Sam hadn't looked embarrassed, like he had been found out, and his attitude toward Isabelle seemed paternal. Paternal could be sick. If Callie had phoned her Monday to discuss a problem, she bet it was related to this pair.

She reached her street, dying to guzzle water. Walter leaned on a rake, gossiping with two men in business suits. They might be Mormon missionaries who could keep him occupied while she slipped into her house. Walter pointed at her. The men wore colored shirts, which was unusual for Mormons.

The tall, broad one strode toward her. "Ma'am." He held up a wallet folder. "I'm Detective Michael Vincelli. This is Detective Brian Novak, from the Calgary Police. We're investigating the murder of Calandra Moss."

His shorter companion also flashed an ID and badge she was too startled to read.

"They were by this morning, looking for you," Walter said. "I didn't know then they were cops, since they weren't in uniform."

The older detective returned his wallet to his pocket. He had a ruddy complexion and looked around her age, in his early fifties. "We'd like to ask you a few questions. Can we step inside?"

"I told them you'd only lived here a month," Walter said. "And didn't know nothing about the murder when I talked to you yesterday."

"My neighbor's right. I first heard about it on the news."

"You heard it from me," Walter said.

"You are an acquaintance of Callie Moss?" the tall man said. He wasn't much older than thirty, with a fashionable stubble beard and shaved head. What did he say his name was?

She glanced at Walter, who looked thrilled by her connection to the case. "Callie and I are friends," she said. "We were friends, I mean."

"When did you last see her?" the young detective said.

"March."

"Have you spoken since then?"

"She left a phone message this week. I didn't return it, unfortunately."

Walter squeezed between the larger men. The dark sedan parked behind his pickup must belong to them. They wore suits and drove an unmarked car. The older one's gut bulged above his belt. Weren't policemen required to keep in shape? How did she know they weren't frauds trying to insinuate their way into her house for a sinister reason?

"Can I see those badges again?" she said.

The young one brushed back his jacket to get his ID, revealing a gun holstered in his belt.

She scrutinized Detective Michael Vincelli's identification. The Calgary Police Services badge looked authentic. His photo showed a man in his late twenties with a drooping mustache. Bushy black hair covered his forehead and ears. She looked up from the picture to the bald head and jaw stubble.

"I need to get a new mug shot," Vincelli said. His badge stated his height was six-foot-four.

Walter craned for a look. She handed the ID back to Vincelli. Detective Novak's photo looked more or less like him: pencil mustache, chubby cheeks, thinning blond hair back-combed to hide a balding crown. Height five-foot-nine. She should have expected the homicide unit to show up. A first step would be to check telephone records. Callie's message on her answering machine would have turned up as a call sent and received.

Walter tried to follow them through her gate. Vincelli blocked his entry. Even Walter wouldn't mess with a man that size. She continued up the sidewalk with Novak, who walked with a limp. Had he been injured while apprehending a criminal?

"I doubt I can offer any useful information," she said. "I haven't talked to Callie in months. I'm kicking myself for not returning her message. I had two full days to do it."

Vincelli caught up with them at the porch. "What about her calls yesterday morning?"

She halted her key in the lock. "What calls?"

"She placed two of them to this number," Vincelli said. "Around 6:40 AM."

"No, she didn't." Paula pushed open the door. "When I got home from work, I checked my messages. There were no new ones from her."

Two pairs of eyes, one brown, one blue, stared at her.

Novak spoke. "Was someone else present in the house, to take the calls?"

"No." She mentally ran through the answering machine messages: Callie's Monday call, Gary's and Hayden's new ones. Between them, some blanks. "I erased a couple I assumed were from telemarketers."

Or had Callie phoned and hung up after the machine connected? Vincelli had said the calls were placed around 6:40 AM. Callie's body was found at seven o'clock. The murder site was at least a half hour jog from Riverdale, which meant Callie had left home by six thirty.

"Did she phone me from the trail on her cell?" she said.

"Two calls were sent to this number," Detective Vincelli said, "We believe she made them minutes before she died."

Chapter Four

Detective Novak limped to the chair facing the kitchen window. Vincelli paused to study the photo magnets on Paula's fridge.

"Those are my daughters," she said.

"The dark-haired one looks like you." He claimed the chair next to the side door, leaving her the one across from him.

When they turned down her offer to make coffee, she got out jugs of water and lemonade and washed some grapes. After the grilling at the door, the detectives had shifted the conversation to small talk, commenting on her home's fresh paint smell, her bare living room walls and her deep backyard. Settled at the table, Novak grabbed a sprig of grapes. Both men took out notepads and pens. Novak nodded at Vincelli, who said they would begin with basic information. He asked for Paula's full name, address, cell phone number, occupation, age, and marital status.

Novak recorded her responses. "How do you spell your surname?"

"S-a-v-a-r-d," she said. "My father was French. I'm from Montreal, like Callie." She couldn't shake the image in her mind of Callie phoning from the trail in darkness. Callie had heard Paula's voice on the answering machine, hung up, and tried again, hoping the rings would wake a friend who wasn't there.

"How do you spell your boss's name?" Novak asked.

She told them and added that Nils van der Vliet Insurance Adjusters was a small firm; she was sure they had never heard of it. The staff currently consisted of Nils, who was the owner, a secretary, and her. It seemed Vincelli would lead the questioning, while Novak took notes. Given Vincelli's age, he might be a trainee. They trained junior adjusters that way, sending them out with someone senior.

"You moved to this house last month?" Vincelli asked.

"I took possession August 24th and moved in the next weekend."

"What was your prior address?"

She supplied it. "The house is registered in my daughter's name, for tax reasons; she and her fellow tenants pay me rent. It's perfectly legal."

Neither cop disagreed. She drank some lemonade. Just because they were cops, she shouldn't be defensive.

Novak glanced at the door. "Do you mind if I open that? It's a bit stuffy in here."

It would be less stuffy if he took off his jacket. Her sweaty blouse and capris made her feel vulnerable against their formal attire. Novak returned to his seat with a groan.

Vincelli loosened his tie. "You should see a doctor about that leg."

"What happened?" Paula refilled her lemonade glass.

"Fell off my horse," Novak said.

She laughed, releasing some tension.

"It's no joke," he said. "That filly's too frisky for an old fart like me."

Vincelli brought them back to business. "When was the last time you saw Callie?"

"In March, at her daughter's play," she said. "We spoke once, about a month afterwards. I left her a few messages over the summer. She didn't get back to me until this week. I found that odd."

"Why?"

"Usually, she returns my calls within a few days. I expect she was busy with Sam and her house renovations. You've met her husband, Sam?" Obviously, they had. She took a sip. Hopefully, the liquid would regenerate her parched brain.

Vincelli continued. "When you talked to Callie in April, did she sound troubled about anything?"

"On the contrary, she was buoyed about her university studies and sounded happy with Sam. Her life couldn't have been better. She'd had a health scare in the winter, though."

Vincelli's raised eyebrow suggested he hadn't heard of this.

"A shadow on a mammogram; it turned out to be nothing."

"She must have been relieved," Novak said.

"Do you suspect some trouble led to her death?" Should she mention her suspicions about Sam? They were based on nothing more than her impressions from a brief meeting. The detectives would have interrogated him and Isabelle and, if anything, seen more than she had.

"Have you known Callie long?" Vincelli asked.

"Forty-two years." With his prompting, she explained that Callie had moved onto her street the summer they were both ten. They became instant friends. Callie attended a Catholic elementary school, but switched to Paula's Protestant high school mainly because it was co-educational. Both attended Concordia University. Paula majored in anthropology, Callie in fine arts.

Novak scribbled notes. In addition to prompting, Vincelli's role was to glare and, presumably, look for nuance in her words and expressions. With his encouragement, she went into details. It felt good to spill everything to an eager listener, even this stranger from the police.

"Callie dropped out of university before her final year," she said. "That is, she moved to Calgary before school started that fall, so she didn't finish."

Vincelli unbuttoned his collar. The pink shirt suited his olive complexion. He hadn't touched his water or the grapes. Despite his writing task, Novak had devoured two sprigs.

Vincelli leafed back through the notebook in which he hadn't written a word. "Callie moved to Calgary in 1973 with her boyfriend."

"Not exactly," Paula said. For her twenty-first birthday Callie's parents gave her a car: a rusted old Chevy that inspired the girls to drive to Vancouver with their then boyfriends. The road trip west was fun. Arriving was not so hot. In Vancouver, they splurged on hotel rooms, rather than stay in a hostel. One night, while Callie nursed cramps, their boyfriends went out to a bar. They picked up some girls and didn't get back until morning.

Novak chuckled, while continuing to write.

"Callie and I were furious," she said. "The guys kept asking us, 'What's your hang-up?' This was the sixties, well, early seventies, free love and all."

Novak looked up. "Being a cop, I missed all that fun."

Her contemporaries at that time would have called him a pig. She had probably used the term herself. During the past thirty years, her worldview had merged with Novak's.

Having finished the pitcher of lemonade, she filled her glass with water. "While the guys were sleeping it off, Callie and I packed our bags and left them with no transportation and an unpaid hotel bill. We even took the cash from their wallets. It was a rotten thing to do."

"It sounds to me like they deserved it," Vincelli said. Did he ever smile?

Later, they learned the boys spent the rest of the summer cleaning hotel rooms and hitchhiking home. In Wawa they waited five hours in driving rain for a ride. Callie's boyfriend caught pneumonia.

Vincelli's lip twitched.

"You're right," she said. "They deserved it."

In Hope, BC, she and Callie treated themselves to a night out at a bar, where a folk rock band performed to their audience of two. After the set, the members joined them at their table.

"I swear," she said, "there were literally sparks between Callie and Owen, the group's front man. The guys invited us to follow them to their gigs in northern BC and Alberta. We said, 'Why not?' School didn't start for two weeks. They taught us harmonies; we played tambourines. What's the matter?" she asked Novak.

He cocked his head at her. "I'm trying to visualize you dancing on stage."

She smoothed her frizzy hair. "Weren't you ever young and foolish?"

"Still am." He patted his leg.

In Calgary, the day they were set to leave, Callie dropped a bombshell. She was staying with Owen and the band. She loved him, couldn't live without him. "They put me on a Greyhound bus," Paula said. "I was—"

Vincelli's eyes narrowed.

Not continuing would seem evasive. She returned his stare. "I was angry at her. Until then, the trip had been a 'we're-in-this-together adventure.' I felt betrayed, like she had broken a pact. I also thought she was stupid to sacrifice her education for a guy she'd only known two weeks. Owen was a selfish jerk, in my opinion. And yet . . ."

Vincelli jotted his first note. So, this was how they operated. She should have seen it. She handled suspicious insurance claimants the same way. Act friendly, gain their trust, share food, and let them ramble until they contradict themselves or blurt something out. Well, she had nothing to hide and her feelings, while petty, had been normal.

She steadied her gaze. "In one of the band's numbers, Owen played the saxophone. It was damn sexy and the one and only time I understood what Callie saw in him. I still thought she was wrong to give up school, but part of me was jealous of her passion. It was a complicated jumble of feelings that all seem irrelevant now."

"What was Owen's surname?" Novak asked.

"Rafferty." She also supplied the name of the lead guitarist, with whom she had shacked up, less ardently than Callie had with Owen. "Both grew up in Vancouver, if that helps."

"I doubt they can add anything," Vincelli said. "But we'll check them out."

Callie and Owen moved in with a group of students they'd met at a music event. Their grand passion fizzled in a few months. At Christmas, Callie sent Paula a card, saying she'd broken up with Owen and was dating one of the students, Kenneth Unsworth, who was majoring in business and geology. They married a few years later. Paula didn't attend the wedding because flying was expensive, she didn't want to use up her vacation time, and she wasn't sure Callie wanted her there. Vincelli waited for her explanation. Spilling to cops was becoming less fun. A cigarette would be handy for stalling and considering replies.

Rather than phone to invite her to the wedding, Callie had sent a note that struck Paula as formal. Callie said it would be a small event, with only immediate family and a few friends present, and Paula needn't feel obligated to come. Kenneth's sister would be maid of honor. "That was understandable," Paula said. "Callie and I hadn't seen each other in three years. Still, I'd known her a lot longer; we'd been best friends since childhood, gone through a lot together." Her voice gave out. She refreshed it with water. "I'm not holding a grudge for that minor slight, if it even was one." That was totally true. Why did it sound like she was covering up?

After the wedding, she and Callie kept in touch through sporadic letters and phone calls. Callie did the books for her husband's struggling business and couldn't take the time to fly out for Paula's wedding. "Tit for tat," Paula said, instantly regretting the remark that made the small hurt seem profoundly meaningful.

As young wives and mothers, both got busy with family responsibilities and jobs. Kenneth's oil company took off. Callie gave up the bookkeeping for volunteer work and, later, interest courses in theater, painting, film studies and music. Paula didn't realize her friend was rich until she visited her in Calgary. Even then, she didn't see it right away, since Callie's house was modest and Paula didn't know Mount Royal was the city's most elite neighborhood. During a second visit, when their children were older and required less attention, she and Callie enjoyed the theater and restaurant scene and the parks, which were far less crowded than the ones back east. It was sunny and warm the whole time; the dry air was comfortable and unpolluted; every hill showcased magnificent mountain views.

Vincelli asked when she moved to Calgary.

"1996," she said. Most people assumed they had moved to escape the sour mood that permeated English Quebec after the 1995 independence referendum. The move was more to rejuvenate their personal lives. She was tired of working for a large insurance firm. Gary, her husband, was tired of being a small insurance agent, but couldn't find anything better due to his lack of fluency in French. Most of their friends had already left Montreal. They decided to hopscotch Ontario and try Calgary. They liked its gung-ho atmosphere. Callie was here; Gary got along with her then husband, Kenneth.

The water jug was empty. She got up to refill it, glad for the opportunity to stretch her legs. With the sun's movement to the front of the house, the kitchen had grown cool and dark. The unstated reason, even at the time, for her and Gary's move to Calgary was a hope that the change would boost their stagnant marriage.

Vincelli asked if the move rekindled her friendship with Callie. For a few years, it did. They met as couples at each others' homes for dinners, board games, and cards. Callie convinced her to join her fitness center, where they met several times a week for exercise and chat. Callie drifted away when she started university; she found it more convenient to work out at the school's facilities.

"She completed her degree last spring," Vincelli said.

"And was so excited about starting her master's this fall," Paula said. "It's ironic and sad. She can't have attended more than a few classes before she died."

The men exchanged glances.

"What's wrong?" she said.

Vincelli's eyes looked puzzled. "What makes you think she went on to her master's degree?"

"She told me all about it last spring. She'd been accepted and was definitely going."

"To the University of Calgary?"

"Where else? Surely Sam, her husband, mentioned this."

Vincelli made a note. "We'll question him again and check the university records."

She crossed her arms. "I can't believe Callie would change her mind.

She was thrilled about going. She said she needed the higher degree to pursue a teaching or performing career."

Novak flipped through his notebook. "You say Callie left an answering machine message on Monday. Did you happen to save it?"

"I can play it right now." Grateful for another chance to get up, she walked to the telephone cabinet. "Callie's tone was casual and breezy, so I didn't feel any pressure to return the message. When I replay it, I notice she asks if I'm free this week and says call me tomorrow. You say she phoned from the trail?"

Why would Callie have wanted to talk to her now, after ignoring her calls all summer? Was it about something urgent, maybe related to the murder? Did anyone know Callie was coming here?

"Could we hear the phone message?" Novak said.

She pressed the play button. *Monday, 2:45 PM.* The metallic male machine voice was followed by the girlish one. *Hi Paula, it's Callie. Long time since we've had lunch. Are you free this week? I want to hear all about your move to Ramsay. There are some new restaurants near there that might be fun to try. Give me a call tomorrow.*

Novak asked her to replay the message so he could copy it verbatim.

"We'll have a technician make a copy," Vincelli said.

"It isn't digital," Paula said. "You can take the tape, as long as you return it."

Vincelli pushed back his chair. "Do they still make them with tapes?"

He pushed all the buttons, seemingly intrigued by the antique. After the replay, he dropped the mini-cassette into a belt pouch. They resettled on their seats.

"One last thing," Vincelli said. "Where were you Thursday, September 23, between 6:00 and 7:00 AM?"

She scraped her chair back. He was asking for her alibi. She looked from him to Novak. How had she missed seeing this from their perspective as investigators? She did this every day when adjusting insurance claims: string together facts to reach a logical conclusion. Two phone calls were placed to her house. For all the cops knew, she received them, had argued with Callie and dashed out to intercept her on the trail. The murder site was a ten minute walk, tops.

She squinted at Vincelli. "My neighbor will confirm I wasn't home yesterday morning."

His dark eyes didn't waver. "He stated your car wasn't parked on the street when he went to bed at midnight and when he looked out at 8:30 AM. You might have returned between those hours or parked in the rear."

"I never use my garage. It's full of boxes. I brought them with me when I moved in and plan to sort through them. Have a look, if you don't believe me."

"There's space to park in the back lane."

They had looked, had probably peered into her garage window, and must be noticing her fidgety hands. She grabbed a sprig of grapes. "Yesterday, between 6:00 and 7:00 AM, I was at my office."

"Do you always go into work that early?" Vincelli said.

"My hours are flexible. I'm there at six o'clock, maybe once a month." Less often. Had she ever got in quite that early?

"Who was with you?"

"No one. Nils, my boss, usually arrives between seven and eight o'clock, the secretary at eight thirty. It's a small company, I told you. That's our entire staff."

"Who else was in the building?"

"It's a small building. The only other tenant is a jeweler. He's never there before ten o'clock." It all sounded so lame.

He asked for the jeweler's name and her office address and phone number. This was crazy. She had no motive for murder, although they could probably extrapolate one from her ramblings. Jealousy? Pettiness? Childish anger at a friend who broke an imagined bond? You didn't kill for that. Did you?

Vincelli took a sip of water. He pulled the grape bowl closer and broke off his first stalk. "What time did you leave your house yesterday morning?"

"I didn't. I spent Wednesday night with a friend. He's a lawyer and had to be in his office by six o'clock. I figured I might as well catch up on paperwork."

"Did this friend drop you off at work or vice versa?"

"We drove in separate cars."

"Did you stop to pick up a coffee or anything along the way?"

"I brought a thermos from Hayden's. This is ridiculous. You can't seriously think I would kill her."

Vincelli requested Hayden's home and office phone numbers and addresses.

"I know that firm," Novak said. "I've dealt with some of their criminal lawyers."

"He does civil litigation."

Novak tapped his leg. "I should sue my horse."

She scowled at his attempt at playing the nice cop. Her grape stem was shredded. Ripping it apart had, no doubt, made her look guilty. She dropped the shreds to her plate.

"What reason could I possibly have for murder?" she said.

Vincelli plucked a grape. "You tell me."

Chapter Five

Hayden looked up from his desk. "First the police; now you. Two surprises in one day."

"They didn't waste time checking my alibi." Paula sank into the visitor's chair. She had given the detectives a few hours to get here and had decided not to warn Hayden they might show up. If he acted too prepared, it might increase their suspicions.

"I was just about to call you." He closed the file he had been reviewing when she came in and placed it on the stack to his left. "Why on earth would they think you did it?"

She explained about Callie's cell phone calls sent from the trail. The file on top of the stack teetered; it tilted more and more and finally spewed its papers onto his blotting pad. Every surface of his desk was covered with folders, paper and pens. By all accounts he was a competent lawyer. She didn't know how he kept on top of his work.

"What kinds of questions did they ask you?" she said.

He stuffed the papers back into the file. "They were here a good half hour and caused quite a stir in this place. I'm sure some of my co-workers were hoping to see me hauled out in handcuffs."

She reached under a folder for the music box, the only personal item in his office aside from photographs. For the second time today, she missed smoking for how it occupied her hands.

"They asked how long I've known you," he said, "how long we've been dating, if I'd seen or talked to Callie. They wanted details of your movements yesterday. I may not have helped when I said you were a bit of a night owl and I'd never known you to go to the office at that hour in the morning. It slipped out . . ."

"Thanks a lot, especially since it was your fault I went in early."

"If it's any consolation, they also wanted details about me, in case we're in cahoots." He got up to close his window blind against the setting sun that blurred the Rocky Mountains zigzagging along the horizon. The mountains looked their best in the morning splashed with eastern light and would be spectacular in a couple of weeks, after a dump of snow.

He returned to his desk. His surroundings were messy, but his person

31

couldn't be more proper and neat. Clean shaven, short dark hair parted to the side with patches of gray above the ears, he wore a business suit, pale blue shirt, and conservative blue and gray tie. The detectives would have to be impressed with the company she kept.

"I wouldn't worry about it," he said. "The police aren't going to impulsively arrest the wrong person."

"You know that's not true. Don't try to make me feel better." She shifted the holograph picture on the music box lid so the trumpet player's cheeks puffed out and in. "I suppose I'm keeping you from work."

"I do have a trial coming up in a couple of weeks."

"Callie's funeral is Monday morning. Can you get the time off?"

"I have a meeting with my client. If you want me to go, I might be able to reschedule—"

"Don't you want to be there for yourself?"

"I only knew Callie in passing, through her husband, Kenneth. I saw her, maybe, twice in the past thirty years. Will your ex be going?"

Was he worried about meeting Gary? About his position in the legal community, if he was connected to her, a potential suspect? "I talked to Gary this afternoon. He's leaving Sunday on a cruise, with his girlfriend."

"Your daughters?"

"Leah might want to go. She used to be close to Skye and Callie. Although Leah always says she's against formal rituals."

"That figures." Hayden glanced at his cluttered desk. He didn't want to rearrange his life to attend the funeral of someone he barely knew, but would do it if she asked.

"Do you realize," she said. "If it weren't for Callie, you and I wouldn't have met?"

He and his nephew had attended Skye's play. Paula had gone with Callie and Leah. Hayden recognized Callie from a charity event she had attended years ago with Kenneth and came up to them during the first intermission.

"I couldn't tell who your nephew was flirting with more," Paula said. "Callie or Leah."

"Either way, he kept them occupied so you and I could get acquainted."

Hayden left the second intermission with her phone number.

"I still can't believe she's dead," Paula said. "Evidently, it happened sometime before 7:00 AM."

"Six forty-eight, to be precise."

"How do you know?"

"A witness heard the gunshot."

"Did the detectives tell you that?"

"It's in the *Sun*."

"You read a tabloid?"

"One of my co-workers does."

He fumbled beneath the files and dug out the newspaper. His telephone rang. While he talked to his client, she studied the tabloid's full front-page picture of the yellow tape running across the entrance to the trail. Superimposed were Callie's photograph and a quote from her husband, Sam: "I didn't know she was there."

She scanned the inside page. Two nearby residents heard a sound . . . initially dismissed as a backfiring car . . . dog walker recognized Callie from the news report. For the past month . . . he passed her daily at that hour on the trail. Police conclude . . . jogged to Ramsay and back at a set time.

But yesterday morning, for some reason, Callie had placed two calls. Was she planning to change her routine and continue to Paula's house?

Paula returned to the article. The murder weapon wasn't found at the site. So, the police couldn't trace it, if it was registered.

Hayden's conversation wound down. He hung up the phone.

She closed the newspaper. "I wish I'd been home to answer her calls, but what difference would it have made? I would have put on a pot of coffee and waited for her to never show up." Her voice broke. She blinked back tears.

Hayden's face softened in sympathy. "It should be over soon. They usually arrest the culprit within a week."

"You know what I hate most about this?"

"You getting arrested and going to jail?"

"Very funny."

"Me going to jail?"

"I hate that all the murder talk, including suspicions against you and me, prevents me from properly thinking about her and grieving. Can't you beg off work tonight?"

He cast another glance at his clutter. "I'd still have to come in tomorrow morning. You don't like me waking you up early on Saturday."

He didn't sleep well in her bed, yet. Nights before work were always spent at his place.

"I'm sure I can wrap it all up by tomorrow noon," he said. "Then, we'll unwind with tennis, cook a great dinner, rent a movie, drink wine, et cetera."

"I can't wait, especially for the et cetera." After last night's restlessness, she could use a good dose of sex. Hopefully, it would send her sailing to sleep.

From his office, Paula drove to the fitness center, even though she was exhausted and didn't need more exercise today after her walk to and from Sam's house. Since she would be busy with Hayden all weekend, this would be her only chance to talk to Anne before the funeral.

During a brief university romance, Anne and Sam had produced a son, Dimitri, now age thirty-one and a prominent federal politician. He won his first seat in the June election. Sam's participation in his son's upbringing had kept Anne and him in contact. Their mutual friends included Kenneth and Callie. When the couple split, Anne had landed on the Kenneth side due to his friendship with her husband. Callie left the fitness center around the same time. Was that a coincidence or not? Paula wondered if Callie's involvement with Sam made her feel awkward with Anne.

The center's sign, Fit for Life, underscored with an infinity symbol, glowed pink and blue neon. Lights shone from the converted church. Anne had bought the building for next to nothing during the 1980s bust. Rather than tear down the one-hundred-year-old structure, she had gutted it, installed beams and floors to support the load of exercise machines and painted the exterior royal blue. The former square steeple became a free weights room with a view of the yuppifying neighborhood. The plumbing and lights could get wonky at times—a burst pipe once closed the center for three days—but during her eight years of membership, Paula had noticed a steady increase in customers. Anne said the business was finally in the black.

Dance music drowned out the whirr of machines, all of which seemed occupied. Paula rarely worked out during the peak evening time, when she tended to be occupied by meetings with insurance claimants. She went through the security gate. Anne rushed toward her. They hugged, which they had never done before. Anne's shoulder muscles felt taut and strong. She spent a good twelve hours at her center every day and pumped machines and weights when she wasn't involved in administrative or supervisory duties. All the way to the changing room, they shared feelings about Callie's murder. "Shock." "Unbelievable." The same words they had used on the phone this morning. Anne's workout gear hugged her hips and thighs. Paula changed into her baggy T-shirt and shorts. What did looks matter in an all-female facility, unless you were the owner and had to project an image? They managed to find two spare adjacent treadmills. Paula's feet moved forward and back on the treadmill belt. "I told you about Callie's phone message on Monday. If I'd returned that damn call, she might have told me what was bothering her, if something was. Maybe I couldn't have prevented the murder, but I'd know enough now to steer the cops in the right direction. They came to my house this morning." She described their visit. Her feet pounded the belt so fast she had no trouble keeping up to Anne's pace. "They can't seriously believe, for one minute, I killed her."

"We all feel guilty for what we might have done," Anne said. "The last time I saw her, Callie told me she was thinking of coming back to the center when the weather got colder. Instead, it got warmer. If only I'd pushed her to rejoin us sooner."

Paula sipped water. "I finally met Sam, today, when I dropped by unexpectedly to pay my respects. Did you know Callie's niece, Isabelle, was living with them?"

"I only found out a few weeks ago. I gather she moved in last May."

"Is she planning to stay on alone with Sam?"

Anne frowned. "Dimitri mentioned she might. He told Sam to consider the optics."

"As Callie's husband, Sam's an automatic suspect. Does he inherit her money?"

"Most of that went into their house."

"Which could be worth a million dollars, after the reno."

"Dimitri didn't tell me the terms of her will. I didn't think to ask about it."

"Do you think Sam is sleeping with Isabelle?" Paula asked.

Anne's hazel eyes flashed surprise, as though she hadn't considered the possibility. "I hope not, for his and Dimitri's sake. He's staying with Sam during this crisis."

Before Dimitri bought his condo in his riding last spring, he had shuttled between Sam's house and Ottawa. Anne had said his relationship with Sam was more like that of two friends than father and son.

"Why did you say, 'for Dimitri's sake'?"

"Dimitri wasn't specific, but he's concerned about Sam. He said the cops have been giving him a hard time."

Paula wished Anne was more curious about people. Callie would have pressed her son for details.

"Dimitri doesn't need this with parliament starting up next week."

They left the treadmills for the elliptical machines. Paula was glad to see some sweat matting Anne's ash-blond bangs. Anne returned to the "shock" and "unbelievable" words that were starting to sound like platitudes. "I shudder at the thought of Callie jogging alone in the dark," Anne said. "I don't much like that creepy area behind the Stampede grounds in daytime, never mind at night."

"Callie didn't tend to worry about such things." Another non-Anne trait.

Anne pressed her machine settings. Paula punched her elliptical panel up two levels. The machines were good for channeling stress. Much of her talk during their tri-weekly workouts involved venting, mainly hers about work, her daughters, parking tickets, incompetent repairmen . . . Anne was a good listener. In the old days, when she and Callie worked out, Callie had listened, too, but was more likely to tell her off. "Get over it," she would say, "Don't be judgmental, see it from his or her point of view." Clearly, at the end of her life, Callie was looking to her for help with a problem that may or may not have been related to the murder. If Paula was in crisis, who would she turn to? Hayden, unless the problem was him. She didn't have many girlfriends. The ones she had acquired after her divorce had remarried and drifted away or stalled in the bitterness. In terms of hours spent together, Anne was probably her current best friend, although they never met outside the fitness center. Of the two, Paula would rather pour her crisis to Callie, despite their distance in recent years. She wiped an eye.

"What's the matter?" Anne said.

"She's gone. There's no one in my life to replace her."

Two minute cool down scrolled across the elliptical panel. Anne maintained her pedaling pace. She always worked vigorously to the end.

"My best memories of Callie are of us being silly," Paula said. "Like that night we went out drinking to celebrate my divorce. I told you about that. We wound up running along Stephen Avenue downtown shouting, 'Death to all husbands.' I can't believe I did that, even when drunk."

"You stumbled into a cop and collapsed in hysterics."

"He threatened to drag us off to jail. Instead, he put us in a cab and sent us home. I told him drunkenly he'd restored my faith in men."

Paula stepped off the elliptical machine. "Now that she's dead, all my petty jealousies seem like a waste of time. I was even jealous of Leah's preference for her, that year after we moved to Calgary. I'm glad I forgot about that when the detectives were grilling me."

Anne led them to ab-cruncher. "I'm sure Leah didn't prefer her—"

"She rubbed it in about how much more fun Callie was, more like a friend than—"

"Normal teenage rebellion," Anne said.

They lay down on the benches and moved up and down in sync.

"Leah blamed me for dragging her here, away from all her friends in Montreal," Paula said. "She let Gary off the hook, although it was as much his fault."

"Kids are never fair," Anne said.

Even at the time, Paula understood Leah's need to heap all the blame on her, so she wouldn't feel betrayed by both parents. It didn't stop Paula from being hurt, and holding back anger wasn't her strong suit. She pulled her body higher to attack her abdominal muscles. So many words she would take back, so much she would change. "I wish I'd said 'screw work' and gone with Leah, Callie, and Skye for that girls' week in Palm Springs. It would have been fun to have had that time together. I might have got grunge."

Anne turned sideways, her heart-shaped face sweaty and perplexed. Paula faced her to work the obliques.

"In Palm Springs, they saw a grunge band in a club," Paula explained.

"What, exactly, is grunge?" Anne said.

"Beats me."

"Could be Dimitri's ear-splitting teenage music," Anne said. "That reminds me, a reporter interviewed him today while he was leaving Sam's house. The clip should be on the eleven o'clock news."

Dressed for bed, Paula flicked on the tv and collapsed into the sofa cushion. Outdoors, a vehicle made a U-turn on her street. Its headlights scanned her dark living room. The light stung her eyes. She was desperate for sleep, but couldn't miss the nightly news for Dimitri's interview and any updates on the murder.

Due to Callie's involvement with Sam, Paula had followed Dimitri's political career through the right wing Reform-turned-Alliance-turned-Conservative party. During his election campaign, the newspaper ran a profile piece in which the interviewer questioned him about his illegitimate birth. Dimitri spun his answer into support of family values by remarking he was glad his parents didn't abort him. The next day a left-leaning columnist implied Dimitri's parents had made an unfortunate choice. The columnist's remark inspired a couple of letters-to-the-editor.

On the screen, the news anchor reported on a hostage's reunion with her family, after days of captivity in Iraq. He segued to a report about United States veterans who opposed a monument honoring draft dodgers in Nelson, BC. Shots of the picturesque mountain town. A sketch of the proposed statue. It could be a half hour before they got to the local stories.

The anchor returned to the screen. "Federal Conservative member of parliament Dimitri Moss was shocked yesterday by the murder of his stepmother."

Paula jerked forward.

"Zoë Jensen talked to Mr. Moss at his father's Calgary residence."

Bathed in sunlight, Dimitri spoke into a microphone. He looked down, not at the reporter or the camera. "I was in my office, answering constituents' mail. My father came in and suggested we go for a coffee. He hadn't done that before, but I didn't think anything of it. I'd heard about the murder on the radio. Names weren't mentioned. I had no idea." His voice trailed.

He wore a leather jacket and held a motorcycle helmet. His hair was thinning on top. Otherwise, he seemed a younger version of Sam; same muscular build and strong cheekbones. Dimitri stood in front of a bow window with closed blinds. The reporter asked for his reaction to the news.

"Disbelief," he said. "I last saw Callie on Labor Day weekend, less than three weeks before it happened, at a barbecue with family and friends. She was full of life."

"How would you describe your stepmother, as a person?"

He looked up. "She wasn't my stepmother. She was my father's wife. There was no reason for anyone to kill her."

"Your party advocates stiffer penalties for criminals. How will this experience influence your views on that issue?"

Dimitri's eyes narrowed. He looked ready to bark out an angry reply.

"I have always been tough on crime," he said. "Nothing has changed."

The reporter signed off. Calgary police had reported no new developments on the case.

So, Dimitri didn't accept Callie as his stepmother. Why would he? He was thirty when his father/friend married her. Still, his response had been sharp, his answer to the crime question sharper. The newspaper profile had referred to his temper as a trait he struggled to control. Callie had confirmed that, adding she thought Sam spoiled him, giving him everything he wanted. Anne worried about his motorcycle riding. He wasn't reckless, she said, but bikes were intrinsically dangerous. The telephone rang. Paula jumped up. It was after eleven. Who would phone at this hour? She hurried to the kitchen. "Hello?"

No one spoke. Someone had called and hung up early this morning, too.

"Hello? Who's there?"

The line went dead.

Chapter Six

Paula finished her morning coffee, her mind numb from two sleepless nights. She got Detective Vincelli's business card from the telephone cabinet. Two hang-up phone calls the day after Callie died might be a coincidence, but Vincelli had told her to phone about anything possibly connected to the murder. Thank God, none had blasted her awake this morning, and Hayden would be staying over tonight. The doorbell made her jump. She glanced at the wall clock. Five past ten. Hayden wouldn't have finished his work already. She hurried through the living room. On tiptoes, she peered through the front door window. The opaque glass obscured the tall, bald man in a business suit—Detective Vincelli.

"I was passing by on my way to the station," he said.

"Is there some news about the murder?"

"Nothing significant. I can only stay a minute." His face looked as tired as hers had this morning in the bathroom mirror. His beard stubble was moving from fashionable to unkempt.

She cinched her bathrobe belt and patted her bed hair. "I was going to call you about some phone calls I received."

"Yesterday morning and last night shortly after eleven o'clock?"

"How did you know about them?"

"They were sent from Callie's cell phone."

She gripped the belt, trying to take this in. Callie had her cell with her when she died. If someone was using the phone now . . . "Did the killer take the phone and gun?"

"The cell might have been dropped and picked up by someone else."

Or the murderer had phoned her last night. Hello. Hello? she had said into the line.

"Did the caller say anything?" Vincelli asked.

"Nothing. The line sounded dead, both times."

"What about breathing?"

"No, I hung up fast. Why would the killer phone me?"

"We don't know that's who it was."

Sweat beads flecked his beard stubble, despite the cool air flowing into the house. She stepped back to let him into the entranceway.

"Your number was the last one Callie phoned," he said. "Someone likely pressed redial as a joke."

"Twice? At sixteen-hour intervals?"

"Did you hear any background sounds? Music? Mumbled voices? Think carefully."

She twisted the belt around her fingers. "I'm sure there was nothing. Why would the murderer joke around with the phone?"

"Why not? The calls would be traced to Callie's cell, not to the person who placed them."

"You could trace them to a cell phone tower."

"That didn't tell us enough."

"Did he do it to scare me? Was it a threat?"

He pulled his tie, as though he found it choking his neck. "Callie may have, inadvertently, placed you in a difficult position. Several people we spoke with had the impression you were her main confidante. It appears she exaggerated the level of your recent friendship."

"To whom? Sam? He called me her best friend."

"She told someone she was having lunch with you this week."

"We didn't because I didn't return her call."

"Who's to know you didn't?"

Now, would he want her alibi for every noon hour this week?

"We don't think Callie was worried about being murdered," he said. "But supposing the two of you had met and Callie had said 'so-and-so's doing this or saying that or otherwise causing me grief.'"

"I would have given her advice, as best I could."

"And if she hadn't taken it, or did take it and was killed?"

"I would have told you about it yesterday, when you questioned me."

"You might have withheld information to spare her embarrassment."

"I didn't." Her voice cracked. She glared up at him. "Are you accusing me again?"

"What if it was subtle?" he said. "Suppose, last week or last month or last year Callie said something, a throw-away remark, that seems trivial, even to us, but with new facts could turn out to be significant. People often know more than they think."

"I don't know anything. I've been racking my brain over this for two nights."

"The bad guy doesn't know that," he said. "For all anyone knows, she told you, her close friend, the one piece of information that would break open the case. Someone out there may be worried you know too much."

"The person who phoned me?"

"One call could have been someone pressing the redial button by accident or to see whose name comes up. A second call sends a message. That's why I advise you to be on guard."

She leaned against the console table, rubbing her throat.

"Let us know instantly about any behavior that strikes you as strange: if someone you hardly know probes you with questions or rings your doorbell or meets you by accident on the river pathway, which I would advise you to stay away from, at all times of the day."

"Yesterday, you thought I'd killed her. Now, you suggest I may be the next victim?"

"I wouldn't jump to conclusions," he said. "It's a matter of taking care. Your office is in a seedy neighborhood. Don't go there alone. Don't go at all after dark. Don't walk around this neighborhood at night. Continue to park on the street, not in your lane, so you come in by the front of the house."

Vincelli bent over to study her doorknob. He gave it a hard turn.

She shivered under her robe. "Are you purposely trying to scare me?"

"This lock looks solid. I'll check the kitchen door, too. Do you have bars on your basement windows?"

"No."

"You should install them. Everyone should. It's common sense."

"I haven't had time. I've just moved in. I didn't expect . . ."

He took several short breaths. "I didn't mean to alarm you." His face relaxed; his voice turned soothing, like a doctor reassuring a patient. "It's wise to be prudent, but you probably aren't in immediate danger."

"Probably?" she said.

"Not yet."

In her dark living room, Paula snuggled against Hayden on the sofa. He flicked off the DVD.

"I'm not sure I bought that ending," he said. "Did you?"

She had lost the plot midway, not being able to focus more than a few minutes. "The movie was meant to be light."

He had chosen the romantic comedy, to take her mind off the murder.

"Even light could use a little meat," he said.

"I forgot to tell you Leah invited us for lunch tomorrow."

"What horrible vegetarian concoction are they planning this time?"

"She wants me to help her install a closet organizer."

"She and Jarrett can't handle that?"

"Jarrett pick up a hammer and nail?"

"True."

"Besides, as Leah says, organizing's my thing." She cocked her head at him.

He seized the opportunity for a kiss. His mouth tasted of buttery popcorn and the garlic sausage they'd had for supper.

"You don't have to go to Leah's," she said.

"I swear, when this trial is done, you come first." He ran his hands down her back. "Can you get time off this November?"

"Why?"

"What would you say to a week in the Caribbean?"

This would be their first trip together. She closed her eyes and pictured turquoise waves on a crescent beach. Palm trees. The water lapping white sand. Waves unearthing a body on the beach. Callie's body on the Elbow River Trail. Isabelle's hand grazing Sam's bare arm. Detective Vincelli's deep voice: *You probably aren't in immediate danger; not yet.*

Hayden raised her T-shirt above her head. *Focus. Forget the rest, for a moment. One moment.* She unbuttoned Hayden's shirt. Was Isabelle doing this to Sam at the moment, in Callie's house? *Focus. Focus.* She kissed Hayden's hairy chest. Did Sam's chest feel like this? Different? From the cling of Sam's polo shirt, his chest looked firmer than Hayden's. Sam's hand through the flowers had felt warm, warm from the shower, and moist. Hayden's were dry. His breathing grew heavy, garlicky hot. This was not going to work, not for her, tonight. She pressed her lips into his. *Fake it.*

Sunday, after breakfast, Hayden left for the office. Paula paid an impromptu visit to the liability claimant who still hadn't returned her calls. His house was a two-story split, with side-facing garage. His front door was open, with the screen door letting in air.

As she rang the bell, a man appeared. "I thought I heard someone."

She introduced herself.

"Oh yeah, I was meaning to call." He pushed past her, onto the driveway, and pointed up to the garage roof. "There's where my neighbor fell from." He led her around the garage to the grassy side.

The garage roof was one-story, with long eaves. If the neighbor had landed with a lucky roll, he might have escaped with a few bruises, as opposed to the concussion and broken arm. Paula asked the homeowner what happened.

"I got my neighbor to help me put up Christmas lights," he said.

"In September?"

"This is Calgary. You take your good weather when you can." He shifted from foot to foot. "I laid a string of lights on the garage roof, by the eaves, and asked him to come over and help me string the higher up ones."

"Can you show me where?"

He trotted to the driveway and pointed to the Christmas lights hooked to the eaves overhanging the second story. "I asked him to bring me the hammer and forgot to tell him about the string in the way."

"Shouldn't he have noticed it?"

"I'm the one who put it there. He was doing me a favor. It was getting dark."

"What do you mean by dark? Was this after dinner?"

"That's when he was available."

They went inside so she could take a written statement. The man's wife hovered nearby, offering coffee and cookies, which Paula refused so she wouldn't spoil her lunch at Leah's. The wife hadn't witnessed the incident; nor had anyone else, to the couples' knowledge. The husband had driven their injured neighbor to emergency.

"I feel so guilty," the wife kept saying. "I hate them going on the roof."

"Do they do it often?" Paula asked.

The husband shot his wife a glance. She pursed her lips.

"How often?"

"We went up the once to hang up lights."

His wife nodded in agreement.

The injured man lived directly across the street. His wife answered Paula's ring and directed her to the backyard. The man reclined in a lounge chair reading a book, his right arm in a cast. He held a beer in his left hand. His torso looked stiff. Bruised ribs. He told Paula to pull up a chair and offered her a beer.

"No thanks." She took out her notebook and asked for his version of the incident.

"We were putting up Christmas lights . . ." His statement matched his friend's almost word for word. He told her his work in graphic design was largely done by computer and raised his right arm. "Can't type. My thinking feels off, too."

"In what way?"

"Hard to explain. It's like the lines don't link. I'm seeing my doctor about it this week."

"Ask him to fill out a medical report. We'll reimburse you the cost." Paula handed him her business card.

She knocked on their adjacent neighbors' doors. No one who was in had witnessed the fall. A man had heard about it, but couldn't add anything. A woman had once seen the injured man carry a case of beer to the homeowner's house. Paula asked if she'd known the pair to go up regularly to the roof.

"Why would they do that?"

"For the view?" Paula suggested.

"The back looks out to a nature park."

Paula returned to the two-story split. Above the dining room the roof sloped back steeply enough that two men could perch up there without being viewed from the street. An odd activity, but it might be relaxing if you didn't mind heights. Had they been drinking, possibly horsing around, and of them slipped? It would be hard to prove.

"I called Skye yesterday," Leah said. "I got her number from her father. He sounded awful."

"In what way?" Paula held up the closet rod. Poor Kenneth. He and Callie had been together for thirty-one years. He had adored her, hadn't wanted her to leave.

From behind, Paula heard the panting of Leah's boyfriend, Jarrett, who was in the corner lifting weights.

"The rod needs to be higher, for my full-length dress," Leah said.

Leah was a few inches taller than Paula. Allowing enough space for shoes on the floor, they marked the spot on the wall. Paula screwed in the rod holder, wishing she had space for a convenience like this. Even with paring down, her clothes barely squeezed into her closet. Leah would have shelves for folded items and bars of varying heights.

"It took Skye's dad ages to figure out who I was," Leah said. "At the end, he seemed to forget again."

"I told Leah he might be senile," Jarrett said from across the room.

Paula wiped sweat from her forehead. The open window let in more noise than air. Rock music blasted from someone's radio. A car in dire need of a new muffler roared down the lane. The apartment building owner was wasting money heating the place during this mild spell.

Kenneth, Callie's ex-husband, wasn't senile. He was distracted and he had to be the most controlled person Paula knew. She suggested they put up the rods for Leah's shirts and pants next.

"We want the shelves in the middle," Leah said. "Jarrett and I will share the shirt and pants rods. We like our clothes mingling together."

Paula suppressed an eye-roll. "Won't that make it hard to find your own things? Why waste time looking through each other's—"

Leah's chin jutted out. Paula picked up a shelf. She shouldn't be telling her grown-up daughter how to organize her life.

She was surprised that Kenneth hadn't returned her condolence phone message, but she would see him tomorrow.

"Did you decide if you're going to the funeral?" Paula said.

"I don't know," Leah said. "I'm not sure Skye's handling this well."

"When you talked to her on the phone—"

"She sounded fine," Leah said. "Chatted away about other things—her acting, her friends. I think it's denial."

"Who can deal with a mother's murder? Even you would grieve a little if your mother was shot." She tapped her daughter's arm.

Leah smiled at the grim joke. "Skye's not the most honest person with herself."

"It always amazes me how self-deceptive people can be." Jarrett raised the barbell above his head.

Paula bit her lip to refrain from pointing out that Jarrett could lift thirty pound weights despite a shoulder injury that allegedly prevented him from installing closet organizers and working at his tile-laying job. Every time she saw him, she felt like reporting him to his disability insurer.

"Any more news about the murder?" Jarrett said. "Aside from what's in the papers, I mean. Any inside scoop?"

She had purposely avoided the subject at lunch, enjoying the eggplant casserole and Leah's and Jarrett's patter about their young lives. It had been a wonderful break.

Jarrett raised the barbell again; sweat matted his underarm hair. "Everyone thinks it's suspicious Callie's husband didn't know she went jogging every morning. I say he was treating her with respect, letting her do her own thing."

If anyone other than Jarrett were saying this, Paula might agree.

"Leah walks to work at worse hours than that," Jarrett said. "I don't insist on going with her."

"Maybe you should, for awhile."

"I'm not a baby or babe." Leah stuck out her jaw.

"You could, at least, stop taking the back lane home at 3:00 AM."

"It's a short-cut," Leah said.

Children's squeals emanated from the lane. Kids were playing street hockey, but this wasn't the safest neighborhood. More than once, Leah had found discarded needles in the lane. Leah and Jarrett liked their neighborhood's "edginess." Paula would have thought the same when she was their age. Maybe she still did. Several friends, including Hayden, had questioned her decision to move to Ramsay, Calgary's former red-light district and now the location of Callie's murder.

Leah laid the paper on the dresser top, next to Jarrett's boxer shorts. "Skye invited me to a private service at her place tomorrow night. I think I'll go to that instead of the church service. Is Hayden going with you?"

"He can't get away from work."

"What about Erin?"

"She has a class she can't miss." That might be an excuse. Her younger daughter was sensitive about death. Erin had cried for days after Gary's father's funeral.

If Gary were in town, Paula would like his company at the service, even more than her daughters' or Hayden's. Gary had known Callie better than they had and had liked her a lot. With Gary not here, maybe it was better for her to go alone and sit by herself in the church, so she could totally focus.

Chapter Seven

Organ music wafted from the sanctuary. The church was about half full. An inverse pyramid of spectators tapered to loners seated by the aisles. The front pews below the pulpit stood empty, reserved for family members. Kenneth Unsworth's balding head bobbed above a group in front of the altar. He leaned forward to speak with Sam. A woman in a red dress wove between them. From Paula's position at the sanctuary entrance, the woman looked the image of Callie in her twenties and could only be Skye, her grown-up daughter.

The back rows were already claimed by those wanting an overview or distance. Paula took her place in the second-to-last pew, in front of two women about her age. For the moment, she had a clear view past the empty rows in front of her. The pulpit stood on a stage-like platform. Behind it, a pianist played a classical piece on an electric piano that mimicked the sound of an organ. A small choir sat in front of stained glass windows portraying Jesus with a group of children and a cross draped with flowers. It had been several years since Paula had been inside a church. Since high school, she had limited her attendance to the rituals: christenings, weddings, funerals. She looked at the memorial card she had been handed after signing the guest book. The front page featured Callie's newspaper portrait, with her name, Calandra (Callie) Lansing Moss, her dates, and the caption "In loving memory." A lump formed in Paula's throat.

"Bev," called one of the women behind her.

"Janice. It's been ages." Bev towered above them in the aisle. She wore an enormous brimmed hat.

"You remember Wendy," Janice said.

"Wendy Watson?" Bev said. "I didn't recognize you as a blonde."

"I've also put on weight." Wendy's high-pitched voice contrasted Bev's husky one. "Are you sitting with anyone? We can squeeze you in."

The women shuffled to make space for their friend. Paula caught a whiff of powerful perfume.

"Isn't it tragic?" Wendy said in a stage whisper. "I'm in shock. I was saying to Janice that I can't stop thinking of Callie and us dropping the kids off at nursery school. That was twenty years ago."

"Don't remind me of time," Bev drawled.

"Remember how that first day Ryan clung to my skirts and cried?" Wendy said. "Skye grabbed his hand and marched him right in. All those kids are grown-ups, now. Look at Skye up there, at the front of the church. I wish I had her figure."

"Did Skye marry or is Ravenshaw a stage name?" Janice asked.

"Who knows," Bev said.

Skye took the name Ravenshaw from a high school boyfriend. At school, she had hated all the kids teasingly calling her "Ucksworth."

"What do you make of Skye wearing red to her mother's funeral?" Wendy said.

"Skye's the blonde in the clingy red?" Bev said. "She always had to be the center of attention. Who's the girl beside her, the one dressed like a tart?"

Janice giggled. "Maybe an actress friend?"

The girl was Isabelle, Callie's niece, whose traditionally black dress ended at her upper thighs. She wore fishnet stockings and black boots. Bev's description was apt, if annoying.

Paula opened the card. The left inside page reprinted the newspaper death notice that offered minimal detail. *Survived by her sister Dorothy and her brother Tony.*

"When I heard about the murder," Wendy squeaked, "I figured, oh well, it's just a hooker or a homeless bum; nothing for us to worry about. I didn't recognize the name Moss. Janice phoned me and said it was Callie. I almost fell off my chair. I hadn't known she was divorced."

"She came into my store last winter," Janice said. "She told me she'd remarried, but didn't add more than that."

"Do you mind if we sit here?" a man asked Paula.

She stood to make way for the elderly couple and considered moving across the aisle to get away from the women's chatter. A trio of youths grabbed the spot. She re-settled on her seat, wondering if the youths were Callie's children's friends. The women's conversation had shifted from Callie to themselves. The organ-like music segued to a folk-rock tune that sounded familiar. One of the women owned an interior design business. Another worked in a clothing boutique in Mount Royal Village. One had divorced and remarried. Someone had given up eggs due to high cholesterol. Wendy had a grandson.

"Ugh," Bev said. "I still think of myself as thirty years old."

"You look it," Wendy said. "So did Callie in her newspaper picture. I wonder how old it was."

"It was recent," Janice said. "At the store, I'd swear she looked the same as she did in our kids' nursery school days."

"The miracle of plastic surgery," Bev laughed.

"I don't think Callie had work," Janice said. "The store lighting is good and I see women our age every day. I can tell when someone's done it, Bev."

It would be interesting to see the face beneath Bev's hat. The church was now about three-quarters full. There must be two hundred people here already. Were they all connected to the family or were many of them voyeurs? Paula hoped some were better friends of Callie than Janice, Wendy, and Bev.

"We Are Lost Together," by Blue Rodeo. That was the name of the familiar song.

Kenneth, the ex-husband, took his place in the third row. The tall, thin gray-haired women flanking him must be his mother and sister. Anne and her husband were behind him. Sam remained in the aisle talking with his son. Both had the straight posture common to short men used to looking up at others. They were joined by an obese man, who patted Dimitri on the back and spoke animatedly, using elaborate hand flourishes.

Blue Rodeo merged into an operatic piece. Callie and Kenneth used to buy season's tickets to the opera. Sam couldn't stand opera, she had said.

Wendy's shrill voice jolted her. "Which one is Sam, the new husband?"

"He's the short one talking with Felix Schoen, the journalist," Bev said.

"Cripes," Wendy said. "Felix sure has packed on the pounds. That scruffy gray hair makes him look like a street person."

Callie had mentioned Felix often, but, for some reason, Paula hadn't met him. He was a good friend of both Callie and Sam. They had lived with him while their Riverdale house was being gutted.

"I don't get out to the charity parties these days," Janice said. "Is that how you know Sam?"

"I did the interiors for a building he designed," Bev said. "We always work with the architect."

"What's he like?"

"All architects are the same," Bev said, "in love with their own importance."

Callie had said something similar about Dimitri, the politician.

The memorial card's right inside page contained the order of service and the names of the pallbearers. Callie's brother, Tony, her son, Cameron, friend Felix, husbands, Kenneth and Sam, and Dimitri, Sam's son. Evidently, women weren't strong enough to wheel a casket down the aisle. Or would it be an urn? Would the casket or urn be brought in or was it hidden behind the people at the front?

The memorial card said the Reverend Ellen Lavigne was officiating at the service. There would be two Bible readings and some music. The memorial card's back page concluded with a Shakespeare poem.

This was going to be hard. Bev's babbling and perfume made Paula gag. A woman in ministerial robes entered from a side door, spoke to the gathering at the front of the church and stepped up to the pulpit. The crowd parted, revealing a trolley supporting a cherry wood box. Candles and flowers decked the altar behind it. The box was about a foot wide and eight inches high, Callie's urn.

The reverend waited for the buzz to subside. Callie's children took their seats in the front pew. The gray-haired couple settling beside them would be Dorothy and Tony, Callie's sister and brother, who must be roughly the ages of their parents when they died. Now, they were burying their baby sister. The redhead next to Tony said something to Dimitri, who moved to the aisle spot to make room for Isabelle and Sam.

Rows of heads bowed. A few pews ahead of her, Felix Schoen's large heaving shoulders suggested he was crying. The church was full. Paula looked back to see if anyone was standing. A man in the last row across the aisle nodded at her. She turned away, feeling guilty for having been caught, although the man was also ignoring the prayer. He was about thirty years old with a shaved head and beard stubble. She spun around. Detective Michael Vincelli smiled.

She hadn't recognized him in this different context. Did detectives normally attend the funeral of a murder victim whose case they were investigating? It made sense that they would. From the back pew, Vincelli could observe Callie's family, friends, and associates for suspicious behavior, such as her checking out the crowd rather than praying.

"I didn't know Callie long," Reverend Lavigne said. "She joined our church a year ago and was a blessing to the choir. Once, while standing in this spot, I heard her clear soprano soaring above the rest. She added a richness that will be missed."

On the platform, several choir heads nodded.

"Callie told me she had been raised in the church," the reverend continued. "As she grew into adulthood, like many of us, she strayed and convinced herself the Lord had no meaning in her life. Marriage, children, work, friends, and other worthwhile activities consumed her time, but in the back of her mind a feeling nagged: this is not enough.

"When she rediscovered our Lord, Callie tried several congregations and chose ours for its music program. She took on the task of directing the children's choir whose presentation you will hear at the end of the service. Now, senior choir members who were able to attend today will grace us with a hymn."

Paula had been stunned when Callie told her she had joined a United Church. "They're more open-minded than the others," Callie had said. "Why any church at all?" Paula asked. Callie changed the subject. Perhaps the reverend's words explained it.

Reverend Lavigne was painting an image of a woman who delighted in life's simple pleasures, savoring the moment. She said Sam had talked about the joy Callie found in gardening. Callie had spent hours with his father discussing ways of producing better tomatoes.

From her brief meeting with Sam, Paula couldn't imagine him using the word "joy" in connection with gardening, if anything. She guessed the word was the reverend's interpretation of whatever he had said. No man Sam's father's age was sitting with the family. Callie had said the old man adored her. Was he ill and unable to attend?

The reverend shared more anecdotes from Callie's family. A holiday in the Yukon . . . Callie stayed up all night to watch the Northern Lights. Amusement park rides . . . Callie laughed and shrieked as much as the kids. The reverend asked them all to rise for a hymn.

"What a boring old dyke," Bev said. Through the rousing chorus, she whispered to her friends, "I've got to split. This has dragged on longer than I expected. It's been great seeing you guys."

"We'll have to do lunch," Wendy said.

"I'll give you my card." The hat brim nudged Paula's head. "Where the hell is it? Did I forget to move my card holder from my regular purse to this one? Shit. This has been one of those days. Oh, here it is."

Choking from Bev's perfume, Paula turned around to tell her to shut up. Detective Vincelli was watching her.

Reverend Lavigne rested her arms on the pulpit. She expounded on grief . . . sudden and violent death that makes no sense. Paula gaze strayed to the urn on the altar. She squinted to read the altar inscription: *Do this in remembrance of me.*

"Ta ta girls, I'm off," Bev said.

Hadn't that bitch already left?

At the front of the church, candles illuminated the altar and urn. Paula wiped her eyes. She couldn't do anything for Callie now.

Chapter Eight

"Are you all right, dear?" a woman asked.

Blood pricked the back of Paula's hand. She must have bitten it while trying to block the tears. She rolled her shoulders in an effort to calm the shaking.

The woman passed her a fresh tissue packet. "Did you know her well?"

"It was more about me than her."

"Isn't it always?"

Paula blew her nose. The pews were emptying into the aisles, front to back. Felix Schoen shuffled by, his eyes red. Hadn't he been listed as a pallbearer? The trolley and urn were long gone. Paula's row was coming up. Paula tried to stand so the couple beside her could pass.

"We're in no rush," the woman said. "The benefits of retirement."

They were the only ones left in the sanctuary, aside from the staff clearing the flowers and candles from the altar. Bev and company were gone. Paula made her way to the lobby crammed with people, some teary-eyed, others chatting in groups. Detective Vincelli had probably left before the procession so the family and suspects wouldn't know he was there. A large group gathered by the far wall. Callie's son's sandy hair hovered above the mass of heads. Sunlight streamed through the open arched doors. Paula needed fresh air and would talk to the family after the crowd thinned.

She wove by strangers to the massive doors and blinked at the bright light. Across the plaza, Kenneth Unsworth chatted with a white-haired man. Kenneth bent closer to catch something the man said. Reporters and cameramen lingered on the fringes, waiting for the family to depart. There had been a lot more of them when Paula arrived at the church.

"Paula."

Anne came up behind her. For the second time since Callie's death, they hugged. Anne introduced Paula to her husband, a sixty-year old man of medium height and weight. Doug's vigorous handshake contrasted Anne's portrait of him as frail. His heart and diabetes conditions were a constant concern for Anne. She had described them to Paula in detail during their workout sessions.

"I was telling Doug, we should have you and Hayden over sometime,"

Anne said. "The service made me realize we shouldn't procrastinate about things. You never know what will happen."

In the park across the street, toddlers scrambled up a jungle gym, surrounded by orange and yellow trees. Marigolds bloomed in planter boxes that lined the plaza. Paula put on her dark glasses, the sun burning through her black dress.

"This is your chance to meet Dimitri," Anne said. "He's inside."

Doug excused himself to go and speak with Kenneth. Paula followed Anne back into the lobby, which was called a narthex, Paula remembered from her childhood churchgoing days. An elderly woman grabbed her arm.

"Paula, my goodness me," she said. "You haven't changed in twenty years."

Paula couldn't say the same about Callie's sister. Dorothy, aged sixty-five, looked like an old lady, in her oxfords, black and mauve shift dress and hair worn weekly-hairdresser-appointment style.

"I'm sorry we missed you Saturday," Dorothy said. "It's been non-stop since we arrived. I hope you're coming to the house."

"I'm sorry; I won't be able to make it." Anne looked up at Dorothy. "I have to get back to work. There's Dimitri. If you'll excuse me . . ."

Dorothy held onto Paula's arm as Anne hurried away. "Now, who is that woman?" Dorothy's wrinkled face was flushed. "I've forgotten. So many people to meet." On top of the strain of burying her little sister, she had to greet all these strangers.

"Anne's the mother of Sam's son, Dimitri. She was also Callie's friend," Paula said. "What's going on at the house?"

"We decided to limit the wake to family and close friends. That's why we didn't announce it at the church. Sam said he was going to call you about it."

"I didn't hear from him."

"I'm sure he meant to, though, Sam has a lot on his mind, naturally. I'm on my way to the house right now to get everything ready before people arrive. There is so much to do."

"Can I help in some way?"

"The food's taken care of. I could use help with the setup."

At the far end of the room, Callie's son stood alone, his hands in his pockets. Paula hadn't seen Cameron since he moved to Vancouver for a job in graphic art. An older couple zeroed in on him. She could probably talk to Cameron at the wake.

"Will Kenneth be there?" she asked.

"He said he had an appointment, but I suspect he would feel uncomfortable. Poor man, the situation is awkward."

Paula spotted Callie's brother standing alone. "I'll say a quick hello to Tony and Kenneth and join you at the house."

"There you are." The minister came up to Dorothy.

Tony's lined, angular face held traces of the young man whose portrait had graced the family mantle while he roamed the continent. Paula introduced herself. "We met at your mother's funeral."

He didn't remember her, although he vaguely recalled hearing about Callie's girlfriend who lived on their street. A scar ran from one eye down his cheek. Callie had said Tony joked, if it was a joke, that he had narrowly escaped jail several times. He credited his wife, Ginette, for settling him down.

Ginette approached them. Still pretty in her late fifties, she wore rimless eyeglasses and a scooped-neck black sweater threaded with glitter. Her black skirt showed off shapely calves. Isabelle dressed somewhat like her, but, in looks, took after the Lansing family side. Paula told Tony and Ginette she'd met their daughter, Isabelle.

Ginette linked her arm around Tony's. "Isabelle reconnected us with Callie, some. Before that, we barely knew her. Tony talked with Callie more these past months than he did his whole adult life."

Paula glanced at Isabelle, who was tapping her black boot and talking with Cameron and the elderly couple. "I gather Isabelle moved here from Montreal last May."

"It was her spur-of-the moment impulse," Ginette said.

"That's my girl." Tony sounded proud. "It felt odd asking Callie if the niece she hardly knew could live with her, but Callie said right away 'Sure, we've got plenty of room.' Now that I've seen the house, I would say that 'plenty' underestimates it. Our duplex could fit into the master bedroom."

"Not quite." Ginette squeezed Tony's arm. "Isabelle loves it here."

"I gather she plans on staying," Paula said.

"No fucking way," Tony said.

Ginette rapped his hand. "Tony. We're in a church."

"Fuck the church. My daughter is not—"

"Tony." Ginette's voice was steel. "This isn't the place."

"I need a smoke," he said.

Ginette shrugged an apology to Paula, who started to follow them outdoors. A man called her name. Dimitri strode over and shook her hand, saying he was glad she had come. Close up, he didn't look totally like Sam. His skin was paler. Traces of Anne were in his hazel eyes and heart shaped face. He told her Anne had run into an old friend.

"Anne pointed me out to you?" Paula said.

"My father did, as we wheeled the urn down the aisle."

Like Sam, Dimitri was more handsome in person than in his photographs. His dark hair was cut short and gelled to tiny points. It was starting to thin on top, which made him look older than his thirty years.

"You've been a support for your father," she said.

"I'm glad I was here for the worst. Her death is hard enough without him being harassed by the cops."

"Have they given him a hard time?"

"They grilled him pretty bad, at first. When they came around yesterday I got the feeling they were easing up."

"Maybe their investigation is proving him innocent."

"Let's hope. Well, I have to catch a plane."

"I'd better get going too, if I'm to help with the wake. I don't see Dorothy or Sam anywhere. They must have already left."

"Sam drove Skye to her place with the ashes," Dimitri said, as they walked toward the arched doors.

"That's right. Skye's holding a service for her mother tonight. I think Callie would appreciate that."

His face darkened, even though they were outside. "Knowing Skye, it's a slam against the funeral Sam arranged. He did his best. It was all very sudden and there were lots of people to accommodate."

"He did fine." So he called his father Sam.

Across the plaza, Anne chatted with Doug and Kenneth. She spotted Paula and Dimitri and disengaged herself to hug her son good-bye. Dimitri flashed Paula a charming good-bye smile and bounded down the plaza stairs. He seemed the opposite of bad-tempered and spoiled. Gone was the hostility he had shown on TV, and his comment about Skye had been surprisingly candid, unless it was all part of a well-honed political image.

"Your son's an impressive young man," Paula told Anne.

"I think so."

"He's very supportive of Sam."

"It flows both ways. Did Callie tell you Sam left the job he loved in the States to move up here for Dimitri?"

"She didn't mention it."

"In university, Dimitri got involved in a religion we considered oppressive, almost cult-like. I credit Sam for getting him away from that bunch."

"Isn't Dimitri still a fundamentalist?"

"Too much for my taste, but he's mellowed the past few years." Anne looked at the men talking across the plaza. "Time for me to drag Doug away. He has a doctor's appointment this afternoon. Would you and Hayden be free to come to dinner this Saturday? I'm sure he and Doug would get along well."

"I'll have to check with Hayden." This would be a shift in her relationship with Anne. Paula enjoyed Anne's company at the fitness center. Why not expand it into the social zone? So far, all of her and Hayden's friends who were couples had come from his side.

Anne hugged her, again, and left her alone with Kenneth, whose hug was always an awkward experience. Today, his arms felt particularly stiff. He looked more funereal than usual in his black suit. His long face reminded Paula of Eeyore, the donkey.

"Callie told me you're seeing an old acquaintance of mine." Kenneth scanned the plaza. "Is he here?"

"Hayden has a trial next week," she said. "He couldn't make it."

"He didn't know Callie so much as he knew me, through the university debating team. We also played chess."

"Hayden didn't tell me he played. I'll have to challenge him to a game." There was so much to learn about a person you'd only dated for six months. With Gary, by the end, there were no surprises, aside from his bombshell confession that he was cheating on her. Callie had once suggested Gary had done it to prove he wasn't as predictable as Paula thought. Paula's neck ached from looking up at Kenneth. What could she say to fill the pause? "I enjoyed the service, especially the music. The classical choices must have come from you."

"He picked the contemporary ones," Kenneth grimaced. Was that distaste for Sam?

"I—" they said simultaneously.

"You first," he insisted.

"I understand your daughter, Skye, is holding a private service tonight."

"She's taking this hard."

"It would be rough on any child, at whatever age."

"Her fight with Callie makes it worse."

"Fight?"

He blinked several times, as though he'd expected Paula to be aware of the fight.

"As usual, it was about Sam," he said. "Obviously, Skye doesn't . . . There's a face I haven't seen in a long time."

An older man shuffled toward them. Damn him for interrupting. Skye doesn't what? Kenneth had assumed Callie had been in touch with Paula this past month.

He introduced her to his cousin as Callie's best friend. She wouldn't have used that term, given their recent disconnection. Detective Vincelli had warned her Callie had overstated the level of their friendship, which might cause someone to worry she knew too much. At the wake, she might get an idea of whom that someone could be.

Chapter Nine

S am started when he opened the door. "I was supposed to call you. Did I?" "Dorothy invited me at the funeral."

He had removed his suit jacket and tie, undone the collar button of his shirt, and rolled his sleeves up his muscular arms covered with dark hair.

She entered the house. "Dorothy asked me to help with the setup."

"What setup?"

"Food, drinks, chairs . . . ?"

Dark circles shaded his eyes. Tension lines etched his forehead. "The caterers are taking care of that. Dorothy must have misunderstood."

Down the long center hallway, servers were setting out bottles on the kitchen table. The dining room's stained glass doors were open. Candles and flowers adorned the table covered in white lace. Sam said Dorothy hadn't arrived. They concluded she must have been detained by the minister or someone else at the church. He added that Skye was skipping the reception, then offered Paula a drink and suggested she wait in the living room, while he got her wine and his beer.

Sam was in his stocking feet. Paula took this as a cue to remove her high heels. She padded into the enormous room. Its rich cranberry walls stretched the full length of the house. White crown moldings bordered the twelve foot high ceiling, which was detailed with flowers and ovals. Cherub faces in the moldings looked out from the room's corners. Light streamed through the plantation blinds. A music stand, stool, and Callie's clarinet stood in the front bow window. The room's middle section contained a baby grand piano and sideboard topped with candles, both pillars and votives. She started counting them and got to eleven when Sam arrived with their drinks.

He looked at the candle display. "It's a little excessive. There are dozens of unopened ones in the drawer."

On their way to the conversation nook in front of the gas fireplace, she complimented him on the room's decor.

"It's comfortable," Sam said. "I would have preferred something more contemporary."

That didn't sound like a bereaved husband's remark. She sat down on a chair facing into the room. Sam took the love seat and remarked on the never ending work involved in renovating an old house. Dorothy would be here in minutes. He paused for a sip of beer.

Paula stared directly at him. "Why did Callie abandon her master's of music plan?"

His left foot was tapping the floor. "The cops asked me about that yesterday. I hadn't known she'd applied."

"And been accepted."

"People keep secrets."

"She told me."

"You were her closest friend."

"Did she tell you I was her best friend?"

"She . . ." He pressed his hand on his leg to stop it jittering and looked over her shoulder, out the window. "I was thinking we should get together for lunch. It might good for us both to talk things over."

Detective Vincelli had warned her to watch out for strangers probing. Callie had told her Sam was the one who encouraged her to go for the higher degree. She might still have kept the application secret from him, but not the acceptance. Had she lied to Paula about any or all of it?

"Are the detectives checking the university records?" she asked.

"I expect they're doing it today. A car's turning in the driveway. That must be Dorothy."

He jumped up and rushed to the door. His edginess didn't jibe with Dimitri's remark that the cops were easing up. Maybe Sam thought they were busy collecting evidence, preparing to pounce.

Isabelle, Dorothy, and Ginette bustled in. They were followed by Tony carrying two wreaths, one round and one cross-shaped.

Dorothy apologized for being late. "The minister asked me to take the leftover funeral flowers. I know you told her you didn't want them, Sam, but they aren't suitable for shut-ins and I hated to see them go to waste."

She directed Tony to set them in front of the fireplace. He placed an arrangement on either side. She told him to move the cross to the left, the circle to the right, the cross an inch forward.

"Do it your fucking self," he said, and headed for the kitchen.

Dorothy flushed.

Ginette patted her sister-in-law's arm. "Tony's wound up from the funeral. A smoke and a beer should calm him down."

Isabelle scratched a black jewel in her navel. "I'm starved."

The doorbell rang. Three women from the church choir trooped in, followed by Felix Schoen, the journalist. His weekly column in the city's newspaper's community section was a chatty mix of personal and social commentary. Paula scanned it now and then.

Felix went directly to the kitchen for a drink. The minister had been invited, but had a prior engagement. No one knew why Callie's son, Cameron, didn't show up. A caterer announced the buffet was ready.

Paula lined up behind Felix and filled her plate with vegetables, dip, coleslaw, and mini sandwiches. In the living room, Felix lumbered toward Isabelle at the baby grand. Dorothy and the church ladies were claiming the love seat and chairs. Ginette hauled in a dining room chair so she could sit with them. Paula considered looking for Sam or Tony in the kitchen or dining room.

"Here's to Callie." Felix raised his glass of Scotch to her. He was about six feet tall and at least two hundred and fifty pounds. His crumpled beige suit and shirt, open at the neck, looked like they had been pulled from a laundry hamper.

"I enjoy your column," she said, struggling to recall a specific thing he had written.

"I've canceled it this week. Who can write drivel in the midst of this? I'm mulling an idea, can't get it started. It's got to be real and not exploit her death."

Isabelle wandered over. "Where is everyone? There were tons of people in the church."

"Most of them came to gawk at the car crash," Felix said.

"It would be fun to report on accidents and stuff." Isabelle toyed with her necklace, dipping it in and out of her cleavage. "Can you get me a job at your newspaper?"

Felix downed some Scotch. "I'm freelance. I don't set foot in that hell hole."

"I've gotta get a job by the end of the week," Isabelle said. "My parents want me to go home with them."

"Where's home?" Felix made it sound like a philosophical question. He looked better in his column photo, which must be an old one taken before his crown went bald; blond or gray locks scraggled down the back of his neck. He had been too broken by Callie's death to serve as pallbearer and left the service with tear-drenched eyes.

"Is my dad with Sam?" Isabelle asked and departed for the kitchen.

Felix turned to Paula. "I remember seeing you in the church. Who are you again?"

"I grew up with Callie in Montreal."

"You came all this way." His voice choked over her dedicated friendship.

She didn't bother to set him straight. "Do you think Sam will stay alone in the house?"

"He'll be gone by Christmas, after the reno's finished."

"It's a shame he has to move the minute the work is done. He must feel sad about that."

"Sam never liked this place." Felix's blush suggested this had been a slip. He drained his Scotch and held up the empty glass. "I need a refill."

Rather than join the ladies in the nook, she followed Felix to the kitchen. No sign of Isabelle or Tony or Sam. It was an odd architect who bought a house he disliked.

They replenished their glasses at the table bar. Felix drifted to the living room. Through the patio doors, Paula spotted Tony on the deck. She slid the glass open.

Tony turned at the sound. "You caught me." His grin revealed a gold eye tooth.

"Sam doesn't let you smoke inside?"

"I figure it's polite in a non-smoking house." He drew on his cigarette.

The house shaded the deck and yard, a jungle of poplar and birch still holding onto their leaves. Through the yellows and greens the Elbow River was barely visible. Tony, like Felix and Sam, had taken his jacket off. He wore a short-sleeved dress shirt. On his upper arm, a tattooed snake coiled around a sword.

He pointed his cigarette at the house. "I didn't know architects made this much bread. I figured the name-brand ones were rich, but Sam only designs offices."

"He's pretty successful at it."

"Kenneth, her first husband, is even richer. His house isn't a mansion, like this, but I get the impression there's a lot stashed in investments. Callie did well for herself."

"Until she got killed."

Tony flicked ash over the railing. "Skye says Callie got a hefty divorce settlement and sank most of it into this place. Sam gets it all after one year of marriage."

"Are you suspicious of him?"

He stared at the trees, dragging on his cigarette.

Paula finished her wine. "At the church, Ginette said you'd talked with Callie a lot these past few months, after your daughter moved in with her. Did she say anything that would lead you to think someone might kill her?"

"Most of our talk was joking or about Isabelle, like how late was she staying out and what job was she quitting now."

"You're sure there wasn't something?"

"Nothing." He dropped the cigarette butt into the yard. "What difference would it make now? The dead are dead. Sending a man to jail won't bring her back."

"It might prevent him from murdering someone else."

Tony took out another cigarette. "Exactly."

"What do you mean by that?"

He turned away and rested his arms on the railing.

She returned to the kitchen and placed her wine glass by the sink. Beyond the arch, Felix expounded to Ginette. His hands flailed so wildly no Scotch could possibly remain in his glass. Rather than cut between them, Paula took the hall route to the living room and passed a door that might lead to a pantry. Muffled sounds flowed through the second closed door. She stopped. Through mahogany arched panels, she heard a man's low tones, a girl's high pitched ones.

Isabelle's voice rose. "We had a deal."

"Ssshhhhhh."

"You . . ." Isabelle's voice trailed.

The den door opened. Paula stepped back. Sam froze, his hand on the knob. He stared at her, his eyes wide, his mouth open, and slammed the door in her face.

She slunk down the hall to the dining room and collapsed on a chair.

We had a deal. The dead are dead. Prevent him from murdering someone else. Sam wasn't upset about the cops preparing to pounce. His plan was unraveling.

Sam entered the dining room and halted. "I didn't know you were here."

Isabelle brushed past him on her way to the table. She loaded a dessert plate with pastries and fruit kabobs. "This stuff is really good. Sam, try the dip."

"It's time I checked out the food." Sam grabbed a dinner plate.

He and Isabelle circled the table, not too close to each other and not deliberately far. Sam said he would ask the caterers to make up take-out boxes for Paula and the other guests, since there was too much food for them to use up. Somehow, Sam had smoothed things over with Isabelle. Their deal, whatever it was, was back in place. They were co-conspirators again.

Sam asked Paula which of the sandwiches she liked. She couldn't stand it anymore and strode across the hall to say good-bye to Dorothy.

"So soon?" Dorothy looked disappointed. "We haven't had a chance to catch up."

Paula bussed cheeks, inhaling old lady perfume. The fake fireplace crackled between the funeral wreaths. Sam entered with his plate. Dorothy told him Paula had to leave. He set his plate on the coffee table and walked Paula to the door, playing the proper host. She thanked him for having her. They stopped in front of the door.

"We talked about getting together for lunch," he said. "Why not tomorrow, if you're free?" His tone was casual, as Callie's had been in the answering machine message when she suggested meeting Paula for lunch. Paula had failed to answer that message. Sam wanted to know what Paula had overheard and what Callie had confided to her closest friend. Paula bet he was already formulating an explanation for his argument with Isabelle. That was easy. She could formulate one herself. "I told Isabelle she couldn't stay and she got melodramatic." If they met for lunch, Paula would assure him she understood and make it clear Callie had told her nothing, all in the guise of friendly conversation. Sam would be on guard, but, perhaps, less guarded than he would be with a cop. There was a chance he would slip. Sam was waiting for her reply. His face said, "Yes, no, either way, I don't care" while his hand opened and closed into a fist, opened and closed against his shaking leg. He was hanging on her answer. Saying "no" would close the door. After talking with Vincelli, she could cancel.

"I can do lunch tomorrow," she said. "Where? What time?"

"Your choice."

She thought of a nearby restaurant. "Do you know Lily's Café?"

"I've heard of it."

"Noon. I'll give you directions."

Chapter Ten

As Paula slit the film cover of a frozen butter chicken dinner, the door bell rang. It couldn't be Hayden, who was working tonight. Leah was at Skye's memorial service and Erin had a class. She hurried to the living room and pulled down some shutter slats. A sedan was parked by the curb between her car and Walter's pickup. From this angle, she couldn't see who was on the porch. The bell rang again. Vincelli had warned her about letting in strangers. How could she live like this, being constantly afraid? She looked through the opaque glass. Detective Vincelli. So far, he was the only stranger who kept turning up. She cinched her bathrobe sash.

"I saw you this morning at the funeral," she said. "You left the service early."

"They didn't need to know I was there."

"They? You mean the suspects?"

"I mean the family. They deserved the break from the investigation. You called me about something?"

Cool evening air flowed into the house. She was hardly dressed for visitors, but stepped back so he could enter.

"You didn't have to stop by," she said as they walked to the kitchen, which seemed to have become their established meeting place at her house.

"It's on my way home from the station," he said.

"Whereabouts do you live?"

"Am I interrupting your dinner?" His nose twitched at the South Asian aroma.

"It's just a microwave meal I can reheat."

Was it significant that he hadn't simply phoned in reply to her message that she wanted to talk to him about some things that had happened at the funeral reception? He was either particularly curious about her observations or seizing the chance to check her out. Surely, he had eliminated her from his suspect list. Sam still had to be on it, but how close was he to the top? Dimitri said the cops seemed to be easing up on him. She offered to make coffee. Vincelli said water would be fine and claimed his chair next to the kitchen side door. She got out a water jug and two glasses and took her place opposite him.

His hands went flat on the table. "What did you want to tell me about the funeral reception?"

"I was the first to show up at Sam's house," she said. "He was there alone. He seemed edgy. I got the feeling he was worried Callie might have told me things."

"What things?"

"Whatever he's hiding. You do think there's something?"

His expression remained the same. He hadn't taken out his notebook.

She rubbed the top of her robe to make sure it wasn't open at the chest. He must think she lived in this outfit when she was home alone. "Sam didn't know Callie had been accepted into the MFA program. He didn't even know she'd applied. You obviously know that. Have you checked the university records yet?"

He paused. Was he considering how much he should share?

"She didn't apply," he said.

"That's odd," Paula said. "Isabelle arrived in May. Did that have something to do with Callie changing her mind about the MFA? What do you think about Isabelle and Sam?"

He sipped water, clearly as an excuse to avoid her questions.

"I overheard an argument between Sam and Isabelle," she said. "They were in the den. Isabelle said angrily to him, 'We had a deal.'"

"About what?"

"That's all I heard. My guess is she agreed to withhold something from you in exchange for his letting her stay in Calgary. Tony, her father, seems in on it, too." When Vincelli didn't respond, she continued. "I've been thinking: why would Tony go along? He wants Isabelle out of that house. He made a remark about preventing someone from murdering again. Maybe Isabelle refused to go home, so he made an opposite deal with Sam. He would stay quiet if Sam could convince Isabelle to leave. That put the squeeze on Sam. Isabelle would tell what she knows if Sam kicks her out; Tony would tell if Isabelle stays. No wonder Sam was edgy."

She refreshed her dry throat with water. There was no point asking Vincelli if he agreed with her theory. He didn't disagree, so must think her speculations were worth his time.

"After the fight in the den, Isabelle came out all sweetness and light. At the door, Sam asked me out for lunch. He was visibly upset by my earlier questions. I think he wants to know what I learned from Callie and how much I overheard between him and Isabelle. That's why I contacted you. Should I have lunch with Sam, or not?" She leaned back on her chair.

"That's your decision."

"You warned me that someone might probe to find out how much I knew. Sam probed at the reception. This lunch is more probing. Would I be safe going out with him?"

"Do you want to?"

With the darkness outside and the room's sole light shining down from the ceiling, this felt like an interrogation room. Yes, she wanted to go. She honestly thought Sam might reveal things to her he wouldn't to a cop. She couldn't shake the image of Sam's stunned stare when he came out of the den. Bewilderment and guilt were all over his face, although she couldn't say if it was guilt for murder. If it was, for Callie's sake, she should do what she could to get him thrown in jail. If it wasn't, whatever his flaws, he had been Callie's husband. Callie would want him out of this mess. Probably. Paula hadn't been there for Callie when she was alive, but she could do this small thing for her. Vincelli wasn't warning her of the risk. Did this mean he didn't think Sam was the killer?

"To answer your question," he said. "It's up to you whom you meet for lunch."

If Sam wasn't the prime suspect, who was? "Would you warn me off anyone in Sam's circle?"

Vincelli averted his eyes for a second, just enough to suggest he would. Who? Someone she had met at the funeral? Her meeting with Sam would give her access to his circle, which could be useful for the homicide unit. This could be Vincelli's first major murder case. He must be eager to solve it.

"Another thing I thought of," she said. "This is similar to what I do for work. At lunch, I could turn the tables on Sam and probe."

"No. That is our job," he said. "For which they pay us the big bucks."

"My job involves probing whiplash claimants suspected of faking or exaggerating injury."

"Stiff necks are a long way from murder."

That hurt. It was also true. Her job might involve similar skills, but it dealt with matters less vital, and less dangerous.

Vincelli's lips narrowed. "If you're going in order to probe, stay home." He finished his water, savoring it to the last drop. "If it's a social visit with the husband of your late friend, I can't object to that."

She was probably going for both reasons, and he hadn't argued strongly enough against the first one.

Lily's Café bustled with lunch patrons. Paula walked past tables ringed with senior citizens and a long-haired artsy-looking group to a vacant two-person table at the back. Altadore, like her Ramsay neighborhood, was aging-turning-trendy, although more upscale and further along in the process.

She removed her jacket and waited for Sam, surrounded by green. A few years ago, when she discovered the café with her daughter, it was called Lily's Pad. Paintings of emerald lakes still graced olive walls; fake ivy wove along a ceiling border; green candles sat on chartreuse tablecloths. It had probably been a mistake to wear her green sweater.

It was twelve fifteen. They had agreed to meet at noon. Was Sam, like Callie, the type who was habitually late? Paula drummed her fingers on the avocado placemat. She hadn't seen that shade since her 1970s apartment fridge that froze her lettuce and thawed her ice. She left the table to check out the crafts for sale on the shelves. Ceramic frogs. Lime candles. Kiwi incense.

The café door chimed. Two young mothers maneuvered in baby strollers. Had Sam forgotten about their lunch? She should have given him her cell phone number so he could call if something came up. At last, something non-green in the place: a candle in the shape of a monkey seated lotus-style. He wore a sailor shirt and looked up at her with an open mouth and wide eyes that reminded her of Sam's deer-in-the-headlights stare before he slammed the door in her face. The monkey's cauliflower ears weren't small and neat like Sam's. The door chimed. Sam burst in and scanned the room. She held up the monkey to catch his attention.

He strode over. "Sorry I'm late," he said between breaths. "I got tied up this morning. The detectives came by, and my father." Raindrops rested on his gray-black hair. He dug his hand in his bomber jacket pocket and jangled the car keys. "I have to leave in half an hour. Let's grab some food. Looks like you order at the counter."

She studied the chalkboard menu and chose a chicken wrap and chai latte. Without looking at the board, Sam asked for the same. She realized she was still holding the candle and told the counter clerk she would return it to the shelf.

"I've already rung it up," the clerk said. "I'll have to redo the bill."

The monkey's wide eyes pleaded; so much for her vow not to clutter her new home with knickknacks. She told the clerk she would take it. Sam insisted on paying for lunch to make up for being late.

At the table, she placed the monkey candle beside the centerpiece. "Is your father sick? I didn't notice him at the funeral."

"He's only sick in the head." Sam took the seat across from her. Not removing his jacket, he tilted his chair back. "The cops came by to tell me they traced the murder weapon to its owner. This was news to me. Last I'd heard the gun hadn't been found."

This was still the official word, according to this morning's newspapers, although she had guessed it had been located with the cell phone. "So, it was a registered gun?"

"Unregistered." Sam rocked the chair. "That's why they can't be sure he's the owner."

"Who's 'he'?"

Sam tilted the chair back so far she thought he would topple to the floor. He jerked it forward. The chair legs landed with a clunk.

"My father," he said.

She glanced at the monkey face and pictured a feeble man nurturing his vegetable garden, which had been Callie's description of her father-in-law.

Sam scraped the chair toward the table. "I thought—hoped—he had gotten rid of the thing. The cops turned up at his house early this morning. They dragged him out of bed, checked the shed and discovered it gone."

"Your father kept a loaded gun in his shed?"

"I don't know if it was loaded; neither does he."

"The cops aren't sure the gun they found was his?"

"I told him years ago he should register it. Did he listen?"

Paula struggled to connect the dots. Callie had told her Sam's father lived in Bridgeland, which was directly across the Bow River from Ramsay and the murder site. A stranger stealing the gun and killing his daughter-in-law would be an unlikely coincidence.

Sam absently reached for the candle monkey. "The cops are checking taxi records and asking bus drivers on the routes near his house if a little old man got on and rode to the Elbow pathway the morning Callie died."

"Could buses have gotten him to the pathway early enough? What time in the morning do they start?"

"I don't think the cops had checked into it yet."

"Do they seriously think he did it?" The detectives might be bluffing or exaggerating the depth of their investigation into bus routes and trips to put pressure on Sam and his dad.

"My father is eighty years old. For his age, he's not in bad shape, a little arthritis. Physically, he is capable. I suppose he might have killed her for some bizarre reason."

"Like what?"

He bounced the monkey from hand to hand. "He told me, once, she reminded him of my mother."

His mother died when he was in university, Callie had said. His father had been devoted to his wife and crushed by her death. Surely, Sam wasn't suggesting his father had killed her?

The counter clerk appeared with their meals. Sam set the candle on the table. His expression seemed a jumble of anger, distress and annoyance.

She picked up her mug. "In what way, did Callie remind—?"

"We can thank Felix for this."

"Felix Schoen?" The morose, heavy-drinking journalist from the funeral.

"The cops visited Felix on Friday. They questioned everyone whose name showed up on our phone records. I guess you know that." He removed his jacket and let it drop to the back of his chair. "Felix is a gun nut. He must have twenty of them all over his house. The cops' questions shook him up. He's the sort who looks guilty when he goes through customs, whether he is or not."

Sam's rust dress shirt coordinated well with the café's green. He twisted his wedding ring around his finger, reminding her he had been married to Callie. He noticed her staring at the ring and stopped turning it.

He picked up the candle. "During the interview, the detectives asked Felix if I owned a gun. Felix, thinking this will help me, tells them not only do I not own one; I'm such an ignoramus I wouldn't be able to tell them the make of my father's gun. 'What gun?' the detectives ask." Sam flashed a wry smile. "For some reason—maybe they took the weekend off or figured it was a long shot, pardon the pun—the cops didn't follow up right away. Today, they descend on my father. Bingo, his gun is gone from the shed."

Paula finished her sandwich bite. "Maybe he moved the gun somewhere and forgot."

"He's tearing the house apart, trying to find it. Even if he didn't kill her, he's in shit due to the illegal possession and storage. Serves the old bugger right." His tone was matter-of-fact, with no hint of malice. He took his first bite of wrap.

"Why wasn't your father at Callie's funeral?" she asked.

"He's an atheist who scorns all religious rituals. He hates cops, too, and institutions. That attitude won't endear him to the police."

"Did he buy the gun to keep squirrels from his garden or something?" That was a dumb suggestion. No one would do that in a city. Well, maybe in Calgary, although they'd be more likely to use a rifle.

Sam placed the wrap on his plate. "He bought it to kill my mother."

She squeezed her mug handle. Foam spilled to the tablecloth. She scrunched up her napkin to clean the mess.

"She had cancer," Sam said. "He bought the gun to end her pain, should it be necessary."

She looked up, stopped wiping liquid from the tablecloth.

"She died quicker than we thought. I doubt he'd have had the guts to use it on her."

She dropped the soiled napkin on her plate. His mother was likely in her forties when she died. If his father's gun was the murder weapon, the killer had to be someone who knew about its existence. Sam did. So did Felix.

"Who knew he kept the gun in his shed?" she asked.

"In theory, everyone, thanks to my big mouth. After my mother died, my father bought a large vase and stored her ashes in it, along with the gun. Every spring, he sprinkles a little of her on his garden for luck. That's how he knows the gun was there on the May long weekend. Whenever the subject of death or cremation comes up, I tell that story. There must be people rolling their eyes from having heard it before and who knows whom they told. My father told his neighbor down the street, which means half of Bridgeland knows."

Half of Bridgeland had no motive for murdering Callie. Sam would want to cast a wide net to keep suspicion far from him. Had he really told the story that often or were those-in-the-know limited to his circle?

"I gather the cops showed your father the gun they found," she said. "Did he identify it as his?"

"He's as dense about guns as me. All he could say was it might be his."

"Where did they find it?"

Sam picked up the candle monkey. "A man out partying Friday night saw someone standing on a bridge drop an object into the Bow River. It struck him as odd. He thought it might be drugs or something and called the police hotline."

"Lucky break."

He scraped the monkey's shirt. "Most Septembers are too cold for parties outside. If it weren't for this unusual mild spell, the gun might have stayed buried forever."

She shivered beneath her sweater. He sounded like he didn't want the gun found.

He picked at the wax eye. Was he an ex-smoker, like her, whose hands turned fidgety when he was tense?

"I doubt they could prove in court it was his gun," Sam said. "I promised the old man I'd come over right away. Sorry to cut out on you. Shit. Isabelle. I was supposed to drop off her stuff at Felix's."

"Isabelle? Felix?" That name was turning up a lot.

He plunked the candle on the table. "Yesterday Tony put his foot down and insisted Isabelle had to go back to Montreal. I was tired of getting caught in the middle and told her she couldn't stay with me. Isabelle was pissed. I came up with the idea of asking Felix to take her in. He has a huge house and is used to friends bunking over."

This would explain the argument she had overheard between him and Isabelle. She nodded her acceptance of the official view. Nothing would be gained by having him think she was suspicious of him.

"Tony and Ginette dragged Isabelle out of bed this morning so they could drop her off on their way to Banff. She didn't have time to pack everything."

"Isabelle's parents have gone to Banff?"

"They figured while they were in Calgary, why not take in the sights."

"Tony is fine about his daughter living with Felix?"

"Not really. I'm sorry, but I've got to leave. This hasn't been much of a lunch. I didn't mean to drag you out to listen to this shit."

He had meant to drag her out to find out what she knew and had overheard. Presumably, the cops' connecting the murder weapon to his father had distracted him from that task.

"Are you busy tonight?" he asked.

"No." Unless Hayden managed to juggle his meeting so they could have dinner.

"My client gave me tickets to the hockey game. Obviously, I wasn't planning to go."

Was this an invitation? "Aren't the Flames locked out of playing?"

"This is the Hitmen, Junior League. Do you like hockey?"

She did. When she was married, she and Gary went to the arena a few times a year. "You'd attend a hockey game the day after your wife's funeral?"

He stroked the monkey's head. "I don't care what people think. It could be a break from all this, take my mind off things."

"Where does Felix live?" Paula said. "I could help you by dropping off her stuff."

"Mission. His townhouse backs on the Elbow." He stopped.

River path, she finished his sentence. Callie would have jogged by Felix's house the morning she died and every morning for the previous month or more. Felix might have seen her and been aware of her habit.

Sam looked at the candle monkey. "Shit. I wrecked this thing. I'll buy you another one."

"It's one of a kind."

"It's strange." He twisted his wedding ring. "From the minute Callie's family arrived, I couldn't wait for them to leave. Dorothy flew out this morning. Tony and Ginette are gone. Even, Isabelle took off. Tonight, the last thing I want is a reheated casserole in an empty house."

A house he disliked, Felix had said. Sam's sympathy plea could be a con, but there might be an element of sincerity. Hayden hadn't called yet about their plans for tonight and juggling was not commitment. After seeing his father this afternoon, Sam might have news about the gun.

"Okay," she said.

"Okay what?"

"I can go to the hockey game tonight."

"That's great." He sounded more distracted than thrilled. "It would help if you would deliver Isabelle's things. If I go, she'll get talking and I don't have the time for that."

"Mission's on my way."

"If neither of them is home, you can leave Isabelle's box on the back deck. By the way, if you see Felix and Isabelle, don't mention the gun being found and traced to my father. The cops asked me to keep it quiet until they have a chance to speak to people."

"You've told me."

Again, the surprised expression of the candle monkey. "I doubt you're a serious suspect."

Unlike Felix and Isabelle.

Chapter Eleven

Isabelle opened Felix's door. "Sam called to say you'd be here." She brightened at the sight of the box Paula held.

On the way to the townhouse, Paula had stopped to check out Isabelle's things. They included assorted mismatching socks, a jacket, several bottles of shampoo and conditioner, bath oils, DVDs, and CDs of punk-looking metal musicians as well as mainstream Coldplay, Usher, and Outkast, whom Paula enjoyed in small doses.

Paula set the box at the foot of Felix's interior stairs. The ground floor was a huge open area. The recliner chair, side table, lamp and TV looked lost in the living room space. No pictures hung on the walls, which were painted builders' white.

"Is Felix home?" she asked.

"He said he'd be back soon."

Paula's nose twitched at the cigarette smell. Behind the recliner, a chandelier hung over the empty bamboo floor. The dining area's sole furnishings were a chair and a student's desk against the wall. Above them hung a rifle rack and glass gun display case.

Isabelle followed her gaze. "They kind of creep me out. Felix says they aren't loaded and the bullets are stored in cupboards behind pots and things."

"Sam says he has about twenty guns."

"There's more?" Isabelle's blue eyes widened.

An island separated the dining area from the kitchen. Three barstools grouped around it. To make room for a plate, you would have to shove aside a foot-high pile of newspapers and mail.

"Sam told me your room is almost a separate apartment upstairs," Paula said.

"It's the attic."

"Can I see it?"

Isabelle stepped over her box and darted up the stairs. Paula bent to pick up Isabelle's things, decided she wasn't the girl's packhorse and left them to follow her up the twelve-foot staircase to the middle floor. Isabelle oozed such innocence. She might be foolishly in love with Sam, but it was almost impossible to think of her as involved in some evil plot.

The back bedroom's door was ajar. Paula glimpsed white pillows plumped on a king sized brass bed covered in a white duvet. The floor's front rooms seemed more suited to the disheveled Felix. The den's computer screen poked above a jumble of paper and dictionaries. Boxes and board games filled the other room. Monopoly. Clue. Risk.

"Felix was talking about us playing one of those games tonight," Isabelle said. "Kid stuff."

"I enjoy a good game now and then."

"You could come over. He says they're better with more people."

Was Isabelle serious? "I'm busy tonight," Paula said. Going to a hockey game.

Isabelle bounded up the staircase to the third floor. Paula plodded behind her to the open attic loft, a long narrow room with sitting areas at each end. Little natural light flowed through the gabled windows.

Isabelle stopped beside the futon at the front of the house. "Dimitri left a DVD and CD player. There's even a microwave and bar fridge. I'm going to use this part for my living room and that other futon for sleeping, like he did. That door over there is the bathroom."

"Sam's son lived here?"

"For a few weeks, until he bought a condo in his political riding." Isabelle crossed to the back window. "See, my view's pretty good."

Paula joined her. From this height, the lone cyclist on the Elbow trail looked like a doll. "Are you sure you'll like it here?"

"Sam's moving at Christmas anyway. I can stay here forever or until I can afford my own apartment."

"You don't mind Sam breaking the deal about your living with him?"

Isabelle's eyelashes flickered, the first indication she was capable of guile. "He came up with something better."

"What does your father think of this?"

"My mom will make him come around."

"Why do your parents think this is better for you than living with Sam?"

Below, something thumped.

"That's Felix," Isabelle said.

By the time Paula got downstairs, Isabelle had explained her presence to Felix, who looked even more rumpled than he had at the funeral. His jeans, belted below his stomach, were frayed at the knees and the hem.

Threads hung from his orange sweater, which had a hole in the arm. He removed his faded Calgary Flames baseball cap and asked Paula if she would like a drink. She hesitated. It would mean rescheduling her first afternoon appointment.

"Maybe a glass of water or juice," she said.

With a swoop of his arm, Felix cleared the kitchen island. Newspapers and envelopes toppled to the floor. He got a jug of orange juice from the fridge, poured three glasses half full, and took a bottle of vodka from an island shelf. Paula turned down his offer of a spike and was glad when Isabelle did too.

"Cheers." Felix raised his glass and downed half his drink. "So, you met Sam for lunch. How's he doing the morning after?"

Reminding herself not to mention the murder weapon discovery, she said Sam seemed okay, all things considered. "This is a great house. I looked at one in this complex last spring that was way beyond my budget."

"Mine too," Felix said. "Magazine and newspaper work pays crap."

"My parents rent," Isabelle said.

"I own," Felix said. "Sam holds the mortgage."

"Really?" Paula looked up from drinking.

"It's no secret."

She took a leap. "Is that why Callie paid for most of her and Sam's house?"

His long sip said he wasn't answering the question. "Are you into guns?" He must have noticed her studying the gun rack and case. Three rifles and three guns.

"Do you hunt or shoot?" she asked.

Isabelle padded to the glass case. "I wouldn't like killing animals. Shooting bottles or birds could be fun."

"Birds are animals," Paula said.

"Someday, I'll take you to the shooting range," Felix said to Isabelle while looking at Paula. He lumbered to the glass case, turned the combination lock, and removed a handgun. "You've got to see this beauty. It's my latest find."

Isabelle stepped back and shook her head, refusing to touch it. Paula would have thought Isabelle would be bolder, although she had seemed startled by the prospect of him owning twenty guns.

Felix cradled the weapon in both hands. "It's a Walther PPK 32."

"Walter?" Paula pictured her next-door neighbor rocking on his porch.

"A widow I interviewed for a quilting article happened to mention, in passing, her husband had brought a Walther semi-automatic home from the war. She was wondering what to do with it, now that he was gone. I offered to take it off her hands."

Paula set her juice glass on the counter. Felix's "beauty" was heavier than she expected. She hadn't held a gun before. The Walther cooled her palm. Felix watched her like a mother releasing her newborn to a stranger. What was so pretty about this gun? It looked like any other semi-automatic.

Isabelle edged closer. "Is it worth a lot of money?"

"I gave the widow a fair price," Felix said. "It even comes with capture papers. Hold your fingers straight." His sweaty hand touched Paula's. "Never on the trigger, unless you plan to shoot. Capture papers authorized soldiers to bring the gun home. I figure the husband stole it from a dead Nazi." Felix scooped the Walther from her hand, apparently unable to tolerate her further mishandling. He returned it to the case.

She picked up her orange juice glass. "Sam says you have about twenty guns. Are they all registered?"

"Of course," he winked at her.

She sipped, not looking up. "I gather the gun that killed Callie wasn't found with her on the trail."

Felix returned to the kitchen island and finished his drink. "Are you and Sam going to the game tonight?"

"How did you know?"

"He said he might ask you."

"When?"

"I don't know. This morning, I guess." So, Sam's invitation wasn't spur-of-the-moment.

"What's the matter with your arm?" Isabelle said to Felix.

His right arm moved stiffly as he refilled his glass with vodka and juice.

"An old hunting injury, acts up in damp weather." Felix leaned back and chugged.

Paula's cell phone rang. Hayden's name appeared on the screen. She told Felix she had to leave and walked with Isabelle to the front door. Would Felix's drinking continue into the evening? Isabelle was wiry, tall, and in good physical shape, but could she handle a drunk who was more than twice her mass and age, owned twenty guns, some illegal and hidden, and was quite possibly under suspicion of murder?

"What did your parents think of Felix's collection of guns?" she said.

"They saw the ones on the wall. They're locked up safe."

"And Felix and Sam forgot to mention all the other ones in the house."

Isabelle's parents had gone off to Banff. She was Callie's niece and had been Callie's responsibility before she died.

Paula rummaged through her purse for a business card and scribbled her home phone number and address on the back. "Call, if you run into problems."

Isabelle took the card. "I won't have any problems when I find a job."

Felix saluted good-bye with his drink.

Paula hurried through the drizzle to her car. She phoned the claimants she was supposed to see this afternoon, apologized with "a close friend died," rescheduled, and returned Hayden's call.

"I have a gap in my day," he said. "Feel like getting together?"

"I'm in Mission heading back to my place."

"I'll grab my car and pop over."

"That's sweet of you."

"I've neglected you these past two days."

She had wanted the time to shower and dress for the evening and phone Leah to enquire about Skye's funeral service.

This impulse from Hayden suggested he hadn't juggled tonight's meeting and she was free to go out with Sam.

It took some effort," Hayden said. "But I got it changed to tomorrow."

He entered the house, dressed in the gray suit she wished he would retire. It tended to wash out his face. The monkey foot poked from under her purse on the console table. If she showed the candle to Hayden, he would ask her why she was buying knickknacks she disdained as dust collectors. While she got their drinks, he settled on the sofa, no doubt expecting her to snuggle beside him. She chose the chair and skirted the issue of tonight's plans by recapping her day: Sam's late arrival at lunch, the detectives' tracing the murder weapon to Sam's father's shed, Isabelle's move to Felix's house, her delivering Isabelle's belongings, and Felix's drinking and guns. Since Hayden seemed attentive, she rambled more. Spewing it out felt so good.

"Sam felt guilty about cutting our lunch short," she said. "He wants to continue the conversation tonight."

Hayden snorted. "I trust you told him no."

"I thought you'd be tied up at a meeting."

"Don't tell me you said yes?"

"I hated to miss the opportunity."

"What opportunity?"

Raindrops blotted her living room window. In fine weather, she could walk to the Saddledome from her house. Sam said he would pick her up at six fifteen. They would grab supper at the game.

"I didn't learn anything from Sam at lunch," she said. "He was too upset about the gun thing."

"I'll bet he was. His father is implicated in a murder."

"It's not certain the gun belonged to him."

"At the bare minimum, he'll be charged with harboring an illegal weapon."

She sipped her wine, searching for more reasons to have said yes. "Sam lost his wife last week. Suddenly, he's alone. I can understand him wanting company."

"Doesn't he have friends?" Hayden said. "What about this Felix?"

"He'll be too drunk to offer any support."

"You've already given Sam lunch. One meal a day for a virtual stranger is enough."

"You and I can have dinner tomorrow."

"I changed my meeting to tomorrow for you, remember? I'm not shifting it again."

"Then we'll make it Thursday."

"I'm not sure about Thursday."

"You're not sure?" She got up. Blood rushed from her head. She dropped to the chair. After five nights of disrupted sleep she was too tired for anyone, never mind a hockey game. "We'll make it Friday or Saturday or whenever. The point is you and I can see each other any time."

"And Sam is only free tonight?"

She dug her fingers in her hair that needed washing and massaged her scalp. "I agreed and I don't like canceling people on short notice."

"You don't mind canceling me or your claimant meetings. How does work fit into your running around?"

"I've got a handle on it." She would be playing catch-up through next week.

"Where are you and Sam meeting tonight? Is it for dinner?"

A hockey game would sound so frivolous and cheerful. How could she be attending one with Callie's husband the day after Callie's funeral? Outside, the rain had stopped. Sun strained to break through the clouds.

"I've told you why I'm doing this," she said.

"Do you really believe you can ferret information out of a man like him?"

"What do you mean 'like him'?"

He clinked his wine glass on the end table. "Why did Sam tell you about the gun ID, when the detectives told him not to?"

"He assumed I was off the suspect list."

"Or, he was putting on a show of openness and sucking you in with tales of his quirky father and his mother's sad death. What woman can resist a man with a childhood wound?"

"Sam was over twenty when his mother died and a father himself already."

"That was careless, getting his girlfriend pregnant."

"What does that have to do with anything?" She rose, slowly this time, and paced to the wall unit. "What's he sucking me into? What would he gain from that?"

Hayden got up, presumably to match her height—more than match, since he was a half foot taller than her. With Sam, she stood face to face, on an equal level.

"I don't know what he gains," Hayden said. "Neither do you. That's my point. The killer has the upper hand because he's the only one who knows what's going on."

"We don't know Sam is the killer."

"If he is, it was clever of him to subtly mention his father may have murdered Callie for some crazy reason, shifting suspicion from himself."

"Would he do that to his own father?"

"If he's a cold-blooded killer, he would, and this murder is starting to sound pre-meditated."

"I agree."

"Sam's father's gun was stolen in advance, with intent to commit the crime."

"The killer knew Callie would be on the trail." She rested her elbow on the wall unit, relaxing at the conversation shift from emotion to reason. "It makes you wonder about Felix. His house has a view of the Elbow River path. Sam implied the police suspect him."

"If Felix knew of Callie's jogging habit, there's a good chance he told Sam about it."

"Sam said in the newspaper he didn't know."

Hayden's smirk implied she was being naïve. "Sam knows you witnessed his argument with his little Lolita-Isabelle. To make a show that there's no hanky-panky between them, he sends her to live with Felix, his friend."

"Hanky-panky?" She mimicked his condescending air. "Isabelle doesn't act like she's interested in Sam that way."

"How do you know she's not a con artist?"

"Isabelle?" Isabelle's blond lashes had flickered at the reference to a deal between her and Sam, and she had been capable of keeping the nature of that deal a secret from the cops.

"I bet the minute her daddy is on the plane Isabelle will run back to Sam's cozy nest."

This was possible and would explain why Isabelle had gladly moved in with Felix.

"Your playing detective will do nothing but mess up the police investigation and put you at risk. Let Isabelle comfort Sam and let the police do their work."

Sam would pull up to her curb in four hours, which left plenty of time to phone him and cancel. Her legs wavered. She returned to her chair. Hayden remained by the wall unit, eyes boring down at her.

She stared up at him. "Give me one day."

"For what?"

"I'll get what I can from Sam tonight, and then I'm finished with him for good."

"I've argued my case."

"Don't be such a lawyer."

"If I hammer it, you'll go out with him to spite me." His face darkened.

"Are you jealous of me spending time with Sam?"

"Ha."

The "ha" was slightly off-key. She had hit a nerve.

Hayden had been the one who pursued her. Despite his work commitments, it was always him, not her, who pushed it to the next level. Why did one in a partnership always want it a bit more?

Slumped on the chair, she softened toward him, just as she had softened toward Sam at lunch. Hayden had been right about that; his case, whatever its motives, made sense. Tonight, she would be careful.

Chapter Twelve

Sam's Acura pulled up behind her Echo. He was five minutes early. Paula let go of the living room shutters, smoothed her burgundy sweater, and answered the doorbell ring. He wore his lunchtime bomber jacket and jeans, but had changed from his T-shirt to a white turtleneck sweater. His shorter hair and its crisp lines indicated he had squeezed a haircut into his busy day.

He held out a paper bag. "I brought these to make up for the monkey one I ruined at lunch. They're ones Callie bought, but didn't get around to using.

She reached into the bag and took out a box.

"If you want more, you can have the rest from the drawer in the sideboard, since you seem to like candles."

She didn't particularly like them, but he had put thought into the gift. A plastic lid covered the set of nine votive candles in colored jars—peach, blue, mint, mauve.

"They may be too pastel for your taste." Sam studied her living room. "I like that cinnamon wall color. I see you haven't got around to putting up pictures. How long did you say you'd lived here?"

"A month. I'm taking my time to see what fits. How's your father?"

"Better. I left him stewing his tomatoes. This house reminds me of his Bridgeland place. Two bedrooms? One in the front, one in the back?"

If he was hinting for a tour, he wouldn't get it.

"Are the kitchen and bathroom redone?" he asked.

"I painted the claw foot tub—pewter."

"Claw foot, sharp."

She adjusted the pendant dangling over the sweater she had chosen because it was her darkest and most subdued. His non-funereal white sweater heightened his dark skin tones. He was missing his wedding ring. Married men who removed their rings when they went out with other women—an airplane roared above them.

"That's my big complaint about this neighborhood." She picked up her purse from the console table.

"There's a new type of window that would block the sound."

"Completely?"

"Like you wouldn't believe. I'll give you my wholesaler's number. He doesn't usually do residential, but I'm sure he'll make an exception."

If nothing else, this would be a practical benefit from the evening.

During the drive through Ramsay, Sam chatted about the architecture in her neighborhood. They entered the Stampede grounds.

She steered the conversation to his father. "Do you think the detectives consider him a suspect or are they convinced his gun was stolen?"

Sam parked between two SUVs. "They told me no bus route could have got him to the site that early in the morning, but he's probably still on their list. I doubt he's number one."

"Who is?"

"Me." He removed the keys from the ignition. "The husband usually has the strongest motive."

Startled by his blunt answer, she got out of the car. A husband's motive would be inheriting money or love gone wrong. They joined the crowd walking toward the Saddledome stairs.

"There'll be more people than usual," Sam said, "on account of the NHL lockout. It could wreck the whole hockey season."

"Some National League players are paid way too much."

"You don't think the ones with talent deserve it?"

Did he relate to the players due to his high salary as an architect? They wove around a group of men in business suits. Young adults and families were the more usual Hitmen patrons. She and Gary used to bring the girls to these junior league games and spring for Calgary Flames' tickets for themselves. It had been over five years since she had seen any hockey game live. Hayden didn't like watching or playing team sports.

Inside, she thrilled to the atmosphere: people milling, out for an evening of fun, the anticipation of a fast-paced game. For dinner, they opted for food court sandwiches. This would be neater to eat on her lap than pizza.

"Do you want a beer?" Sam asked.

"Of course."

Music geared to a young audience blared from the dark arena. They made their way up the steps to the second level.

"They aren't the greatest seats," Sam said.

"They're center ice. Good overview." Assuming she would focus on the game.

Sam settled into his seat beside a seven- or eight-year-old girl. His hand brushed Paula's as he passed her his jacket to place on the spare seat next to her. She draped her jacket over her shoulders, breathing the cool air. Strobe lights swirled over the ice; a ticker tape circled the arena. The clash of the metallic musical tones reminded her that the point of this evening wasn't enjoyment: it was to probe Sam.

"Nice to get away," he said.

"It's bad enough for you to go through a loved one's death," she said. "On top of that, to be the brunt of the cops' suspicions—"

"It's fair."

"What do you mean?"

"I'd think the same in their place."

"Please rise for the national anthem," the announcer said. "And remove your hats."

Sam sang along with "Oh, Canada," one of the few people she knew who did that. His voice was deep and strong and could carry a tune. With the puck drop, the game began. Intently, Sam followed the play, while eating his sandwich. He moaned with the crowd when the puck missed the net.

"Did you play hockey as a kid?" she asked.

"Just on the neighborhood rink, not in organized leagues, like they do today."

"Did Dimitri play?"

"For a few years. He was pretty good. I liked taking him to games."

"You were quite involved in his upbringing." She knew this from Callie and Anne. "A lot of guys would have buggered off."

"It was the timing, I guess." His gaze stayed fixed on the ice. "Yeah."

The Calgary Hitmen had scored. The crowd cheered. The strobe lights went wild. The girl beside Sam blew her plastic red alp horn. Paula watched the goal on the instant replay.

"Dimitri's upset that my father's gun might be the murder weapon," Sam said. "He and the old man are close. Dimitri's worried he did it."

"Do you think he did?"

"I don't know or especially care."

"That's odd."

He nursed his beer, either reflecting on or avoiding her remark. "Worst case scenario: my father goes to jail. If they give him a patch of earth to garden, he won't find it much different from being at home. He's eighty and has lived out his life."

"You're hard on your father."

"He would say the same about me, if he thought I was guilty." His tone was neutral, with no trace of resentment. "In fact, he did say it this afternoon."

"He suspects you?"

He took another sip, probably stalling for more time. "Callie and I used to visit him together. Once, while she went to the washroom, he told me I was cool and not good enough for her."

Again, his flat tone suggested no pain. Acceptance or denial? His ringless hand grazed her arm. She felt a chill through her sweater. "Were you cool toward her?"

Sam jumped. The girl beside him had spilled her Coke on his jeans. Her mother leaned over and apologized, over and over.

"It's okay." Sam wiped his jeans with his hand, barely seeming bothered. "I do that all the time," he told the girl.

Paula passed him her napkin. He cleaned his sticky fingers. The whistle brought the period to a close. Girls carrying sticks and rings skated onto the ice.

"My daughters played ringette," Paula said. "I coached a few years." And spent umpteen motherhood hours in arenas watching games.

Paula stayed for the ringette demonstration, while Sam went out to buy them each a second beer. In the old days, Leah used to fly across the ice, scoring goals. When Paula called her this afternoon, Leah described Skye's memorial service for Callie as weird. The urn was placed on the coffee table that a dozen or so of them grouped around, snacking on hors d'oeuvres and acting like it was a party. Aside from Cameron, Skye's brother, none of the others knew Callie. Most of the talk was about theater.

Sam returned with two plastic cups of beer. She expected him to start into small talk. Instead, he picked up on her earlier question.

"Callie and I . . ." he said. "Our marriage, essentially, ended ten months ago. There was no more than casual friendship between us since Christmas."

No sex. "You'd barely returned from your honeymoon."

"It was a classic case. Anyone, except the people involved, could have predicted it. The minute we had it all, we didn't want it any more. Instead of exploding, our romance fizzled, which was lucky in the sense that it allowed us to live together until we figured out what to do."

He was looking straight at her, his expression obscured by the darkness of the arena. Clearly, he wanted her to know this and may have rehearsed his explanation while getting the beers. His hand minus its wedding ring rested on her sweater. He was interested. She ought to shake his hand off, but letting it linger might encourage him to tell her more.

"We were also lucky to have a big house," he said. "I set up residence in the basement. There's a bedroom, bathroom, microwave, fridge, den. Sometimes I joined her for meals upstairs. We got along okay. We even shared some laughs now and then."

Last Friday, when Paula walked to his house and met him and Isabelle, Sam had come up from showering in the basement. When Callie was murdered, he had been exercising down there. If they were, effectively, living separate lives, it would explain why he didn't know where she went in the mornings. Their passion had been strong enough to break up Callie's twenty-eight-year marriage. It may have been the excitement of the forbidden, but what were the odds such passion would mutually fizzle into easy friendship? Isabelle lived with them the last four months. She must have witnessed things.

"Was Isabelle aware of your situation?" she said.

"She couldn't have missed it. Callie was glad to have her move in last spring. She liked the company. In her weird way, Isabelle fit right in."

"With Callie, or you?"

His eyes narrowed and, to her surprise, crinkled in amusement. "I'm not suicidal. Isabelle's high maintenance. She also has a father who would take out my liver if I laid a hand on her." He stared directly into her eyes. "Besides, I'm not interested. For all my faults, I prefer women my own age."

She looked away and let go of the pendant she had, apparently, being toying with. They stood to let a group returning from the intermission squeeze by. The second period began. The action on the ice was too slow for even Sam's attention.

"Are the police aware of your living arrangement?" she said.

"They looked through the house. I knew it would have been obvious from her bedroom and other stuff, so I leveled with them. I think they're satisfied I didn't kill her in a passionate rage."

"You said you were the prime suspect."

The collective murmur in the arena rose. Sam turned his gaze to the fight on the ice. The referees pulled two players off each other. The police must figure Sam's motive was money. He would inherit the house Callie had bought. A million dollars was a lot of money, even for someone with his income. And he could have debts, a gambling addiction . . . The cops would be checking every cranny of his life. It was strange that Sam didn't deny he had killed Callie. Maybe he felt there was no point in denying, since he would claim innocence whether he did it or not. Likewise, he would say he wasn't involved with Isabelle and, in Paula's view, that was still the most likely problem Callie had wanted to discuss with her. Something immediate might have happened to make Callie call on impulse from the trail. Isabelle pregnant?

The crowd cheered and groaned at a near goal. The ice action died down again. Sam asked about her daughters, switching the conversation to her. She passed it back to him and found out he had offered to marry Anne those thirty-one years ago when she told him she was pregnant. She turned him down because "She knew I wasn't marriage material." Dimitri was born two months after Sam's mother died. That's what he had meant by timing. He didn't expect to become involved with the baby, but guessed he wanted something to hang onto. Anne chose the name, Dimitri, because it was different. She baptized him with her surname. When he was ten, she married and asked Dimitri if he wanted to remain a Hawthorn or take his father's name. She had meant his stepfather, and was "a little pissed" when he opted for Sam's surname.

Sam chuckled. "Anne couldn't go back on it, since she gave him the choice and wanted him to accept her marriage. Doug's been a real father to him. I'm somewhere between a father and friend."

"Anne's told me many times how much she appreciated your help with Dimitri all these years," Paula said. "She says you gave up a job in the States to move closer to him."

"Yeah," he said. "It was also a handy excuse to escape a woman I was living with at the time." In response to her probing, he confessed to having lived with four, no five, women in his life. The longest arrangement had lasted three years.

The hockey game second period ended. The intermission entertainment would be a wild chicken run. People in chicken costumes slid onto the ice.

Men set up barrels. Rather than watch the chickens chase around, Paula chose to walk in the concourse with Sam. He bought a third beer; she'd had enough. As they were leaving the concession stand, Sam was hailed by a client. He introduced him to Paula. She recognized the name as one of the city's construction giants.

The man expressed his condolences to Sam. "Glad to see you're not letting it get you down." He shot a questioning glance at Paula. "I mean, naturally, you're . . ." His voice trailed. He said good-bye and returned to the arena.

"That was a bit awkward," Sam said.

His suppressed smile made her think he was glad to have been noticed in public with her.

Sam steered the Acura onto her quiet, dark street. The timer light glowed from Paula's living room, making the place look occupied. That wouldn't ensure her safety, if the danger was in this car. She had learned quite a bit about Sam tonight, but nothing that brought her closer to knowing whether or not he had murdered Callie. He parked in front of Walter's pickup. Light from the street lamp flickered across Sam's face as he said how much he had enjoyed the evening. "Even though we talked about the murder, it felt like a break."

Paula thanked him for inviting her to the game. "I'd forgotten how much I like them." Not that she had absorbed more than a few minutes of the play.

"We should do it again sometime."

"I don't think so."

His forehead creased. She touched the door handle, preparing to leave. Hayden was right. From now on, she would leave the detecting to the detectives. Did Sam know she was seeing someone? She hadn't once mentioned Hayden's name. That was equivalent to his removing his wedding ring.

He rested his hands on the steering wheel. "Felix and I are planning a hike in Kananaskis this Saturday. It would be another break, a real getaway. He and Callie were good friends. I think he's more broken up about this than I am. It would be more fun if you came along."

Felix again. If Paula spent a whole day with him and Sam, she could learn a lot. What was the matter with her? Hadn't she just decided she would let the police do the figuring out? Hayden wouldn't tolerate being dropped a second time for Sam. "I can't."

"You don't have to decide right away," he said. "I'll call you later this week."

Sam had been Callie's husband, albeit estranged, according to him, and Callie, her friend, had been dead less than week. Paula was committed to Hayden. Sam's attitude toward his father and the woman he dumped in the States was a warning flag. Romantic involvement with him was not an option.

The street light rippled across Sam's forehead lines. She could almost see his mind churning in thought. His lips tightened, apparently, in decision. She waited for the revelation.

"I'll walk you to your door," he said.

That was it? "Don't bother." That was sharp. Tough. He deserved it.

"You can leave the decision about Kananaskis to the last minute."

"I've decided now."

"A lot could happen between now and then."

Despite her protests, he got out of the car. They passed through her gate on their way to the porch. In another life, she would have invited him in for coffee. Good chance they would have wound up in bed. But the complications were there. So were his lips and eyes framed by laugh wrinkles, his high cheekbones, and his solid chin. Under the porch light, he leaned toward her.

She drew back, her lip's tingling, and banged her leg on the railing. She muttered good night. He said he'd call her Friday about Kananaskis and trotted down the stairs, seemingly undisturbed. She wished she'd given him a shove.

Without watching him drive off, she entered the house and closed the door to the sound of the revving of his car engine. The living room seemed unusually bright. She set her purse next to the box of candles he had brought, hung up her jacket and unlaced her sneakers. Light was shining into the room from the hall. Had she forgotten to turn that light off? Footsteps sounded in the kitchen. Paula grabbed the candle box. The steps moved to the hall. She raised the box to hurl it. A figure entered the doorframe.

Paula gasped. "What are you doing here?"

Chapter Thirteen

"Do you want popcorn?" Isabelle said. "I was putting a bag in the microwave when you came in."

Paula realized she was still holding the candles. She placed the box on the console table, still shaken by the apparition in a fuchsia tank top and yoga pants. "How did you get in? I'm sure I locked the doors. I spent Saturday installing bars on my basement windows."

"The man next door used his key."

"Walter?"

"Whatever. He's old. He saw me ringing your bell and yelled from his porch."

"Walter has a key?"

"He wasn't sure it would work. He thought you might have changed the locks after you moved in." Isabelle brushed her blond hair behind her shoulders. "I'll make one bag of popcorn. We can always do more."

Presumably, the previous owners had given her neighbor a key. Neither they, nor Walter, nor her realtor had mentioned that little fact. How many times had Walter offered to pick up her newspapers and mail when she was away? Never once had he said he had a key, or that he'd put the papers and mail in her house. He had kept this from her deliberately. She would give him shit about letting strangers in. Paula strode through the living room to the kitchen.

Isabelle was searching through the fridge. "Do you have any real Coke? I only see Diet."

"You're out of luck."

"I can drink Diet, then."

"Why aren't you at Felix's place?"

Isabelle peered over the fridge door. She had the widest blue eyes. "I didn't feel like staying there overnight."

"Why not?" Paula passed behind Isabelle to check the side door lock. Her business card lay on the kitchen table. She had given one to Isabelle today. "That's how you knew where I lived."

"It took two buses to get here," Isabelle said. "I could have walked as fast, but I had my bag and this area's kind of creepy after dark."

"What time did you get here?"

"About nine o'clock. It was your card that convinced the man next door I was legit. You wouldn't give your card to everyone."

"I do. I give it to everyone."

"He said you'd gone out with a man in a red car. I told him that was Sam and explained I was Callie's niece. He knew all about her and you being friends. He said it was nice of you to ask me to move in with you after she died."

"I did not ask you to move in. I said to call if you ran into trouble."

"What good would calling do when you were out?"

"My cell number's on the card."

Isabelle's eyelashes flickered. "I didn't think of that."

Paula's heartbeat had returned to normal. So, Isabelle wanted to move in. Why? Had Felix done something? Paula couldn't seriously see Isabelle as a murderer, even though she was probably on the suspect list. "While I change, can you get a bottle of red wine from the basement? It's at the foot of the stairs, on the shelves to the right."

"I had enough booze at Felix's," Isabelle said.

"The wine's for me." Paula opened the door for Isabelle. Even with the light on and the window bars, she didn't envy Isabelle's tread down that staircase tonight. And she herself wouldn't feel completely comfortable in this house, accessible to people like Isabelle and Sam, until the murder was solved.

In the bathroom, a pink comb trailed long, blond hairs onto the sink. More strands clung to the basin. Paula washed them down the drain. Isabelle's toothbrush nestled next to hers. This wasn't a two-person counter. Bath oils Paula didn't recognize lined the shelf by the claw foot tub. Isabelle had brought her essentials.

A tote bag spilled thongs, shorts, and CDs onto the den's single bed. A trio of pastel Beanie Babies perched on the pillow. Isabelle had helped herself to Paula's laptop and had, evidently, spent part of the past hour on MSN, chatting with friends in Montreal. Her last entry read, *My dad's been hassling me since I got here.* He might have good reason.

It felt good to get out of her bra and into her sleep-shirt. Even better would be a crawl into the sheets, but no way could Paula sleep before she cleared up some details with Isabelle. She followed the popcorn smell to the kitchen, closing the basement door on the way. Isabelle opened the steaming bag and dumped the popcorn into bowls. Paula uncorked the merlot. She carried the food tray to the living room ottoman. The light timer had clicked off.

Isabelle wandered to the wall unit and picked up the monkey candle. "We can light this."

"No, it's too cute to burn."

"The back of its shirt is gouged. It only has one eye. Did you drop it?"

"Let's turn on the regular lights. I spent all night in a dark arena."

Isabelle returned the monkey to the shelf. "How was your date with Sam?"

"It wasn't a date. Why didn't you stay with Felix?"

Isabelle settled into the armchair. "Stuff. Mostly, his drinking and acting weird."

Paula turned on the table lamp. Isabelle twirled a strand of hair, dipping it into her tank top. Her navel peeked out of her skin-tight yoga pants. She and Felix had been drinking.

Isabelle dug her hand into the popcorn bowl. "His guns were creeping me out."

"You seemed all right with them this afternoon."

"That was daytime. My room had no door. What if Felix went psycho and came upstairs to murder me?"

"What made you think he'd go psycho?"

Isabelle munched popcorn. "After you left, the detectives came by. They sent me upstairs so they could talk to Felix alone. I tried to listen, but they were too far away. When they finished with him, they called me down and asked about . . . stuff. They didn't grill me as long as Felix. I don't know why. I'm as much of a suspect as he is."

"Are you?" Paula picked up the merlot from the tray.

Isabelle wiped her greasy fingers on her pants. "I don't have an alibi. I was asleep when Callie was killed, but I could have snuck out. Sam was in the basement and wouldn't have seen me."

"Which means you wouldn't have seen him sneaking out."

"None of us has alibis. Like Felix says, at six thirty in the morning everyone's either alone or sleeping with someone who'd lie for them."

Paula took a sip. "What did the police grill you about?"

Isabelle chewed pink glitter from her fingernail. "If Sam and I had some kind of deal about my staying with him."

"Did you?"

"My dad made him change his mind. Sam said I could move in with Felix, which I thought was better, only it turned out it wasn't."

Sam and Isabelle had done an adequate job of coordinating stories. Paula set the tray on the floor so she could prop her legs on the ottoman. "Do you know what they asked Felix?"

Isabelle's eyes widened. "They found out who owned the gun that murdered Callie." She paused for effect. "It was Sam's father." She waited. "You don't look surprised."

"Sam told me about it."

Isabelle's face dropped in disappointment.

Paula picked up a piece of popcorn. After her small dinner, this tasted good.

Isabelle resumed eating. "It's weird about him sticking the gun in a jar with Sam's mother's ashes."

"It was more like a vase."

"Felix says Sam's father loved Sam's mother totally." Isabelle raised her leg and twirled her foot clad in a ballet slipper. "Felix thinks Sam messes up his romances with women because they don't measure up to the one he imagines his parents had."

Paula finished her glass of wine. She could learn a lot about Sam from Isabelle. She made a guess about the cops' reduced grilling of Isabelle. "Why did they question Felix, and not you, about the gun?"

"They wanted to know where he was Friday night, when the person witnessed the killer tossing the gun in the Bow River. Felix said he was home alone. That's kind of suspicious when he has all these friends. They were phoning all afternoon."

"About what?"

"Mostly about his writing work. Boring."

Paula poured herself another glass of wine. Two would be enough on top of her two glasses of beer. With a witness to the probable disposal of the gun, the murderer needed two alibis. "Where was Sam Friday night?"

Isabelle licked butter from her fingers. "That was the night I quit my job at the video store. Sam drove me there around nine. He went home, I guess." She started. "I couldn't have done it. They could alibi me at work." Her face dropped. Another disappointment.

Paula ate a handful of popcorn. "What else did the detectives ask Felix?"

Isabelle bit the skin around her index fingernail, like Callie used to do when she was deep in thought. Clearly, the cops considered Felix a major suspect. Isabelle was either innocent or a gifted actress.

"He was too freaked to tell me much about it," Isabelle said. "Do you want more popcorn? There was hardly anything to eat at his house. I finally found a can of Alphaghetti and had to look all over for the pots and pans. He doesn't keep them where you'd logically think. I opened a drawer and there was this gun staring up at me. I freaked. Felix told me, don't worry, you have to cock the safety to use it and he hides the bullets in the cupboard above the stove, but I mean, shit."

Paula finished her second glass of wine. Since she was feeling no effects, she poured a third. "In what way was Felix freaked?"

Isabelle shrugged her bony shoulders. "He kept staring at his guns in the wall racks and drinking. He took out that old gun he showed you and me and turned it over and over in his hand. I let him make me some screwdrivers, figuring it would help if I joined in." She adjusted her tank top strap.

"Did Felix make a pass at you?"

Isabelle looked up. "No. That would be gross."

"What about you and Sam?" Paula tensed, dreading the answer more than she should. Her hunch that Callie's problem was Isabelle's pregnancy made perfect sense. Isabelle's stomach couldn't be flatter, but she wouldn't show for the first few months.

Isabelle fingered up the dregs from her popcorn bowl. "My dad asked me that, too. Why do old people always think these things? He'll be glad when I tell him I moved in with you."

"It's only temporary. Did Sam—"

Isabelle jumped up. "I'll go make some more popcorn."

Was she hungry or avoiding an answer or eating for two? Paula gnawed the corn kernels that hadn't totally popped. She was exhausted and half drunk, but before bed she had to find out about Sam and Isabelle. Isabelle returned with the fresh batch. Paula held out her bowl for a topping up. The wine was making her light-headed.

She poured a fourth glass anyway. "Sam told me, when Callie died, he was living in the basement. He said their marriage effectively ended last Christmas."

Isabelle crossed her legs, lotus style. "He ate with us sometimes, when he wasn't working late, and read the paper in the den. I thought them not sleeping together was weird at first, but these friends of my parents have separate bedrooms because the husband snores."

Did Sam snore? She shouldn't get distracted. "Do your parents know about his and Callie's arrangement?

"I didn't tell them," Isabelle said. "Sam pretended to them he and Callie were still together. He gave them her bedroom upstairs. My mom thinks he's too broken up by her death to sleep there. She likes thinking Callie was happy with him. Why disillusion her?"

"Sam doesn't seem too broken up. How did he and Callie get along?"

"They were friendly."

"Did they argue?"

Isabelle chewed her finger skin. "The detectives asked me that. I couldn't think of an example of them arguing. If they did, it wasn't so that you noticed."

"Did you tell the detectives about their living arrangement?"

"Sam already told them he and Callie weren't sleeping together. That wasn't a secret."

"What was?"

Isabelle's finger was bleeding around the nail. She sucked the blood.

"Why was your father so eager for you leave Sam's house that he thought Felix's place was better?"

Isabelle examined her finger and appeared satisfied the bleeding had stopped. "My dad doesn't believe Sam will sell the house. He thinks Dimitri will move in and take Callie's room. Or Sam will move upstairs and give Dimitri the basement."

Paula's head started spinning. "Dimitri, Sam's son? So what if he moves in? Doesn't he own a condo in his riding?"

"My dad says that's for show, so people in the area will vote for him. After Callie died, Dimitri stayed with us all the time."

"To support Sam." Paula set her wine glass and popcorn bowl down on the tray. The light hurt her eyes. She switched off the lamp.

Isabelle's fuchsia yoga suit was so bright it glowed in the neon of the DVD digital clock. "On the weekend, Dimitri and I went out to a bar. He got stinking drunk. My dad waited up for us, pacing all over the place. He gave

Dimitri hell for driving me home on his bike when he was plastered."

Paula leaned into the sofa cushion, her feet on the ottoman. "Did Dimitri argue back?"

"Dimitri ignored him and went down to the basement, where he was staying with Sam. My dad called him an arrogant prick."

Paula tittered.

"After Dimitri left, my dad lit into me. I kept telling him Dimitri's okay, that I'm not into him like that. My dad thinks he's transferring it from Callie to me."

"Transferring what?" Her body swayed.

Isabelle beamed. "Sam didn't tell you that. He doesn't want anyone to know. I wish I hadn't told my parents. I didn't think they'd care."

"Are you saying—?"

"He was into her."

"Dimitri . . . had the hots for Callie?"

"When Sam told me she was killed, I asked if he'd told the cops about Dimitri's thing for Callie. Sam was surprised I knew and said it would wreck Dimitri's political career if people found out, with him being so religious and all. Sam said if I didn't tell the cops I could keep living with him."

"That was your deal. Have you told the detectives this?"

"I promised Sam I wouldn't."

"Sam reneged on your deal."

"What's reneged? Like I said, I thought living with Felix would be okay, but it's better living with you. My dad will like that, and he's wrong about Dimitri's being into me. He just wanted company his own age."

Paula found herself reaching down for her wine glass. Somehow, Dimitri's hots were significant. She couldn't think why. "What did you and Dimitri talk about at the bar?"

"Movies . . . music . . . when I tried to talk about Callie, he told me to fuck off."

Dimitri, Sam's son, interested in Callie? At the funeral, Dimitri had been friendly and charming and had gone out of his way to talk to Paula because she was Callie's friend. Paula struggled to remember what he had said: the cops were easing up on Sam. Yet, Sam had seemed frantic at the reception. The cops' easing up should have made him more relaxed, unless Sam was worried their focus was shifting to his son. Did he think the cops had learned about Dimitri's hots? Learned it from Paula? That's why Sam asked her out to lunch. He wanted to know if Callie had confided this to her and if she had told the police. So, Dimitri had a thing for Callie, his stepmother twice his age. Well, not twice. Dimitri was thirty, maybe thirty-one. Callie was fifty-two. That made her, what? Two-thirds older than him? Paula couldn't do the math half drunk. Or was she three-quarters drunk? In last week's TV interview, Dimitri had objected to the reporter's use of the word "stepmother" not because he had disliked Callie. "How did you find out about Dimitri's interest?"

"By accident. I was coming down the hall and heard Callie and Dimitri fighting in the kitchen. I stopped to listen. They were arguing about him following her around the folk fest. After, I asked Callie about it. She said it was just a crush he'd get over, that he hadn't had that much experience with girls, on account of his religion and all."

"The folk festival was in late July. When did this fight take place?"

"I'd started work at the video store. Early August, I guess."

"Did he come by the house again?"

"Not until after she died. At least, I didn't see him there."

Paula drained her wine glass. That fight was two months ago. Dimitri had a temper, the newspapers said. Callie described him as self-centered and spoiled. "Was it this past Saturday night that you went out with Dimitri?

"Sunday," Isabelle said. "My dad's prejudiced. He hates politicians and religious nuts. He says you can't trust them not to go psycho."

"The politicians or nuts?" Paula giggled. Definitely too much wine. "Why didn't your father tell the police about this?"

"He hates cops more."

Paula picked popcorn from her teeth. Dimitri had stalked Callie. This was relevant to the case. "The cops need to know about this."

"I was wondering if I should tell them about the other woman."

Paula stopped picking. "What other woman?"

"I didn't before, since I wasn't sure that's what she was."

"What other woman?"

In the darkness, Isabelle brightened at her second scoop. "The morning after Callie died, I woke up early. It was all the excitement, I guess. Aunt Dorothy and Cameron and Skye were in the living room talking about the funeral. On my way to the kitchen, I heard Sam's voice in the den."

Sam's hallway seemed to be the place for discovering secrets.

"The door was open a crack," Isabelle said. "I heard Sam say, 'Beth, I promise I won't tell them about you.' Then, he looked over and saw me and started talking to her about business."

"Did you ask Sam about this?"

Isabelle shook her head. "He went out after the phone call. When he came back, he acted like nothing happened and I thought, maybe it was business."

"Without knowing the context, we can't assume." Given his nine-month estrangement from Callie, it wasn't unlikely Sam would have an affair; it was more than likely. Surely the cops were looking into this.

"She'd be a suspect," Isabelle said. "She could have killed Callie out of jealousy or to get Sam for herself."

"He called her Beth?"

"He went out again that afternoon. Remember, that was the day you came over? He didn't get back until late. While he was gone, I went down to the basement and found his address book. There wasn't anyone in it named Beth."

"What about Elizabeth?"

"I tried that, too."

"Are you certain that was the name you heard: Beth?"

"Bev," Paula said.

Shadows floated across the ceiling of her dark bedroom. She shook her head on the pillow, recalling the woman seated behind her at the funeral, who had chatted with her two friends. "Bev" could have sounded like "Beth" in an overheard phone call.

Paula rolled onto her side and curled her legs into a fetal position. What a coincidence if she was Sam's "Beth." Or would it be? Didn't mistresses traditionally attend the wife's funeral, sit in the back pew and cattily discuss the deceased? Paula struggled to recall the women's conversation. Her head throbbed. She was almost sure Bev was the one who left early. Did she leave so she wouldn't be seen? By whom? Sam? Detective Vincelli, who was sitting across the aisle in the other back pew? Bev had arrived after the other two friends. One had called out "Bev" and asked the woman in the wide-brimmed hat to join them. So, technically, Bev hadn't chosen the back pew. She probably wasn't Sam's mistress. But what if she was?

One of the three women knew Sam. Paula bet that was Bev, the interior decorator, who had worked with him on a building. She had called him full of himself or something equally negative. That sounded like a mistress scorned. The woman in the wide-brimmed hat was at least six feet tall. Paula giggled, imagining her with diminutive Sam. Giggling made her head ache more. Wouldn't it be delicious if that bitch was Sam's "Beth"? It would serve him right for the problems he had caused the cops by holding back the information on his son. Bev was the bitchiest of the three bitches.

Paula clutched the blankets to her knees. The women and Callie had been friends when their kids were growing up. They had probably been her neighbors in Mount Royal. Hadn't one mentioned that she worked in a Mount Royal Village boutique? That was Janet or Janice. The third woman had a sweet voice and seemed a homey type. What was her name? Never mind.

The digits of the bedside clock rolled to 4:00 AM. In a few hours, Paula would be officially hung-over and facing a day packed with meetings, some already postponed twice, but she could squeeze in a shopping trip to Mount Royal Village. The clerks in those upscale shops worked on commission. She could ask for one named Janet or Janice, explaining she had dealt with her last week and wanted to give her the sale. The three women had talked about meeting for lunch. When she left, Bev gave them her card. Paula could get Bev's phone number and address from Janice or Janet by saying she wanted to question her about the murder case. But why would she, not the cops, be doing the questioning? She needed a pretext.

No. Paula should tell Detective Vincelli about this, but if Bev was "Beth" he probably already knew. If she wasn't, he would think Paula nuts to jump to the conclusion. She would check it out first. The likelihood that Bev was "Beth" was one in a million, or more like one in a thousand. Paula bet one in ten. Still not high enough odds to tell Vincelli and she really wanted to meet this ball-breaking Bev, if she was Sam's "Beth."

Chapter Fourteen

Drum beats pounded Paula's brain. The rhythms blasted through her bedroom door. Blades of light cut through the shutters. It was 9:23 AM. She crawled out of the covers, staggered into the hall. The den door was open. The fuchsia yoga suit lay heaped on the floor. She stalked toward the rhythmic blare. Isabelle sat at the kitchen table, bopping her head. Paula flicked off the radio.

"Hey," Isabelle said. "I like that song."

"It's my house."

Newspaper littered the kitchen table. Callie's picture stared up from the City and Region section.

"Any news?" Paula asked.

"A rehash of the old stuff." Isabelle brushed toast crumbs from the sleep shirt she had borrowed from Paula. "They don't mention the murder weapon or say Sam's father owned it."

"They like keeping their little secrets." Outside the window, clouds blurred the crab apple tree. That might be her fuzzy eyes. The thermometer tacked to her garage strained toward forty-five degrees.

"Your hair's all sticking up," Isabelle said.

"Who cares? Can you make coffee while I shower?"

"I couldn't find where you keep it, so I made juice. I don't like coffee much, except in cafés, where it comes with foam and chocolate. My mother loves coffee."

"Stop talking about coffee until I've had some." Paula rubbed her pounding head.

"You're a grizzly-grump in the morning."

"Get used to it." Paula got the coffee from the fridge, where anyone might have thought to look for it, and ran cold water into the carafe. When she fell into bed, around 2:00 AM, Isabelle had been tapping away on the computer. "Don't people your age sleep all morning?"

"I got up early to look for work. I forgot to tell you last night. Your friend called while you were out with Sam."

"What friend?"

"I forget his name. I wrote it on the pad by the phone." Isabelle picked up her juice glass.

"Can you walk over and get it for me?" The brew began its merciful drip. After some food—Paula couldn't handle more than toast—she would down an Aspirin or two. Or three.

"Hayden." Isabelle ripped the sheet from the notepad. "He was surprised that I answered. At first, he thought I was your daughter. He knew all about Callie and me, but didn't believe it when I said I was moving in with you."

"You aren't." Would the fucking drip ever finish?

"He said to call after you got home from your date with Sam."

She had got home before ten o'clock. Hayden would think she had been out later than that. "Did Hayden call it a date?"

"He did or I did. I forget which."

"Thanks a lot." Paula massaged her spiky hair in an effort to smooth her sore brain. The coffee dripped at glacial speed. She grabbed the carafe. Black liquid sizzled on the warming tray. Hayden was one more thing to take care of today on top of work, Isabelle, arranging for new door locks, telling off Walter for letting Isabelle in, and tracking down Bev.

"Can I borrow some clothes?" Isabelle said. "There wasn't room in my sports bag to squish dresses or skirts. Can you drive me to Felix's this afternoon to pick up the rest of my stuff?"

"I'm busy." Coffee wove through Paula's brain, mending the ache.

"I could borrow your car. I have a license."

"I need my car."

"I guess I should phone Felix before he notices I'm gone."

"Felix doesn't know you're here?"

"He fell asleep in his chair. I shouted at him. He'd taken some pills that conked him out after all those screwdrivers. I decided to split. He probably figures I'm still asleep upstairs."

Last night Isabelle had said Felix's drinking increased, if that was possible, after the detectives left. They had started a few board games, but he couldn't concentrate and ended up pacing the house, mumbling words Isabelle couldn't make out.

"If Felix goes out, he might not notice I'm gone until tonight," Isabelle said. "But what if my parents phone from Banff to check up on me? They'll freak if Felix checks my room and tells them I'm missing. My dad will feel better when he finds out I've moved in with you."

Paula drained her mug of coffee. "I need a shower. After that, we'll talk."

You can't live here. Not permanently," she said. "It might work if this were a monstrous house, like Felix's. There isn't space. We're different ages, with conflicting lifestyles."

From the seat Paula usually occupied, Isabelle stared out the kitchen window. She hadn't changed out of the pale blue sleep shirt with teddy bear decals on the chest. Paula had bought the shirt on sale, but had never worn it. The teddy bears looked more corny than cute when she got home.

"When I get a job, I'll find an apartment," Isabelle said.

"Could you afford one?"

"Waitresses get tips. I could share an apartment with someone. I'd like that better than living alone."

Paula sipped coffee, wondering how Isabelle would support herself on McJobs she regularly quit. She should go home with her parents. "Montreal has plenty of restaurant jobs. You're bilingual, which would be a plus. Apartments are cheaper there. You don't have to live at home. You could share with a friend."

They had touched on Isabelle's love life last night. Isabelle confirmed she wasn't involved with Sam. Her sudden departure from Montreal last May hadn't stemmed from a failed romance. Among her wide circle of Montreal friends were some male ones with occasional benefits. Paula told her that she didn't understand that kind of casual friendship-sex. "Montreal is old," Isabelle also said. "The buildings are old. People complain all the time. Calgary's more fun."

Paula finished her toast. "Montreal is bigger, more exciting and multi-cultural, with real action downtown. If I were your age, I'd find it more interesting."

Isabelle twirled a strand of blond hair. "Flying to Calgary was my first time on a plane. I got to talking to the guy beside me. He owns a company that makes computer games. We flew past the airport and circled the city about six times. There was this grinding noise under the plane. The computer guy said the landing gear wasn't working, the wheels weren't coming down, any minute they'd tell us to prepare for a crash landing."

"That must have been scary."

"It was exciting, you know, something was happening. We kept circling toward the mountains. They were shining white. The day before there'd been a huge snowstorm. The whole city was white. I mean, a snowstorm in May. Whoever heard of that?"

"Not a great start to your visit."

"All that white around the shiny downtown buildings looked like," Isabelle let go of the twisted hair strand, "like an egg dropped sunny side up from space. Sam picked me up at the airport. He told me he designed some of those buildings and I thought, wow, you can do that here."

"You can, after years of school."

"I hate school," Isabelle said. "I don't want to design buildings, but you know what I mean."

She might, once the coffee kicked in. Paula refilled her mug. "You should have asked that computer guy for a job."

"I wasn't thinking about staying in Calgary then." Isabelle bolted up. "I have to get ready to look for work. The restaurants around here will be open soon."

While Isabelle showered in the adjacent room, Paula popped herself another piece of toast. Odds were Isabelle wouldn't be hired for a restaurant job by Friday, when her parents returned from Banff. Between the three of them, they should be able to convince her go home. Paula could tolerate a roommate for two more nights, and it would be an excuse to avoid seeing Hayden those evenings. Not that she would go out with Sam again. This morning, she would phone Hayden to reassure him there would be no more Sam dates. Hayden didn't need to know about Sam's invitation to go hiking in Kananaskis.

The shower water stopped. Paula loaded the dishwasher. Isabelle came into the kitchen, her hair bouncing on Paula's navy dress. Since she was taller, the skirt stopped several inches above her knees. A belt cinched it to her narrow waist. The blue color brightened her eyes.

"You look better in that outfit than me." Paula smoothed her magenta slacks. Her black suit jacket would hide the trace of pot she hadn't managed to work off since her divorce. Today was Wednesday, wasn't it? She wouldn't have time for her usual workout. Before she forgot, she phoned Anne to let her know. Isabelle wandered back to Paula's bedroom. Anne answered from her office in the fitness center.

"My day is packed," Paula said. "Meetings with claimants, appraisers, a traffic cop . . . I also want to stop in at Mount Royal Village." Why had she brought that up? Anne would find her snooping weird.

"I was thinking of looking at stores there for a dress," Anne said.

"Those places are expensive."

"I need something special for the reception in Ottawa next month."

Dimitri was bringing his mother, in place of a wife, to the reception for new members of parliament. Anne was excited about meeting the Governor General.

"I can't shake hands with the Queen's representative wearing department store clothes."

Paula laughed and realized Anne was serious. How would Anne react to the news about Dimitri's crush on Callie? From everything Anne had ever said about him, there was no chance she suspected.

"How about I meet you at Mount Royal Village?" Anne suggested. "What time?"

They agreed on 4:30 PM.

"This will be fun," Anne said. "I never do girlfriend things like shopping together."

Would it be fair to dump the news about Dimitri on Anne when it was only hearsay from Isabelle, not the most trustworthy source?

Isabelle returned to the kitchen, Paula's best purse draped over her shoulder. "We wear the same shoe size. Isn't that lucky?" She raised a foot. "These look cool with this dress. And the purse matches."

Paula handed her the phone receiver. "Call Felix.""

Isabelle backed up as though the phone were poison. "Could you do it? He might get mad at me for splitting."

"Tough."

"What if he turns psycho?"

"Better you than me."

"I'll print my résumés first."

"Stalling won't let you off the hook."

Paula studied price tags and ran her hands over fabric, pretending to browse for clothes. She was the only customer in the boutique, the fifth one she had tried. A young sales clerk had said Janice was on her coffee break. When Paula turned down her offer to help, the clerk retreated to the rear of the shop to steam iron wrinkles out of blouses. To calm herself, Paula hummed to the sound system's instrumental "Softly as I Leave You." At 4:00 AM, the plan she plotted in bed had felt completely plausible. It seemed ridiculous now. Or was this last-minute jitters? She tried to focus on the clothes.

Black and red, Paula's colors, seemed in vogue this fall. She examined a pair of wool slacks: $179.00. Last month she had balked at paying seventy dollars for a pair of pants that looked better than these. She paused at a strapless, floor-length teal-blue dress hanging flush against the wall. $595.99.

"Would you like to try it on?" A clone of the stylishly dressed young clerk appeared behind her. For these prices you got service.

"I'm waiting for my friend." She had called Anne to give her the name of the store. Paula had rushed through her last meeting to get to the Village early, approving her hit-and-run victim's medical expenses even though his accident statement raised questions: why didn't he report the collision to the police? What was the point, he said, when there were no witnesses and he couldn't recognize the other car? Why was he taking a different route home in the middle of the night? Paula would have to question him without his wife present.

The outside door jangled. Anne entered, precisely on time. Her face lit up at the sight of Paula, who cursed herself for not bringing Anne into the plan. She had hoped to be finished with her fake investigation before Anne arrived. The clone clerk reached Paula's side before Anne. Paula hustled the two of them off to look at outfits before the next door jangle. A gray-haired woman strode to the back of the boutique. The clerk at the ironing board hailed her. The women spoke. Paula tensed as Janice approached.

"You were looking for me?" Janice was roughly her height. Her gray pageboy shimmered. She spoke in the moderately toned voice Paula recalled from the funeral.

She gave Janice her business card and introduced herself as an insurance adjuster. "I'm assisting the Calgary Police Service investigation into a murder that took place last Thursday."

Janice's plucked eyebrows rose. "Callie?"

This was ridiculous, but she was here and might as well continue until Anne blew her ruse. "I understand you are acquainted with a woman named Bev."

Worry shot through Janice's hazel eyes. "The police? What do they want with Bev?"

"Routine questioning; we understand she is acquainted with the victim's husband, Sam Moss."

"Why are you asking me? I hadn't seen Bev in years, until the funeral."

"A detective attending the funeral noticed you sitting with her."

Janice coiled her fingers around her pearl necklace. "How did he know it was me?"

That was sharp of Janice. Shit. She wouldn't fall for this. "The detective entered the church directly after you and got your name from the guest book."

Janice's frown caused no forehead creases or lines between her eyebrows. At the funeral, the women had chatted about plastic surgery. Janice claimed to be an expert on the subject. Hopefully, she wouldn't ask how the cops had traced her to Mount Royal Village.

"Why is an insurance adjuster involved in a murder case?" Janice said.

"To reduce costs the Calgary Police Service is outsourcing work that can be handled on a semi-professional basis." If you didn't think it through, it almost made sense.

"Paula," Anne called. She held up a taupe suit and a dress with layers of ruffles. "Which do you prefer?"

"Try on both," Paula said.

Janice clenched the pearls. "Outsourcing is the trend these days. My nephew's worried about losing his job to India."

Paula stared into the hazel eyes. "CPS is trying it as an experiment."

"You couldn't outsource police work to India." Janice giggled, presumably from nervousness about being questioned by a representative of the police. "I doubt Bev could tell you much about Sam. She only knew him through work."

"We cover all bases. Can you give me her phone number and address?"

The door jangled. A young clerk clacked by them to greet the new customer. Janice wore two inch pumps, rather than the stilettos her colleagues favored. The clone clerk waited outside the changing room for Anne.

Janice's hands relaxed on the pearls. The winding turned leisurely. "Is Sam a suspect?" she said.

"In a homicide, everyone connected to the victim is investigated."

"Some people find it strange that Sam didn't know where his wife went in the mornings. I like men who aren't possessive, who don't keep tabs on a woman."

Paula's neck felt as tight as Janice's looked. The number, please, just the fucking number, or Bev's surname.

"I guess there's no harm in your having Bev's address," Janice said. "Her company's probably listed in the phone book. Did you look it up?"

Paula and Isabelle had searched the Internet for "Bev–Interior Decorating–Calgary." No luck.

Janice tugged at the necklace. If it burst, spewing pearls to the floor, Janice would be on her knees, searching for rolling pearls, with time to think about the request. Anne was out of the changing room. Never again would Paula follow through on a plan hatched while drunk. She shook her head at Anne in the ruffled dress. It made Anne look like a Christmas tree.

"Bev used to work out of her home," Janice said. "I expect she still does, if her company's a small operation. I always found her house by sight. Now, what is the address? I can't even remember the street name." She tapped a patch of dry skin on her cheek.

"Would you have Bev's business card?"

"I forgot about that. She gave it to me so I could call about lunch. It must be in my purse. Do you want me to get the card?"

"Please."

Janice walked to the back of the store. She stopped to talk with the ironing clerk, who shot glances at Paula while Janice, presumably, told her about the pseudo-cop visit. Anne emerged in the suit. Paula judged it too serious.

"We'll find her something lighter but not frothy," the clone clerk said.

Anne disappeared into the changing room. Paula fingered the evening gown. Silky, slinky, smooth, the color of a mountain lake, $595.99 and of no conceivable use. Since it was strapless, she would have to buy a new bra, necklace or choker, drop earrings, dressy shoes, matching handbag. And cut off that stupid hip bow, which would be fifty dollars of wasted material.

Janice approached holding a card worth more than a useless dress.

"I think that's her home address," Janice said. "You can keep it. I jotted down her number, in case I decide to call her about lunch. I was thinking I wouldn't."

"Why not?"

Janice fanned her face with the card. "Bev has this way of bringing out the worst in me. I don't like how I am when I'm with her. I'm not saying she's a criminal."

"I think I met Bev once. Isn't she fairly tall?"

Janice laughed. "That's an understatement. She's six-foot-two."

"Her voice is husky and deep."

"Maybe it's her voice and height that intimidate me. And her personality."

Paula took a breath. "Is she still married?"

"As far as I know."

The clone clerk was carrying an armload of dresses to Anne's changing room.

"I wish I'd been closer to Callie," Janice said. "I knew her as a neighbor and the mom of my son's friend. She was a lot nicer than Bev but we didn't click, for no particular reason."

"Who were her close friends, at that time?"

Janice's forehead managed a faint pucker. "When I think of us all as young mothers, I see Callie hovering on the fringe. She might have had friends outside our clique. I hope she did." Janice toyed with the necklace. "My niece is in insurance. I didn't know insurance work could be so interesting. How long have you been assisting the police?"

"Not long." Paula held out her hand, willing Janice to hand over the card.

"I should tell my niece about you. She might want to apply for the same job. Are they hiring more people?

"Not at the moment."

Janice stared over Paula's shoulder. "I saw you admiring that ball gown. I love the color: cosmic blue. Would you like to try it on?"

"I'm only here for the police . . . and my friend." She nodded at the changing room.

"It's the exact shade of your eyes and would suit any formal affair, like a wedding."

"Both of my daughters claim they aren't into marriage."

Janice shifted the card to her left hand and took the dress down from the wall. "Let's have a look. For fun."

Was Janice enough of a salesperson to be offering the card in exchange for Paula's trying on the dress? Paula wanted that card enough to deal. Janice led her to the second changing room. Paula slipped on the gown and fiddled with the bodice she didn't trust to stay up.

"Hey," Janice said as she emerged. "The dress is you. The color brings out eyes and your hair's red highlights. And doesn't the material cling to all the right places?"

"And don't you work on commission?"

Janice laughed. "This is one time I mean it. That dress is a perfect fit for you."

Paula studied herself from all angles. She hadn't looked this svelte since before she had kids. Cosmic blue hugged her mature model's back. Was this a trick mirror? Her stomach was almost flat. How could she look slim and voluptuous at the same time? Even the stupid bow enhanced the curve of her hip.

"I bought a house last month," she said. "I can't spend six hundred dollars on a dress."

"It's great value. I've seen hundreds more expensive that aren't as well made. The cut is flawless."

Paula smoothed the bodice over her breasts that would be stunning in a push-up bra. "I can't afford your Mount Royal lifestyle."

"Neither can I on my sales clerk's salary." Janice had a pleasant laugh. "I'd hate to see someone else take it."

Music flowed from the sound system. Michael Bublé. "The Way You Look Tonight." Latino rhythms. Was one of the clerks in the back room pressing the sound system buttons? Paula wouldn't sell out just to get Bev's address.

"Accessories would double the cost," she said.

"Easily."

She turned sideways. "It's slightly tight at the waist."

"A body shaper would take care of that."

"More money."

"We should treat ourselves sometimes. Life is short."

What next? Injecting Botox into her forehead and doing whatever women did for turkey neck? The smoothness looked pretty good on Janice, who was fanning her neck with the business card. Who was playing whom?

Anne came out in a lime two-piece. Her clerk gushed that it cried out for an orchid corsage.

"Perfect for the Governor General," Paula said.

Anne frowned at the price tag. "It's out of my range."

"Not any more. Your business is going strong."

"You look fantastic in that, Paula."

"I have nowhere to wear it."

"You'll find the occasion." Janice handed Paula the card: *Beverly Berwell Interior Design.* Underneath was Bev's Mount Royal address. Paula dropped the card in her purse. "Maybe the dress will bring me luck."

Anne studied her back in the mirror. "Dimitri would be proud to show me off in this. All right. You've twisted my arm. I'll do it for Dimitri and his new career."

Anne's grin was wider than Paula had ever seen it. She couldn't spoil Anne's mood today by revealing Dimitri's interest in Callie. Someone else could break the news.

Janice wrapped tissue around the Cosmic Blue dress. "Poor Callie. She didn't deserve what happened. I hope you get to the bottom of it."

Anne nodded. "We're counting on the police to do their job."

She might regret that remark when the police hauled in her son.

Chapter Fifteen

Morning light glanced off her rear windshield. Paula drove across Macleod Trail, which was jammed with rush-hour traffic. She crossed the Elbow River and Mission's main street alive with pedestrians and cars. As her car climbed the curving avenue to Mount Royal, she wondered if talking to Bev before the cops got to her would compromise the investigation. Paula didn't see how it could as long as she didn't give away secrets, like the tracing of the murder weapon to Sam's father. True, the police would want Bev's fresh, unguarded response. But how unguarded would Bev be, if she was Sam's mistress? Bev had to expect that the homicide unit would find her eventually and have prepared her answers days ago.

Paula drove through tranquil crescents lined with wide properties, one-hundred-year-old homes, and luxury vehicles. She stopped in front of Bev's house, which seemed too modern for Mount Royal. The large eaves, stained wood siding, and glass room perched on the roof made it look like a squished pagoda. A patterned concrete driveway forked to a double garage and front door. Paula hadn't called in advance and could drive away. Had she told Hayden her plan when they talked last night, he would have pointed out hazards of meddling in the case. Luckily, she hadn't told him.

Paula rang the bell. Inside, a dog barked. A second dog joined in, and another. The door opened to a cacophony of yaps. Three toy dogs darted between a woman's legs.

Paula looked up at the face framed by cropped, black hair. "Bev Berwell?"

"What can I do for you?" The deep, husky voice brought back memories of the funeral where a wide-brimmed hat had concealed Bev's square face. Shaped eyebrows arched perfectly over unwrinkled eyes. Was the crimson sneer her usual expression or one aimed at strangers who disturbed her morning work? A fourth dog, identical to the rest, was chasing its mates. Paula introduced herself.

Bev accepted her business card. "I thought you might turn up. Cappuccino?"

Evidently, Janice had phoned Bev last night. Paula had anticipated that, but not this easy invite in. Bev led her down a center hall, its walls covered in black and gold embossed wallpaper. Watercolor sketches of Asian landscapes hung between closed doors. One of the dogs hobbled beside Paula. Bev's spicy perfume recalled the catty woman behind Paula at the funeral. Was it good or bad that Bev was prepared for her visit? Good, so far, since it had got her in.

Bev's haircut was 1920s flapper-style. She wore a man's tailored shirt tucked into beige, linen slacks. Her broad shoulders and muscular limbs made her seem taller than six-foot-two. The hallway's ceramic tiles flowed into a kitchen. Its black cupboards and appliances matched the adjacent family room's black walls.

The dogs were a good distraction. Paula squatted to pat one. "Are these shih tzu?" A second dog nuzzled in. "What are their names?"

"Tao, Xiang, Chu-Hua and Fred."

Paula laughed. This wouldn't work if she couldn't reign in the nervousness. A third dog squeezed through the others and almost toppled her.

"My husband chose little Fred's name." Bev's voice rose to a baby pitch. "Him's hurt his paw jumping off Mommy's and Daddy's bed." The tone sounded weird on someone her size. The voice plummeted to normal. "I can see you're a dog-person."

Paula untangled herself from the shih tzu. "We had a family dog. My daughter kept her when I moved into my new place. I miss her. The dog, I mean. I miss my daughter, too. Sometimes."

Bev smiled as much as plastic surgery would allow. "What breed is she? I mean the dog."

"Mutt, German shepherd-ish." So what if Bev caught onto the ruse. All she could do was throw Paula out.

Bev took a knife from the chopping block and cut into a pan of apple strudel. She placed two plates with strudel and glasses of cappuccinos on a tray.

Paula followed her to the family room. "Black paint in a house is different. Your decor seems to have an Asian theme."

"You think?" Bev opened the patio window blinds, exposing a Japanese garden with bonsai trees, ponds, waterfalls, and bridges back-dropped by distant downtown high-rises.

"What a lovely yard," Paula said. "I like those lion statues guarding the pathway entrance."

"They're lion dogs. Shih tzu, to ward off evil spirits." Bev carried a cappuccino and pate of strudel to the sofa facing the patio doors. She lifted Fred onto a cushion.

This left Paula the love seat. She faced a fireplace flanked by enormous painted silk wall hangings, one of a pagoda, the other a pair of giggling geisha. Two of the dogs trotted out of the family room; a third one settled on the Oriental carpet. Paula balanced her plate on her lap. The situation felt similar to an interview with an insurance claimant—aside from the creepiness and the fact she was here under a false pretense to discuss murder, not whiplash or theft. Bev stretched her long legs on the sofa's built-in hassock. Fred snuggled next to her.

Paula finished a first bite of strudel. "This is delicious. Did you make it?"

"My cleaning lady did," Bev said. "Let's cut to the chase. Why are you here?"

"I'm an insurance adjuster who has been retained—"

"Cut the crap." Bev's lips curled into a peculiar smile. "What's your interest in Callie's murder? More importantly, what's my interest in someone I haven't seen in years?"

Hands shaking, Paula set her plate on the coffee table and grabbed her cappuccino glass for support. Fred's eyes peered through strands of fur, following her movements. Bev would have had all night to consider the logic of Paula's police outsourcing pretext. Paula had thought it through all night as well.

"You must have heard about the city's shortage of police staff?" she said.

"The cops are always complaining so they'll get more money."

"It makes sense for trained civilians to handle minor police work matters, in this case, interviewing outside witnesses."

"How did you get my name?"

Paula sipped cappuccino to appear hesitant. "From Kenneth Unsworth, Callie's ex-husband, who lives a few blocks from here."

Bev's forehead grew impossibly tighter. She strode toward Paula, who forced herself not to cringe. Wafting spicy perfume, Bev took her cigarettes and lighter from the coffee table. She held the pack out to Paula.

Paula hesitated. Even during the highest stress of her divorce, she hadn't slipped off the track. Bev's smirk taunted: goody-two-shoes. This was so high-school, but could be good for bonding and calming her nerves. Paula slid the cylinder from the pack. Bev lit the cigarette for her. Paula dragged on it. Bitter. She willed herself not to cough, as she had that first time she and Callie tried it behind her house.

Bev returned to her seat next to Fred. "So, this is about me and Sam."

Paula coughed. She bit the cigarette tip to stop.

"Have you told the police?" Bev said.

"Not yet." Damn. That implied the cops hadn't sent her.

Bev's red lips crooked up in a smile.

"I presume Kenneth has kept quiet, too, or the real cops would have come after me."

Paula flicked the cigarette into the ashtray. The shih tzu on the carpet buried his muzzle in his paws. Fred appeared to be dozing.

"That is precisely why I stayed home to meet you," Bev said. "My involvement with Sam is irrelevant to Callie's murder. Why spoil dearly departed Callie's happily married image?"

Paula dragged on the cigarette to stall. "Are you sleeping with Sam?"

"No."

"That's not what Kenneth said."

Bev stroked Fred's flowing mane. "Our affair ended two months ago."

"When did it start?"

"January."

Six months. "How often did you meet?"

Bev drew on her cigarette, not replying.

Paula looked at the Asian screens. "Did you meet here?"

"God no, never. I'm not nuts. We met in hotels."

"What ended the affair?"

Bev shrugged and flashed a smile that was probably meant to be worldly. "They always end."

"Did Callie or your husband find out?"

Bev stood, causing Fred to slither down the sofa. He dropped to the carpet with a yap of pain and hobbled to a collection of rubber toys by the window. Two other dogs ran into the room. One joined Bev on the sofa; the other sniffed the strudel on the coffee table.

"Chu-Hua has a sweet tooth," Bev said. "He usually ends up eating half the pan."

Paula inhaled the cigarette. She had never been hooked on the taste.

What had kept her smoking through her twenties was the feel of the cigarette in her hand, its link to coffee and the fact most of the people in her Montreal office smoked. She gave it up mainly to set a good example for her kids.

Paula had got what she came for: confirmation of Bev's and Sam's affair. This was a murder case. Nothing could convince her to keep this from the police. She should finish her snack and drink and smoke as fast as possible and get out.

Bev dragged on her cigarette. "My husband and I are a couple in every sense of the word, but have our separate needs." Smoke billowed from her nostrils. "He appreciates other women. I appreciate other men. We have two ground rules: safe sex and discretion. We're both prominent in the community and do not wish to be the subject of gossip."

"Unfortunately, that's hard to avoid when your lover's wife is murdered."

"Ex-lover."

"Did Sam break it off or did you?"

Bev's lips smiled; her eyes stayed hard. "I wish I could say it was me. I accepted Sam's decision and moved on. It turned out to be extremely easy."

"No hard feelings?"

"If you think I was angry and murdered Callie in a jealous rage, you're barking up the wrong tree." Fred's ears perked up. Bev patted the head of the dog beside her. "Had I still been sleeping with Sam at the time, which I wasn't, the last thing I would have wanted was Callie's death. I only date married men."

"No commitment?"

"Singles go into it agreeing to no strings, but they have this habit of getting involved and trying to ruin my marriage, when my marriage satisfies me in every other respect."

Coming from Bev, it seemed strangely believable. "Why did Sam break up with you?"

Bev squeezed her eyes shut. Had her pride been hurt and not yet recovered? The dog crawled onto Bev's lap. Chu-Hua nuzzled Paula's legs. She patted the love seat, inviting him to join her. Fred, on the floor, looked back and forth between her and Bev. The fourth dog gnawed a hard plastic rope.

Bev stroked Tao or Xiang. "Sam told me he wanted to work on his marriage. I didn't believe it, but when a man doesn't want me, I don't beg."

"Why didn't you believe him?"

"I have an instinct about men who are basically alone. There was no marriage to work on."

This fit Sam's and Isabelle's reports. "Aren't men in empty marriages at risk for getting involved?"

"Not the ones I pick."

Something else Isabelle had said. "Did Sam wear a wedding ring when you and he met?"

"At the hotels? No. Before that? I don't recall him wearing a ring. For men, it's a personal choice."

According to Isabelle, Sam only started wearing one after Callie's death.

"I see you're not married," Bev said.

"Divorced." Paula butted out her cigarette. "What did Sam tell you about his marriage?"

"Before your divorce, did you have affairs?"

"No."

"Too bad, they can be refreshing." Bev's lip curled. "You would also know that cheating spouses avoid discussing their partners."

"I hear some talk obsessively about the spouse."

"What would be the purpose of that? Sam told me nothing about his marriage. I assumed the spark died and he looked elsewhere. Old story."

Paula scratched Chu-Hua under the ear. She might like a dog if they weren't so much work and didn't tie you down and shed over everything, like these slacks she would be wearing to work. "If the affair was over, why did you phone Sam after Callie's murder?"

"To find out what he told the cops so I could be ready for any police visits. Sam forgot to warn me about insurance adjusters."

Paula smiled. She could enjoy Bev, in small doses. "When you were together what did you and Sam talk about?"

Bev snubbed out her cigarette. "We weren't much into talk."

Paula felt herself blush, which would confirm Bev's goody-goody image of her. "Did he ever mention his son, Dimitri?"

Bev's eyebrows rose, "The politician? He ran for office last spring. Sam mentioned him occasionally. Why?"

"What did he say about him?"

Bev slid a new cigarette from the pack, without offering to share this time.

"He seemed fond of him, as parents are, and proud of his achievements, although I don't think Sam's into politics. More cappuccino or strudel?"

Paula shook her head. "Do you think Sam is capable of murder?"

"I believe anyone is, if pushed to his or her limits."

"What are Sam's limits?"

"I wouldn't know. Ours was not a soul mates affair, which is why there is no point dragging me into this. I can't tell the police anything of relevance. It's over between me and Sam. I didn't kill Callie to get him and he sure as hell didn't kill her to get me."

Such anger hinted at more than damaged pride.

Bev shuddered. "It would be horrible to have this splashed in the press."

"You could ask the police to keep it quiet."

"Would you trust them? I don't. Some cop will leak it to the media, which adores taking down the successful and rich." Bev looked at Fred on the carpet. His ears wriggled with her rising voice. She lowered it to the husky drawl. "About five years ago, the newspaper published a photo taken at an architecture awards gala. This was before our affair, when I knew Sam casually. I was wearing high heels. He stood a little behind me, and with the perspective and my heels he looked like, well, Xiang here trying to hump a Great Dane."

Paula laughed.

"All of Calgary will laugh if they dig that picture up from the archives. And they will. Do I want that photo staring at me beside that image of sweet, dead Callie? I'd be Camilla to her Lady Di."

Tao bounded to the sofa. After several attempts, he hoisted himself onto the cushion.

"You're going to tell the cops about me," Bev said.

"I'm not sure."

"Or do you plan to use this against Sam?"

"I wouldn't blackmail."

"Or do you want something else from him?" Bev drew on the cigarette. Her unlined face scrutinized Paula so intently that Paula turned to Chu-Hua. The dog's eyes closed as she scratched beneath his ears. Paula wanted nothing from Sam for herself. She was doing this for Callie.

Smoke streamed from Bev's perfect nose. "If you stay away from the cops, I'll tell you something interesting."

Lots of deals were being made these days.

"It concerns Sam," Bev said. "This might encourage you to keep it from the cops for a few days, while you investigate a little more."

Paula wondered if she was still doing this only for Callie. She would ponder that later. "Okay."

"What is your connection to Callie and Sam?"

"What is it you have to say?"

Bev mashed out her cigarette. "If I were you, I'd be interested to know why Kenneth hasn't told them."

"Kenneth Unsworth? Callie's ex-husband?"

"He has a dog," Bev said. "A golden retriever he walks every day along the same route through this neighborhood. You could set your watch by it. Being naturally curious about the murder, I decided to run into him yesterday, and took Chu-Hua and Tao." The latter looked up at the mention of his name, his tongue out of his mouth. He panted as though in agreement. "We met up with Kenneth. I gave him my Callie condolences. He spewed appropriate replies and looked miserable, like a basset hound. I had this urge to cheer him up and tried to think of something nice to say."

Nice and Bev didn't mesh.

"I thought, if my husband ever ditched me, I'd want his romance to tank. So, I told Kenneth I knew with certainty there was nothing between Callie and Sam. Kenneth asked how I could be so sure. I told him about my affair. He looked surprised."

"I'm surprised you'd reveal it."

"I don't know what came over me. I thought if anyone could be discreet it would be Kenneth. He never tells you anything you don't need to know."

Fred limped to the sofa. Bev lifted him onto her lap. She stroked Fred with her right hand, Xiang with her left.

"We babbled good-byes," Bev continued. "I said I was glad I had my dogs to walk with for protection. Kenneth stared at little Chu-Hua and said no dog could protect her from him. I assumed he meant Sam and rushed to his defense, saying Sam wasn't the type to murder for money and he certainly didn't kill Callie for love, since their marriage was dead. Kenneth said husbands who cheated always claimed that. That's when I lost it. Sam lied to me? I ranted at Kenneth. He backed off."

Paula patted Chu-Hua's head, stifling a smile. Bev didn't sound like she had totally moved on from Sam. Chu-Hua growled at Tao, on the floor.

Bev stroked Fred, who dozed on her legs. "Afterwards, I wondered if Kenneth was talking about someone other than Sam, somebody else who had feelings for her. I think he just said 'him,' not specifically 'Sam.'" Bev swung her legs from the footrest, startling Fred and knocking him to the carpet. Xiang bared his teeth. He leapt on top of Fred. Chu-Hua and Tao joined the scuffle. The dogs barked and growled and nipped each other.

"See what I mean?" Bev said. "Killing is instinct."

Chapter Sixteen

They slid to the ends of the park bench. Hayden set out the picnic between them. Paula dropped her sandals to the dirt and swung her legs, inhaling the sweet fall air. They were surrounded by poplars specked with yellow and green leaves. Paula's dark glasses couldn't block the glare of the sun shining across the Elbow River. Hayden had suggested they meet for lunch to make up for his being unavailable tonight. His evening commitment freed her to phone Kenneth Unsworth and invite herself over for a condolence visit. Kenneth said he would be home and might have something to give to her.

"I wonder what it is," she said to Hayden. "He wouldn't explain over the phone."

"Callie could have left you something in her will." Hayden held out two submarine sandwiches. "Chicken or tuna?"

Paula took the fish. "Sam told Isabelle he's not starting work on her estate until next week. He's the executor."

Hayden scowled at Paula's reference to Sam. She let it go, being in too good spirits. Partly it was the weather and partly a sense of zeroing in on what she wanted to know about Sam. The uncertainty was driving her nuts. Hayden removed his suit jacket, but left his tie on and his collar buttoned. Given the heat, she was grateful for her loose cotton blouse that fluttered like the feathers of the Canada geese parading past their bench to the rocky shore.

She unwrapped the sandwich's wax paper. "Why the delay with the will, do you think?"

"I expect Sam's too busy squiring Callie's girlfriends to hockey games." Hayden took a huge bite of submarine.

Paula couldn't resist his dry humor. So far, Sam had made her laugh by the things he did, like his involvement with Amazon Bev. Should she tell Hayden about her? Would he be amused or annoyed by anything related to Sam? She hadn't mentioned Bev when they talked last night for fear he would accuse her of heading off on a wild goose chase. She giggled at the geese lined up on the shore.

"What's so funny?" he said.

She chewed potato salad, avoiding an answer. The geese honked at their comrades perched on stones, splashing in the river, dipping their beaks into the water. Fewer complexities in her life would be nice. Since leaving Bev's house, all she had thought of was Kenneth's remark "no dog could save her from him."

"I wonder if Kenneth knows about Dimitri's crush," she said. "If he does, you'd think he'd have told the cops about it for no other reason than to hurt Sam."

"Some of us are above petty revenge." With apparent nonchalance, he dipped his fork into the coleslaw.

Would he take the high road with Sam, if given the opportunity to hurt him? "Since the cops suspect Felix Schoen, it makes me wonder if Kenneth told them something about Felix. Maybe he is the 'him' Kenneth was talking about."

"Are you suggesting Callie had an affair with him? Potato salad?"

She finished off the container. "I wouldn't think Felix was her type. He's heavy, drinks too much, and is a major slob, although she might go for his artistic side. He's a writer."

Hayden chewed his salad.

"If Callie had an affair," she said, "it would equalize matters between her and Sam. This morning, I learned he had an affair during their marriage."

"There's a shocker."

His dry humor could be irritating. She could wipe off his smug expression by telling him about Sam's estrangement from Callie, another thing she had neglected to mention last night. Why make him feel even more threatened by Sam? The point of this lunch was to smooth things out; gloss over. Sweep everything under a pile of leaves.

"Was Sam's affair in addition to whatever he's got going with Isabelle?" Hayden said.

"I told you, they aren't involved."

"You believe her about that?"

"I can judge people."

"Hmpph."

Paula resented his insinuation that she lacked judgment about Sam. So far, she had that involvement under control. More or less.

The Elbow River current carried a pair of geese sideways down river.

On the opposite bank, another goose waddled up to explore a lawn that was far trimmer than Sam's backyard. A week ago this morning, Callie had left her home upstream to jog the winding path that followed this river. Had anyone seen her from those houses lining the bank?

Hayden popped open a can of diet Coke. "If I work tomorrow night, I can clear the weekend for us. Are you free Saturday—I'd love a good game of tennis—or do you need to catch up on work?"

On Saturday, Sam was hiking in Kananaskis. Anne had invited her and Hayden to dinner. Shit. She had forgotten about that. If she brought it up—he was bound to say yes—she would be stuck and she wanted to keep her options open until she talked to Kenneth.

"I'm not sure," she said.

"This Indian summer is supposed to hold. It would be great for tennis."

Saturday's weather would be perfect for a fall hike with Felix and Sam, who had been foolish to withhold Dimitri's crush from the cops. Its coming out now would make his son's situation ten times worse. Why hadn't he seen that? Dimitri was on public record for being hot-tempered, and Isabelle would report Callie's accusation that he had stalked her at the Calgary Folk Festival. What had Callie meant by stalking? Isabelle didn't know. It could have been anything from running into her by fake accident to following her around the park, harassing, threatening. Had there been other incidents? Was Sam aware of them? He must be, to risk trusting Isabelle to conceal her information.

"I'll be glad when this business about murder is over," Hayden said. "I'm tired of talking about Sam and his bunch."

"We were talking about tennis."

"Thinking about him counts."

She flushed, which was stupid. She tossed her sandwich remains to the geese.

Hayden sniffed. "I smell cigarette smoke."

"I slipped and bummed one from a friend this morning."

His eyebrow shot up, "How come?"

"Stress. I'll be glad, too, when this is done and I can focus on work."

Nils van der Vliet sucked his pipe behind the stack of claim files. Twenty-plus were piled on his desk, in contrast to the usual three or four. In the visitors' chair, Paula inhaled the room's sweet tobacco aroma that reminded her of her long deceased grandfather.

"I don't blame you for taking a few days off," Nils said, "but this is one hell of a time for it to happen when we're short staffed."

"I was in yesterday."

"For all of an hour."

"I was running around all day meeting claimants, and whose fault, anyway, is the short staffing?"

"I'm not hiring someone with the wrong chemistry for this firm."

Nils' telephone rang. While he talked, Paula swiveled her chair. During the past two months he had vetoed five suitable candidates for the junior adjuster's job. The workload might teach him to be less particular next time. Outside his smudgy window, vehicles streamed by the freight cars parked in the 9th Avenue railway yard. Beyond them, blue sky framed the Saddledome's curved roof. A homeless man shuffled along the sidewalk, his arms weighted by shopping bags. His yellow vest looked familiar. She had probably seen him in her neighborhood, a twenty-minute walk away.

Nils chatted with his business friend about football, while Paula sat here wasting her time. Unlike her, he didn't have Alice, their secretary, screen calls. With no interruptions, and prioritizing claims, Nils could cut that stack in half. Yesterday, they had agreed on the ones that didn't require immediate attention. One was the Jensen file sitting on top of the pile. He was going to spend hours on that and let slide ones that claimants, lawyers, and insurance agents had been calling about. His third flaw—or was she up to four?—smoking in the office, bothered her less than it amused her. She chuckled at Alice's battles to keep his door closed and visitors' futile attempts to explain that people did not smoke in today's offices.

Nils hung up the phone and pulled out a file from the stack as deftly as a magician. "I sense we're close to settling with your friend, Roy Turner."

"One of our rare, honest claimants."

"Which is fortunate or our job would be boring."

"As if it's not boring enough."

"What's the matter with you today?" Nils took another call.

Paula rubbed her head. Maybe she was simply tired or annoyed by the police report that had come in this morning. Someone had reported a hit-and-run in the neighborhood of her alleged hit-and-run claimant's accident.

The damage matched up with her claimant's damages, which meant her guy was possibly lying. He was the hit-and-run perpetrator, not the victim. Had he been drinking? It wouldn't surprise her. Normally, she loved nailing liars and cheats. Today, it was all extra work. Her gaze shifted from Nils' files to his off-white office walls that hadn't been painted since the 1970s, when he purchased the metal desks. The room's only art was a sketch so small you couldn't see it from more than a foot away. The venetian blind permanently drooped. Paula had taken the job with his little firm, in part, because it seemed a flashback in time. Nils refused to deal with computers. Alice printed everything out for his thickening files. Nils viewed the firm as David fighting Goliath insurance adjusting chains and multinational staff adjusters. All they needed was a niche, he said over and over.

Nils kept talking to his lawyer-friend. Paula walked to the room's far side. She never came in here without her cell phone and a paper report to occupy her during Nils' calls. She phoned Anne to ask about her husband's heart palpitations. As they left the boutique yesterday, Anne said he was going in for tests, a routine occurrence for him that still stressed Anne.

"They're keeping him in." Anne's voice shook. "I'm going to have to cancel our dinner on Saturday night. I hope Hayden understands. I'm really sorry. We'll make it another time."

Paula felt relief and guilt because she hadn't mentioned the dinner to Hayden and Anne seemed to think it was a done deal. Events were pointing to the hike with Sam.

Anne suggested they take advantage of the fine weather and replace tomorrow's workout with a walk to the hospital. Paula said she would come by the fitness center at one o'clock. By then, Anne would probably have found out about her son's interest in Callie and its implications for the murder case. Poor Anne having to deal with that on top of her husband's problems. A weaker person would crack. Paula herself felt close to cracking these days, while dealing with less.

Nils hung up and placed another call. She stared at his sketch of the Lloyd's of London coffee house circa 1688, where modern insurance began. Nils' office door opened. Alice tiptoed across the room to Paula and whispered that she had a visitor.

"Who? I'm not expecting anyone." A claimant angry enough to come to her office was the last thing she needed.

"Shall I tell him to wait?" Alice asked.

Nils looked entrenched in his discussion about whiplash. Paula signaled him she was leaving. He nodded and motioned them to leave the door open. Paula closed it behind her.

Alice scanned the reception room. "That's funny. He was here a minute ago. In fact, he stopped in this morning and made a special trip to return. Your door's open."

"I'm sure I closed it." Paula walked in to find a man standing next to her desk, holding a picture frame. "Sam?"

He wore a white shirt and shorts. Sunglasses arced over his head. He returned the photo of Leah to the bookshelf. He couldn't have missed the picture of Hayden she had added only last month.

"I was checking out a building near here," he said. "I remembered you worked in the East Village and figured I'd look you up."

"You don't look dressed for work." Had she told him the name of the firm she worked for? She closed her office door. Alice was a bigger eavesdropper than Isabelle.

"I'm on my way to play squash."

Where was her second visitor's chair? Alice must have borrowed it for the reception area. If Paula offered Sam this one, she would have to talk to him from behind her desk, which might feel too business-like. Clearly, he had made a special trip to see her. Why?

"I hear you've inherited Isabelle," he said.

"Only until Saturday, I hope."

He studied her bookshelves, rubber tree plants and wall paintings. One featured a mountain scene, the other a field with oil pump under a wide open prairie sky. "Your office looks homier than your home."

"I've worked here longer than I've lived there." She pushed her penholder away so she could lean against the desk. "Isabelle told me about Dimitri."

Sam didn't flinch. "I kind of figured she would, she's not so good with secrets."

"She kept a good one from the police."

"It seems she's capable, when she wants to be." From the bookshelf, he picked up her souvenir of Mount Saint Helens. "I was there, too. It was amazing, the trees all crashed down in the direction of the blast. They didn't know what hit them."

"Sam, I have to tell the police about your son's interest in Callie. Or you could do it today. That would be better."

"For whom?"

"For you, I guess. They'd appreciate your coming clean."

"What difference would that make?" Sam returned the miniature volcano to the shelf.

Paula waited for him to turn around. "Were Callie and Dimitri involved?"

"Why would you ever think that?" His eyebrows rose in surprise that appeared genuine. "She was twice his age."

"Women go for younger men."

"Callie wouldn't, for him. She found him too priggish and too religious."

"She joined a church last year."

"Not Dimitri's fundamentalist one. Even if she was interested, he'd have been too prudish to follow through. It was a fantasy. Now that Callie's dead, it's over."

"His feelings wouldn't end with her death. Have you discussed them with him?"

"Not recently."

"Since she died?"

"No."

He was so close she could see a faint dent in his left cheek. It made his face look so vulnerable at the moment.

She leaned harder against the desk. "After Callie died, you and Dimitri agreed not to tell the cops about his interest. So you and he did talk."

Sam turned away to look at or pretend to look at her shelf full of photographs.

Paula pressed her hand on the desk so hard her knuckles went white. "What about Callie and Felix Schoen?"

"What about them?" The back of his shirt was bunched around his shorts belt.

"Why do the cops suspect Felix?" she asked.

"Felix is nervous. He's got a house load of guns. His house backs on the Elbow River and he saw her jogging every day."

"Did he?"

Sam turned around. "Felix has a weird sleeping routine. Out like a rock for a few hours, prowling around the rest of the night. He saw her jog by each morning at the same time. In the summer, when she started, she would have set out in daylight. I guess she got used to leaving at that time, even when it was dark. She wasn't a nervous sort of woman, that way."

Unfortunately, as it turned out. "Did you know about her routine before her death?"

"Felix told me afterwards."

"Did he tell the cops?"

"Yes. That's likely why they suspect him. He knew her habits and could easily have followed her along the trail or driven to your neighborhood to intercept her at the murder spot. I'm sure he didn't."

"How do you know?"

"For starters, he had no reason to kill her."

"Could they have been having an affair?"

Sam chuckled. "That's impossible."

"Nothing's impossible."

"Felix would have told me about it, for sure."

"Men don't usually confide their affairs to their lover's husband."

He averted his eyes. "Felix knew about Callie's and my situation."

"Did he know about you and Bev Berwell?"

Sam's face grew pink. He raked his hand through his hair, knocking the sunglasses to the carpet. "Shit. Isabelle told you? How did she find out? From Felix? Bev. Fuck. Biggest mistake in my life." He squatted to pick up the sunglasses. "Scratch that. I've made worse ones. My whole life's a mistake." He placed the sunglasses on his head. They pushed his hair back so it stood up like a giant cowlick. "You must think I'm a complete shit."

"I wouldn't have thought Bev was your type."

"Do you know Bev? Shit. Don't tell me she's your friend."

"Hardly, I met her this morning."

"Where? What do you think of her?"

She faced him squarely. How to sum up Bev? "I didn't totally dislike her."

"I found her scary toward the end."

"Only toward the end?"

He shook his head. "This is so totally screwed up. I don't think it can get any worse." He spun toward her mountain painting. "This reminds me of the reason I dropped by. The Kananaskis hike with Felix is a definite go for Saturday. Did you decide if you're interested?"

Nils opened the door. "There you are."

Alice appeared behind him. "I tried to keep him away."

"I was just leaving." Sam startled Paula by extending his hand for her to shake. It seemed oddly formal. "I'll call you tomorrow about the hike." He squeezed between Alice and Nils and out the door.

"Who was that?" Nils said.

"I thought he looked familiar," Alice said. "He's better looking in person than in his newspaper pictures where he looks so somber. I find his face pleasant."

"Is he one of our claimants?" Nils said.

Paula sunk to her chair.

"There's something delicate, yet strong, about his hands." Alice stroked her own palm. "He could be a surgeon or violinist."

"He's an architect." Paula jiggled her computer mouse to get rid of the screensaver.

"For God's sake," Nils said. "I'll be in my office when you're finished."

"Not many men can wear shorts without looking foolish," Alice said.

Paula recalled Sam's shirt bunched in the back above his shorts, the T-shirt sleeves hugging his biceps

"He's got the full package," Alice said. "Legs, bum, arms, chest."

"I didn't notice."

Chapter Seventeen

For the second time in one day, Paula entered Mount Royal's winding streets, which had been designed to thwart traffic. The major city routes bypassed these wealthy homes. The few pedestrians she drove past today almost certainly either lived here or had come to service the residences. This wasn't Ramsay. No homeless people roamed the streets; no airplanes roared overhead; no trains enclosed the neighborhood and whistled when they passed.

She parked in front of Kenneth's house. Nothing had changed since she was here three years ago. A dozen mature trees drained the front lawn of nourishment. Patchy grass struggled through dirt in the sunken yard. The walkway bridge connecting the city sidewalk to the porch had been the highlight for her young daughters during their first family visit from Montreal. They called it a drawbridge and the yard, a moat, and played endless games of castle and fort with Callie's children and their friends. Gary, Paula's ex, kept an eye on the kids, while Paula and Callie went for walks that always ended up in 17th Avenue cafés. She and Gary had left thinking Calgary wouldn't be a bad place to live.

When she was halfway across the drawbridge, Kenneth opened the door. He greeted her with a hug that was slightly less stiff than the one they had shared at Callie's funeral. Inside, the house also looked the same. In contrast to the modern decor of her Riverdale home with Sam, Callie had furnished this earlier one with antiques, many of them purchased at estate auctions. She had reupholstered the French provincial sofa in 1990s mauve and gray. Perhaps the Riverdale decor had been a compromise, since Sam didn't find it contemporary enough.

Kenneth had set out a plate of cookies on the coffee table. He offered her a drink. She asked what he was having.

"Milk." He tapped his long leg. "I have a touch of osteoporosis. I know it's unusual for a man."

It wouldn't hurt to join him in a glass. The dog barked in the kitchen. Callie and Kenneth always gated the golden retriever when they had visitors. She followed Kenneth to the gate and petted Mandy, who had sprouted white fur around the muzzle. Bev had compared Kenneth's face to a basset hound's. Paula still thought Eeyore was closer to the mark. Kenneth was her age, fifty-two, but his bald crown, cardigan, and slippers made him look older. She hoped she didn't look that old.

She returned to the living room with Kenneth who had, evidently, been reading when she arrived. The lamp on the end table illuminated *Paris 1919*, a book Hayden had found fascinating. It was supposed to explain the modern, political world. She couldn't get past page three. Kenneth set the glasses on the coffee table beside a cigarette pack and ashtray with two butts. The room had a mild acrid odor.

"I thought you gave up smoking after college," she said.

"I slipped back into the nasty vice a couple of years ago." When Callie left him for Sam.

Paula turned down his offer of a cigarette; this morning's slip with Bev had been enough. "On the phone, you said you might have something for me."

"I wasn't sure then. The kids and I have argued about it back and forth since the funeral. Finally, we reached an agreement." He led her to the piano against the inside wall. The family photographs had been cleared away from the upright top. The only objects on it now were five boxes, lined up like stairs and painted with brightly-colored ovals and circles.

"Callie made these in IA." Paula reached for the largest one.

Kenneth pulled her arm away from it. "IA?"

"Industrial Arts, at high school. Callie and I took that instead of Home Ec. like most of the other girls, to make a statement, I guess, but really to meet boys." Paula waited. Kenneth didn't smile at her joke, if it was a joke. She and Callie had enjoyed IA and, between them, had picked up several boyfriends, Callie more than her, naturally. Kenneth's boney fingers let go of her arm. "Most of the class made practical objects like napkin holders and pencil boxes," she said. "I made a tea chest for my mother. She still uses it. Did Callie's sister bring these out here? She must have found them when they cleared out their parents' home." She touched the middle box, caught his glare and retreated. He must be really in love with Callie if he couldn't bear anyone's hands on something she had made.

"They've been here all along," Kenneth said. "I kept them at the office, to remind me of what was important."

The four largest boxes gleamed thanks to forty-year-old IA shellac. Paula would have expected the largest one to fade first, since it had probably been exposed to more air than the little blue and green one. The boxes would normally be displayed nested like Russian dolls.

"Do you remember the boxes from Callie's and my wedding?" Kenneth said.

"I wasn't there."

His forehead lines deepened, as he considered this. "You're right. I'd forgotten. She presented them to me at the ceremony, as part of the vows."

"Like exchanging rings? A ring would fit in the smallest box."

Kenneth no longer wore a wedding band. "That one is for you, if you'll accept it."

The box had been made by Callie's young hands. It could hold paper clips or safety pins and would look good with the pictures and souvenirs Paula had put on her office bookshelf to remind her of what was important. Evidently, Kenneth and his children placed great sentimental value on these creations if they had argued for three days about what to do with them. God knew how long it would take them to dispose of the remaining Callie artifacts. She picked up the faded, small box, with its crooked fastener and hinges that somehow managed to work. Callie didn't have the knack for woodworking. The boys had been glad to help her, while Paula produced her more complicated tea chest on her own. Did that sound bitter?

"Are you sure you want to break up the set?" she said.

"Don't open it." Kenneth's bark made her shake the box. Something shifted inside. "The kids and I debated it endlessly, but couldn't agree on what to do with her ashes. We all had different ideas."

"Ashes?"

"They call them cremains these days."

"They're in here?"

Paula clunked the box on the piano top. She struggled to fiddle it back into position, knocking the next ones out of place. The stairs zigzagged to the largest box, painted yellow and orange and roughly the size of the elegant cherry wood urn at the funeral. Had they squeezed all of Callie's ashes into the blue and green box? What did he mean by it being for Paula?

"Skye wanted the ashes tossed to the sky," Kenneth said.

"That seems appropriate. For Skye, that is."

"Her argument was that her mother chose the name, so it must have meaning for her. Of course, Skye's name really came from the island in Scotland."

Callie had liked the sound of it. Why were her ex-husband and children deciding on the disposal of her ashes with no apparent input from Sam? He was her husband, albeit estranged, which Kenneth had learned from Bev. Would someone as shrewd as he was believe a mistress scorned?

Kenneth's bony face was obscured by shadows. Even in daytime, this room was dark due to its northern exposure, sheer-covered windows and forested front yard.

"Cameron wanted to work them into a sculpture," Kenneth said. "He feels his mother would appreciate becoming an object of art, especially one made by her son."

"What . . . what would be the design?"

"Possibly something related to music; whatever it is, I'm sure I'll find it hideous."

His whole body shudder made her stifle a smile, while tending to agree.

"I'm conventional in this matter," Kenneth said. "I want her buried in a place I can visit. That left the three of us in deadlock. Do you mind if I smoke?"

While he got the cigarettes, she straightened the staircase of boxes. The colors got brighter on the way to the top. Was he asking her to break the deadlock?

"Shouldn't Sam be involved in this decision?" she said.

Kenneth returned with a lit cigarette and ashtray he placed on the piano, beside box number two, the orange and red. He either hadn't heard her question or ignored it. "My children inherited their mother's artistic sensibility and my stubbornness. Fortunately, last night, I thought of these."

Both turned to the boxes on the piano.

"Skye insisted it would be bad luck if we didn't use all five in the set."

"Why?"

"Who knows? This meant we had to include two more people. My kids said Sam should get one. I was, frankly, surprised. I thought Skye despised him."

"I thought she did, too, and wonder why." Paula touched the piano keys.

"She didn't like his coolness toward Callie."

"Sam's father also noticed that."

"They weren't great at disguising it. I don't know how they pulled it off." He blew smoke sideways, away from her. "I don't much like him getting a box, but deep down I knew the kids were right. She would want him to have a part."

"Even though they were estranged, he was still—"

"This left us with an extra box," Kenneth said. "I suggested you. Cameron and Skye couldn't come up with anyone more suitable."

"What about Callie's sister or brother?"

"They would find it a nuisance. Tony would probably throw her down the drain."

That did seem like Tony, especially when there would be no money for him in it. "Dorothy is responsible."

"She did her sisterly duty but is glad it's over so she can go back to her real life."

"What about Isabelle?"

"Too immature for the responsibility; Callie's cousins weren't close enough to her to attend the funeral. I can trust you to do the right thing, to counterbalance Sam's inevitable action."

Piano tones clashed. She had pressed the keys. Kenneth's anger at Sam was understandable, but it was unfair to assume Sam would mistreat the ashes. He had been deemed responsible enough to plan her funeral. Callie had chosen him to execute her will and hadn't changed his status on that.

"This is probably nosey of me," she said. It was super nosey, but if he was entrusting her with a portion of the ashes . . . "Does he inherit all her money and property?"

"That goes to the kids. He gets nothing. Why should he? He didn't contribute a penny to that house."

"Do the police know this?"

"They requested the will."

Sam had no motive for murder. The cops knew it. That was why he wasn't the prime suspect. "I'm sure he'll treat his box of ashes with respect."

"He can take it to hell with him, for all I care. Shall we sit down?"

Bev's intuition about another murderous "he" must have been wrong. Kenneth was simply a man who despised his rival and, fairly or unfairly, saw the worst in him. She took her place on the sofa, facing the window and a railroad clock she didn't recall from her previous visits. She asked if it was new.

"A family portrait used to hang there," Kenneth said. "It was easier to buy the clock than plug the hole and repaint."

She remembered the portrait now: Callie with him and the children in a happy family pose. She bit into an oatmeal cookie. "This is good. Is it homemade?"

"I bought them at a store on 17th Ave." Kenneth butted out his cigarette and turned his attention to cookies and milk. He had never been good at small talk.

Taking her cue from Bev, Paula cut to the chase. "I ran into a neighbor of yours, a former friend of Callie's, Bev Berwell."

Kenneth looked confused. "Bev's more Sam's friend."

Paula waited for him to bad-mouth Sam for cheating on Callie.

Kenneth crossed one long leg over the other. "The detectives were by to see me yesterday. Or was it Tuesday? I lose track of time. Did they talk to you?"

"Not since they located the gun."

"That changes the whole complexion, don't you think?"

Paula took a sip of milk. "It suggests the killer was someone close."

"He knew the gun was in the shed."

"Did you?"

"Not before the police told me."

"Sam says he blabbed the story to everyone."

"I don't recall hearing about it." Kenneth caught her glance and attempted a wan smile. "There's no proof Sam didn't tell me. As the jilted husband, I'm the obvious suspect."

"You're not the only one. There's him." Paula grabbed a cookie.

"You must have been shocked when Callie told you about her and him," Kenneth's face darkened. The only light in the room came from the reading lamp beside him. "Did you try to discourage her, convince her she's throwing her life away? I'm sure you did and she refused to listen."

Paula nibbled the cookie. Like everyone, he thought Callie had confided in her.

Kenneth took another cigarette from the pack. "I assumed, from the start, the murder was random. And Sam and I were friends. That's why I went along. Presumably, you felt the same. The gun changes all that."

She nodded her mouth full of cookie.

"As of yesterday or whenever it was, you hadn't told the police," he said.

Told them what? About Callie and someone who wasn't Sam, whom Sam would like to protect? Paula washed down her cookie with milk. "I wanted to think through the implications."

"Me too, we're both rational types. Callie was impulsive." A faint line of milk coated his upper lip. He twirled the unlit cigarette. "I thought, why drag her reputation through the muck when it's unrelated to the crime. But if it was him, he deserves to fry."

She took a stab. "Dimitri?"

"Sam assured me it was over between them and he hadn't come near her since spring."

"That isn't true." It had been more than a crush. Callie and Dimitri had had an affair. Kenneth knew about it. Sam had persuaded him to keep it quiet, as he had persuaded Isabelle. "Callie's niece told me Dimitri followed Callie around the folk festival this summer. Callie didn't like it."

"Even as a kid, he wouldn't take no for an answer."

The grandfather clock in the hall bonged the half hour. The dog barked from the kitchen. The railroad clock chimed Westminster Chimes. Kenneth, as Anne's and Sam's friend, would have seen Dimitri growing up. He might have toddled around this room.

"Callie believed he would eventually go public with their affair," Kenneth said. "I told her he never would. It was all about image with him."

"You say the affair ended last spring. When did it start?"

Kenneth stopped twirling the cigarette. He stared at her.

Damn. She had forgotten her role as Callie's confidant. Paula said, "It wasn't clear to me which of them strayed from the marriage first. Sam can't have taken her fooling around with his son lightly."

The peculiar smile returned to Kenneth's face. "You don't know. Now, I understand. I couldn't see why you would go along with Sam and keep it from the police. It all makes sense."

"What don't I know?" Paula took another cookie.

"Callie didn't tell you because you have common sense. You would have told her the truth: that she was out of her mind to leave a good marriage for him."

"Callie planned to leave Sam for Dimitri?"

"He's a pompous, conceited kid."

"You thought her marriage to Sam was good?"

"I told her when she left me she would live to regret it. I didn't know how much." The weird smile soured to one more suited to his face. "You still don't get it. There was no marriage."

"Callie and Sam weren't married?" Her voice croaked. She reached for the milk. "They were living common-law?"

"They never existed," Kenneth said. "It was her and him from the start. Sam was the cover for their affair. Callie left me for the kid."

Paula tipped the glass. Milk spilled to the carpet. "Shit." She grabbed a napkin, squatted, and wiped the stain. After the funeral, Dimitri had gone out of his way to talk to her, not out of politeness, as she had thought, but because she was Callie's friend. On TV, he had snapped at a reporter who called Callie his stepmother but not because he didn't accept her—he didn't see her in that role. After Callie's death, Dimitri got drunk. Sam seemed barely grieved. At the hockey game, Sam had talked about the son he had loved since infancy. He would do anything for him.

Paula looked up at Kenneth. "Callie gave me the impression she disliked him. She described Dimitri as self-centered and spoiled. She lied to me." Callie had purposely kept her from Sam because she might notice their indifference to one another and guess the truth. "What do you mean, there was no marriage? She told me they got married in Hawaii."

"Callie assumed his surname socially, not wanting mine anymore." The cigarette lit up his snarled and beaten face. "She and I aren't divorced. It's a legal separation."

The carpet looked reasonably clean. Paula got up and paced to the fireplace. Sam and Dimitri had the same surname. Who would know that when she called herself "Moss" she had meant the son? "They faked all this to protect Dimitri's political image."

"His family values party would never have accepted his involvement with a married woman."

"Sam did it to help his son."

"I sympathize with Sam," Kenneth said, "but he'll have to get used to seeing the little fucker in prison."

Chapter Eighteen

The shop doubled as a second-hand bookstore. Mystery novels lined the alcove around their table. Detective Vincelli arranged the four donuts on his plate into a square. He looked as exhausted as Paula felt after her night of restless sleep. Vincelli's olive face was pale, the whites of his eyes reddened. His maroon shirt was so creased Paula doubted he'd washed it since their last meeting.

Vincelli picked up a donut. "So, what information do you have for me?"

After getting home from Kenneth's last night, Paula had called Vincelli. He had suggested the donut shop. Yes, he said, he knew donuts and cops were a cliché, but who cared when the shop made ones exactly like his grandmother's?

Where to begin? With Bev or the lovers, Callie and Dimitri? Paula still couldn't get used to not thinking the lovers were Callie and Sam. "I located a woman who had an affair with Sam, Bev Berwell."

He paused, mid-donut. "We spoke to her yesterday."

"After I saw her?"

He finished the donut.

Bev must have been certain Paula would call the police and had contacted them first to pre-empt her, which meant Bev would have told them about Kenneth's cryptic reference to "he" during the dog walk. A homicide team was probably interviewing Kenneth now and discovering what Paula had learned last night. All Paula could offer the police were reports of her conversations with Isabelle and Sam in light of Kenneth's revelation. She felt like Isabelle during their talk Tuesday night, losing her scoop.

"What did you think of Bev?" she said. "My impression was, if she had killed anyone, it would have been Sam, not Callie."

"I wasn't involved in the interview." He picked up his teacup. "We could arrest you for impersonating a police officer." His dark eyes looked grim.

"I was impersonating an adjuster working for the police." That sounded flippant.

"This is serious."

"I know it is."

"Your interference could have screwed up our investigation and prevented us from making our case."

"I'm sorry. I wasn't thinking straight."

"Don't ever do it again." He bit hard into his donut.

Vincelli was right, but Paula didn't appreciate being chewed out by this man twenty years her junior. "You'll probably want my take on things, after someone in your unit has talked to Kenneth."

Sugar flecked his lips. "Kenneth Unsworth, Callie's former husband?"

"When did Bev call you? Yesterday afternoon or last night? You must have gone out to Kenneth's right away. I'm surprised our paths didn't cross."

"What are you talking about? Did Bev say something about Kenneth?"

"She must have told your colleagues the same thing, knowing I'd bring it up."

"Bring up what?" Vincelli's eyes were blank.

"I thought you and Novak were primary on this case."

"We are. Our colleagues gave a full report at the unit meeting."

"When was that?"

"About an hour ago."

"That's odd. They wouldn't keep this from you."

"Not when we're fucking primary." He wiped sugar from his chin stubble, but missed the powder on his lips.

Bev had no motive to withhold Kenneth's "he" reference from the cops. There was nothing in it for her, which seemed to be her operating principle. It could only benefit her, publicity-wise, if the media shifted its attention from Sam. She had no reason to think "he" was Sam's son. Knowing Bev, it might have been a whim. Maybe she didn't like the interviewer's face. He might have tried to push her around. Bev would balk at that. Vincelli was waiting for Paula's explanation. A flash through his dark eyes suggested he didn't like her trumping the cops once again. So, he was competitive and she had lingered long enough for a drum roll effect.

"Sam and Callie were never together," she said, "they weren't married."

"We've known that from the start, having requested the marriage certificate." His face relaxed. Presumably, he thought this was it.

"Sam inherits no money or property. Callie paid for the house with her settlement from Kenneth. She had full ownership."

"We also requested her will and the title deeds." He couldn't conceal a triumphant smirk as he tackled his second donut.

Paula was competitive, too, and would love to take him on in tennis. Imagine the reach of those arms and the power of his stroke. Hayden was a more even match for her.

"Everything goes to her children," she said, "as well as a charity that helps street kids. You know all that, and also know that she and Kenneth are still legally married, having requested the divorce papers."

Vincelli continued eating, presuming she had no volleys to slam.

"Did you interview Dimitri, Sam's son?" she said.

His eyes implied "what-do-you-take-us-for?"

"Did he tell you about his affair with Callie?"

He stopped mid-bite.

"It began two summers ago, at the Calgary Folk Festival."

His eyes narrowed. "Bev Berwell told you this?"

"Kenneth did, last night. Callie and Dimitri ran into each other at the festival. Both were alone. They decided to keep each other company at the performances."

He set the donut remains on the plate. "Two years ago?"

"It led to an affair. They met at Felix's house, where Sam and Dimitri were living. Their liaisons took place while Sam and Felix were out."

"Sam and Felix didn't know?"

"Not until the night she told Kenneth about the affair. It led to a fight. Callie left and showed up at Felix's place, insisting she would never go back. That put Dimitri in a pickle."

"Goddammit," Vincelli said. "Sam, Dimitri, Felix, Kenneth—the four of them kept this from us."

The four original conspirators—Dimitri, Sam, Felix, and Callie— spent the night drinking and debating how to deal with the problem. Dimitri was being groomed to run in the next federal election and the Conservatives had their pick of aspiring candidates. The party would turf him out. Between them, they hatched the plan of pretending Callie left her marriage for Sam. Kenneth believed he sparked the idea during their fight, when he railed he could understand her getting involved with Sam, but she was an idiot to mess around with a kid. A year later, the same gang of four vacationed in Hawaii, where Felix and Sam witnessed the beach commitment ceremony performed by Dimitri's preacher friend.

"It wasn't legal, of course," Paula said.

Vincelli's hand banged the remaining donuts, squashing them flat. "This has cost us a week's work. I'll charge the lot of them with Obstruction of a Peace Officer. Had we known . . . why the hell didn't Kenneth tell us this?"

"He was a bit fuzzy about that."

"Why protect the man who ruined his marriage? You'd think he would hate the son of a bitch."

"He does." Paula finished her first donut and wiped her mouth, hoping Vincelli would take the hint and wipe the sugar from his. He didn't. As Kenneth explained it, Sam was the first person the police interviewed after her death. He lied about his son's affair on impulse, out of confusion, he claimed, when he told Kenneth about her death. Kenneth believed Sam honestly thought it was a random crime that would be solved within days, eliminating the need for deep investigation into Callie's personal life. Kenneth felt nothing would be gained by bringing Dimitri down. What did any of that matter anymore? Callie was gone.

"Kenneth hoped to the end that she'd come back," Paula said. "You have to credit him for not seeking revenge on Dimitri. Kenneth could have seized the chance to cause Dimitri a lot of public embarrassment."

"Kenneth wouldn't relish the publicity for himself."

"I was thinking that, too. He's a private person—"

"—who wouldn't like seeing his picture in the paper as the spouse dumped for a virile young man."

"I suppose that's why Kenneth went along with the marriage charade in the first place. He never really answered that."

Vincelli studied his flattened donuts as though he wondered if they were worth eating. "Who else knows about this?"

"No one, Kenneth says, not even Dimitri's mother, Anne. I can confirm that, unless Kenneth called her after last night. Anne will be broken up. The murder rap aside, Anne wouldn't like his having been involved with a woman her age."

"Why?"

Sweet of him to ask and appear to mean it; Vincelli was roughly Dimitri's age. Dating a younger man was the trend, but what would she and a man Vincelli's age have in common, aside from donuts and tennis, assuming he played?

"Isabelle knows Dimitri was interested in Callie," Paula said. "Isabelle believes it was all on his side. Sam convinced her to withhold this from you. It's a miracle she managed that."

"It's a sad day when Isabelle can deceive a trained cop."

"Isabelle's living with me now," she said. "Do you mind if I tell her all this or should I keep it secret?"

He rubbed his lips, reflecting. "Don't say anything to anyone until we've had time to assess the new situation."

"Another thing, Sam invited me to go hiking with Felix and him this Saturday."

Vincelli's eyebrow shot up. "Are you going?"

"I . . . I haven't decided yet. With his son in a jam, Sam may not even want to go."

"Would you be impersonating a police officer on this trip?"

"Very funny." But she could learn so much. Sam or Felix might drop some evidence incriminating Dimitri, sad as that would be. She had liked Dimitri at the funeral. He was the son of Anne, her closest girlfriend, now. And Callie had loved him once. "If the hike is still on, would it interfere with the case if I went?"

He rubbed his jaw stubble. "I doubt it. We'll get to Felix and Sam today. But, I have to advise against your going on the hike."

"Why?"

He bit into a squished donut, washed it down with tea.

"Are you saying I wouldn't be safe? Sam has no motive for Callie's murder." Vincelli wiped his lips. "This could change things."

"Are you saying Sam didn't like his son's involvement with Callie and finished her off? That's so unlikely. Or do you still suspect Felix?"

His eyelashes flickered. "Stay home and let us take care of this."

They finished their donuts in silence.

Paula squeezed her Echo between Walter's pickup and the white Grand Am that occupied her usual parking spot in front of the house. Walter and Isabelle and Paula's daughter Erin stood on her porch flinging plastic hoops onto stakes planted in her yard. Tony stood beside them, smoking.

"I didn't know you were coming over," she called to Erin.

"My class was canceled this afternoon."

She ducked a wild shot by Isabelle. "How'd you get here?"

"Bus." Erin ringed a plastic stake. "I win."

Isabelle groaned. "You've had more practice. I get the game now. Let's play again."

"How was Banff?" Paula asked Tony.

"Expensive." He butted his cigarette on the freshly painted railing. "Now that you're here, we can eat. Lunch must be ready." He coaxed the girls into the house.

Walter came down the stairs to collect the plastic stakes. "I haven't played that since my kids were little."

He had kids? Paula followed him around her yard. "You should not have let Isabelle into my house the other night. Why didn't you tell me you had a spare key?"

"You didn't ask."

"How did you get one? From the previous owner?"

"They were always locking themselves out. It's not safe leaving a spare in the garage."

"I've arranged to change all the locks next week."

"Good idea. You can't trust anyone these days."

"Until then, don't let anyone in, except Isabelle and she's leaving tomorrow."

"Is she? That's not what I hear. I'll look after your new key for you."

"No thanks." It was time she got to know her other neighbors, so she could leave a key with one of them. The yuppies in the house across the street spent long hours at work. Her neighbors on the other side weren't chatty types, but she might try them.

She entered her house to the sound of a *Cheers* rerun. Tony sat on the chair, Isabelle and Erin on the sofa, legs propped on the ottoman. Ginette came in with a beer for Tony. She and Paula hugged.

"Banff was wonderful," Ginette said. "Warm enough for shorts. I can't get over those turquoise lakes. The mountains are even more amazing than they are in pictures."

"Are there mountains in Banff?" Tony said. "All we saw were boutiques."

Ginette tapped his shoulder. "Don't listen to him. I just bought a few souvenirs."

"Paula and I are going to Banff tomorrow," Isabelle said.

"Kananaskis," Paula said. "We'll discuss that over lunch."

Tony raised his beer bottle. "No need for discussion. Everything's settled."

"We need Paula's permission, first," Ginette said.

"For what?"

Isabelle stood. She adjusted her skort and sports bra top. "I'm moving in with Erin."

Paula turned to her daughter. "How did that happen?"

"I kicked out my roommates."

"All of them?"

"Only the ones in the small front room."

"My old den?"

"They trashed it," Isabelle said.

Paula looked at Erin. "I knew those ones sounded like bad news."

"It isn't so bad." Erin stuck her thumbs under the bib of her jeans. "Mainly marks on the wall. It was also about all their arguing that bothered everyone else. I was afraid the others would leave."

"How many of you are there in this house?" Ginette asked.

"Six," Erin replied, "including me; well, now three plus Isabelle."

"How big is this place?" Tony said.

"It's a bungalow with a finished basement," Paula said. "Erin and two tenants had the upstairs rooms, three others the down."

"The couple I kicked out was getting the room cheap," Erin said. "Isabelle can afford to pay as much they did together."

"I'll be affording it," Tony said, "until she finds work."

The den in her former home trashed. Erin was probably underestimating the damage so Paula wouldn't get mad. She should have sold the place rather than give her daughter responsibility for renting it to students.

"We're fine with Isabelle living with your daughter," Ginette said. "If you have a problem—"

"Erin says there are tons of restaurants and stores near there," Isabelle said. "Or I'll look for an office job at the university."

"She can't move in 'til the room is fixed," Erin said. "Could you do it tomorrow, Mom?"

That explained the surprise visit and Erin's taking the trouble to get to Ramsay by bus. "I already have two other offers for tomorrow." Going to

Kananaskis with Sam and tennis with Hayden, who would also help with the house repairs if she asked.

"Is the pizza ready?" Tony asked Ginette.

"I started it late. It will take another ten minutes." Ginette turned to Paula. "Isabelle says you've been shopping, too. I'd love to see the evening dress you bought."

"That was money down the drain," Paula said.

"We'll trade you the dress for a hundred Banff souvenirs," Tony said.

"You'll be getting a bargain."

"Want to bet?" he said. "Overpriced junk."

She led Ginette to her bedroom, took the dress out of the closet and laid it on the bed.

Ginette stroked the silky fabric. "The color reminds me of those lakes in Banff. It's beautiful."

The shade would highlight Ginette's dyed red hair and porcelain complexion. The latter was the only obvious physical trait she had passed down to Isabelle, who had inherited Callie's mouth and nose.

"Where did you buy it?" Ginette said. "I might drag Tony to some stores this afternoon. Since you and I live across the country, we wouldn't have to worry about running into each wearing the same dress at a society bash." She laughed.

"I suppose I could wear it to the Stampede parade," Paula said.

"That would be more fun."

Paula could buy charity event tickets as a surprise for Hayden, to make up for her recent rotten treatment. Callie had willed her money to a street kids' charity that might host a ball. With his dark hair and muscular build, Hayden would look striking in a tux.

Ginette let go of the dress and faced Paula. "Do you mind having Isabelle living with your daughter? You can be honest with me."

Paula reflected. Isabelle would get her wish to stay in Calgary and would be, basically, out of Paula's hair, assuming Tony came through with the rent. Isabelle and Erin were the same age. "I don't know if she'll fit in. The others are all students. She says she hates school."

"Isabelle gets along with everyone. I'm not worried about that." Ginette adjusted her glasses.

Would she be a bad influence on Erin? Isabelle had a casual attitude toward sex; a lot of students were worse. The skimpy clothes? Erin could use a little panache in her wardrobe that largely consisted of T-shirts, sneakers and bib jeans. Isabelle didn't smoke. She didn't appear to drink much and hadn't mentioned doing drugs. She seemed to enjoy innocent amusements like games. She was impulsive and naïve. Those weren't terrible traits. "She's bound to be an improvement over the renters who trashed the room. I dread seeing the mess."

"Kids exaggerate."

"Is Tony really okay with her staying in Calgary?"

"She's twenty-one. What choice does he have? I think it will be good for her to be on her own in a new city. I didn't like Isabelle living with those men."

"They're too old for her," Paula agreed.

"It's not only that." Ginette looked at the dresser mirror.

"Isabelle told me about your concerns with Sam's son."

Ginette walked to the long, low dresser and touched the jewelry box. "What would an ambitious politician do with a girl like her? We know what he'd do. That's part of it, but it isn't the whole point." She trailed her finger across the dresser surface toward the blue and green box containing Callie's ashes. Paula hoped she wouldn't have to explain that Tony had, once again, missed out on an inheritance from his sister. Tony and Ginette would be stunned when they learned that their brother-in-law-in-effect was Dimitri, not Sam. Paula wondered if Sam would tell them tonight.

Ginette stroked the mini-urn. "Tony's afraid if Isabelle stays in Calgary she'll become like Callie, getting in with these rich, aspiring people and turning her back on her family."

"Callie didn't do that," Paula said. But she had. During her thirty years of living here, Callie had only returned twice to Montreal, for her parents' funerals. Who did she have there to visit, aside from Paula? Her sister and brother were much older. She hadn't grown up with them. Tony left home when she was a kid.

"That box," Paula said. "Don't pick it up. It's fragile."

Ginette stopped stroking, but pressed her fingers on the box. "Tony still sees Callie as eight years old. He sees Isabelle that way, too, sometimes. In his mind, I think he connects them. Callie's murder has hit him harder than he shows."

"You and Tony are much warmer than Callie's parents were. Isabelle finds Tony stifling now, but she knows you both care. She won't turn away from you."

Mercifully, Ginette lifted her fingers from the box. "You're all going hiking tomorrow in Kananaskis? That's the mountain range we passed on the way to Banff."

"It's almost as nice and is less crowded than Banff, but not so many boutiques."

Ginette smiled. "I'm glad Isabelle will have a chance to see the mountains."

"There will be other opportunities. She doesn't have to go with Felix and Sam."

"Don't get me wrong. I like Sam and Felix is a funny drunk. I don't think either of them killed Callie."

"How do you know?"

"They aren't the type."

"Who is?"

Ginette glanced at the blue and green box. Had Isabelle told her what was in it? "Dimitri," Ginette said. "Sam's son."

Paula shivered. "What makes you think that?"

"I can see he's capable."

"How can you see—?"

"Tony agrees. He's been around."

"Even if you're right, capable doesn't mean—" To get moving, Paula grabbed the dress. She hung it in the closet, leaving space between it and the adjacent skirts so the dress wouldn't wrinkle. If Sam saw this trait in Dimitri it would explain why he so easily believed his son did it.

"Dimitri's always hanging around Sam's house," Ginette said. "That's why we didn't want Isabelle to continue living there. She was getting too friendly with Dimitri."

"She says they're just friends."

"Isabelle's gullible; he could convince her of anything."

"Dimitri's in Ottawa now."

"He comes back often enough. Parliament only sits about half the year."

"The cops might be arresting him as we speak. If he's guilty, he'll go to jail."

"Do you really believe that? Sam and his friends will take care of it."

"How?"

"People with money and power know how to handle the cops."

"Pizza's ready." Erin poked her head in the door frame.

Ginette tousled Erin's blond head, "I'm glad Isabelle's moving in with you. You seem grounded."

Erin stuck her tongue out at Paula. "Tell that to my mom."

Erin was gullible and naïve, too. She would give the T-shirt off her back to anyone. What had she got her daughter into? If he wasn't arrested, Dimitri could follow Isabelle to Erin's house. Paula might choose a dangerous situation for herself; she did not want her daughter involved.

Chapter Nineteen

On her way to meet Anne, Paula stopped to question her hit-and-run claimant at his place of work. His office looked out to a high-rise building under construction. He was an accountant who handled the payroll for a large oil company. Paula noted him move with ease as he closed his office door. He wore no cervical collar.

"You seem to have recovered from your whiplash," she said.

He massaged his neck. "It flares up at night. Painkillers hardly help."

From her chair, she stared across his desk, into his close-set eyes. "I received a police report. A man claims he was sideswiped by a driver who took off. He's got damage along the left side, in addition to whiplash."

"What does that have to do with me? This must happen a lot."

"On the same night? Around the same time? Two blocks from your accident?"

He frowned so intently that his eyebrows met above his nose bridge. "Two blocks . . . I might have got the street wrong." He yanked a finger; his knuckle cracked. "The fellow is lying. He's the one who hit me. Did he get any witnesses?"

"Neither did you."

"It's his word against mine."

"He reported the accident; you didn't."

"It's not required for damages under one thousand dollars. I—"

"Your appraisal is thirty-two hundred dollars."

"Those garages rip you off."

"In your statement, you said you were taking a different route home. Why?"

"I told you already, for variety, and it wasn't so different. I try something new every few weeks. My wife confirmed that for you."

"She believes you were working until eleven thirty?"

"Why wouldn't she?" He glanced at the photo on his side table. Blond wife. Two blond smiling kids.

"I noticed a security camera downstairs. It will show the time you left."

He pulled on his finger.

She winced, waiting for the crack. "It would be better for you to come clean."

"You insurers. I pay premiums year after year and the first time I make a claim all you do is look for ways not to pay." He pointed his finger at her. "If you don't mind, I have a ton of work to finish today."

Paula wished her desk looked so clear. He claimed he'd worked late that night to get in the payroll. His department was short-staffed due to downsizing. It didn't matter if he'd left his office or his girlfriend's house, except that catching him in a lie might make him crack.

"I'm going to talk to my lawyer." He touched his neck, which now looked rigid.

"That's not a bad idea."

"The Kid is Hot Tonight" blared through the fitness center speakers. Women, of various ages and shapes, worked the machines. Anne was in her glass office arguing with the machine maintenance contractor, who had shown up unexpectedly. Paula waited for her at the reception desk. Entrepreneurship was a hassle, Anne said repeatedly during their workout sessions, yet it was obvious she thrived on those hassles, like Paula's boss, Nils, did. Both worked ridiculous hours and were taking on the big guys, in Anne's case the fitness chains. Unlike Nils, Anne was starting to win, thanks to her better organizational skills and expansion into whole health that appealed to the local Kensington yuppie residents. Fit for Life offered everything from yoga to counseling to body talk, whatever that was. Paula avoided the fruity getting-in-touch-with-yourself stuff. She and Anne preferred pounding the treadmills while discussing the struggles of the small firm.

Sometimes, Paula had wondered if Callie left their trio because she felt excluded. Now she knew Callie quit because she was involved with Anne's son. Did Anne know about this yet? Dimitri was well acquainted with guns. When Dimitri was a boy, he and Anne went out shooting with Anne's father, an avid sportsman. Next month, he was going hunting with a group of cabinet ministers—good networking for him, Anne said. Dimitri had to have known about the gun in his other grandfather's shed. He could easily have stolen it to use on Callie.

In the glass office, Anne and the maintenance man rose to shake hands. He lugged his equipment to an elliptical machine. Anne hurried over to

Paula and apologized for the delay. They hugged. Anne had dressed for the walk in capri pants, a V-neck T-shirt with capped sleeves, and no sweater, despite the cool temperature. Paula asked how her husband was doing.

"They still can't find the cause of his heart palpitations," Anne said.

They crossed the parking lot and crunched over gravel down the lane. Both put on sunglasses; the hospital was due west.

"Have you heard from Dimitri since he went to Ottawa?" Paula asked.

"He's having the time of his life." Anne smiled over at Paula. "Isn't it wonderful to be young and embarking on a new adventure?" Her face sobered. "Of course, Dimitri's concerned about Doug. I told him not to worry. It will be okay. I've been so preoccupied—"

A garbage truck roared by. Callie's involvement with Dimitri wasn't something Paula wanted to shout above the stream of cars. But the police were certain to act soon. Anne might take the news better from a friend and she'd be furious at Paula for knowing about this and holding it back.

"I saw Kenneth last night," Paula said.

"Callie's death has knocked him flat. Kenneth told us the only thing that's kept him going the past two years was the hope she'd come back. Doug asked me to keep an eye on him, in case he does something desperate."

"I don't think Kenneth's the type to sink to suicide."

"Anyone is."

Anne's legs were around the same length as Paula's, but they were moving fast. Paula did a quickstep to catch up. She had known Anne for five years and this was the first time they'd walked together outside.

"Did Kenneth tell you about their peculiar plan for disposing of Callie's ashes?"

"The boxes of cremains."

"Kenneth said they were the boxes from their wedding." Anne lifted her elbows to power walk. She described the wedding as a hippie-like ceremony on Sandy Beach that must have been Callie's idea. "It sure wasn't Kenneth." Callie wore a flower wreath in her hair and a Greek-goddess dress that Anne helped her make. The day was perfect August weather. The affair was limited to family and close friends—about a dozen people—and Sam was best man.

"So he and Kenneth were that close?" Paula said.

"Dimitri was the ring bearer. He'd just turned three. Sam and I had to keep grabbing him so he wouldn't run up to the front and wreck the ceremony."

They stopped for the 14th Street lights. Paula was glad to catch her breath. She squatted to stuff her sweater into her backpack.

Anne marched on the spot, arms moving power-walk-style. "Felix told me you and Sam are an item. Is that true?"

"Totally not. Where did Felix get that idea?"

"I heard you're all going hiking in Kananaskis."

"Felix told you that?"

Anne's hazel eyes flashed a mix of girlfriend curiosity and concern.

The light changed. They crossed 14th Street. Anne barely puffed up the hill.

"I can see Sam being attracted to you," Anne said. "For starters, he leans toward dark-haired women."

Anne's hair had been dark before it went gray and she lightened it to ash-blond. She kept telling Paula to go blond, claiming it softened the aging face.

"Sam also likes women who seem independent," Anne said. "Seem being the operative word. Half the time he gets it wrong and they turn out to be high maintenance. I suspect he secretly enjoys the drama. That's why, in the end, he's not for you."

"Who is?"

"Probably Hayden, if you give him a chance. It isn't all rockets out of the starting gate."

Paula's impression was it wasn't rockets for Anne and Doug. They had separate bedrooms due to Doug's snoring and restlessness sleeping.

Anne pointed at the brown brick school. "There's Dimitri's junior high; how many hours I spent in that principal's office."

Busy 5th had turned into broad, quiet 6th Avenue. Here was a spot to drop the bomb, although Anne had provided an opening for more information. A few more minutes delay wouldn't hurt. "Did Dimitri get into trouble at school?"

"Nothing serious," Anne said. "Stuff like throwing spitballs, failing to hand in assignments, cutting classes. He settled down in high school, got his energy out in a garage band he formed. My God, the noise, I felt sorry for my neighbors."

Music was an interest he and Callie shared. They had met at the folk fest. "Did Dimitri give up the band after high school?"

"Thank God he did. There was no future in it."

"I've never asked before. How did Dimitri happen?"

"The usual way," Anne smiled.

"I'd have thought you would be more careful."

Anne stopped to check for traffic. "I tried the pill, but it made me feel bloated and fat. Sam and I were using condoms, but you know guys in those days. They liked it better without them. I was foolish to go along, but I don't regret Dimitri, not for one second. He's the best thing that ever happened to me." She jaywalked toward the community center. "I like to detour down this street. It's quieter."

The avenue had a suburban flavor. Its houses were newer than the ones in Kensington and Hillhurst, the yards larger. Few cars cruised by. Anne power walked, chin forward in determination. It must have been hard, at twenty-one, to raise a child on your own. With the baby's arrival, Anne had abandoned her plan to do an MBA. She worked at jobs that fit the growing child's schedule, while Sam rose up the architectural ranks. True, he had stuck around to help with the child, but he had been a cad to get her pregnant.

They veered around a toddler riding a tricycle. The bike clanged over the sidewalk joints behind them. The child sped up, passed them on the grass, and pedaled up his driveway.

"If I hadn't had Dimitri," Anne said, "I might not have had children at all. Doug was wary of having kids of his own. His father and uncles all died in their forties and fifties from heart disease and diabetes, which Doug inherited. It sounds calculating, but Dimitri benefited from getting Sam's genetics and Doug's parenting."

The dead-end street led to a sidewalk. They climbed up the stairs to the pedestrian overpass. Even Anne was puffing by the top. Traffic roared beneath them down the Crowchild Trail. Clouds covered the sky. They removed their sunglasses. The hospital jutted like a castle behind the trees. If Paula didn't raise the issue now, there might not be another chance. No one else had rushed to be the first to tell Anne.

Paula stared at Anne's profile: pointed nose, small round chin. "Kenneth told me something else last night."

"What?" Anne turned toward her, heart-shaped face alert.

"It's about Dimitri."

Worry clouded Anne's hazel eyes.

"Callie and Sam were never involved. Their marriage was a cover for her affair with Dimitri. It began over two years ago and ended last spring."

Anne's mouth opened. She didn't speak.

"I still hardly believe it myself," Paula said.

"Dimitri," Anne croaked. "Callie."

"I know."

Anne coughed to clear her throat. "She's twice his age. She's my age."

But looked and acted much younger than Anne, whose stunned face was more wrinkled than Paula had noticed before.

Anne rocked from foot to foot, trying to steady herself. "Kenneth told you this?"

"He was in on it from the start. Sam convinced him to go along."

"I see Kenneth at least once a month. He's never said anything. It can't be true. Someone would have told me."

"Kenneth thinks the only other person who knows is Felix."

"Felix?" Anne shrieked above the traffic din. "He kept this from me, too?"

"They probably figured why worry you, since it was bound to end, which it did about five months ago, when Callie broke it off."

Anne gripped the railing and stared down. She looked ready to somersault onto the cars. No wonder the others had hidden the affair from her. She hadn't yet grasped the worst: her son was now a prime suspect for murder.

"Here I was afraid Dimitri had something going on with Callie's niece," Anne said.

"Isabelle? I know they're friendly—"

"Felix had a barbecue Labor Day weekend, a bon voyage party for Dimitri."

Anne had told Paula about the barbecue; she hadn't mentioned Isabelle.

"You should have seen Dimitri and Isabelle together. I worried he was throwing his career away for that silly girl. Callie was a married woman, twenty years older than him. It would have been disastrous."

"That was the reason for the cover."

"Whose idea was that? Sam's, I bet. It explains so many things. Dimitri always stayed at Sam's house when he was in town." Anne's jaw went slack. Her face turned white. "Did you say Callie broke it off? When? Do the police know about this?"

Paula touched Anne's hand. "They do now." How would Paula feel if one of her daughters was in this kind of trouble? Anne's fingers were cold and shaking.

"Have they arrested him?" Anne's voice was barely audible above the cars.

"Not that I'm aware. This is only circumstantial evidence against him. Maybe he has an alibi."

Anne's eyes lit up with hope, but if Dimitri had one, Sam wouldn't be so worried.

"Dimitri's in Ottawa now," Anne said. "Will the cops there talk to him?"

"Probably."

"I'm sure he's innocent."

Paula ran her hand through her hair, avoiding the expected agreement.

"You don't believe he is?" Anne looked panicked. "Did Callie tell you something? Did you hide it from me, too? What did she say?"

"Nothing."

"Tell me."

"I swear." Paula backed into the railing.

Anne raised her arms as though to grab Paula by the shirt. Paula moved sideways. It was a twenty foot drop to the freeway and she didn't want Anne pushing her over the railing by accident.

"Callie told me nothing," Paula insisted. "It bugs me she didn't. We were supposed to be friends. Didn't she trust me?"

Anne took deep, heaving breaths. The white left her face. She looked calmer, almost normal. Still, it would be wise to get off the overpass.

"I suppose," Anne said, "Callie was afraid if you knew, you'd let something slip during our workouts."

"That might be part of it."

"A sham marriage," Anne said. "Trust Sam to come up with a scheme like that."

"Kenneth says Sam, Callie, Felix, and Dimitri planned it together."

"It was Sam. He's the worst drama queen. Why solve a problem with a simple approach when there's a convoluted, complicated way."

"Drama queen?"

"Why didn't Sam tell the cops about this . . . arrangement?"

"He knew it would make Dimitri a suspect."

"Didn't he realize keeping it secret makes it worse when it finally comes out?"

"Sam was hoping the murder would be settled before it did."

"Why didn't Kenneth come out with it, then?"

"That's a good question."

"Felix goes along with whatever Sam says. Kenneth . . . I can't understand him. Yes, I do. He loves Callie. He must be furious at Dimitri for stealing her. He's also smart enough to see that holding it back would put the screws on his rival."

"I don't think Kenneth would be so cruel." Although he could be ruthless in business; Anne's theory made sense.

Anne rolled her hands into fists. "I hate him."

"Kenneth?"

The anger drifted from Anne's face as she struggled to regain control. "I don't really mean that. He's a good friend, my husband's best friend and, in a way, I admire his devotion to Callie. I just feel so . . ."

"Helpless?"

Anne thrust her chin forward. "Dimitri didn't kill her. I'm his mother. I know."

Chapter Twenty

"I'm going to try Dimitri's assistant." Anne flipped open her cell phone. "He didn't answer the last two times," Paula said. Nor had Dimitri answered Anne's calls to his cell phone and Ottawa residence.

They continued through St. Andrew's Heights. While house hunting, Paula had considered a bungalow here. Its location near the hospital might have been useful for her old age, but the house hadn't grabbed her. Anne punched her cell phone keys. To Paula's surprise, this time Dimitri's assistant picked up.

"He did?" Anne spoke into cell. "Why? . . . When? . . . If he contacts you, tell him I'd like to talk to him tonight . . ." Anne closed her cell. "Dimitri is flying home for the weekend. His plane arrives around four thirty."

"He just left for Ottawa on Monday."

"He told the assistant he had to see his father."

"Sam?"

"Doug, in hospital." Anne's lips narrowed. "That's an excuse. Dimitri and I specifically agreed he didn't need to be here."

They reached the ledge overlooking the Bow River. Across the river, evergreens rose up to homes sparkling white in the afternoon sun.

"Do you think the police contacted him?" Paula said.

"Or someone did."

"Sam—"

"Dimitri's assistant overheard him call the woman who takes care of his condo while he's away. He asked her to air the place out for his arrival." Anne opened her cell. "I'll try him again."

"Won't he be on the plane?"

"Something's happened. I know it. I'd go meet him at the house if it weren't for Doug . . . and the maintenance man. I don't trust him to fix those machines."

"That can wait until tomorrow."

"I can't let my customers down. They've been complaining about the elliptical."

"Phone him when the plane gets in."

"He won't answer." Anne shook her head. "If this were a normal visit, he'd go to Sam's house. When Dimitri's deeply in trouble, he retreats. It isn't healthy for him to brood."

"You could ask Sam to go see him."

"No." Anne's eyes slit. "He's caused enough problems already."

"I could go." Where had that come from?

Anne's face brightened. "Would you?"

"I've cleared my workload for the rest of the day," Paula said. "I don't know what I can do."

"You'd ease my mind that he's all right."

"Where is his condo?"

"Over there." Anne motioned across the river. "I really appreciate this, Paula. You're a good friend."

Or a curious one.

Since it wasn't much past two o'clock, Paula could walk back to the fitness center, pick up her car, drive home, then go see Dimitri. But her former home wasn't far from here. She decided to kill the remaining afternoon hours by hopping a bus to check out the damage Erin's tenants had caused to the bedroom.

The bus dropped her off on familiar streets shaded by poplars and willows. When she and Gary moved to Calgary, they had chosen a renovated bungalow over the larger, newer homes farther from the city center. The girls' bedrooms and TV space were in the basement. She and Gary had a master suite on the main floor. The house had served them well, but, while there, had she ever been content? She had spent the first few years settling in and the rest dealing with Gary's betrayal. He was the last man she would have picked to have an affair. Maybe not the very last, but he was fundamentally decent. He couldn't pass a street person without tossing him a dollar and treated some of them regularly to coffee and lunch. Who would have thought a scheming bitch would take advantage of his kindness, sucking him in with feigned helplessness?

She crunched over dry, fallen leaves. The bitch part was true, but the woman couldn't have schemed her way into a vital relationship. After his confession, in the midst of Paula's rants Gary had lobbed his share of barbs. "You know, Paula," he said, "you left the marriage first." And she had, involving herself in work, children, friends, extended family responsibilities to the point where all she talked about with him was work, kids, friends, family. Never them, as a couple. Could she and Gary have worked through the affair and possibly made the marriage stronger? Callie had urged her to give it a try. Anne agreed with Paula to boot Gary out. Gary said, "I knew we'd be finished the minute you found out. You don't cut people slack." Callie didn't understand why that barb had hurt. "Paula, you admit, yourself, you're judgmental." Well, shouldn't there be standards? Most important was she happy now with the end result? Before Hayden, there had been lonely nights when she'd wished she'd cut Gary slack, worked through their problems. But, even then, what she'd missed was companionship, not Gary in particular. Gary was right; she had left the marriage first.

Finding herself on her porch, she pressed the doorbell. No answer. She rang it again. Erin and her renters must be off at university. Paula let herself into the usual jumble of shoes piled in the entranceway and closet jammed with jackets, more shoes, and soccer balls. A smell of rotten eggs made her nose twitch. Newspapers and clothes littered the living room coffee table and sofa. Dirty dishes covered the kitchen counter. More of them filled the sink, where they were rinsed by a dripping faucet that could easily be fixed if one of them bothered to buy a washer.

She followed the odor to the small bedroom in the front. Whew. Why hadn't they thought to open the window? The room was empty, the couple having taken their furnishings. They had bashed in the wall next to the closet with what might have been a baseball bat. Felt marker sketches covered the walls. Some were cartoons. Superman flew above the window. The Road Runner chased Bugs Bunny to the light switch. Other drawings looked like illustrations from the Kama Sutra. One showed a couple doing it doggy-style. She cocked her head, unable to determine either participant's gender. The artwork was actually pretty good. It was almost a shame to paint over it. She and Hayden could easily patch the bashed hole this weekend. The illustrations might inspire them. The truth was she would rather go to Kananaskis with Sam, and that would be pushing Hayden too far. She and Hayden were compatible. It was a little boring, but why break off a reasonably satisfying six-month relationship for a man who preferred drama to commitment? Callie would ask, "Is 'reasonably satisfying' enough? Why are you staying with Hayden?"

Because he can't hurt me, not to the core as Gary had. So could Sam, if I let him.

Dimitri squinted at her. Even after Paula introduced herself, it took him a few seconds to remember who she was. "Did Sam send you?"

He looked angry enough to slam the door in her face. Instead, he motioned her into the condo with his bottle of beer. An L-shaped counter separated the kitchen from the dining area and living room, which was at the back. No lights were on. Closed blinds made the main floor even darker. Folk music wafted from the CD player. Dimitri's feet were bare. His black muscle shirt clung to his arms and pecs; blue jeans hugged his hips. His tousled hair framed a handsome young face, with Sam's strong bones. Paula could see his appeal to Callie.

His breath reeked of beer. Spidery red veins crawled through the whites of his hazel eyes. Four empty Corona bottles sat on the countertop. She accepted his offer of a beer. He led her into the living room, flicked off the CD and settled on the white love seat facing the fireplace. She took the matching one that lined the back wall. A Bible lay on the glass coffee table. A bookmark stuck out of it, near the beginning of the book.

"What passage are you reading?" she said.

"Nothing particular." He yanked the bookmark out. Both sipped their beer. Behind her, the wind clacked the vertical blinds against the screen.

He stared at the unlit fireplace. "I guess everyone knows. Or they will in a couple of days." He raised his bottle, as though making a toast, "Who the fuck cares? It's over."

She adjusted her position on the hard cushion. "Did the police visit you in Ottawa? Is that why you flew home?"

"I was getting ready to go to the airport when they showed up. I told them if they want to talk, okay, but it would be in the taxi or nowhere. Not a smart move on my part." He swigged more beer.

"Why were you coming home, even before—?"

"Why are you asking all these questions?" He kept staring straight ahead.

A gust of wind banged the blinds out toward her head. If the Ottawa cops had solid evidence, wouldn't they have taken him into custody? Later, she would think about why he had assumed Sam had sent her.

"What's the next step?" she said.

"For me?"

"The cops."

"I expect the Calgary ones will grill me. When you rang the door, I assumed it was them. Sam left a message, saying they'd been to see him. My mother has left, like forty messages, on all my phones. I don't feel like talking to anyone. I don't feel like talking to you either, if that's okay."

Despite his protests, he had invited her in, offered her a beer and had said a fair bit so far. Clack, clack, clack went the blinds.

"Do you mind if I open the blinds to let in more air?" she asked.

"I prefer it dark."

"Can I ask you a few questions about Callie?"

"I'd rather you didn't. The cops asked me enough." He scratched his thinning hair.

"Did you—"

"It's bad enough she was shot to death." His voice wavered. "To be dragged in as a suspect. You don't know what that's like. I'd never kill her, no matter what she did."

"What did she do?"

"It was my fault. Why didn't I do what she wanted? My career's shot now, anyway. I could have lost it as easily with her alive." He stared at her, his eyes wild and red. "Have you ever looked at your life and watched it get sucked down the toilet and there's not one fucking thing you can do about it?" He slumped back on the love seat. It was hard to picture him as the affable politician who had spoken to her at the funeral.

The clack behind her was starting to drive her nuts. "Did you see much of Callie after she broke up with you last spring?"

"We met a couple of times."

"I heard you stalked her at the folk festival."

Anger flashed through his eyes. "Who said that? Isabelle? I didn't stalk her. It was a public place. I bought my ticket. So she happened to be there." He leapt up. "Do you want another beer?" Without waiting for her reply, he strode to the kitchen.

If the cops came by later tonight, what would they think of him in this drunken state? He got a Corona from the fridge and plunked it on the counter.

Paula set her beer on the coffee table next to the Bible. "What did you and Callie talk about those last two or three times you met?"

He popped off the beer bottle cap. "The usual stuff. Music, the house, her studies, that is, what she'd do now that she was finished her BFA." He sounded surprisingly sober.

"Did she apply to an Ottawa university MFA program and then withdraw after the breakup, not wanting to move there without you?"

"I felt shitty about that. I told her to try teaching for awhile and apply to the University of Calgary next year. Or chuck the university thing and form a band, get some gigs. Who cares if they don't pay very much? She wasn't doing this for the money." He remained behind the counter. "Who would kill her? That's what I want to know. She didn't have problems with anyone except—well, I'm not accusing him. Her husband was still hung up on her, was always calling with some kind of excuse and working on her guilt about leaving him. I told her she shouldn't go back to him on account of that."

"Was she considering it?" Paula reached for her beer bottle.

"She said it wasn't about him. The guilt was something else."

"Guilt about something besides leaving Kenneth?"

"She refused to tell me." He dumped the remaining quarter bottle of beer into the sink and got a fresh one from the fridge, opened it, and returned to the love seat.

Clearly, he did want to talk. He struck her as the extroverted type, inclined to turn to people when troubled rather than retreat, as Anne had said. Maybe he retreated when sober; reached out when drunk.

"Let me get this straight," she said. "This conversation about the something other than Kenneth, did she bring it up repeatedly or just one time?"

He closed his eyes and swayed his head, as if he were listening to imagined music. "It started around last April, before she dumped me, and got worse."

"What do you mean by worse?"

He leaned his head back and tapped his toes on the coffee table. "More nervous about it, or hyper, like it was getting hold of her. I said if she couldn't tell me, she should talk to her minister or someone. If you don't get it off your chest, sin eats away at you."

She glanced at the Bible. "Did you tell the police any of this?"

"Not yet." His eyes shot open.

"When was the last time you and Callie discussed it?"

"A couple of weeks before she died. I really think it was the Kenneth thing, but she insisted it wasn't so I wouldn't feel guilty about it."

"Did you?"

"I should have, but didn't, somehow." He looked at the Bible.

"You and she met three or four times since spring."

He took a sip of beer. "So what if we did? It was talk, not sex."

"Did she call you or you her?"

"I don't remember. It doesn't matter who did. We both wanted to be together."

"Really?"

He stared ahead, not answering.

"Were you hoping to patch things up?" she said.

"Maybe, but I was playing it, cautious-like. Fuck." He banged the bottle on the table, spilling drops on the book. "None of this matters any more. Don't you get it? She's dead. People say I'll get over her. Sure, I will. It isn't that."

She sipped her beer. Let him spill his thoughts out.

"I don't care that much about fucking politics. I can find legal work. I've got great connections. Politics gets you that." He picked up his bottle. "I'm not even worried about a criminal charge. I'll get off. I'm fucking friends with the best defense lawyer in town."

She squinted at him. "What is it you care about?"

"Nothing."

"So, why consume, like, forty bottles of beer in one night?"

He swished the beer around his bottle. "She was on her way to talk to you, wasn't she, the day she died?"

"It looks that way."

"I told her to confide in someone. She picked you."

The guilt needled Paula. "Do you feel guilty about sending her on the trail that morning?"

"Fuck, no. I couldn't predict that would happen. No one could." He jumped up, walked to the counter and turned. "I didn't invite you here. Why did you turn up? Maybe she sent you."

"Anne, your mother?"

"The soul lives on. I can't escape, couldn't escape her in Ottawa."

Did he mean Callie? He thought Callie had sent Paula?

He rubbed his head. His thin hairs stuck up as though electrically shocked. "I'm the one who told her to confess. I should do the same: get it out, before it eats me to death." His words were beginning to slur.

She held her breath. Would he confess to the murder? Did he think she wouldn't report it to the cops, or was he past caring? What if he stabbed her once it was off his chest? The knife block was awfully close to his hand. If the patio door was unlocked, she could make a quick dash.

Dimitri leaned against the kitchen counter, crossing one leg over the other. "My mother will stand by me to the end. She thinks I shit gold bricks."

His voice had regained the calmness that interspersed his outbursts. It was hard to adapt to the swings. She relaxed, tentatively.

"My dad is almost as bad," he said. "They'll both believe I'm innocent until they see me behind bars and even then they'll call it justice miscarried."

She stared straight up at him. "You're lucky to have their support. By your dad, you mean—"

"Sam thinks I did it."

"He's worried you did."

"He knows I did. He has no doubt of it. He says he believes me. I know he doesn't. It's all over his eyes and face: it's in his words. There's not one fucking thing I can do to convince him."

"Of your innocence?"

"Fuck yes. What else?"

She felt a mix of relief, disappointment, and confusion. "What is it you want to confess to me?"

"That was it."

"What?"

"Confess, confide, what's the fucking difference?" He paced to the love seat and back, with the swift, jerky movements of a teenager. "Like I said, I'm going to be okay. You can't have everything you want. Monday, I'll meet with the party leader and resign my seat. One way or another, the affair shit will hit the public fan. They'll turn on me, throw me out. I deserve it. I shouldn't have done what I did. If I could take it back . . ." He halted, eyes red, hair wild. His face suddenly eased into an ironic smile that reminded her of Sam's. "So much for my political image."

She stood and faced him. "Sometimes the public likes things real. People might find the affair romantic and appreciate your vulnerable, human side."

He grinned. "That's what she always said."

"You mean Callie?"

"Who else?"

"And what bothers you most is Sam's lack of faith in you."

"What bothers me most is her fucking murder."

"You didn't kill her?"

"Sam's convinced you I did."

"No, he didn't."

Faint hope lit his hazel eyes. "You believe I'm innocent?"

"I . . . I don't know."

"That's why she sent you."

"Callie?"

"You're open to the possibilities."

"You think her spirit is acting on this?"

"I don't want to talk about it. Didn't I say that already a million times? Would you all leave me alone?"

Paula rode the elevator to Hayden's office floor. He was waiting. As she exited, he kissed her.

"I thought we were saving ourselves for tomorrow," he said.

"Something's come up."

"Nothing serious?"

His shirt sleeves were rolled up; he wore no jacket or tie; a five-o'clock shadow shaded his jaw. They walked down the corridor lined with dark, empty cubicles

"I had breakfast with Detective Vincelli," she said. "I told him all I've learned over the past few days."

"I'm glad you finally contacted him. You've done your bit. The cops can take it from here."

"Isabelle's moving in with Erin. Long story. It involves drywall and painting."

"The point is Isabelle will no longer be living with you." He smiled.

"It turns out Dimitri, Sam's son, was more involved with Callie than I imagined."

"That house was a sick situation, everyone screwing each other."

"It wasn't like that. Or maybe it was. I still don't know. There are too many possibilities."

A single file folder and a few scattered papers remained on his desk. He had been working hard to free his weekend for her. Outside his corner windows, city lights shimmered along the highways and streets toward the mountains buried in darkness. Paula took her place in the visitors' chair, across from him, willing herself not to grab his New Orleans souvenir music box to fiddle with. This was going to be hard.

"I can't play tennis tomorrow," she said. "I have to go to Kananaskis."

"To interview a claimant?" Hayden looked puzzled, then brightened. "I'll go with you. We could stay overnight; turn it into a little holiday. God knows we both need it."

Paula rocked the chair. "Sam asked me to go hiking with him and his friend, Felix."

Hayden's face dulled.

"Isabelle's coming along," she added.

"A double date? Cute."

"You could join us, if you like."

"And be a fifth wheel?" he said. "No bloody way."

Paula exhaled in relief. Dealing with Hayden and Sam in one place would be like juggling matter and antimatter. As it was, she had probably made a mistake, giving into Isabelle's pleadings. Paula would have said no, if Tony and Ginette hadn't been so agreeable to Isabelle's going. They must truly believe Sam and Felix were innocent. They also seemed to think Paula was a good influence on Isabelle, which likely showed their bad judgment.

"It's not a date," Paula said. "This might sound silly, but I think the cops need my help."

"More than silly, it's arrogant to believe you can do more than the professionals."

"It's not a case of doing more, but doing something different. I can attack from inside. Sam didn't ask the cops to go on a hike."

"I wish Sam would take a hike."

"I'll have a whole day with Sam as well as Felix, whom the cops consider major suspects, for reasons they won't explain. Sam might keep his cool, but Felix is a blabbermouth. One slip could provide all the evidence they need to nail whoever did this. Felix and Sam will be less on guard with me on a friendly hike."

Hayden slammed his hands to his desk.

Paula got up and walked to the window. "I've just come from visiting Sam's son, Dimitri. He seems on the brink of cracking up, mainly because it bugs him that Sam, his father, believes he killed her."

"Quite possibly Dimitri did, unless Sam killed her himself."

"Dimitri was Callie's lover. It seems Callie had feelings of, at least, friendship toward him to the end. She'd hate to see him in this state, if he's innocent. This could ruin his life."

"Callie can't see him when she's dead." Hayden approached Paula.

"In her final minutes, Callie was reaching to me for help. I wasn't there for her then. I can be now."

"D-e-a-d. Dead. Let her rest in peace."

"That's what I'm trying to do."

Hayden was so close Paula could smell the garlic and mushrooms on the pizza he must have ordered in for dinner. She wasn't religious, but since the funeral she couldn't shake the feeling that Callie wanted her to pursue this. And, so far, nothing she'd done had been a burden, aside from the conflicts with Hayden, the disruptive involvement with Sam and his family, and the time taken from her work. It would help if dead souls, if they existed, were more specific in their requests so she would know the right thing to do.

"And then there's Anne, Dimitri's mother and my friend," she said. "Anne is devastated by the prospect of her son's arrest. She says she believes in him, but might be kidding herself. She's overwhelmed by her husband's illness. I don't know how much she's got left to give Dimitri."

"Dimitri deserves what he gets if he killed Callie."

"What if he didn't?" She picked up the book lying on top of his bookcase. A thousand or so court cases and legal precedents. The legal system crawled through details. She would not have the patience for that line of work. "How long does it take for a murder case to go to trial? One year?"

"The hearing could take up to a year; the trial, about another six months. Why?"

"Once someone is charged, the murder disappears from the newspapers. Unless it's spectacular in some way, the public loses interest."

"That's human nature."

"The cops continue to gather evidence secretly."

"It's better without media attention. The accused will get a fairer trial if prospective jurors know little about the case. Where are you leading with this?"

She looked up at his shadowed chin. "It could be a year and half or more before we know if a person charged is guilty or not. Would he get bail?"

"Usually not with murder; unless someone puts up a lot of money."

"Sam and Anne would put up everything they have. Anne's business is just starting to make a profit. If she digs too deep into her savings, this could set it back."

"Sam probably has a lot socked away."

"What if Dimitri is wrongly convicted?" she said. "The killer's still out there."

"Wrong convictions happen less than the media implies; they can also be overturned."

"Sam and Anne will push for it. If you think I'm determined, you don't know Anne. But it would take forever. Meanwhile, Dimitri's life drains away in jail."

Hayden returned to his desk, moving his hands in circles. "This is all hypothetical speculation."

That was true, to a point. "It's a long time for an accused and his loved ones to sweat."

"There's often a plea bargain. That would end it much sooner."

"In which case, we would never find out the details. What if the accused gets off on a technicality? What if the cops can't find enough evidence to build a case and they let him go? We'll never know for sure what happened. Even if Dimitri's off the hook, Sam will always believe, deep down, his son did it."

"I don't give a flying shit what Sam believes."

"I do."

Hayden's nostrils twitched. "That's what this hike is really about. Forget justice. Forget helping your girlfriends, living and dead. You want to make it with Sam."

"That's part of it." She hadn't meant to say it. Not now. Hayden looked shocked. How to backtrack? "I don't mean 'make it' in that sense."

"What other sense is there?"

Hayden's jaw was too square, his complexion too pasty, he wore socks with sandals, his shirts pinched his thick neck, but not long ago she had found him attractive. She set the law book on the bookcase. "If I don't go, part of me will always wish that I had. Do you want that between us? It wouldn't be fair to you."

"None of this is fair to me."

She sidestepped him to get her purse lying next to the chair. "We can't end it like this. I want to talk about it, but not tonight. I can't think straight."

"That's obvious." He grabbed her elbow.

"We've both had a long day. I'll call you Sunday."

"You're not getting away that easily."

"Let go." After several shakes, Paula sloughed off his hand.

"Go with Sam and his murderous friends," Hayden said. "Then sleep with him—"

"I'm not—"

"If you do, have the courtesy to tell me."

"I realize my sleeping with him would end it with us."

"We still might salvage things." He raised his hands, fingertips aimed at her. "Can I offer you some free advice?"

"Whatever you say will be designed to put me off Sam and this trip."

"It will be the truth."

"As you see it." She tucked her purse under her arm. "I'm sorry to do this. Have a good night and weekend."

Hayden flinched. Paula regretted her newscaster sign-off remark. A peck on the cheek would be equally cruel. She said good-bye and strode into the dark corridor, not looking back. His advice would probably be a lie, intentional or not, to convince her to change her mind. Not hearing him out would nag her and make the evening feel inconclusive. At the end of the hallway, she turned. He stood in his office door frame. An eager young lawyer working late gazed from his office. How much had he overheard? She took a step. To her surprise, Hayden met her halfway down the hall. He would hate acting out his personal life in front of a colleague.

"I don't know most of the details." Hayden lowered his voice so the watcher would have trouble hearing. "No doubt, I'm prejudiced against Sam, but my impression, from all you've told me, is he's a manipulator."

Sam had manipulated Kenneth to go along with the fake marriage; he had manipulated Isabelle, Tony, and Kenneth to withhold evidence from the cops. Hayden didn't know the half of it.

"You told me the cops suspect Felix, his babbling friend, for no apparent reason," Hayden said. "They may not suspect him, but rather are leaning on him to get information about Sam or his son."

Felix's house backed on the Elbow River pathway. He may have seen someone follow Callie the morning she died.

"Sam might have a hold on his friend that keeps him quiet," Hayden said.

"What kind of hold?"

He fluttered his hands in a motion that said keep your voice down. "Perhaps something Felix doesn't want revealed. It might be irrelevant, but embarrassing to him if it came out. The hike may be part of Sam's plan to keep a lid on him."

"How?"

"I haven't a clue. My advice is this: watch out and don't let Sam use you."

"I won't."

"He already has."

"The hell with that."

The young associate's face perked up; the hell with him. Paula whirled, clutched her purse to her ribs and clacked down the corridor, aware she was being a drama queen. Hayden didn't call after her. She punched the elevator buttons; tears stung her eyes and throat. Some of what he'd said was right.

Chapter Twenty-one

Sam shuffled his feet on her front porch as he apologized for being late. He had already called to say it had taken about ten doorbell rings to wake Felix. Then, he'd had to wait for him to eat breakfast and dress. Paula could see why dressing had taken Felix so long. He was decked out in Bavarian lederhosen: a white blouse and brown suede knickers, tied below his knees, with a button front flap. A hunting knife stuck out of a side pocket. Patterned knee socks, hiking boots, and peaked cap with a feather completed the outfit.

Felix turned around to display the suspenders crossed in the back and the embroidery arc that made his ass look enormous in this getup.

"I bought it on eBay," he said, "in honor of my German heritage."

"Is your heritage Bavarian or Prussian?" Sam asked.

"Who the fuck cares?" Felix said.

Paula laughed. Like Sam and Isabelle, she had had settled for a light jacket, T-shirt, and jeans. Sam's shirt was plain white. Across Isabelle's chest, *Calgary* scrolled in rope letters. Paula's red T-shirt, bought last year in Banff, sported a mountain sheep decal. Sam chatted about the warm, sunny weather and Felix fussed with his knee socks and cap as though nothing had changed in the past few days. Did they know she knew the truth about Callie and Dimitri? Or had the police told Sam they had found out from Kenneth to protect her? Isabelle was still in the dark, which meant Sam, Felix, or Paula would decide when to bring the subject up.

"Just a minute," Isabelle said, and dashed into the house.

"Morning," Walter called from his front porch. "Who are your friends?"

"Relatives from Europe," Paula said to avoid explanations.

Walter grinned at Felix. "All you need is a walking stick."

"It's in the boot." Felix mimicked an English accent.

Isabelle re-emerged with her tote bag. "I was thinking we could stop at Felix's on the way home to pick up my stuff. I really miss all my CDs."

Paula stuck her cooler into the "boot," lunch being her contribution to the outing. Felix and Isabelle hopped into the back seat. Sam logged their destination into the car's GPS, despite Paula's offer to explain the best route out of town. Walter waved them off. They left Ramsay and Inglewood and sped past Saturday shoppers and office towers glistening in morning sun. Across the Crowchild Trail, Foothills Hospital loomed on the right. They merged onto the Trans-Canada Highway and passed the western suburban fringe: pale houses packed on treeless lots. The men discussed the benefits of the Acura's gadgets. Paula gathered Sam had bought the car a year ago, around the time he *hadn't* married Callie.

Felix poked his capped head between the bucket seats. He smelled of toothpaste. "Did you ever tell me how much you paid for these wheels?"

"Too much," Sam said. "You should probably be wearing a seatbelt."

"Can we talk about something besides cars?" Isabelle said. "How about some music? Do you have any good CDs?"

"I feel like Elvis." Felix started singing "Love Me Tender" with an Elvis quiver.

"I know that one." Isabelle's voice joined his.

On this clear morning, with the pure mountains ahead, Paula found it hard to believe she might be sitting in a car with a criminal. They entered ranchland: rugged coulees and rolling hills, and cruised past the few vehicles on the road. No one passed them. Sam was driving above the limit, which she wouldn't have guessed from the smooth ride. Isabelle's soprano trills from the back seat contrasted Felix's assaults to the ears. Paula glanced back. Isabelle's blond hair grazed Felix's cheek. He seemed far from Isabelle's type. Paula wondered what she would say if Isabelle asked to be dropped off at Felix's tonight. Isabelle was twenty-one, an adult. Sam stared ahead, in silence, his hands steady on the wheel. His profile was classic: smooth forehead, straight nose, strong chin so cleanly shaved Paula bet he had taken the trouble to use a manual razor today. His brushed up and gelled hairstyle suited the upturned lines on his face. She still couldn't quite wrap her head around his never having been involved romantically with Callie. Callie had been sort-of married to his son, making Sam Callie's sort-of-father-in-law. Paula giggled.

"What's so funny?" He glanced at her through his sunglasses.

"Nothing."

He smiled. "I agree. Felix sounds like a gravel truck."

The pair behind them crooned to a close.

"I'm surprised you know Elvis," Felix said to Isabelle. "You weren't even born when he died."

"My parents have been playing that crap all my life. Do you know this one?" Isabelle's voice lowered to the steady rhythms of the "Duke of Earl."

"That's my favorite." Felix jumped in with the main lyric's whiny falsetto.

Sam flashed a conspiratorial wince at Paula. "I'm not sure if I can stand this all the way to Kananaskis."

They were like parents taking the children on a day trip. Any minute now Isabelle and Felix would start quarreling.

"What hike are we going on?" Paula asked.

"We haven't planned that far," Sam said. "It was all I could do to get Felix out."

Felix botched a lyric. Isabelle laughed. They resumed singing. Both muddled lines. "Duke of Earl" limped to an end. Sam turned off the highway to the two-lane road.

"I was up all night working on my column." Felix's cap was between them. "It is going to be awesome."

"What's the topic?" Paula said.

"I can't tell you." He slumped back.

To the right was turquoise Barrier Lake. They drove straight into the Kananaskis mountain range. Evergreens hugged the road.

Felix thumped the back of her seat. "It's going to be the best column I've ever written, the best fucking thing ever. They'll print it on the front page."

"You'll be famous," Isabelle said.

"Page One of the whole fucking newspaper. Numero Uno." Felix lurched between their seats. "Turn the car around, Sam. We can't waste time on this trip. I've got to finish my column."

"You have all week to write it," Sam said.

"The deadline is Tuesday, for fuck's sake. I've got to keep going while I'm on a roll. I should never have come today. Why didn't I think it through?"

"How far along are you on the column?" Paula asked.

"I haven't started it yet. Where to begin? That's the hard part."

Sam steered past a line of cyclists struggling up the hill. "The hike will clear your head. You'll feel fresh enough to start tomorrow."

Was Felix's newspaper column related in any way to the murder? Sam hadn't sounded worried that it might be an exposé on Callie and Dimitri. If anything, Sam seemed amused by Felix's struggles to write the column, and Felix didn't seem the type to blatantly exploit his friends' secrets for front page newspaper fame.

"What happened to the singing?" Isabelle said.

"Fuck singing," Felix said.

"When do we eat?" Isabelle said.

Felix's grabbed Paula's head rest. "Let's eat at home, so I can work on my piece. If I don't start right away, it won't be ready in time."

"If I'd brought my purse," Paula said, "I could give you a notebook and pen. I always carry them in case I get an idea about a claim."

Felix let go of her headrest. "I can't write in a car. I need my proper space."

Sam winked at Paula. "Ten dollars says we don't make it to a hike."

"I want eleven to one odds."

The picnic lunch at the Visitors' Center assuaged Isabelle's hunger and Felix's desire to work on his column. His behavior had certainly been erratic. Now, he leaned attentively over Sam's shoulder as they consulted the trail guide book.

Sam suggested they hike up Mount Indefatigable for the spectacular views. "I did it about twenty years ago," he said. "You might find it too strenuous."

That sounded condescending. "I'm not in such terrible shape," Paula said.

"I was thinking of Felix."

She glanced at Felix's suspenders straining over his gut that hung over the waistband of his knickers.

Felix read the trail description. "Rigorous, steep climb, loose rocky sections, upper altitude might bother people with breathing difficulties."

Hayden had warned that Felix might know too much and Sam might be using her for some plan. Was this it: push Felix beyond his limits? An accident? A heart attack? A fall? Paula and Isabelle present as witnesses? Sam looked so innocent studying the park map spread on the picnic table. He had claimed the point of this trip was to get a break from their concerns. She could either submit to paranoia or accept his words on faith.

Felix closed the guide book. "We've come all this fucking way. Let's go for it."

"If we're lucky, we might see bears," Isabelle said.

Paula didn't want them to think she was wimping out.

A dozen cars were parked in the trailhead parking lot. They hoisted on their backpacks, which contained water bottles and space for their jackets when they warmed up from the climb. Felix hadn't worn a jacket and refused to carry a pack so his lederhosen look wouldn't be ruined. He grabbed his walking stick and led them across the dam between the upper and lower lakes. Puffy clouds floated over the mountaintops. The rest of the sky was clear blue against rocky tips and evergreens. Beyond the dam, they caught a whiff of wild animal scent.

Sam passed Felix and halted at an opening in the woods. "Here's the turnoff."

It looked like the start of a beaten path, not a major trail listed in a guide book. There was no trailhead sign.

Paula pointed ahead. "I'm sure we follow the main trail."

"A friend of mine was here a few weeks ago," Sam said. "He told me the sign was down. The main trail just takes you around the lake. For Indefatigable, you turn right, after the dam."

"I don't remember Felix reading that," Paula said.

"We shouldn't have left the guide book in the car," Felix said. "I'll go back—"

"No," Sam said. "We'll never get to the top if we lose more time."

Paranoia crept into Paula again. Felix hailed a group of backpackers returning on the main trail. They didn't know if the turnoff led to Mount Indefatigable, as they were coming from the campsite.

"The book didn't mention a campsite on Indefatigable," Felix said. "Sam must be right." He plunged into the woods.

Isabelle disappeared behind him. Paula shot Sam a glance she hoped he would interpret as either "I'm game" or "I know what you're up to," depending on his purpose for the trip. The opening enlarged to a wide path cooled by deep shade. Isabelle and Felix took the lead; Sam walked silently beside Paula. Pine cones and dried pine needles cracked beneath their feet. A butterfly flew by. She inhaled aromas of Douglas fir and kept her gaze on the forest floor so she wouldn't trip over rocks and roots.

They crossed a log bridge over a dry creek to a hill so steep they had to grab onto rocks for support. Puffing heavily, Felix gripped with one hand, his walking stick dragging beside him in the dry dirt. At the top, he dropped down to a rock and planted the walking stick in the ground.

His left hand rested on his heaving chest. His face was red; perspiration drenched his forehead and scraggly hair. Paula stood beside him, catching her breath, her back sweating beneath the pack. She took it off and got out a water bottle. Isabelle looked barely fazed by the exertion. Paula had never seen Sam's face this relaxed. His Adam's apple bobbed as he guzzled enough water to make her think he needed as much refreshment as she did.

"Let's get going," Isabelle said.

"I'm ready." Felix leapt up. He thrust his water bottle at Paula and bolted ahead, leaving her to screw on both of their caps.

Sam watched Felix climb. "I wish he'd take off that stupid Robin Hood hat. It's driving me nuts."

Her hand brushed Sam's as she passed him Felix's water bottle to return to his pack. They took off their jackets.

"Felix seems to run to extremes," she said. "Is he often this hyper?"

"He takes his work more seriously than people think."

"It's almost like he was looking for excuses not to write his column."

"He does that all the time; claims writers will do anything to avoid the blank page."

Paula hoisted the pack onto her back. "I wonder what his awesome column is about."

"Probably something more thrilling to him than to you—or me."

Was Sam worried about the content of the piece? They rounded the path and found Felix stopped at the base of a rock pile that Isabelle was scrambling up.

Felix held a cigarette; he pointed it at the hill. "Are you sure this is a legitimate trail?"

"Dimitri described parts of it as being rugged like this," Sam said.

"Dimitri was here?" Paula said. "Was he your friend who was here a few weeks ago?"

Sam looked from her to Felix and back. "He hiked it with Callie last fall. It was the only place they went together alone outside Felix's house."

Paula stared at him, unsure what to say. Sam was too careful to have dropped his son's name by accident.

Felix lit the cigarette. "Dimitri phoned me last night. All I got out of it was that he came home because all this was haunting him in Ottawa. He was pretty tanked."

Sam looked startled. "Dimitri's in Calgary?"

Felix nodded, the cigarette in his mouth.

"When did he get back?"

"Sometime yesterday, before midnight, when he called me."

"I left him a message in the afternoon. When he didn't answer, I assumed he was still in Ottawa. Why didn't you tell me he called you when I picked you up this morning?"

Felix drew on the cigarette. "I didn't want you bothering the poor boy with a phone call. He's probably still sleeping it off."

Sam pulled out his cell phone from his jeans pocket, opened it and closed it. "No reception. Why did he call you and not me?"

"Dimitri knows I stay up late."

"He might have phoned me from Ottawa before he left."

Felix shrugged. Interesting that Sam didn't like his son turning to Felix ahead of him. Jealousy?

Felix mashed his half-finished smoke in the gravelly dirt. His right arm was shaking. When she stopped by his house, hadn't he said something about an old hunting injury that acted up in damp weather? Today couldn't be dryer.

"Hey," Isabelle hollered from the crest of the hill. "What's keeping you guys?"

Felix took out the hunting knife from his knickers pocket. He slid the blade from the sheath and slashed at a sapling.

"What did you do that for?" Paula said.

Felix held up a yellow leaf. "It would have fallen anyway."

"Would you hurry up," Isabelle yelled. "What if there are bears? I don't want to run into them alone."

Felix took out another cigarette. "I need a few more minutes to get my breath."

"I'll stay," Sam said to Paula. "You go and save her from bears."

The rocks were sharply inclined. The covering of dry gravel and dirt made them slippery. Paula edged up on her hands and feet, using stray roots as steps. Her foot slipped, stomach sank. She hated that out of control feeling of falling. If Gary, her ex, had dragged her onto this hike, she would be swearing at him now. She refused to show such weakness to Sam. Even worse would be to fall on her ass, which the men were getting a good view of, if they were looking. She climbed faster to get it over with. On the ledge, she looked down at Felix and Sam, their heads together like conspirators.

Isabelle darted across the rock to the far side. "There's a better view from over here."

This one was spectacular enough. Paula scanned the panorama of lakes bordered by rocky peaks. Evergreens and yellow deciduous trees crept up the mountainsides. Avalanche trails cut through them; glaciers and snow nestled in crevices. Her hair blew all over her face. She rubbed her arms, chilled by the wind and her body cooling after the exertion. Scraggly trees beside her cast long shadows over the rock.

Sam started walking up the hill. No hands. He made it look easy. Show-off. Felix plodded, his walking stick probing the rock. It slipped. His cap blew off. He should be scrambling up on his hands and feet, but either wouldn't ditch the stupid stick or was imitating Sam. The walking stick slipped. Paula held her breath. Felix would fall down the hill to the rock. She was standing here, a witness to the "accident." This was the plan. Sam was approaching the ledge. Below, Felix's walking stick shot to the side. He tottered. Paula gasped, stepped forward, and bumped Sam. He grabbed her arms. They swayed sideways. Her heart plunged to her stomach. They would crash, rolling into Felix.

Her body steadied against Sam's. His breath warmed her face. She clutched his T-shirt, feeling his chest underneath. Felix regained his balance; he continued up the rock.

There was no plan. She had come foolishly close to pushing Sam down the hill, maybe into his friend. She might have gone with him, causing serious injury or death.

Felix hoisted himself to the ledge. "Damn arm. Gives out when I'm tired." He stomped his stick on the rock.

"I'm sorry I knocked you," she told Sam.

"I wouldn't have fallen. But if you want to hold onto me, I don't mind."

Paula let go. Over Sam's shoulder, she saw Felix watching. She stepped back and stumbled onto higher rock, where it was safer.

Chapter Twenty-two

Paula found the hike down the mountain as treacherous as the climb. She focused on not sliding on the loose gravel and dirt. With Sam, she chatted about everything other than Dimitri and Callie. Felix kept up with the others thanks to his walking stick. A few times she held onto Sam's arm, wishing she wasn't such a typically female wimp.

At the car, Sam stripped off his sweaty shirt. Dark hair formed a T that crossed his chest and scrolled down his abdomen to his belt. He got a fresh T-shirt from the trunk, plain navy blue. The fresh shirt didn't mask the scent of musky fir lingering on his body.

After a washroom break at the Visitors' Center, Isabelle and Felix fell asleep in the car. The fresh air, exercise, and vehicle motion would have sent Paula to sleep if she weren't sitting across the console from Sam. He leaned into the rear-view mirror, presumably for a view of the sleeping couple. Paula glanced back. Isabelle's hand rested on Felix's chest, the feather cap they had retrieved on the hike down the hill slipped over his eyes. He was snoring.

Sam stared ahead, at the narrow road. "When did you find out about Dimitri and Callie?"

"From Kenneth, Thursday night. I told the cops about it."

"They said they heard from Kenneth. I was surprised he kept quiet so long."

"What a perfect setup. Dimitri could stay at your house as often as he liked and no one would suspect he was with her. It never once crossed my mind."

"In hindsight, it was a stupid idea. We must have been drunk when we thought it up. It was even stupider to withhold it from the cops. I take the entire blame."

"The others went along," she said. "Why did Kenneth agree to the plan at all? He'd hate the public scandal, sure, but I'd have thought he'd grab the chance to put the screws to Dimitri, his rival, who had far more to lose, publicly, than him."

Behind them, Isabelle murmured.

Sam craned his neck to check the mirror. "Kenneth hates Dimitri, but he's basically rational and made the practical choice. My guess is, he thought taking the high road would win Callie back. It might have, eventually."

"Did Kenneth speak to you about the boxes of her ashes?"

Sam's face relaxed into a smile. "I understand you received one of those gifts."

"Did you give yours to Dimitri?"

"Not yet. I'm waiting . . ."

A van was stopped on the other side of the road. A man stood beside it, snapping pictures of curly-horned Rocky Mountain sheep.

Sam didn't slow down. "Dimitri told me that if he had charge of her ashes, he'd sprinkle them on the mountain we just hiked. It was their special place."

"Her resting place would be the spot where I almost toppled you?"

"At the summit. We only made it to the first lookout."

Felix snored a series of sputters. Isabelle groaned. Paula glanced at the pair shifting positions in their sleep. The cap rolled to Isabelle's lap.

"Callie broke up with Dimitri last spring," Paula said. "How many times did they meet after that?"

"Once or twice."

"Off the record. I won't tell the cops."

Sam frowned. He steered onto the main Kananaskis road. "He admits to a half dozen times. It wasn't just him making the moves. She sometimes called him, suggesting they meet for coffee and a friendly chat. No doubt, the cops will dig up witnesses who saw them together. The heat's on him totally now. I would do anything to get rid of it."

"Anything?"

"What?" Felix muttered in the back seat. "What? Get rid of what?"

Sam looked in the rear-view mirror. "I was telling Paula about the great view of the mountains behind us. The sun is lighting them up."

Paula looked around. Against the backdrop of orange peaks, Felix and Isabelle squirmed, moved apart, and settled into sleep against the doors. The feather cap lay between them on the seat. Before they woke up, she wanted to ask Sam about some of Dimitri's comments from last night. It would be quicker to avoid mentioning her visit to Dimitri's, as Sam would want to know what brought her there.

"During the summer," she said. "Callie told Kenneth she felt guilty about something. He sensed it was about more than her leaving him."

"I wouldn't know anything about that. She didn't confide much in me."

"Me neither, it seems."

They passed Barrier Lake sparkling in the late daylight. A canoeist paddled over the smooth turquoise water.

She stared at his dashboard full of instruments and dials. "I can understand why Callie hid her romance from the public."

"Dimitri was sure it would end his career."

"What I don't understand is why she hid it from me. I wouldn't have told the media. I guess I might have told Anne, his mother, and you all seemed to want to keep it from her."

"We figured the fewer people who knew the better."

"Kenneth suggested Callie hid her romance with Dimitri from me because I would have told her she was nuts to leave a good marriage for someone half her age. I don't know if I would have. I might have been supportive, if not intrigued by her fling."

"She didn't see it as a fling," Sam said. "Would you have believed it would last?"

"Did you?"

"Not really, but I knew enough to keep my mouth shut."

"And I wouldn't have?"

He took his eyes from the road, looking her up and down. "Probably not. Or your opinion would have slipped out in some way, like it just did. People in love don't want to hear the truth. It isn't your fault Callie found you . . ."

"What?"

They turned onto the Trans-Canada Highway.

"Let me guess," she said. "God knows she told me a number of times. Callie found me judgmental."

Sam grinned. "I like women with strong opinions."

"What." Felix snorted. His voice rose. "What? What?"

"Are we there yet?" Isabelle yawned noisily. "Don't forget to drop me off at Erin's."

Paula turned around. "My daughter, Erin's? You're not moving in until next week."

"She's having a party." Isabelle yawned again. "Didn't I tell you?"

"No."

"She also said you don't have to go there tomorrow to fix the trashed room. Her sister's boyfriend is taking care of it. His name is Jason or something."

"Jarrett is doing physical labor? I doubt that."

"Erin convinced him to do it, so you wouldn't crab."

Sam was chuckling through this. Felix's head was leaned back on the seat, his nose pointed at the car roof. His snoring sounded like farts.

"I told Erin you'd drop me off on the way back from the hike," Isabelle said. "You don't have to worry about my getting home. I can crash on her sofa."

"Where does Erin live?" Sam asked.

"Brentwood," Paula said.

"Screw Brentwood." Felix, suddenly awake, gripped Paula's headrest. "I have to work on my column."

"We can go to your place first," Isabelle said. "The party won't get going until later. This way we can pick up my things."

"I've got to get started." Felix shook Paula's headrest. "I've already wasted this whole day."

They entered the Calgary city limits. The skyline shimmered ahead. All the way to his house, Felix insisted there wasn't time to collect Isabelle's belongings. Sam said they would do the collecting, so he could start writing immediately.

"You'll be running around, thumping, distracting me," Felix said. "I need complete silence to work."

When they reached his Mission neighborhood, Paula's head was pulsing. She liked Felix, but didn't have Sam's patience with his erratic moods. Rather than argue, she said she and Isabelle would swing by tomorrow on their way from Erin's place. Sam pulled up in front of the townhouse. Felix bolted from the car. Halfway up the yard, he halted; he trotted back, and leaned down to the open window, with a friendly smile. "I forgot my walking stick," he said. "Thank you all for the amazing day. You were right. All that nature has totally recharged me." He sounded calmer.

Sam popped open the trunk to get the stick. They watched Felix walk up his steps and made sure he got into the house, then Sam drove on.

"Felix forgot his hat," Isabelle said. "I put it on and forgot I was wearing it."

"God forbid we return and distract him," Sam said.

"We'll deliver the cap tomorrow," Paula said. "I doubt he'll go hiking before then."

Isabelle leaned between them to preen in the mirror. She fluffed the feather. "Cool. I'll wear it to the party."

"That should finish the dumb thing off," Sam said.

They took 17th Avenue to Crowchild Trail North and crossed the Bow River to Brentwood. Leah's Civic and a pickup truck were parked in the driveway. Jarrett must be at work on the room. This Paula had to see. Isabelle got her tote bag from the trunk and caught up to Paula on the sidewalk. They heard Pepper barking inside. Erin answered the doorbell, dressed in her usual baggy bib jeans that did nothing for her youthful figure. Pepper scurried in circles, her tail beating the porch. Paula stooped to pat her, laughing as the mutt licked her face.

"I think you miss Pepper more than you miss me," Erin said. From her solemn face, it was hard to tell if she was joking. Her feelings were easily hurt.

Paula reached out to hug Erin as Leah appeared.

"I have to use the bathroom." Isabelle scooted between the girls.

Leah peered over Paula's shoulder. "Is that Sam in his car? Didn't he want to meet us?" She wore her usual too-short skirt and clinging blouse. Clothes-wise, couldn't her daughters meet in the middle?

"Sam's phoning his son."

"Mom, he's a criminal, for God's sake," Leah said. "Why are you dating him?"

"This was a friendly hike, not a date, and he isn't a criminal."

"He's obviously guilty," Leah said. "Everyone at the bar wonders why the cops are taking so long to arrest him."

"The cops might know something everyone at the bar doesn't."

"Callie was your best friend. She's been dead, like, a week and already you're screwing her husband."

Paula flinched at the word, which felt crude coming from her daughter. Leah stood six inches taller than her thanks to the height she had inherited from her father and the fact she was standing in the house, while Paula was out on the porch.

"Sam wasn't Callie's husband," Paula said. "It's complicated. He's going straight home after he drops me off." That sounded prudish and she didn't have to defend her love life to her daughters.

Erin wrapped her fingers around the straps of her jeans' bib. "That's not what Isabelle said when she asked to stay over tonight."

"You mean, after the party?"

"What party?" Erin said.

Leah placed a hand on her hip. "Isabelle told Erin that you two wanted to be alone so you could get it on in private."

"For God's sake. Where is Isabelle?"

Erin raked back her cropped, blond hair. "Mom, you aren't becoming one of these weirdoes who write to men in prison, are you?"

"Look, whatever Isabelle told you about Sam and me is exaggerated." She glanced at Sam waiting in the car. "I'll explain tomorrow when I pick her up."

Jarrett came up beside Leah and offered his usual greetings that always struck Paula as false. Tall, dark, handsome, bare-chested in skin-tight jeans. She could tell Leah that sex wasn't everything, but today that message coming from her might not ring true.

"You're here to work on the trashed bedroom?" she asked Jarrett.

"I'm more like supervising some friends who do that kind of work."

Paula nodded. That made sense.

"Jarrett's concerned about you," Leah said.

Paula looked at Jarrett.

He slouched to the side. "Menopause does strange things to women."

"How would you know about that?"

"It hits certain women your age, a kind of craziness. You should talk to your doctor about it."

"I should?"

"He can give you a simple prescription."

"I don't need drugs for what ails me."

"Mental illness is nothing to be ashamed of. I was reading this article—"

"Oh, fuck off."

Leah's and Erin's eyes popped open in shapes so identical it made Paula laugh. Her daughters gaped more. Mother/daughter conversations had certainly changed these days. Jarrett looked smug. He might be right that she was going nuts. She scratched her hair, which felt windblown and sticky from the hike. A shower would be wonderful.

"I'm sorry," she said. "I'm tired and it's been a long day." A long ten days since Callie's death. She relaxed as Jarrett disappeared down the hall to his supervisory tasks.

"Did you dump Hayden?" Leah said. "I know he's boring, but he's better than this." She motioned toward Sam's car.

Leah never let up once she got her jaw on a bone. And talk about judgmental. Where did those traits come from? Paula smiled.

Isabelle, the scheming minx, appeared between her daughters. "Can I open the bag of chips in the cupboard? I haven't eaten since lunch."

"I have to get to work," Leah said.

What could Paula do but give her daughters a hug? Leah felt stiff, Erin softer and relaxed. "I'll be by tomorrow around ten thirty. Since there isn't a party, I don't have to nag about drinking and drugs and people trashing the house more than it already is."

Erin smiled at the sort-of joke and retreated into the house; Leah remained grim. Another week of this and Paula would be desperate enough for pills. She returned to the car.

"That took awhile," Sam said.

She buckled her seatbelt. "You always swear you will never become your parents. When it comes to being judgmental and stubborn, my mother's worse than me."

"Is that possible?" he teased.

"Did you reach Dimitri?"

He turned the car ignition. "He's hung-over as hell. The cops were by; they woke him up this morning."

"And?"

"Do you want to grab dinner? You must know some good places nearby."

The dash clock said 5:58 PM. All the references to food made Paula realize how hungry she was, and dinner would delay the inevitable walk up to her door, where he might try to kiss her again and she might give in this time. She suggested her favorite Greek restaurant. He steered the car down the street with purpose and control. Or, maybe everyone drove like that, if you watched them, but not everyone had his muscled arms and a T of dark hair under a shirt that perfectly hugged his pecs.

"You asked me earlier if I would do anything to get Dimitri off the hook," Sam said without looking at her. "The answer is, no. I wouldn't let the cops arrest someone who was innocent."

"Unless that innocent person was you."

"Since I didn't do it, I figured I'd get off. If didn't get off, better me than him. I have less life ahead to waste in jail."

At the hockey game, he had said something similar about his father. When the gun was traced to his father, he must have hoped that the killer was the father he disliked and not the son he loved.

"There's the restaurant," she said. "You can park on the street."

Two hours later he was driving her home. Over Greek salad and moussaka, retsina and ouzo, they had avoided talk of the murder and worries about their respective children. He told her about his relationship with a volatile, insecure woman that ended a year ago and led him to think clinical, unemotional sex with Bev was the answer. He hadn't been with anyone since breaking up with Bev. "She was meticulous about safe sex," he added for no apparent reason except to assure her he was disease-free. Rather than respond directly, Paula said she'd been with Hayden for six months, but they had separated to work things through. Too much ouzo led her to mention the evening dress she had impulsively bought in Mount Royal Village. Sam suggested she model it for him when they got to her place.

He parked between her car and Walter's truck. Her living room timer lights were still on. Inside, she left Sam and went to the bedroom to change. It was foolish to put on a ball gown for him alone, but where else would she wear the thing? At least, she would use it once, but probably only once, as it would remind her of this night. On the off chance she got back with Hayden, she couldn't wear it with him now. If tonight flopped, which it probably would, she couldn't wear it ever again. What a waste of a $595.99 dress, but it would look stupid to tell Sam she had changed her mind. Might as well go through with it. Light had stopped shining through the bedroom door frame. Sam must have turned off the timer.

Paula rolled off her sensible cotton underwear and rifled through her drawer for the bikini nylon lace ones Leah had given her as a joke. She struggled to zip up the back of the gown and adjusted the bodice, studying herself in the dresser mirror. Without a strapless bra, her boobs sagged. The hip bow looked dorky. Her ass was too wide. She tried a few necklaces, but all looked too clunky or thin and cheap. The hell with them. She would go with a bare neck and ears. After all the fussing, there was no time for make-up. She plumped up her sweaty, tangled hair and turned around again. Her ass wasn't so bad. The hip bow might pass for elegant. Her boobs were reasonably perky for someone her age. She smoothed her hair a final time and opened the bedroom door. Music wafted from the living room. Ray Charles. Good choice, except that the CD had been a gift from Hayden. She remembered the condoms she and Hayden had stopped using and probably didn't need with Sam, but grabbed one from her bedside table and dropped it into her cleavage in case they didn't make it back to the bedroom. It was wise to be prudent. She followed the music down the hall to the living room. Sam stood at the far end of the sofa, his back to her, lighting a candle on the end table.

Sam turned around and said something. Paula couldn't tell what from the buzz in her ears. He had slid the ottoman toward the front window so there was nothing between them but open floor. Five candles in glass jars lit up the wall unit shelves. The jars shimmered peach, green, pink, yellow, blue. Mint glowed from the glass on the far end table. Sam lit the mauve candle on the table between the sofa and chair. Ray Charles sang from the CD speakers.

Sam walked toward her and held out a match. "You light the last one for luck."

She shook her head. Her hands would drop it to the wood floor and burn the house down. From the speakers, piano notes rippled down a keyboard. Sam took her hand and placed his other one on the hip without the bow. They moved, rather than waltzed, to the room's center. The ninth candle shone white from the entry console table. Sam had closed the living room shutters. His cheek was rough against hers. When they set out this morning his face had looked so smooth.

They kissed; his mouth and tongue tasted like Mediterranean food and mountain air. His hands were all over her back. He slid her zipper down. She pressed closer to keep her dress from falling and felt him harden against her. He kissed her hair, her ear, her throat. She stepped back, wanting his lips on her breasts. The dress slid to floor. He sucked her nipples. She fumbled with his belt buckle. He drew back and stripped off his shirt the same way he had this afternoon. All she had on now were the nylon lace bikini panties. She stepped out of the bunched dress so it wouldn't get more creased and turned to the candles staggered on the wall unit shelves. Peach, green, pink, yellow, and blue quivered in colored jars. Behind her came the thud-thud-thud of him hopping out of his pants. For him, this was fun, a release from stress, a chance to get laid after two dry months. He had nothing to lose, while she could wreck everything with Hayden, if she hadn't done that already. Hayden had warned that Sam was using her. For what? She couldn't remember, with Sam nuzzling her neck and rubbing her and sliding his hand down her thighs, down her calves. She blew out a candle for luck, turned around, and kissed him. They sank to the pile of clothing on the floor. She straddled his thighs, remembering the condom that was buried somewhere under the dress. Forget it.

"Ouch," Sam said.

"What?"

"My buckle jabbed me in the back." He shifted position. "Ooh. I think that was your dress bow." Gingerly, he edged their bodies sideways.

"We could go to the bedroom," she said.

"That might be safer for me."

"In that case . . ."

Colored candlelight danced on his face and chest. She loved how it shimmered on his silver hairs. She kissed his skin shining yellow and green and blue and mauve. Hands fumbling, she slipped him in. Quivers shot through her arms, her thighs, her whole being. She loved this. Make it last forever, Sam. She loved it, loved it, loved it.

Chapter Twenty-three

He was gone from her bed. Paula spread her arm across the cold sheets. Had she imagined last night? She hoped so. No, she didn't and she hadn't. Their empty orange juice glasses sat on the bedside tables. The clock rolled to 7:43 AM. Dim light flowed through her window. The door was ajar. No sounds streamed in. Sam must be in the kitchen or living room. She crawled from the covers and put on her sleep shirt.

In the bathroom, she dabbed water on her morning hair, patted it down as best she could and padded to the kitchen, where Sam wasn't sitting. Nor was he in the living room that reeked of acrid candle smoke. Her cosmic blue evening gown was draped on the chair, where they had placed it after waking up. Wrinkled and smelling of sweet sex, it would need to be dry-cleaned. Sam's T-shirt and jeans and briefs were missing. The Sunday newspaper lay on the console table. He must have brought it in. She opened the shutters. His Acura was parked on the street. Drizzle coated its metallic red. Where the fuck was he? She rolled the ottoman back to its spot in front of the sofa and checked the kitchen again. He hadn't made coffee. There were no signs he'd had breakfast. He wasn't on the back deck. The only place left was the basement. She opened the door and shouted his name. No reply. She called again and rechecked all the rooms, peered into closets, looked under the beds, which was nuts. How could you lose someone in this little house? The hell with him. His car was here. He had to turn up. She started the coffeemaker and carried the newspaper to the kitchen table. The City section featured a recap of Callie's murder with her usual photograph. No news. The front door creaked. Sam stood in the entry, removing his windbreaker.

She stopped beside the ottoman. "Where were you?"

"I went for a walk," he said. "Didn't you see my note?"

"No."

"I left it on the telephone table."

"Why would I look there?"

"Sorry." He moved toward her. "I assumed you'd guess I didn't go too far."

"Why did you go out at all in weather like this?" She crossed her arms.

His hair was rumpled and damp. "You were sound asleep. I didn't want to disturb you with the radio or TV. I felt like stretching my legs. It wasn't raining when I left. It still isn't. Just a little mist." He smelled mustier than her evening dress.

She stepped back. "Where did you go?" Her hand rested on a glass jar.

"I planned to look at the old commercial buildings on 9th Ave, but got blocked by a train. So, I went to the murder site. I hadn't seen it, since the murder, that is."

Paula picked up the jar. The mauve candle had burned halfway down while they slept on their clothing. She had woken with a jolt, rousing Sam. He'd got their orange juice, while she used the bathroom. He was waiting for her in bed, where they did it again, slowly this time.

"The place where she was killed looked so normal," he said.

"It always does, whenever I go there. I can't believe I didn't notice you leave. How long were you gone?"

He glanced at his watch. "About an hour, I guess."

"The site's ten minutes away."

"I continued to Macleod Trail and circled back through the streets."

She plunked the jar on the table. "Would you like breakfast? The coffee smells ready. There's cereal and toast, maybe fruit if we're lucky. Orange juice."

"I'm meeting Dimitri at ten o'clock for brunch. I could have a coffee."

She had to leave around ten o'clock to pick up Isabelle. He would want to go home to shower and change. They both conveniently had excuses to avoid the question of what to do the morning after. Had he made up the brunch date with Dimitri? He would be more used to these first-time situations than she was, having changed women every two or three years. Over thirty years of adult life that would make . . . how many? She was too tired to do the math. She poured their coffees and sat down across table from him.

He added milk to his mug. "I did a lot of thinking on the walk."

"About what?" She sipped, dreading whatever he had to say.

"About you and me and other things. I'd like to see you again."

Paula ran her fingers through her matted hair. In the bathroom mirror, her skin had looked sallow, her eyes red. He didn't look much better, on the whole, although his tousled hair was splendid. So were his eyes that were way too eager for this hour of day. In that first newspaper article, he had said he was an early riser. That figured.

"We really clicked last night," Sam said.

A flush warmed her neck and face. "I've been thinking, maybe I should be alone for awhile, to sort things through."

"If it's about that guy you're with, I wouldn't mind sharing with him while you're sorting."

"I'd mind. And he certainly would." How could Sam understand her so little? Last night, they had been so connected. She knew what was under his T-shirt and jeans now, but didn't get what was in his head, like was he willing to share because he wanted her that much or because he just wanted a partner to click with? Had he loved any of his previous women, aside from those moments during sex when the body tricked you into feeling love? She didn't love him beyond those moments yet, but to continue with him she would have to believe there was potential.

"I'll phone you tonight," he said. "Are you still planning to swing by Felix's today?"

She nodded, finishing her coffee.

"He was acting weird yesterday, even for him. Give me a call if he still seems off balance."

He cared about Felix, his friend. He cared a great deal about his son. He looked after his father who disliked him and whom he didn't like very much. He had showed concern for Callie and Isabelle. There was potential.

Paula pressed the doorbell again and heard it ring inside the house. Felix didn't answer. His living room blinds were drawn.

Isabelle put her ear to the door. "I can hear the TV. He probably fell asleep watching it, like he did the night I left."

"Sam said he had to ring ten times yesterday before waking him up. Felix might have been up all night, struggling with his newspaper column, and only fallen asleep this morning."

Isabelle looked down the street, the feather cap perched on her head. "He could have gone for a walk, like Sam did with you this morning."

During the drive, Paula had filled Isabelle in on some of last night's details. At Erin's house, she had stuck to the minimum facts: Sam stayed over. They might get together again. Hayden was probably toast. Leah would have pushed for details, but Erin implied this was more than she wanted to know about her mother's sex life.

"Felix could be sleeping upstairs," Paula said. "Or in his den, too absorbed in his work to hear the bell."

Isabelle bounded down the stairs to the sidewalk and squinted up at the second floor. "I don't see a head in the window. I'll check the deck." She ran around the side of the townhouse.

Paula zipped up her jacket. She doubted Felix would be sitting outside on this chilly morning that threatened rain. It was possible yesterday's hike had inspired him to use the pool or gym at the Talisman Center down the street. Most likely he had gone on a quick errand and not bothered to turn off the TV. Paula should have phoned, but had assumed Felix was expecting them and would be at home all day working on his urgent column.

Isabelle reappeared. "I looked through the window. His chair is leaned back, like he's lying in it. I think I saw the top of his head. The house is all dark, except for the TV. I was right about him falling asleep."

"Do you have his phone number? The ringing might wake him up."

Isabelle shook her head. Her blue eyes brightened. She squatted and unsnapped the side pocket of her tote back. "I kept it when I left his house, in case you weren't home and I had to come back here." She held up a brass key.

"Is that Felix's? We can't use it. That would be almost breaking in."

"We'll sneak upstairs, get my things, and split before he sees us."

Paula pressed the bell and waited. The lack of reply from Felix didn't say "all is well." He didn't seem the sort to fuss about friends breaking in, provided they didn't disturb his work. And she didn't want to make another trip.

Isabelle turned the key in the lock and entered the house. She stopped so abruptly that Paula bumped into her.

"What's that smell?" Isabelle said.

Paula's nose twitched at the rank odor. Voices chattered from the TV. Felix lay on the recliner chair, his face covered with blood. Drops spattered the floor. Isabelle screamed.

"Oh my God." Paula covered her mouth.

Felix's mouth was all blood. Paula searched her purse. She had to call . . . whom? The paramedics or cops or the morgue? Emergency would know. She pressed 911. No answer. Was no one answering anywhere today? Shit. She had pressed the wrong digits. She punched them slowly. Why was no one picking up?

"I see something." Isabelle ran to the dining room.

Felix's lower face and his shirt were covered in blood. He held something blue in his left hand, something black in the other. Isabelle stood beside the dining room gun rack and case, reading a piece of paper. A woman's voice came on the line.

"He's dead," Paula said. "We need someone here. Now."

"Who's dead?"

"Felix. He shot himself. He's holding a gun."

"Try to calm down, ma'am, and tell us where you are."

"At his house."

"What's the address?"

"I don't know. Can't you tell from the phone number? Don't you have call display?"

"We can't tell from a cell phone."

"What's Felix's address?" Paula called to Isabelle, who didn't look up from her reading. "Never mind." She hurried through the dining room to the pile of mail on the kitchen counter. No guns were missing from the wall rack and case. He must have used one of his twenty other ones. She rattled off an address in a window envelope. At the other end of the line she heard computer taps.

"Are you at the residence of Felix Schoen?" the woman said.

"He's dead."

"How did he die?" The tapping continued.

"He killed himself. Didn't I say that?" She paced through the dining room. Felix's body on the chair looked rigid. How long did it take for rigor mortis to set in? At room temperature, three to six hours, according to what she learned in an insurance course. He'd have died before 9:00 AM.

"We'll send someone right away," the woman said. "Please go out of the house and wait on the sidewalk. Don't touch anything."

She had touched the counter and mail. Isabelle was touching the sheet of paper.

"Is it a suicide note?" Paula asked.

"I think so," Isabelle said.

Yesterday, Felix had acted weird but upbeat, determined to finish the column he was struggling to start. Had he killed himself over frustration with it? A half glass of Scotch sat on the table beside him. Drink might have contributed, depressing him enough to take his life. Suicides often used drink to bolster their courage for the act. On the hike, he had sliced off a large leaf. "It was going to fall anyway," he had said. She had to phone Sam. He had wanted to know if his friend was still off balance. "They said to get out of here," she told Isabelle.

Isabelle chewed her nail, not looking up. "I'm almost finished."

"Why are you taking so long? It's only one page."

"His writing's all wavy, like an old person's. I can't figure out all the words, but for sure he offed himself."

Two men on the TV screen babbled about rain and crops. A voice blared, "More about canola after the break." She would zap the annoying voice if the remote wasn't on the table beside the body, and she wasn't supposed to touch anything. The Bavarian costume lay heaped in front of the TV. The walking stick rested on top. Dark stains spattered the bamboo floor. Blood. Felix's blood. She stayed behind the chair where she couldn't see the body, only the bald top of his head.

"What's that stink?" Isabelle wrinkled her nose. "It smells like piss and shit."

"The sphincters relax with death."

"Is Felix Catholic?" Isabelle said.

Paula edged toward Isabelle, who still wore the feather cap.

Isabelle fluttered the sheet of paper. "This is that newspaper article Felix was raving about. The start of it anyway. It's like a confession you make to a priest. I'll read it to you 'Forgive me, Father, for I have sinned. It's been thirty-five years since I've been to confession and almost as long since I've attended . . .' I think the next word is 'mass.' 'That isn't my confession, nor do I want or deserve forgiveness. To . . .' I can't read the next few words. 'Understand me, Readers, for I have sinned. Two weeks ago a woman was murdered on the . . .' this must be 'Elbow River pathway.' Something, something, something 'Callie Moss. I am responsible for her death. Why did I . . .' something something . . . 'come forward? How to explain my crime? Will explanation bring peace? I hope it brings . . .' something. 'To understand, we must return to the start. The story begins with love.'" Isabelle looked up. "That's as far as it goes. He murdered Callie."

"Does he say that? Let me see."

"They told us not to touch."

"You've already touched it." Paula skimmed the page. The peacock blue writing was shaky, but not that hard to decipher. "'Her name is Callie Moss. Why did I wait all this time to come forward?' Does he mean wait the two weeks since her death?"

"I don't know."

"Callie died ten days ago. Of course, the column would run this Thursday. That would be exactly two weeks."

"Was Felix saying he was in love with Callie?"

"Sam insisted he viewed her as a friend." Although Felix was notably upset, if not broken, by her death. Was this a classic case of a man killing the woman who rejected him, and later killing himself? Much later, in this case. Ten days.

They walked to the house entry. Isabelle gaped at the body Paula avoided looking at. A siren shrieked down the street. An Emergency Services van pulled to the curb. Two paramedics leapt out. One dashed up the stairs and told them to wait on the sidewalk. A patrol car roared up. They met the policewoman on the sidewalk.

"Is this your car?" she asked Paula. "Can you move it down the street?"

"I forgot my purse. The keys are there. I'll get it." She turned around.

The policewoman's arm blocked her. "Nobody goes in. I'll have someone retrieve them." She spoke into her walkie-talkie.

Isabelle was talking with a passerby who was walking her dog. Felix's cap was still perched on her head. They should have left it in the house. It belonged to him, except that would be disturbing the scene. A male constable got a roll of tape from the patrol car and started running it around the perimeter of Felix's yard. Ten days ago, it all began with yellow tape across the Elbow Pathway entrance. Another constable handed the policewoman the keys. She gave them to Paula, who got into her car, feeling too shaken to drive.

"Don't go away," the policewoman said. "We'll want your statements."

Paula parked her car down the block and walked back through a corridor of curious neighbors on doorsteps. A second police car zoomed by.

A dark sedan wove slowly through the gathering crowd and stopped across the street from Felix's house. A constable ran to greet the new arrivals. He pointed at Paula and Isabelle. The man and woman dressed in suits came over, flashed IDs, and introduced themselves as detectives.

"Where's Mike?" Isabelle asked.

"Detective Vincelli," Paula explained.

The female detective glanced at the house. "He must be inside. Do you know him?"

"Well enough to know he's not here."

The woman led Isabelle to a quiet spot across the street. The short man with the crew cut and mustache remained with Paula beside the unmarked car.

He took out his notebook and pen. "How did you come to discover the body?"

"We were picking up Isabelle's belongings. She lived here a day before she moved in with me."

He demanded precise dates and times. Was Paula a suspect all over again? This time, Sam would be her alibi and she would be his, apart from that hour he was away for his walk.

"What time do they think Felix died?" she asked.

The detective looked up from his writing. "Isabelle is the niece of Callie Moss, who was recently murdered?"

"Yes. I already told you that."

"Sam Moss is Mrs. Moss's husband?"

"Yes. No. Your unit is aware of his marital situation."

He either didn't know or was pretending or had forgotten.

"Sam is also a friend of Felix Schoen. He would want to know about this. Has anyone contacted him?"

"When did you last see Felix Schoen?"

"Yesterday, around 5:00 PM. We dropped him off after our hike in Kananaskis."

"We? That would be you and who else?"

"Isabelle and Sam Moss."

He looked up. "I'll need a full description of your day."

Three people in coveralls got out of a police van. They draped cameras around their necks and carried boxes and machines into Felix's house.

"Do they always go to this much trouble for suicide?" she said.

"What time yesterday did the four of you leave for Kananaskis?"

Not surprised by his non-answer, she went into details about the hike, including Felix's Bavarian costume and his excitement about his newspaper column. "His suicide note seemed to be the beginning of the piece."

"How do you know that?" the detective asked.

"We read the note when we were in the house."

"You should not have contaminated the crime scene."

This detective was annoying. His pointed face reminded her of a coyote's.

Another patrol car pulled up. The officers jogged down the block to control traffic entering the street. Isabelle mingled with other spectators, her interview concluded. Lucky her to get the less picky cop. A man from the crime scene unit scoured the lawn and went around the side to the backyard that bordered the Elbow River. Presumably, the morning Callie died, Felix had taken the gun he had stolen from Sam's father's shed, followed Callie to a secluded spot and shot her. A premeditated crime, executed coolly enough to leave no evidence.

Paula concluded her story of the Kananaskis hike. "Felix slept all the way home. We watched him walk into the house. It was the last time any of us saw him. Alive." Her voice croaked.

"After you left Felix, where did the three of you go?" the detective asked.

"We drove Isabelle to my daughter Erin's house, where she was spending the night." In a sense, Paula owned the house, but this would take forever to explain in the detail he was bound to require.

"From your daughter's house, you and Sam went where?"

"To dinner." She provided the restaurant's name and location. "Sam drove me home and stayed the night."

The detective looked up, smirking.

She balled her hands into fists. "He left around eight forty-five this morning."

He returned to his notes. "You can vouch for Sam Moss the whole time, between 10:00 AM yesterday and 8:45 AM this morning?"

"Aside from about an hour between 6:55 and 7:55 AM, when he went for a walk to the Elbow River. That is, he told me he did. I didn't know he had gone until around seven forty, when I woke up. His car was still parked in front."

"What time did you and Sam fall asleep last night?"

"Around two o'clock, I guess." Surely, if Sam had left her bed much earlier than 6:00 AM she would have noticed.

The detective closed his notebook. "That's enough for the moment."

Did he think Sam had snuck out of her house, drove to Felix's and killed him, then returned the car and went for a walk so she would wake up to see it there and find his absence believable?

Two more vehicles entered the street. One turned into a driveway. The sedan continued and parked behind a patrol car. A tall, broad man in a business suit got out. Dark complexion. Shaved head. Beard stubble.

"Don't go away." The short detective said to Paula. He went over to talk with Detective Vincelli, who kept nodding and glancing in her direction. The men strode toward her.

"I didn't expect to find you here," Vincelli said.

"Since homicide is involved, does this mean you think it might not be suicide?"

"After I look inside, I want to take you to the station."

This not sharing of information was such a cop power-trip. "What for?" she said.

"Fingerprinting and questioning."

"I've been answering questions for an hour. Fingerprints? Am I a suspect?"

"We need your prints to eliminate ones found in the house."

"You contaminated the scene," the short detective said.

"While you're inside," Paula said, "can you see about getting my purse and Isabelle's tote bag with her clothes?"

"I'll do my best," Vincelli said.

The men walked together to the yard, talked with various constables and disappeared into the house. A television van appeared. Reporters jumped out. One carried a mic to the sidewalk. A cameraman panned the scene. Isabelle held court with a group of spectators, no doubt detailing and embellishing her involvement in the event. Paula hung back across the street, surveying the scene from a distance.

Eventually, Vincelli came out. "You can pick up your purse and Isabelle's bag at the station, after they're checked."

"We should return that hat Isabelle's wearing to Felix's family," Paula said. "He left it in the car last night." After an hour of talking, her throat was dry. She coughed to clear it. "We were sure we'd see him again. Soon. He won't need it now." Her eyes watered. She pictured the bulky corpse flopped on the recliner chair. "He held something in his hand. It looked like a silk scarf. Navy with yellow dots."

"They're stars."

"Did it belong to Callie?"

"We don't know, yet."

"You think he killed her and, ten days later, killed himself?"

Vincelli didn't reply.

"Sam doesn't think Felix had a romantic interest in her. The note was the start of his newspaper column, not a suicide note. I found it ambiguous."

"You read it?"

"He didn't say, explicitly, that he killed her. The note isn't conclusive proof."

"I agree, but it fits with other things."

"What?"

"Additional evidence."

Chapter Twenty-four

The interview room was twelve feet square, its only furnishings two chairs and a table. Seated across from Vincelli, Paula described the hike and dinner with Sam. While talking, she could see it was possible that Sam had planned their whole evening so he could murder his friend, using her as an alibi.

"After we woke up in the living room, I went to the bathroom," she said. "Sam made orange juice in the kitchen. I found him waiting for me in bed with the glasses of juice on the bedside tables. Maybe he spiked mine so I'd sleep through his trip to Felix's house."

Vincelli rolled his chair back. He placed his fingers together in a display of concentration. "We could examine the juice glasses."

Was he teasing because her suggestion was so implausible? She couldn't tell from his straight face. "I ran them through the dishwasher this morning," she said. "Besides, I don't believe Sam did that. He isn't that calculating."

"How long have you known him?"

She hesitated, "A week."

He raised a brow. Did he think her a silly woman who had fallen for a man's false sincerity?

She changed the subject. "What is this evidence you have supporting Felix as Callie's murderer? Did he or someone else tell you he was in love with her?"

Vincelli wheeled his chair toward her. He'd ignored that question twice during the drive from Felix's house.

She glanced at the camera mounted on the wall facing her. "A few days ago, Sam told me he was sure Felix had no interest in Callie beyond friendship. Have you talked to Sam?"

"How could Sam be sure?"

"Felix was his best friend. From the little I saw of Felix, he struck me as the open type, who'd wear his heart on his sleeve. I doubt he could hide his feelings if they were strong enough for him to kill Callie."

"No one's completely open," Vincelli said. "Everyone has secrets. Matters closest to the heart are often the last ones we share." He grabbed a mushy egg sandwich from the platter he had ordered in.

She helped herself to one composed of limp lettuce and meat spread. "Felix had the opportunity. He knew of her morning jogging habit. I presume he had no alibi. None of us do." Including Sam. "It seems hard to get an alibi that's iron-tight."

"Too iron-tight can be suspicious."

"Nobody wins with you people."

"Everyone wins except the bad guys. And victims."

"Felix isn't a bad guy."

Vincelli wheeled back from the table. If his constant movement was designed to drive her nuts, it was working. So did the sterile room and camera recording her every word and movement.

"You asked for the evidence," he said. "During the weeks preceding Callie's death, numerous phone calls were placed between her home and Felix's. Sam couldn't account for them all."

"What about ones from her cell phone?"

"She rarely used it and kept it mainly for emergencies."

True. Callie had a touch of the Luddite, not being into e-mail either, which was unfortunate. E-mail could have provided heaps of evidence about what she'd been up to lately. The police experts were doing a forensics check of Felix's computer. Even deleted e-mails and writing could be retrieved from the hard drive.

Vincelli wheeled forward to get a meat spread sandwich, the only ones left on the plate because they tasted even worse than the salmon and egg. She would have expected the cops to be more competent at selecting food.

"Dimitri had access to Sam's house," she said. "He might have placed those calls. That reminds me, I saw Dimitri Friday night."

He nodded, chewing his sandwich. So, Dimitri had told the police about her visit.

Paula finished her tepid coffee. "Dimitri talked with Callie during the summer. She told him she felt guilty about something. He sensed it wasn't related to her leaving Kenneth. Felix's note talked about guilt. It might be guilt about his murdering Callie, but what if he and Callie both felt guilty about something else?"

"Such as a love affair?"

"Why would they care about that? Callie had broken up with Dimitri. Felix was single. They were free agents."

"Dimitri would have been hurt by their involvement."

On the hike, Felix had shown a concern for Dimitri that was almost paternal. It seemed Callie still had feelings for Dimitri, too.

Vincelli's cell phone or beeper rang. He excused himself and left. His notebook lay on the table. If she peeked the camera would catch her. She rubbed her fingertips. A tiny spot of dye remained, after scrubbing with the police soap. Isabelle was in a room similar to this one answering questions. Were they suspects? Was Sam? The questions aimed at her suggested the police leaned strongly toward thinking it was a murder followed by suicide from guilt. Felix's body—he had been shot in the mouth—was still in that chair, surrounded by crime scene unit members dusting for fingerprints and rooting through his garbage. His family had been notified. One of his sisters was flying from Winnipeg today. His mother and two other sisters would drive from Saskatchewan.

The interview room door opened. Vincelli entered with fresh coffee in Styrofoam cups.

He returned to his chair. "Where were we?"

"Discussing your evidence against Felix."

Vincelli's olive complexion looked sallow in the room's white glare. His trendy unshaven look was growing closer to Felix's unkempt stubble. This was Sunday. He had said he was called in from his first day off since starting work on the case.

He laid his large hands on the table, palms down. "A few weeks ago, Felix's neighbor saw him standing by his backyard fence, arguing with a woman who fits Callie's general description."

"A lot of women do. What were they arguing about?"

"Since she was inside her house, the neighbor couldn't hear."

"How did she know they were arguing?"

"Both were gesturing wildly. The woman, in particular, was shaking and thrusting her arms. At one point, Felix looked around, as though to check for someone overhearing. In the end, the woman whirled and ran off. Felix stood watching her."

"Circumstantial. You don't know if the woman was Callie or if it was a romantic argument."

He was blocking the camera. Was that by accident or on purpose?

"After the murder, a man called the police hotline," Vincelli said. "He recognized Callie from her newspaper photo and said he had passed her every morning on his walk to work. One day, he noticed her talking with Felix, whom he knew by sight as a prominent journalist. They were engaged in, as he put it, spirited conversation."

"A fight? Like the one the neighbor had noticed?"

"He wouldn't commit to that. He didn't hear any words. This man is very precise. He makes an excellent witness."

Vincelli slid his chair to the side. The camera stared straight at her.

"Do you believe Callie and Felix had an affair?" she said.

"By many accounts, he was in love with her thirty years ago. Some people never let go. His obsession might explain why he never married or lived with a woman."

"Who told you he'd been in love with her?"

Vincelli stroked his Styrofoam cup. "Believe it or not, I like Felix. Liked him, that is, and I don't think he's a bad guy. His remorse shows he wasn't a natural killer."

"I still say his so-called suicide note wasn't conclusive."

"It provides the missing piece. The motive. Everything fits."

"Neat and tidy."

"As it should be."

"Too tidy can be suspicious." Paula placed a half-finished sandwich on her plate. "If alibis can be too iron-tight, can't the same be said for evidence? What if Felix didn't do it? What if he didn't kill Callie and didn't kill himself?"

"At the moment, we're ninety-five percent certain his death was suicide."

"What about the other five percent?" She stood. Her leg buckled after so much sitting. She rubbed the cramped muscle. "Suppose, for a minute, it wasn't suicide. Pretend one of your experts rules it out. What would this mean?"

Vincelli looked up at her, scratching his beard stubble. "Someone murdered him, setting it up to look like suicide."

"Was there evidence of break and enter into his house? There can't have been or you wouldn't be thinking suicide. He must have let the person in."

"Felix kept a spare key under a statue in his backyard," Vincelli said. "He told Isabelle to use it if she lost the one he gave her. That reminds me to make sure Isabelle gives us that other key."

"Who else knew about the spare under the statue?"

"All of his friends we've talked with so far. He would tell them to let themselves in if he thought he might be late getting home to meet them. It seems he used it regularly when he locked himself out. Anyone passing on the Elbow trail might have observed him or someone else removing the key. It was an incredibly careless practice and completely in character."

She paced to a white wall. "Was Felix killed by one of his own guns?"

"The one he was holding was registered to him."

"You'll check it against the bullet."

"I'll be surprised if they don't match."

"The killer would have known about his gun collection."

"That narrows it down to a few hundred friends and acquaintances."

"And whoever they told," she said. "Is it easy to set up a murder to look like suicide? You could probably find the information you need on the Net, but to do it convincingly . . ."

"If this was a setup, we'll find out."

Paula returned to her chair, to face him. "The reason for doing it is obvious: the case is closed with Felix declared guilty of Callie's murder; her killer is off the hook."

"Don't forget his note confessing to the crime."

"The writing was wavy. Could it have been forged?"

"Our handwriting expert will determine that." Vincelli wrapped his hands around his cup. "Your turn to suppose. Let's say our expert confirms Felix's handwriting."

"In the note, he didn't directly state he murdered Callie."

"He states he was responsible for her death."

"You can feel responsible without being literally guilty. I've felt responsible for her death, for not returning her call. If I was unstable, it could have nagged at me until I went crazy with guilt." She brushed back her sweaty hair. "Maybe Felix was in a position to have prevented her murder. He might have seen someone following her on the trail and didn't say or do anything. Or something else relatively innocent preyed on him. Guilt works in mysterious ways."

"You don't need to tell me about guilt," he said. "I was raised Catholic." Again the deadpan expression.

"The note was the start of his column. Did you find more of it, earlier drafts in the wastebasket?"

Vincelli stared, lips tight. He had shared the information about the witnesses and gun registration. She guessed he didn't know if they found anything in the basket.

"If it wasn't suicide, Callie's murderer is still out there," Paula said. "It's someone who planned ahead enough to steal Sam's father's gun and scout the river trail for the best murder site. Someone brazen enough to enter Felix's house at the risk of being seen by neighbors or waking him up. That suggests, by the way, it was someone who knew him to be a deep sleeper. Sam told me he had a particular sleep pattern. I forget the details."

"He was an insomniac who got by on a few hours of rock-solid sleep."

"Sam said Felix was up every morning when Callie jogged by his house, around 6:15 AM. I bet that wasn't the time of his murder. The killer would have got him during his period of deep sleep."

"That's assuming he was murdered."

"He was a snorer. His mouth would have been open." Paula pictured the body on the chair, its bloodied head leaning back. Would she ever get over the image? "Whoever killed him was knowledgeable enough or skilled enough in Internet research to set up a suicide that was ninety-five percent convincing to a homicide unit. And heartless enough to kill a friend or acquaintance."

She took a breath. Vincelli was edging back. He probably thought her obsessed, but this was her chance to make a point. The whole unit would watch and listen to the camera recording.

"Felix raved about his explosive column," she said. "What if he planned to expose Callie's murderer and that person found out and felt a need to silence him? Felix talked a lot. He probably talked even more than usual when he was drinking in bars. What if he confided his knowledge of Callie's murder to someone he met there and Callie's murderer learned about that? He murdered Felix to shut him up. What's to stop him from killing that other innocent person?"

Vincelli's chair stopped a few feet from the wall. Even to her, the theory sounded like an improbable chain of events. Vincelli and his colleagues would think her unhinged. Now, she understood why he had shared police information. There was no need to keep it secret. The case was almost closed.

He wheeled the chair toward her. "We'll know more, as information filters in. Felix's friends might corroborate his suicidal mood, as you did when you described his behavior on the hike: his unnatural buoyancy, magnified sense of purpose."

After the high came the crash. Everything fit so well.

Outside the interview room, they were met by the short detective who had questioned Paula on Felix's street. He told them Isabelle had been sent home in a taxi an hour earlier.

"Once again, she scores the shorter grilling," Paula said.

His jaw tightened. "We need to investigate thoroughly."

"I hope you do."

"You'd be wise to curb that attitude."

Vincelli said he'd drive Paula back to her car parked on Felix's street.

"Your colleague rubs me the wrong way," she told him on their way to his vehicle. Without replying, he unlocked the doors.

They drove under the railway tracks and entered the Beltline district humming with people out shopping or enjoying a Sunday stroll. While they had been stuck in the police station, gray skies had given way to a burst of sun.

"I gather Felix has been a prime suspect from the start," she said. "Murder-suicide fits your expectations. All that remains is to wait for the evidence to roll in and prove it."

"Can we leave it, Paula, for one minute?" His tone was harsh. Was he annoyed by her attitude, too, or simply tired?

She switched gears, slightly. "What happened to your partner, Novak? I haven't seen him since you both interviewed me that first Friday." It felt like a year ago.

"Novak's on sick leave. Doctor's ordered him to rest his leg and do physio. I wouldn't count on him doing either of those things."

"It puts more burden on you when you're short-staffed."

"That's chronic in all police departments, but don't think we're rushing the case. We'd do a proper job if we were down to a single person. Still, you notice it with three missing; including Novak, who's by far the most experienced, and the staff sergeant, out with cancer."

"I'm sorry about your staff sergeant," she said. "Who's replacing him?"

"Thinking of going over my head?" His lip twitched.

It had crossed her mind, but his supervisor would watch the video and all she could do was repeat that Sam had told her that Callie and Felix were merely friends. Close as he was to Felix, Sam might welcome a murder-suicide verdict that would lift suspicion from his son. A quick conclusion to the case could even keep Dimitri's affair with Callie out of the media and salvage his political career.

The Beltline merged into Mission, which was even more bustling with people.

Vincelli turned east on 25th Avenue. "The acting staff sergeant is the detective who rubs you the wrong way."

Not Coyote-face. "When he questioned me, all he did was pester me for details. He struck me as someone who'd miss the forest for the trees."

"He's competent."

They reached Felix's street. Vincelli parked behind her car. The crime scene van and one patrol car remained. The yellow tape was still up.

"Felix's body has been removed," Vincelli said. "We must have just missed it."

"I wish someone who knew him had been here to watch. It seems appropriate."

His eyes flickered in sympathy. "I'll phone you when the autopsy results are in."

"When will that be?"

"Probably tomorrow afternoon."

Walter rocked and smoked on his porch. For once Paula wanted to talk to him. She grabbed her purse from the front passenger seat. He mashed his cigarette on the railing. They met on his sidewalk. Despite today's relatively cool weather, his parka seemed overkill.

"Have your relatives from Europe gone?" he said. "I saw their car drive away this morning."

"At what time?"

"Just before you left. Didn't you see them off?"

"Did you notice their car leave earlier in the morning, before 8:00 AM, and return?"

"I wasn't up 'til eight thirty."

"That late? I thought people your age got up with the birds."

"Why should I do that when I'm retired?"

Trust him not to oblige the one time his snooping would have helped. She would question her other neighbors. Some, she knew, slept late on Sunday mornings. If Sam had driven to Felix's house and back, probably no one had seen him. It was unlikely he'd done that and she didn't want Callie's murderer to be Sam. She didn't want it to be Dimitri, either. For everyone, her included, settling on Felix as the killer would be easiest.

Chapter Twenty-five

The 6:00 PM news blared from the TV set. Isabelle sprawled on the chair, one leg draped over a chair arm.

She looked up from filing her nails. "You just missed the report. They showed Felix's house and people hanging around the street. I couldn't see you or me or Mike. They didn't say Felix knew Callie or that he murdered her or even that he offed himself."

"That isn't proven yet," Paula said.

"What did the cops ask you?" Isabelle said. "They kept you forever."

"I'll tell you over dinner," Paula said. "I need a break first."

"I'm eating out." Isabelle followed her into the kitchen. "A lot of people phoned this afternoon."

"Who?" Paula took out a bottle of wine from the fridge, a chilled Riesling for a change.

"Your boss. He said it wasn't important and he'd see you at work tomorrow morning."

Paula uncorked the wine. "Do you want a glass?"

Isabelle shook her head. "I'll probably be drinking enough tonight."

"Where are you going?"

"We aren't sure. Dimitri said we'd decide in the car."

Paula froze. "You're going out with Dimitri?"

"He was another one who called, looking for Sam. He already knew about Felix. He said he'd canceled his trip to Ottawa and felt like going out and I wasn't doing anything."

Pouring wine into her glass, Paula said, "I don't think you should go."

"Why not?" Isabelle picked up some scraps of paper from the telephone table. "Also, your mother called. She was wondering where you were, since you usually phone her on Sunday. I said you were at the police station being questioned about Felix's death."

"That should reassure her."

"Erin called, wondering why the cops came by her house to alibi me for last night. Isn't that exciting? I called Leah, your other daughter, to tell her about Felix, but didn't say Sam stayed over here last night. I figured you'd want to tell her yourself. The last one was Hayden. I told him about Felix and about the cops questioning us."

"But not about me and Sam?"

"I wasn't sure you'd want me to, since he's your boyfriend. I've got to get dressed. Can I borrow the flowery skirt in your closet? The purple blouse, too. I don't have anything fancy enough."

"Call Dimitri and say you've changed your mind."

"I won't stay out late or drink too much since I've got a job interview in the morning."

"Where? Did one of the restaurants you applied to call back?"

Isabelle was already dashing down the hall. At least the blouse and skirt would be less skimpy than her usual clothes. Outdoors, a pink glow illuminated the crabapple tree, now almost bare of leaves. When Dimitri arrived, Paula would suggest the three of them order pizza and talk about Felix here. She owed it to Isabelle's parents not to let her go out with him until his part, or non-part, in the murders was settled. She glanced at the clock. It was after 8:00 PM in Montreal; she would return her mother's call first.

The doorbell rang. "Can you get it?" Isabelle yelled from the den.

"Sure I can, since it's my house." Which she couldn't wait to claim back for herself.

She crossed through the living room, preparing her comments for Dimitri, and opened the door. It was Hayden.

"Isabelle told me about you and her finding the body," he said. "That must have been a shock."

Isabelle reappeared, looking gorgeous in the flower skirt, mauve blouse, and pendant Paula had worn on many dates with Hayden. He didn't seem to recognize the outfit. After introductions, she poured him a glass of Riesling. He wore his best casual clothes: a yellow golf shirt and freshly pressed corduroy pants. He ironed way more than she did. Isabelle launched into her story of their discovery of Felix's body.

"It was lucky I had a key," she said. "We can use it tomorrow when we get my things."

"Didn't you give the key to the cops?" Paula said.

"No one asked me for it." Isabelle jumped up. "Is that a car?"

She and Paula went to the door. Dimitri looked sharp in a long-sleeved navy shirt and white Dockers pants. "I'm sorry and stunned by Felix's death," he said. "I can't imagine him committing suicide."

They shook hands. His fingers felt eerily like Sam's.

"Can you imagine him in love with Callie?" she said.

He jerked his hand away. "I'm sure the interest was entirely on his side. She must have been aware of it, but didn't tell me to spare my feelings." He looked over Paula's shoulder. "I didn't realize you had company."

Paula introduced him to Hayden. The men shook hands firmly. Dimitri had certainly composed himself since her visit on Friday night.

She glanced out the window. "I see you brought your car, rather than your motorbike."

"Isabelle can't drive the bike, but she can drive the car if I drink too much, which I have no intention of doing," Dimitri said. "I've learned my lesson, the hard way, several lessons, in fact."

She liked him better when he was falling apart. What was his interest in Isabelle? It would be hard to convince Isabelle to stay home without Dimitri; sharing pizza with Hayden and Dimitri would not be fun. On balance, Paula had to let Isabelle go. She suggested they be back by eleven o'clock so Isabelle would be fresh for her interview.

"What kind of job are you getting?" Dimitri asked with apparent interest as Paula closed the door behind them.

"What a phony," Hayden said, returning to the sofa.

Paula took the armchair. "I can't help feeling responsible for her."

"He'll fly off to Ottawa soon and chase after some classier woman. Why isn't he in Ottawa already? Aren't federal MPs required to attend parliamentary sessions, on occasion?"

"Dimitri told me Friday he would resign his seat. I wonder if he's changed his mind."

They sipped the sweet Riesling. Hayden was obviously waiting for the Sam report and she was too tired to circle around it. She set her glass on the end table, on the spot where Sam had lit the last candle before they tumbled to the floor. Not so many hours ago her evening dress was draped on this chair. Now, it hung in the front closet waiting to be dry-cleaned. Hayden's brown eyes looked hopeful.

"I owe you the truth." She took a breath. "The hike was okay. When we got back to Calgary, we dropped Felix off at his house and Isabelle at Erin's, where she was spending the night. Sam and I went to dinner. He drove me home and stayed over."

Hayden went pale. "You slept with him?"

"Feel free to say 'I told you so'."

"There are times I'd prefer to be wrong." He placed his wine glass on the ottoman. "What was it like?"

"I'm not answering that."

"This is the end."

"I'm sorry."

"And the beginning of you and Sam."

"I don't know about that. Felix's death changes things."

"In what way? I expect Sam will be looking for comfort after his friend's suicide."

"I'm not sure it was suicide."

"An accident? When I called, Isabelle said Felix had been drinking."

"I think it might have been murder."

A pickup truck lumbered down the street. An airplane roared overhead.

"It wasn't likely Sam," she said. "I can give him an alibi for the probable time of death, aside from an hour when he disappeared."

"Disappeared?" Hayden said. "Was that some kind of kinky sex thing?"

She studied his self-deprecating smile. "You seem calmer about this than I had expected."

"I've had all weekend to prepare. I knew I was finished the moment you decided to go on that hike."

"I didn't know we were finished then. I don't even know it now."

Hayden stood and marched to the wall unit, his nostrils twitching in anger—or at the acrid odor that lingered from last night.

"I still care about you," Paula said.

"If you say let's be friends, I'll puke." His hand brushed over the feather cap Isabelle had placed on the shelf. He picked up the monkey candle. "Is this new?"

"I bought it on impulse earlier this week."

He stared at the startled monkey face and mumbled something that sounded like "monkey in the middle."

"It's not your fault you're stuck in the middle of this," she said. "Don't be hard on yourself."

"See no evil, hear no evil, speak no evil," he said. His hands shook. This breakup was bothering him more than he let on. She edged toward him and touched his arm.

"Do the cops really suspect Felix was murdered?" he asked.

"They lean strongly toward thinking he killed Callie and committed suicide from remorse. I'm the one who's more skeptical."

"Why?"

"A hunch?" She shrugged. "Yesterday, Felix went on and on about a great column he was going to write that was so vitally important the newspaper would splash it on the front page. Suddenly, he's dead. If it wasn't suicide, someone wanted desperately to shut him up."

Hayden plunked the candle on the shelf.

"They might find more of his column in his wastebasket or on his computer. If they don't . . . I feel so helpless. I wish I could do something."

"No." He walked to the sofa, his legs steady, the shaking gone. "You've done your bit. The cops can take it from here. If they rule it suicide, you agree, whether you believe it or not."

"But—"

"Keep your eyes, ears, and mouth shut."

See no evil, hear no evil, speak no evil. "Why did that candle upset you so much?"

"Keep your doubts to yourself. Don't tell anyone."

"Not even Sam?"

"Especially Sam."

"I don't know if I can."

"Then stay away from him and his bunch."

"You would like that."

Hayden crossed one leg over the other. "It isn't jealousy this time, I swear. I don't want the cops barging into my office demanding my alibi because you've turned up as the next probable suicide."

Paula shivered. "I wish you would lay off these warnings."

"I wish you'd lay off Sam, rather than lay him."

"There's no need to be crude."

He bolted up. "I should leave before we end on an even uglier note."

"You always avoid arguments." Did he? She was too tired to remember. "I'd like us to talk when things are more settled."

"We'll see."

After he left, the house felt strangely silent. She returned her mother's and daughters' phone calls. Everyone was out. Where would her mother go at 9:00 PM? Paula left them both messages saying she was fine and would call when she had a chance. Not in the mood for TV, she paced from the living room to the den, to the kitchen and bedroom. She wouldn't rest until Isabelle was back safe from her dinner with Dimitri, who was probably pumping her for information relating to their findings at Felix's house. Paula felt herself wear a track in the hardwood floor. Her house shrank to the size of the interview room and was almost as stark: no pictures or plants, minimal knickknacks. She would go nuts if she didn't get out, but didn't dare walk through her neighborhood at night. The murder had ruined the place for her. Would she ever feel safe here again? She grabbed her car keys and purse, double-checked the locks on her front and side doors. In the car, she drove, not knowing which way she would turn until she reached 8th Street.

Cool night air flowed into her window. She passed the sandstone school, rounded the corner below the Stampede grounds, bumped over the C-train tracks, crossed MacLeod Trail and steered onto Felix's street. House lights shone down the block to his home and yard, which were dark. No police vehicles remained, no yellow tape; no crime scene guys prowled the grounds.

If it wasn't suicide, Felix's killer had probably entered via the trail at the back after midnight, when most of the neighbors were asleep. He would have helped himself to a gun and bullets from Felix's cupboards, tiptoed to the recliner chair and fired into the snoring mouth. He had to count on Felix staying asleep or, failing that, account for his own presence. It all pointed to an acquaintance or friend. Both Dimitri and Sam had lived with Felix for two or three years. Sam had said he would call her tonight and hadn't. No surprises there, considering what had happened. His house was a ten-minute drive away.

She crossed the Elbow River Bridge, entered Riverdale, and parked in front of Sam's home. Light streamed through the living room's plantation blinds. She had been here twice. The first time she had met Sam and Isabelle. The second visit, six days ago, she had come for the funeral reception. So much had happened since then.

Sam answered the doorbell. "I was going to call you."

Hadn't he said something similar the last time? "I know you've heard about Felix's death."

"I'm sorry you had to find him," he said.

"It was a shock. You must be stunned." They repeated Dimitri's platitudes.

Sam offered her a drink and left her in the living room, which looked essentially the same: baby grand piano, candle collection on the sideboard, cranberry walls, fireplace beneath a painting of a beach café bought to remember not Sam's and Callie's marriage, but Callie's and Dimitri's commitment ceremony witnessed by Felix and Sam. During that week the four of them stayed in Hawaii, had Felix loved Callie to the point of obsession, without either Sam or Dimitri noticing? How dense could two men be?

A change to the room was the addition of clutter. Newspaper sections covered the love seat. A half-finished bottle of beer sat on the glass coffee table next to a bowl of Hershey kisses. White sports socks lay on the floor.

Sam returned with two glasses of ice water. He was barefoot and wore jeans and a T-shirt. He gathered the newspaper sections into a pile to make space for himself on the love seat.

Like the previous time, Paula took a chair facing the piano and him. "How did you learn about Felix's death?"

"Dimitri and I were clearing the shrubs in the back," he said.

"A damp, dreary day for yard work."

"We were filling in time before his Ottawa flight."

"Dimitri changed his mind about that trip," she said. "He's out with Isabelle."

Sam nodded. "He finds her amusing. She takes his mind off things. Dimitri's the one who heard the doorbell. I ran around to the front and caught the detective getting into his car. While he was talking, I kept thinking, if Dimitri hadn't heard the bell, if I'd walked not run, this wouldn't be happening. Felix wouldn't be dead." He paused for a sip of water. "They took us downtown to get our statements."

"Isabelle and I were at the downtown station. I'm surprised we missed you."

"The reason for Felix's death didn't hit me until they asked about the scarf that was found in his hand."

"It was navy with stars. Did it belong to Callie?"

"I couldn't identify it. Dimitri said it was her type. He hadn't a clue Felix was in love with her and insists there was no affair. Naturally, he wants to think that. I can't be sure."

The bowl of chocolate kisses reminded her that she hadn't eaten anything since this afternoon's sandwiches. She took one and peeled off the foil wrap. "Three days ago you were sure there was nothing like that between Callie and Felix. You were sure his interest was strictly friendship."

He flushed. "Who knows what people get up to in their private lives or what they really feel? You think you know someone, but you never truly do, in the end."

"You'd think Dimitri would notice another man taking an interest in the woman he loved."

Sam tossed a red foil kiss from hand to hand. "Like I said, Felix kept his feelings close."

"Was that his style?"

"Everyone knew he was in love with her years ago. I'd assumed he'd gotten over it. Maybe he did for awhile and something re-triggered it."

"This is so convenient for you and Dimitri. The killer is someone who can't answer for himself. It makes everything easy."

"It's hardly easy to lose your best friend. You, of all people, should know that." He twirled a foil kiss open.

She got up and paced to the sideboard. "Do you really think Felix would commit murder?"

"I can see him as a crime-of-passion type."

"Anyone could buy a scarf that's Callie's style and plant it in a dead man's hand. Whoever murdered Callie stole your father's gun in advance. That's not a crime of passion. It also took planning to leave no clues at the site."

Sam walked over and faced her by the sideboard. His chest moved up and down beneath his green shirt. "Crimes of passion can involve a series of impulses," he said. "Impulse one: Felix steals the gun. Dithers for awhile. Typical Felix. Impulse two: he follows her on the trail to see where she goes. More dithering. Impulse three: follows her and does the deed."

"Do you really think Felix would carry a torch for thirty years with no one suspecting?"

He touched her arm. "In hindsight, there were signs."

"Such as?" She shook off his hand.

"Why are you hassling me? It's the cops, not me, who are calling it suicide."

"And you're going along."

"What else can I do?"

"You could tell them you're convinced Felix didn't love her."

"I'm not convinced, not anymore, and the evidence is there. The scarf. His note. You found him with the bloody gun in his hand. Stress was obviously building in him since her death. You saw his weird mood yesterday."

"How convenient I was there to see it."

"What does that mean?"

She rested her hand on a candlestick. The crystal felt solid and thick. "Yesterday, you told me there were limits to how far you would go to protect your son. You said you wouldn't let them arrest an innocent person."

"They can't arrest Felix. He's dead."

"Pin the rap on the dead man." She fingered the candlestick's glass grooves. "Is it fair that Felix's family and friends will falsely remember him as a murderer?"

"Would they feel better remembering him as a murder victim? That sucks, too, in my opinion. Whatever he's pinned with sucks."

"If Dimitri is guilty—"

"He's not."

"Are you sure? You never truly know someone, in the end."

He scowled.

"Talk about stress," she said. "Dimitri was a basket-case on Friday night. With his religion, he's big on sin. If he's guilty, don't you think it will prey on him the rest of his life and catch him eventually?"

"So, it's better he catches it now and spends the prime of his life in jail? I don't think so. If he's guilty, that is, which he's not."

"You're not sure of that in your heart. You'll never be sure."

Sam turned away. Paula picked up the candlestick. If she could only beat the truth into his head.

"The uncertainty will eat at your feelings for Dimitri," she said, "just as it's eating at my feelings for you."

"What's eating you? Last night, you thought I was innocent."

"I'm less sure this morning."

"Don't forget I was in your bed when Felix died."

"You were gone an hour and possibly more. How do I know you didn't slip over to Felix's house to set up a suicide to protect your son? You've told me there are no limits."

He scanned her face. "If you believe I'm capable of that, there's no hope for us."

"Until the crime is settled beyond any doubt, I can't trust either you or your son. You adore him and I can't stand the sight of him at the moment. It makes me sick to think he's with Isabelle."

"That's your problem, not mine. You don't trust any men."

She clutched the candlestick. "Where do you get that? You don't know me one bit."

"I knew you pretty well last night."

"Push the cops, Sam, convince them to dig deeper into Felix's death. If you won't do it for Felix or Dimitri or yourself, do it for us. I can't be with you until I'm sure."

His gaze took in the fireplace, the piano, the candle-topped sideboard and resettled on her. "Look, the bottom line is this: we had sex. It was nice, but I can't ruin my son's life for that."

"Nice?" She raised the candlestick. It was heavy and hard. Good.

Sam's eyes widened. She hurled the candlestick. He ducked sideways. The crystal bounced off the piano edge and landed next to his foot. Had she really done that? She might have killed him. The piano's black enamel looked chipped.

He squatted to examine the candlestick. "I can't see any damage, except, possibly, this tiny nick. That was a lucky break. Or non-break, as it happens." He looked up, head cocked, an odd smile on his face. He was enjoying this.

"Do you want me to throw another one at you?" Shit. She had played into his drama queen fetish. Her storming out would thrill him, but she couldn't help herself.

"Fine," she said as she marched down the hall. "If that's how you feel, I'll go elsewhere for help."

"Where?"

She struggled to squeeze her heel in the fucking shoe. Hardly a smooth exit.

"Stay," he said. "We'll—"

She was out the front door, slamming it behind her. She breathed in the cold night air. Where else would she go for help? Good question.

Chapter Twenty-six

The dog barked before Paula rang the bell. Kenneth answered the door and grabbed Mandy's collar as she lunged for Paula's skirt. On the way to the living room, she thanked him for fitting her into his morning, adding she was sorry about Felix's death.

"You and he go a long way back," she said.

"Some thirty years, to university." Kenneth's face looked as gray as his suit, shirt, and tie.

Ever the host, he had set the table with coffee and muffins. Mandy ran around in circles until she settled beside his armchair. Dim light filtered through the window sheers. There was no ashtray on the table, but she detected a faint acrid odor. The railroad clock beside the window chimed 9:00 AM. Like her, he would be dashing to work when their meeting was done. She had to get down to business.

"Were you and Felix close in recent years?" she asked.

Kenneth leaned down to pat the golden retriever's head. "I wouldn't say so. We saw each other every few months, usually in social rather than intimate settings."

"Everyone seems to know about his old romantic interest in Callie. Were you aware it had continued?"

"Like I said, I hadn't seen much of him lately, or him and her together, for obvious reasons." Frowning, he leaned lower to scratch Mandy behind her ear. "The police said he left a note confessing his love and regret for murdering her."

"I read the note. He didn't directly state that." She wished she could see more than the top of his bald head so she could read his expression.

"People tend to confess in a roundabout way, in an effort to explain themselves or avoid getting to the point. As a lapsed Catholic, I should know." He looked up, flashing his awkward smile.

"I was with Felix the day before he died," she said. "He talked about struggling with a newspaper column, an explosive one he claimed would get him on the front page."

Kenneth leaned forward to pour himself a coffee. He added cream and stirred. "Felix mentioned it Friday night when he dropped by."

"Here? He told us he'd spent all Friday night working on the column."

"Felix's idea of work mainly involved thinking about it." Again, the smile on his long face.

On the drive to Kananaskis, Felix had admitted he hadn't accomplished any actual writing.

"What did he tell you about the column?" she asked.

Kenneth touched Mandy's head, prompting her to leap up and rest her forepaws on his lap. In the past, he had always gated the dog in the kitchen. It was odd he hadn't done that today, when she would shed over their work clothes. A glow appeared on his bald pate. Perspiration? His coffee sat on the table, untouched.

"Felix never discussed his newspaper columns with me," Kenneth said. "He knows I consider them fluff."

"Then why did he drop by Friday night?"

"No reason. He just wanted to ramble and clear his head."

"Out of the blue, a day or two before he allegedly commits suicide, he drops by to talk about nothing?"

"It may have been his way of saying good-bye."

"Dimitri phoned him late Friday night."

Kenneth looked up, his lips narrowed to a slit.

"Dimitri told him Callie felt guilty about something unrelated to her leaving you. Do you know what it would be?"

He scowled, presumably at the reference to the hated Dimitri. "Perhaps, about living a lie with Sam? It confused our kids, especially Skye, who couldn't understand why she stayed with someone so indifferent to her."

It was cruel to return to Dimitri, but couldn't be helped. "I suppose, if the cops decide Felix didn't commit suicide, the heat will be on Dimitri again."

"Much as I'd like that, I can't escape the facts. The bastard's probably innocent."

"Did you tell the cops about Felix's Friday night visit?"

"Of course. Did you see the newspaper today? Felix told you he would make the front page? He got that part right."

A brief article had announced the popular weekly columnist's suicide. A friend was quoted as saying Felix had been depressed by another unnamed friend's death. Thursday's Community section would feature a one-page spread of his best columns.

With a napkin, she brushed muffin crumbs from her mouth. "I'm not convinced Felix's death was suicide. You said Dimitri's probably innocent. If you aren't convinced, you're in a position to push the cops to dig deeper."

Kenneth's hand slid down Mandy's head. The dog's eyes closed in delight. "I was in rough shape after Callie left me," he said. "That's why I understand a man killing a woman who rejects him and turning the gun on himself. If Felix held onto this obsession for thirty years, the only surprise is that it didn't explode sooner."

"You really believe that?"

"I do." He scratched the dog's back hard. "Much as I'd rather they hang the kid for it."

While driving from Kenneth's house, it struck her that he hadn't asked her what Felix had revealed to her about his column. Did he assume Felix didn't discuss his columns in progress with anyone or not care what the column was about, or had he learned from Sam that Felix had told them nothing? Their little group seemed to operate an effective grapevine. She got to the office at ten o'clock. Alice's reception desk was empty. The smell of tobacco flowed through Nils's open doorway. A woman sat in his visitor's chair, her long blond hair draped over the back. Nils rose to greet Paula as she walked in. The woman turned around.

Paula halted, stunned. "What are you doing here?"

Isabelle tucked hair behind her ear dotted with one of Paula's pearl earrings. She wore Paula's navy suit. "I told you I had a job interview."

"You didn't say it was in my office."

"You didn't ask."

"You, you . . ." She turned to Nils for an explanation.

He pointed his pipe at Isabelle. "When I phoned your house yesterday, Isabelle here happened to mention she was looking for a job. We're looking for an employee."

Paula glared down at Isabelle, who was chewing a fingernail painted with Paula's pearl polish. "You purposely kept this from me because you knew I wouldn't like it."

Isabelle's wide blue eyes flashed innocence. "Don't you want me to find work so I can pay you and Erin rent? This job pays better than the other crap-jobs I've had."

Nils motioned his pipe toward the visitor's chair. "Sit down, Paula, and we'll discuss the plan."

"Where's Alice? Don't tell me Isabelle's her replacement. We'll never get our telephone messages."

"Alice called in sick," Nils said. "That's just what we need with you off gallivanting around. We need somebody steady in here."

"I've been dealing with a couple of dead friends."

"I sympathize with your loss." Nils looked sympathetic. "Both losses; Isabelle's been telling me about the one yesterday. But this has been one hell of week for me, taking care of the whole shop. We need to stop dithering about whom to hire for this junior position."

"You're the one who's been dithering."

A two-foot pile of claim folders sat on his desk. He must be desperate to be considering someone so unsuitable for the work. For starters, Isabelle had no insurance experience or even office experience.

Isabelle swiveled her chair toward Paula. "Your boss's computer reminded me of Felix's laptop. Do you remember seeing it when we found him dead yesterday?"

Paula blinked at the non sequitur. "Where did he usually keep the laptop?"

"He always put it away in the downstairs desk drawer when he wasn't using it. That's why I didn't notice if it was missing or not."

Paula glanced at Nils. "We can discuss this later."

Nils circled the air with his pipe. "Go ahead. Life and death is more important than work."

Coming from him, this was crazier than hiring Isabelle.

"I saw them take out Felix's big computer," Isabelle said. "All the time I lived there, I never saw him go upstairs to use it. He probably wrote his newspaper stuff on the laptop."

"If it was gone, someone stole it." The laptop might be in the shop or anywhere. "I need to call Detective Vincelli about this."

Nils set his pipe beside the stack of claim files. "While you're doing that, I'll discuss details with Isabelle. I give her points, Paula, for concealing this job interview from you. Reading people is key to our work. A certain amount of deviousness also helps. As far as I'm concerned, Isabelle's in. She can start as a trainee, fill in for Alice, and help with some clerical tasks. I'll leave the decision to you."

In her office, Paula left a message for Vincelli. She tried to concentrate on claim files, her thoughts flitting from Felix's missing laptop to this morning's visit with Kenneth to the pros and cons of hiring Isabelle. The main pros were the rent money and the fact it would satisfy both Isabelle and Nils. If she vetoed his choice, it could be months before he agreed to another candidate and she would be saddled with the extra work. The main con was that training and dealing with Isabelle would probably be more hindrance than help. If and when Isabelle got too frustrated with the job, she would probably quit. If, by some miracle, she grasped the work and stuck with it and Paula couldn't stand it, well, that might provide the impetus she needed to leave this place for something better.

In the midst of her mulling, Gary phoned. She had forgotten all about his return from the cruise yesterday. That must be progress, not thinking about your ex-spouse for a week. The trip had gone well, he said, not elaborating further, and now he was swamped with post-vacation work. Equally swamped, she suggested they meet Friday for lunch.

"Sounds great." Gary chuckled. "Unless you're too busy having lunch with some gangster. The girls tell me you've become a moll."

"My moll career was short-lived."

"Too bad. It sounded intriguing and not at all like you."

"Thanks."

Paula hung up and opened the file for her claimant who fell off the roof. The medical report had come in. His broken arm and ribs were coming along as expected; his doctor confirmed no physical damage from the concussion and was referring him to a neurologist to evaluate his complaints about mental fuzziness.

She scanned the initial report from the insurer. The homeowner had no history of claims, but his injured neighbor might have tried putting one over another insurance firm. She made a note to ask him for his insurance agent's name when she went to his street to poll more neighbors about the fall. The phone rang.

"I assume you're wondering about the autopsy," Vincelli said. "It came in and is what we expected. Consistent with suicide."

"Consistent?"

"That's sufficient to rule on suicide, with the supporting evidence."

"I was actually calling about Felix's laptop. Did your people find one in his house?"

"Isabelle phoned about that ten minutes ago. I checked. None was taken."

"She definitely saw Felix use one."

"It would have been better if she had brought this up at the station. It makes you question her memory."

That didn't seem fair. "Felix told me he worked freelance, so no colleagues can confirm his work habits, but his friends might know if he wrote his columns on the laptop or desktop."

"We're looking into it."

"Kenneth Unsworth said Felix visited him Friday night."

"Kenneth told us."

"Did Felix visit other friends?"

"We're talking with all of his friends and acquaintances. He had a lot of them." Vincelli sounded tired. "If there was a laptop, or if there were other visits, we'll dig them out."

"When I was at Kenneth's this morning, something struck me as interesting."

He waited.

"On all my earlier visits, he barricaded the dog in the kitchen. Today, she was with us in the living room. He kept bending over to pat her and I wondered if he wanted her there so I couldn't see his face when he answered certain questions."

"When we talked to him yesterday, the dog was gated."

"Kenneth seems so willing to accept Felix as Callie's killer. You'd think he would seize every opportunity to get you guys to target Dimitri, his rival."

"I'll make a note of your canine concern."

Was he trying to be funny?

"Is that all?" he said. "We're busy here."

"Isabelle wants to stop by Felix's house to pick up her belongings."

"She also brought that up. Apparently, she didn't turn in her key to his place."

"Apparently, you have to ask her for everything."

"Felix's sister is fine about Isabelle going in. I trust you'll be with her."

"Is his sister staying in the house?"

"She and the rest of the family prefer to stay with friends in town. I advised her to have his house re-keyed as soon as possible. Isabelle's key should work, if you go tonight."

"I know it sounds trivial," Paula said, "but I hope you'll question Kenneth about his keeping the dog in the room."

"I'll phone you with any significant developments."

Nils appeared in her office doorway. "What's the decision?"

She studied her homey office. Rubber trees in the corners, mountain and prairie paintings on the walls, travel knickknacks and family pictures on the bookshelves. This had been her place for eight years. She liked her friendship with Alice and the respect she had earned from Nils, who was a father figure, of sorts, filling in for her dad who had died only four years before she started this job. Like her dad, Nils didn't cut colleagues slack when they failed to come through. If it came down to Isabelle and the welfare of his insurance firm, Isabelle would be out.

Paula clasped her hands on the desk. "Here's the deal: You hire her and you train her. I stay out of it and do my work."

"Terrific. I'll be caught up by the end of the week. She can start next Monday." Nils saluted her with his pipe. "This will be fun. It's been a long time since I've had a protégé who's green enough to mould."

"Don't count on it."

Paula rushed through the rest of her claims and squeezed in an afternoon workout with Anne to get her take on Felix's death. After their standard commiserations on the treadmill, Anne said Felix hadn't visited her Friday night. She didn't know if he had a laptop or not, but wouldn't be surprised if he did. "Like most guys, he was into electronic gadgets." Anne confirmed his youthful infatuation for Callie. "It started when he was at university. I didn't realize he'd carried it forward to the present." She echoed Sam's words on the subject. "You never know a person, do you?"

Anne and Sam had the same vested interest in protecting Dimitri.

"I guess the heat's off him now," Paula said.

Anne smiled. "I can't deny I'm glad about that."

Hayden looked up from his office desk. "I must say, I'm surprised. I thought we'd broken up. Did I miss something?" His eyes managed a self-effacing twinkle of amusement, while he nervously twiddled his thumbs.

"I thought we left it ambiguous." She slumped into the visitors' chair.

"Is that our problem?" he said. "Lack of communication?"

"I'm sure our problem is me." Why was she here? Because he was all she had left. "It feels like a conspiracy," she said. "Sam, Kenneth, Anne, everyone wants the investigation to end with Felix as Callie's killer who then killed himself. Even the cops are in on it. They're short-staffed and overworked. I suspect they're tired of the investigation and figure this is as good a way as any to bring it to a close."

"I doubt they'd let it go if they had evidence pointing in another direction."

"How can they get the evidence, if they don't look for it?"

He rocked back and forward on his chair. "You know, it occurred to me you might be clinging to this murder investigation to avoid dealing with your personal issues."

"What issues?"

"The loss of your oldest and closest friend. The loss of you and me. Your dissatisfactions with your job. How are things working out between you and Sam?"

"I wish people would stop analyzing me."

"It was just a suggestion."

"So, I'm not intriguing. So, I don't trust men."

"I didn't say that."

"Tonight, I'm taking Isabelle to Felix's place. It's a huge house. The cops didn't take everything out. Maybe we'll look around."

"Don't." His tone was sharp. "Let go of this thing and deal with your grief."

"Don't tell me what to do."

They stared at each other across the desk. His thumbs stopped twirling; the tips rested together.

"It's advice," he said. "Obviously, not an order. If I encouraged you to snoop through his house, would you do the opposite?"

"Probably." She smiled to imply she was joking, and really she was. "I swear I'll give it up, after tonight."

"Why do I doubt that?" His wry expression returned. "So, have we broken up?"

"I don't know."

"Let's keep it ambiguous."

She followed Isabelle up Felix's stairs, pausing at the middle floor for a peek at the master bedroom. The gold and maroon colors, king-sized brass bed, plumped pillows, and chaise lounge screamed Callie's decor. Felix had given Callie and Dimitri this space until she bought the house in Riverdale. If Felix had loved her, it seemed a bit kinky of him to preserve it as a shrine.

The clunky old computer was gone from the front den. The other front room contained a maze of boxes the police would have searched if they were looking at probable murder instead of probable suicide. The boxes were labeled in felt pen. She passed over the one marked "university essays" and opened "Saskatchewan," where Felix was born and grew up. Inside were Matchbox cars, a Slinky, and assorted balls: a football, soccer ball, basketball, and baseball. Leaving Isabelle to collect her belongings in the attic, Paula sat on the hall floor between the two front rooms and zoomed the mini cars to the master bedroom door. The Corvette did a triple flip.

Isabelle came down the stairs carrying her box of movies and CDs. "Cool. I used to play with those when I was a kid." She dropped to the floor and grabbed a mini pickup truck. Paula wandered back to the box-filled room. What if Felix's sister threw out those boxes without checking the memorabilia inside? That's what Paula would do if she had a packrat brother. Searching through them would help the overworked police. How was that for a rationalization? So many boxes. Where to start? At university, where his crush on Callie began and he formed a close group of friends.

Paula lugged the "university essays" box to the hall. It turned out to be full of yellowed newspaper clippings on subjects ranging from Saskatoon berries to travel destinations to racing cars to Barbie dolls to, not surprisingly, guns. These were probably ideas for magazine pieces. Evidently, the box labels didn't necessarily match the contents.

Isabelle zoomed two cars across the hall and squealed at their mid-air collision.

Paula slid the first box to the hall corner by the den, carried an unmarked one from the room and plunked it beside Isabelle. "Since you want to work for me, stop playing and look through this."

"For what?"

"I don't know."

Kneeling, Isabelle opened the flap and pulled out a bottle of Old Spice cologne. She screwed off the top and sniffed. "Phew."

Paula smiled. "My great-aunt gave my dad a bottle of that for his birthday every year. He recycled it at his Christmas gift exchange at work. I wouldn't think it would be Felix's taste either, assuming he'd ever wear cologne."

"Hey." Isabelle held up a wallet. "I need a new one."

"We aren't taking anything."

"It's not like Felix can use it now."

"It's a matter of ethics." Was snooping ethical? "Put everything back and pile the finished boxes in the corner so they don't get mixed up with the ones we haven't searched through yet."

The next box was full of 1960s car and *Playboy* magazines. If time weren't limited, the *Playboys* would be interesting to browse. The plan was to drive Isabelle to Erin's house tonight. They couldn't be too late; Erin had an early class tomorrow morning.

An hour later, about a third of the boxes were piled in the hall corner. Paula stretched and rubbed the small of her back.

Isabelle opened a box filled with books on Eastern religions. "Who'd have thought Felix would be into this junk? You learn a lot about him from what's here."

"And from what isn't here. We haven't found one single thing related to Callie, the so-called love of his life. If I'd carried a torch for thirty years, I'd keep sentimental things connected to my loved one over car magazines."

Isabelle disappeared into the box room. "This one's too heavy," she said. "Since half of them are in the hall now, there's space to sit down here."

Paula joined her. She took a light box from the top of the tall pile.

Seated lotus-style, Isabelle opened the box of university texts. She removed the musty books one by one, turned each one upside down, shook it, and scrutinized every scrap of paper that fell out. If she applied the same focus to insurance claims, hiring her might turn out to not be a horrible mistake. Paula's box contained a crunched sombrero and photographs. One showed a man, aged about thirty, wearing the sombrero in an outdoor market. It must have been taken on a trip to Mexico. Was that slim man with the head of bushy, blond hair really Felix? Isabelle squinted at the photo and agreed it was. Another shot showed him with an unknown woman on a palm-treed beach. Black and white photos went back to his childhood. Something bumped downstairs.

Paula looked up. "Is that Felix's sister? Vincelli didn't say she'd be coming."

"I'll check."

Isabelle thudded down the stairs. Paula closed the box. If it was the sister, she would imply they had found the boxes already out in the hall, where the cops had left them after their presumed search. She leafed through the pictures of little Felix, a curly-headed boy with mischievous eyes. In some, he posed with his sisters, two older, one younger. What was keeping Isabelle? Should Paula have let her go down there alone? Footsteps sounded on the stairs and approached the room.

Isabelle stopped in the doorway. "I couldn't see anything."

"Might have been the furnace."

Isabelle held out two apples. "It's all there was in the fridge. They're kind of wrinkled."

Paula wiped her hands on her skirt. "My hands are covered with dust. Yours are, too. We'll wash them along with the apples."

The wizened fruit flesh tasted better than she had expected. Hard work must have piqued her appetite. She wouldn't mind a coffee break or a shot of vodka from Felix's stash downstairs, if the cops hadn't taken it for evidence, but stopping would kill her momentum. From a box labeled "work distractions," Isabelle pulled out a Rubik's cube.

"What is this?" she said.

"You haven't seen one before? You twist the colored shapes to get a single color on each side. We don't have time to fool around with that." She would have loved to try.

Isabelle tossed the cube. It bounced down the bamboo floor. She started working on a metal puzzle, losing her focus for the task at hand. Who could blame her? Paula sat down to examine her box full of paper. Her ass ached on the hardwood. Across the hall was a comfortable bed. Why hadn't she thought of it before? She carried the box to Callie's and Dimitri's bedroom and plumped the pillows against the headboard. She sank into the mattress. "Ahhh."

The top essay was titled, "Jay Gatsby and Billy Budd: American Dreamers." It made sense that Felix, a journalist, would have majored in English. Term papers underneath analyzed classic novels, poems, and

Shakespeare plays. At university, Paula had avoided literature as much as possible. Wading through those essays now would be torture.

Spinning, "a novel-in-progress." She turned over the title page and read the first line: *The day was golden.* She finished the paragraph. This wasn't a school assignment. She skimmed the page and went on to the next and next. Her heart raced to *The End.*

"Isabelle," she shouted. "Isabelle. We found it."

Chapter Twenty-seven

Pre-dawn sky silhouetted her crabapple tree, now bare of all but the most tenacious leaves. Paula sipped coffee, waiting for Detective Vincelli to arrive. When she called him last night, he said he would pick up the manuscript around seven o'clock, on his way to the station.

She flipped the corners of the sixteen pages, now wrinkled from so many readings that she could recite key passages by heart. The manuscript's date stared up from the title page. October, 1979. Felix would have been in his late twenties. Evidently, he had set out to write a book, but rushed the story to the end. The result was a novel synopsis in semi-legible handwriting with numerous misspellings and crossed out words. The first pages chronicled an idyllic boyhood spent shooting gophers in wheat fields that led to Felix's love affair with guns. *I blame the Y-chromosome for inspiring my passion for shiny cylinders that go "pow" and explode with the force of death.*

A creak down the hall made Paula turn. She hoped it wasn't Isabelle waking up. After her first skim of the story, Paula had read it aloud to Isabelle to make sure she wasn't exaggerating its significance. She phoned Detective Vincelli's cell and caught him at home, apparently watching TV. She summarized Felix's story and their discovery of it. Vincelli didn't see an urgent need for her to drop it off at the station and said he would stop by for it this morning on his way to work.

No more sounds. With luck, Isabelle would sleep through Vincelli's visit. Paula had told her he wouldn't be coming until eight o'clock, so Paula and Vincelli could have a quick, serious talk without Isabelle butting in. It might help that Paula had disrupted Isabelle's sleep at 3:00 AM to use the copier in the den. Paula would have a copy of the manuscript to peruse during the day. A second one lay in her underwear drawer for safe-keeping. The police would get the original sitting on the kitchen table.

She refreshed her coffee and got out a bowl of grapes—she'd served the same thing to Vincelli and his partner Novak during their first visit here—how long ago was that?—eleven days. Grapes were fitting since this new evidence might bring about the end of the case. One thing was sure: Felix hadn't murdered Callie for love. If he had murdered, it was to cover up a thirty-year old crime, and odds were the killer wasn't him. Three or four others had equal motives.

For the umpteenth time, she turned over the title page. While he had changed the names, clearly Felix had modeled the story characters on himself and his university friends. He was the unnamed "I" narrator, a sensitive, aspiring writer. Callie and Owen, her rock-singer boyfriend, were Cassie and Ozzy, two non-students living in the house. The character named Kendall seemed loosely based on Kenneth. Samantha, an architecture student, might be a composite of Sam and Anne. Who was the sixth resident named Merritt? A friend who had moved away after university?

She flipped to page six, where the narrator introduces the street kid. *The boy told us he was sixteen. He looked younger and we didn't ask. He was skinny and short, with bright yellow dyed hair. He wore bellbottom jeans and scuffed cowboy boots. He said he had run away from back east. We didn't ask from where.*

The gay student, Merritt, had brought the boy to the house. That was the moment Merritt came out to the group. Felix, sleeping in the bedroom next to Merritt and the boy, got to listen to moans and bed creaks all night. A virgin, Felix wished he was getting it on. *During the day, the boy helped Cassie with the cooking and cleaning and grocery shopping.* The story really began about a week after the boy's arrival. *It was a Saturday night. We were all home, which was rare. Usually Samantha was out on a date. Cassie and Ozzy had a music gig. I often went to movies with friends. Kendall did things like play chess. That night, he was studying in the basement. Cassie, Ozzy, Samantha, and I were in the living room listening to music, burning incense and smoking up. Cowboy boots stomped toward us, from the hall. Merritt followed the boy. They got into a screaming match. Merritt explained the boy had dropped acid.*

"*Is there any left?*" *Ozzy asked.*

Acid was another thing I was afraid to try.

Paula took off her reading glasses. She got up to microwave her coffee. The wall clock said seven ten. Vincelli should be here any second. The microwave hummed. Felix described the boy as moving his arms over his torso and legs, moaning that he was full of holes. *Merritt ordered him out of the house. Cassie said they couldn't kick him out on the street.* "*That's where he came from and where he belongs,*" *Merritt said.* Paula didn't know

Merritt, but the others sounded true to their real-life counterparts. Twice, Felix had slipped into Callie's real name.

The boy ducked into Felix's bedroom and emerged with the box of guns Felix had stashed under his bed. He'd locked the box and locked the bullets in another box in the closet, but had used obvious combinations: Callie's birth date and gun caliber numbers. The boy had figured them out. He was obviously smart. *"I know everyone's secrets,"* he had taunted them in the living room.

Paula took her coffee from the microwave. In her rush back to the table, she spilled coffee drops on the linoleum. She rubbed them clean with her stocking foot. In the manuscript, she found the line where the boy sat cross-legged on the floor, pulling guns from the box. *Smith and Wesson Model 10 revolver in .38 Special . . . Colt Woodsman semi-automatic in .22 caliber, the "Woody," the first gun I ever bought, my sentimental favorite.*

"Are they loaded?" Callie asked.

"Of course not," I said. "I'm not stupid."

The boy pointed a revolver at me. Samantha wrestled it away from him.

Such wrestling seemed a Sam/masculine action. Merritt refused to take a gun until the boy threatened to tell his father he was gay. Cassie accepted a Colt Pocket Hammerless. Why? Because she was stoned? Because the little gun seemed like a toy? Because everyone else was doing it and, like the others, she didn't know it was loaded? Because she was attracted to the danger?

The boy gave Ozzy the prettiest gun. "You're all glitter, all on the surface. You're empty inside and you know it."

"Shut up with the insults," Samantha said. "Loser."

The boy smirked at her. "You're ugly and fat. Porky Pig."

I giggled, from nervousness and marijuana and, I admit, a little cruelty toward Samantha, who had confessed to Cassie she had been fat as a child. The other kids ridiculed her, calling her Porky Pig. Her mother put her on diets. She had slimmed down, but told Cassie she still felt like the fat girl and only did it with her boyfriend in the dark. Samantha glared at Cassie for telling her secret.

Had Anne or Sam been fat kids? Anne was slim now. In all their talk during workouts, Anne hadn't said she was ever overweight. Sam had a husky build and kept his weight down by working out. Even though it was over between them, Paula hated to think Sam was involved in this grubby crime. It would also give him a double motive to murder Felix: to both protect the secret as well as his son from being accused of the Callie's murder.

The boy rotated toward me. "You're a coward."

I stepped back. Someone else giggled. Did everyone know? I was a coward at heart, scared to try hard drugs, scared to have sex, afraid of everything.

"Stop this," Cassie said.

The boy whirled. "'Stop pretending you're so nice. You're greedy and ambitious, like the rest of them."

Paula looked up at the clock. 7:20 AM. Vincelli had better arrive soon or they might have Isabelle barging in. Outside the window, pink streaked through a puffy cloud. She returned to the six youths circling the boy. Kendall had heard the commotion from the basement and had come up.

"We ought to teach him a lesson," someone said.

I don't know who started it. The room was black, except for light from incense and reefer smoke. We raised our guns one by one and closed in on the boy.

"No, no, no." The boy spun, aiming his gun wildly. He started to cry.

"The big talker's a baby," someone said.

We moved closer. I bumped Callie's shoulder. A gun blasted. Smoke lit up the boy falling down. Another blast. My arm collapsed. Everything went silent and dark.

Felix had claimed his arm had been injured in a hunting mishap. This must have been the real cause. Paula skimmed to the part where he woke up in his bed. The gay friend was bandaging his arm. Felix fell asleep and resurfaced to find Samantha on a chair next to his bed. She told him the boy had been killed. They had put the body and guns in garbage bags, which they dumped in the Bow River. The boy was a runaway, she said, and wouldn't be missed. The others were removing the living room carpet, which was drenched in blood. Monday, they would varnish the hardwood underneath. The carpet had been crap, anyway. The landlord would find the new floor an improvement.

Pain seared Felix-the-narrator's arm. He argued they should call the cops.

"None of us wants to go to trial or jail," Samantha said. "That's why we can't take you to hospital. They'd question the bullet in your arm. The only problem will be if it gets infected."

Paula got up to re-zap her coffee. The roommates managed to dispose of the body without the neighbors noticing. None of the neighbors had made friends with the boy. If they thought about him at all, they would assume he was a newcomer, like Cassie and Ozzy, crashing with the group. The roommates were reasonably sure the boy hadn't been in touch with his family back east. To their knowledge, he had mailed no letters and placed no calls. This was long before e-mail and cell phones. Even if the body washed up, nothing would connect it to the group.

Felix portrayed himself as being against the cover-up. Was that self-white-wash or had that been the truth?

"We'll tell the cops we were playing around," I said. "We were stoned."

"On illegal drugs," Samantha argued.

"No one does jail for pot."

"Kendall says we'd be charged with manslaughter," she said. "You do jail for that. The case would drag on all winter. We'd flunk out of school and have criminal records. Who would hire us?"

"I don't want a real job. I want to write."

"Think of the rest of us. Think of Merritt. They print trial details in the papers. The whole world will know he's a fag."

The whole world would know I was a coward and virgin. That seemed worse than doing jail and losing my guns.

The incident changed all their lives. Felix-the-narrator quit school, moved to Italy, and became a novelist. Ozzy took off to avoid the mess. He later committed suicide, which Owen did in real life. Was that partly caused by guilt from this event? Kendall went into law to fight crime. Cassie turned to Kendall for support and eventually married him. Samantha got pregnant. Felix wrote, *She called it an accident, but I wondered if she did it on purpose, creating a new life to replace the one we'd snuffed out.* The gay roommate went into medicine, as he had planned, but rather than pursue a lucrative career he went on to treat the down-and-out in San Francisco. Was that his response to the guilt, a more positive one than Ozzy's?

The doorbell rang. She returned the pages she had been reading to the top of the pile.

Vincelli apologized for being late. "Something came up."

His dark suit and white shirt were wrinkled, his chin so bristly she wondered if he was growing a beard. His bare, shaved head needed trimming.

In the kitchen, she poured them each coffee. He selected the chair under the clock, reversing their positions of the previous visits. It threw her off balance to take his usual place facing the sink. Was this his point? She slid Felix's manuscript across the table. She had summarized the story over the phone.

Vincelli looked at the title page. "'Spivving'?"

"That's 'Spinning,'" Paula said. "Felix's writing's hard to read."

"I'll say. It's worse than Novak's." He returned to the page. "'Spinning, a novel-in-progress. Fiction.'"

"The narrator grew up in Saskatchewan, like Felix," she said. "He's a writer, a gun nut, and had a crush on a character much like Callie. All the others resemble his university friends. He barely disguises the names. There's one named Merritt the others might have lost touch with, as people do after they finish school. If the shooting happened, it gives the lot of them, including Felix, a motive for murder."

Vincelli leaned back in his chair, his thumbs stuck in his belt, gunslinger-style. His jacket flipped back, revealing his gun. "My partner when I walked the beat dabbled in fiction. He called police work grist for his mill. I appeared in one of his stories as a character named Matt, a womanizing cop on the take. Definitely fiction." He grinned.

A fully grown head of hair would nicely frame his handsome face that was irritating her at the moment.

He tapped the belt with his large fingers. "I told my partner about a scrape my cousin and I got into when we were kids. He blew our prank into a crime that would bar me forever from police work. Borrowing your uncle's car for a joy ride is not the same as driving while drunk, killing a pedestrian and leaving the scene. I'd hate to have that story held up against me."

"I know all that, but—"

"Luckily, Novak can barely churn out police reports." He chuckled.

She glanced at the manuscript. "You don't think this is worth investigating?"

"I'll decide after I read it." He reached for a grape.

"Will you have time today?"

"We've got a murder case going to trial. We're short-staffed. My partner—"

"I know. Novak's off with a bum leg. Somebody else is on vacation. Your staff sergeant has been replaced by a coyote."

"What I'm saying is, don't get your hopes up about this fiction changing the course of the investigation."

"I hope you'll re-interview Kenneth, Anne, and Sam."

"If it's appropriate, you can be sure we will."

"And look for Merritt in San Francisco. It would be easy to get the name of his real life counterpart from one of the others."

"Don't you go doing that. Such interference could destroy the case."

"I know. I'm not that stupid." Paula sipped her coffee to hide any anger in her face. She debated if she should share her ideas while he was in this haughty cop mood. There might not be another chance if he dismissed the manuscript as valid evidence. "I've come up with some theories about the various people in Felix's story," she said.

"Shoot." Again the gunslinger mode.

"Some are obvious. The Samantha character could be a composite of Anne and Sam, although would Sam be so convinced of his son's guilt if he knew all these others had equally strong motives? Why would any of them murder Callie after all this time? I thought about that all night. Callie talked to Dimitri about guilt. People saw her arguing with Felix. Was she pressuring her friends to come forward with the truth about that old crime? If so, why now, after keeping silent for thirty years?"

He stared, chewing grapes. She was rambling, but couldn't stop. "A year ago, Callie found religion, after ignoring it most of her life. It could be that Dimitri got her back to the church. Religion is core to his life. They must have discussed it."

"Are you saying her newfound religion prompted her guilt?"

"She also had a health scare, a spot on her mammogram during the winter. That can prompt people to make amends."

"We'll investigate all possibilities," Vincelli said. "That reminds me, we located Felix's laptop. He gave it to a friend on Friday to fix a bug."

"Damn." A missing laptop would have pointed to murder, not suicide.

"The friend also told us that Felix wrote first drafts in longhand. That jibes with our forensic expert findings. So far, there's nothing on his computers related to his alleged column."

"Obviously, you would have checked wastebaskets for discarded paper."

"There was a can by his desk. Empty."

"Don't you find that odd, given the clutter of mail on the kitchen counter? Does Felix strike you as the type who would empty his wastebasket before everything was spilling out? Did you check his other garbage?"

"We know how to do our job." His lip twitched.

She would rather he show anger at her arrogance than amusement. "I think his killer took his earlier draft attempts from the wastebasket."

"Why are you so determined to prove us wrong?"

"Why are you so determined to wrap up this case? Is it because the acting staff sergeant wants this settled on his watch, so he'll impress the higher-ups and get the permanent position if and when it becomes vacant?" She waited for his denial or annoyance with her uppity remark.

He scraped back his chair. "I've got to get going. The staff meeting starts at seven thirty."

"Will you bring the manuscript to the meeting?"

"I'd prefer to read it first." He headed for the hall.

"Aren't you taking the story with you?" she asked.

He halted and turned around. "I forgot."

"You will try to read it this afternoon?"

He scooped up the rumpled pages. "I may get it typed up first."

"How long will that take?"

"Like I said, don't expect too much."

Chapter Twenty-eight

While driving around the city to meetings with claimants, Paula wondered if there was a way to get Kenneth or Anne to admit the critical parts of the story were true, without jeopardizing the case. After tossing the candlestick at Sam, she wouldn't approach him again. Only one of those three, at most, was the killer. The others weren't involved in Callie's and Felix's deaths, unless they had acted together, an unlikely event. The easiest one to talk to would be Anne. Paula could just show up for their usual workout-chat and maneuver their conversation to the subject.

She drove across the Bow River. Being early for her meeting in the city's northwest, she detoured past Fit For Life. The bright blue building sparkled in the afternoon sun. She stopped the car across the street. No way could she face her friend who might be guilty of horrible deeds without a plan. As for Kenneth, she was sure now that he had kept his dog with him yesterday to conceal his facial expressions. He knew Felix hadn't killed himself for love and she would bet money Felix had revealed his plan to "out" the murder in his newspaper column when he visited Kenneth Friday night. Kenneth may have told the others Felix intended to expose the truth behind Callie's death. It was a stupid move on Felix's part. He must have been too drunk to think the consequences through.

Of the three or four suspects, Felix seemed the one least likely to be concerned about the story of the old murder coming out. He might even view a criminal charge or jail time as grist for his writing mill. That was why she didn't believe he was the killer. She wasn't clinging to the case for psychological reasons, as Hayden had suggested, or out of a stubborn determination to be right. And what if Merritt, whoever he was, had come out of hiding and was bumping off his co-conspirators one by one, either to silence the old crime forever or for a crazy sense of justice that would end with him taking his own life? That was a wild theory she would not share with Vincelli. He would say she'd gone over the top, but anything was possible.

Paula approached the claimant's house on a hill. The Rockies stretched along the horizon. Her cell phone rang. She pulled to the curb to take Hayden's call.

"I found some evidence at Felix's house last night," she said. "The cops say they will check it out. I'm not sure I trust them to."

"Why not?"

"I don't know. It's a piece of writing Felix labeled fiction."

"Writing about what?"

"An old crime that may have happened when Felix was in university. It's too complicated to get into over the phone."

He paused. "If you want someone to talk it over with, I'll be at the office tonight."

Sweet of him. Did he really think they could get back together after Sam and all the rest? Possibly they could.

The claimant shook her hand, his too-satisfied grin a stabbing reminder that she had settled his hail damage claim too high. She suspected some of the damage was pre-existing and not due to hail, but hadn't been in the mood to argue. The creep had lucked out, but thought he had put one over on her. When all this was over, her professional self would be back. For now, thank God, today's meetings were ended. Since it was past rush hour, the quickest route home was through downtown. She took Memorial Drive to the Louise Bridge. Should she phone Vincelli to enquire about the day's progress with the case? Stopping at his office might exert more pressure. Police headquarters was on her way.

The security guard said Vincelli was in, but took ages to locate him. Policemen and civilian employees streamed past to the elevator. Finally, he reached Vincelli, who approved her entry to the premises he had hauled her to for questioning after Felix's death.

The receptionist directed her into the large room that looked like any office. No uniforms in Major Crimes. Vincelli's head popped above the last workstation as he stood to greet her. He had his jacket and tie off, his collar open.

"I was in the area," she said, "and wondered if you had any news about the case."

"No more than I told you an hour ago."

"An hour? I haven't seen you since the morning."

"Didn't Isabelle pass my comments on?"

"Isabelle?" She settled in the visitors' chair, prompting him to sit down.

He looked at her across the desk. "She's phoned me it seems like a dozen times today."

"About what?"

"It's always some little thing or other. She thinks she's some God-damn Nancy Drew. Can you find her a job to keep her occupied?"

"She found herself one, in my office."

He blinked in apparent surprise. "Good luck."

His desk phone rang. Not Isabelle again, she hoped.

"Yes . . . no . . . no . . ." he said. "I told you . . ." Something about his tone made her think it was a personal call. Did he have a girlfriend, or a wife? There were no photos in the cubicle. A calendar with a waterfall scene was the only remotely personal item. A handful of papers lay neatly stacked on his desk. He hung up the phone.

"By the way," she said, "have you had a chance to read Felix's story yet?"

"This day has been hairier than I expected." He scanned his uncluttered desk. His cell phone rang. "Excuse me." He took it out of the pouch on his belt. This call appeared related to police work. "Noon tomorrow," he said, jotting the details on his notepad.

He finished the call and apologized for the interruption. "Felix's writing is impossible. I'm waiting for the typed version."

"It shouldn't take long to type it up, if you give it priority."

"We're a busy place, as I've told you, what with people being off."

"I had an idea about that," she said. "Maybe Novak, your partner, could read it while he's recuperating with his leg. I'd be willing to drop it off at his house, if you give me his address."

"Are you out of your mind?"

Her face grew warm. The idea had seemed more brilliant as a mere thought, but it wasn't stupid. "Calgary Police is paying Novak's salary. Why not get something for it? That's what we'd do in my office."

"We aren't a two-bit insurance firm."

"You don't have to insult me."

"I'm sorry." Not looking too sorry, he clasped his hands on his desk as they waited out a third telephone ring. "There's no time to discuss this right now. I've got a staff meeting in ten minutes."

"Your staff meeting was this morning." That sounded accusing. "I mean—"

"When we're busy there can be two or three a day."

"I know you're busy. That's why I suggested—"

He stood up. "I can't miss this meeting." His tone was almost shrill for him. He really was stressed and shaking. His face turned sheepish; as though he was embarrassed he'd lost control—by his standards.

"I am sorry," he said. "It isn't your fault. I have this meeting and . . . I promise to phone you about any further developments. Pass that along to Isabelle. You'll have to trust us to handle this. Now, I've got to get to that meeting."

She doubted the staff meeting's existence. Why was everyone accusing her of mistrust? She trusted everyone, she decided on the way down the elevator to her car, except for overworked policemen and suspected killers. And men who slept with you and blew you off the next day. Greedy insurance claimants. Cheating ex-husbands. Isabelle, who might blab to the wrong person about Felix's story. Who was left? Her daughters, her co-workers, Alice and Nils, and Hayden, who had offered to listen. This past week Hayden had given her lots of advice, most of it annoying and spawned by his jealousy. Yet, every time, it had helped her decide what she wanted to do.

Hayden listened to her garbled recap of the story with surprising attention, considering the litter of work on his desk.

"There's a copy in your briefcase?" he said when she paused for a breath. "Can I have a look at it?" He pushed the paper and files in front of him out of the way.

She dug out the story. "You can skip the first five pages about wheat and little boys playing with guns."

He put on his reading glasses, squared the corners of the sixteen-page stack and turned over the title page.

"I know his writing's hard to read," Paula said.

"I've seen worse."

Aside from the hum of florescent lights, the office was silent. All his co-workers had left for the day, even though it was only 8:00 PM. That must be some kind of record for a law firm. He skimmed page six and the next page, turning the sheets over to a neat, upside down pile.

"Are you really reading it?" she said.

He nodded at the page. Her gaze strayed to the windows concealed by horizontal blinds he had closed against the afternoon sun, now gone. Beneath the blinds, legal texts filled his bookshelves topped by photos of his daughter and son, his first grandchild, and her. His kids lived on the east and west coasts. The plan was she would meet them at Christmas. Paula turned back to his desk. Hayden's reading pace slowed. From the size of the remaining pile, he had hit the story meat.

"Do you—?"

He raised his hand, palm toward her, not looking up. His brow creased. Was it possible that, unlike Vincelli, he could see the value in pursuing this?"

To occupy her hands, she fished the music box out from under a pile of papers. His souvenir from New Orleans, a city she'd love to visit some-day. *The day was golden* Felix's story began. She tried to picture a young Hayden beneath the graying hair, filled-out jowls, and deepening facial creases. Like the rest of them, he had once been a student, with hopes and dreams. He had known Kenneth at university.

The discard pile was growing. Over halfway through, he would have reached the shooting of the boy. His forehead was pale, his reading pace snail-slow.

She set the paperweight on his desk. "It's hard to believe—"

He seemed stuck on the last page; the paper wavered in his hands.

"What's the matter?" She hadn't seen him shake like that since Sunday, when he came to her house and picked up the monkey-shaped candle. "Monkey in the middle," she had thought he said. In the story, the circle closed in on the boy in the middle. The character she assumed was Kenneth later became a lawyer. If Samantha was a composite of Sam and Anne, that other character might be a composite of Kenneth and—

Hayden's forehead glowed with sweat.

"You were there," she said.

He took off his glasses. Fear, resignation, everything but denial rushed over his face. The morning of Callie's death, they both had come to their offices alone. The cops had questioned him, checked for an alibi. She and Hayden had joked about it. When Felix died, she was with Sam and Hayden was—?

Hayden pushed back his chair. She grabbed her purse. He sprinted around his desk and caught her at the door, thudding it back to the wall.

His arm shot out to block her exit.

"Let me go." Paula pushed her shoulder into his rigid arm. She tried to duck the other way. Hayden's right arm wedged her to the door. His chin scraped her nose. She breathed in his odor of sweat along with the onions he must have eaten for dinner.

"Come back and sit down," he said.

"I'm not crazy." She had to get herself down that corridor, past the empty workstations, to the elevator, out the building door.

"I want to explain," he said.

"And then kill me like you murdered Callie and Felix?" This was surreal. Not Hayden, her Hayden couldn't be Callie's killer.

"You're safer here than anywhere else tonight," he said.

She raised her purse to shove him away. He squeezed it between them. The clasp dug into her chest.

"If I wanted to kill you, which I don't, it wouldn't be here," he said. "The cops would link it to me in a minute."

Was there a gun in his desk drawer, on his belt? Would he press it to her back, lead her out of the office, and kill her on some anonymous street? His beard stubble grated her nose. How could she have been with him for six months, shared his bed, and missed this whole side of him?

"Who are you?" she said.

"Don't you see? The cops have the original of Felix's story. If you're found dead anywhere tonight, they'll make the connection and investigate to the limits, starting with me, your jilted ex. I'd be insane to murder you knowing that."

"Are you insane?"

"You shouldn't need to ask."

"Were you there when the boy was shot?"

"Yes and no."

"That doesn't make sense." None of this did.

"I'll let you go, if that's what you want." His grip didn't slacken. "But if you call the police, I'll deny everything and make up a story to explain your accusations against me. I imagine they've pegged you as someone hysterical and obsessed."

She shoved his arm. How could she escape when he was stronger than her?

"I'll tell you what I know because it might save your life," he said.

"How?"

"By preventing you from poking your nose into things you know nothing about."

"Things that happened in Felix's story?"

His dark eyes studied her face. "You were right. There's a conspiracy going on. It will block the cops from solving the case."

He dropped his arms. She froze to the door. He turned and walked toward his desk, shoulders slumped, looking so normal, so Hayden, behind his cluttered desk. The insane could look normal. So could sociopaths.

She held her purse like a shield. "Who's involved in this conspiracy?"

"Kenneth, Anne," he counted them off on his fingers, "Sam, his son, me and, I'm hoping, you."

"Was Sam there when they shot the boy?"

Hayden crossed his arms. "It's always about Sam."

He wasn't reaching for a gun. Paula could make a clear break down the corridor to her car and home, where she would bolt the doors and stay light years away from anyone connected to this case. Sam would be definitely out of her life, as would Anne, her friend. She would send Isabelle packing to Montreal. With luck, she would return to her life from before, aside from the absence of Hayden and a nagging wish to know exactly what had happened.

Hayden looked up at her, like a friend, not a lunatic or cold-hearted killer. "You'll have to swear to keep all I tell you a secret. No spilling it to the cops or Isabelle or Sam."

"If Sam's a conspirator, isn't he already in the loop?"

Hayden raised an eyebrow, his sign he wouldn't say another word unless she came back to the chair. She was free to run down the hall, but this was Hayden. She had to believe he wouldn't kill her.

Chapter Twenty-nine

Hayden moved the folders and papers to the side table. His penholder, jazz music box, and Felix's manuscript were the only objects on the desk between Paula and him. She reconsidered the option of running down the corridor to her car. His jaw shaded by five-o'clock shadow, which she had once found attractive, now felt threatening. He squared the manuscript corners to form the sixteen pages into a solid block.

"You know Kenneth and I were on the debating team at university," he said, pushing the top sheets out of alignment. "One day, at the start of our final year, we got to talking about chess. He invited me to his place for a game on Saturday night. I wasn't doing anything." His voice trailed. "I could use a coffee." He stared as though he expected her to fetch it for him.

"Get it yourself."

His heavy eyebrows shot up.

"What do you expect after you brutalized me?"

He rolled back his chair to stand. She held her breath, half-expecting him to grab the music box and attack. His walk to the thermos on his legal bookcase seemed slower than normal. Was that a wobble in his leg? She hoped so. Even with the door ajar, she felt claustrophobic. She asked him to open the blinds.

As Hayden carried their coffee mugs back, he described his arrival at Kenneth's house. His recollection was that Kenneth answered the door and took him downstairs without introducing him to his roommates. Hayden and Kenneth played chess in the basement rec room while music, laughter and the scent of patchouli and marijuana wafted from the main floor. Here he was on Saturday night playing a nerd game. "I wished Kenneth would suggest we join the fun," he said with a wan smile.

Paula realized why her coffee tasted too heavy and sweet. Hayden had mixed up the mugs. He continued his story, not appearing to notice his coffee contained only milk.

Shouting upstairs distracted them from the game; they heard a loud blast. He and Kenneth ran up to the living room full of people shrieking and running around. "The smoke lit up what I thought was a scarlet blanket crumpled on the floor. Then, I realized it was a body covered in blood. My stomached heaved. I ran out to the yard and puked. Got to the bus stop and home and didn't tell anyone anything. Ever." He spilled coffee onto the manuscript.

"Why not?"

He blotted the coffee with his handkerchief. "Kenneth stayed in there, mopping up the mess. I suppose I felt incompetent, in comparison."

"Are you telling me you and he weren't involved in the shooting? Felix's story placed Kenneth, a law student like you, there." Her hand shook. She glanced at the dark sky outside his windows. How did she know he wasn't lying?

"Kenneth took control of the cover-up," Hayden said. "As an accessory, he could be charged along with the rest of them."

"Why would he do that?"

"I think, from all he said, he was secretly in love with Callie and did it for her."

"Said when? Have you talked to him recently?"

Hayden realigned the manuscript. He rolled the corner of the top sheet, which was covered with damp, brown smudges. "I met Kenneth a few days after the shooting, at the debating club. He said they took care of it. I didn't ask questions. I think we both wanted to avoid the whole thing. We avoided each other from then on, too."

"I hadn't known you played chess until Kenneth mentioned it at the funeral."

"I don't. To this day, the sight of a pawn makes me nauseous." Hayden added that he assumed, or convinced himself, that taking care of it meant they had called the police, who judged the incident an accident, which he'd thought it was.

"Wasn't it?" Paula said. "They didn't know the guns were loaded."

"They knew."

"In Felix's story—"

"The boy told them he'd loaded the guns."

"Why?"

"Who knows? He was a troubled kid. Probably self-destructive."

"I mean, why would the others fool around with loaded—"

"Young people can be stupid, especially in groups when they're doped on drugs."

"I can't believe Callie—"

"That's why she never told you about it, Kenneth thinks. She was so ashamed she could barely discuss it with him."

Paula banged her mug on the desk. "The day after Callie's murder, the cops questioned you, in this very room. Did you tell them any of this?"

"I didn't think it was relevant."

"Had they known, they would have grilled that whole group. Felix, for one, might have caved. It would have saved him."

"Don't you think I feel guilty about that?" His jowls quivered. "I swear to God, it didn't occur to me this old event was connected to Callie's murder until two days ago, when I saw that monkey-shaped candle at your house. It reminded me of a game . . ."

Monkey in the middle, he had said. Hear no evil, see no evil, speak no evil. His body had been shaking. Why hadn't she clued in? She got up and tottered on rubbery legs to the corner windows. Fourteen stories down, street lights fanned south and west through blackness. They tapered at the suburban fringe. She heard Hayden's footsteps behind her.

"When the cops were here, it did cross my mind to tell them." His low tones flowed with his onion breath to her ears. "To be honest, I was ashamed, too, by my weakness and not doing anything. I knew there was something fishy about Kenneth's 'take care of it' remark."

"Your response was normal."

"Would you have puked and run away?"

She pictured Felix dead on his recliner chair. "I might have puked at that young age."

"And told your parents or someone about it, or more likely, marched back into the house and helped deal with the mess."

"I don't know." Even at twenty, she couldn't imagine herself not getting involved. "My way's not the only way."

"You do give that impression sometimes," he said.

Her stomach knotted. Hayden's words echoed her daughters' complaint that she expected everyone to live up to her standards. Paula had always answered, "What's so wrong with that?" What was wrong was that Hayden had withheld information from the cops and Callie had kept the grubby crime secret for thirty-one years because Callie and Hayden believed, if Paula knew, she would judge them harshly. And she might have. Wasn't she judging them now? What if one of her daughters got into a jam some day and, fearing her judgment, didn't come out in the open or turn to her for help?

Hayden segued to his first meeting with Callie. A few months after the shooting, she showed up to watch a debate. Kenneth introduced her as his girlfriend. "I remember wondering how a geek like him got someone so hot." Hayden next saw Callie about five years later, at a charity ball, shortly after his marriage. She looked stunning in her off-the-shoulder dress, her hair up in a French twist, jewels dripping from her ears.

"Don't tell me you were in love with her, too?" Paula said.

"Callie wasn't my type. When she saw me, she turned white. It was so obvious my wife later asked if I'd dated her in university. As if I could have gotten a girl like that."

"Thanks."

He fluffed his gray sideburns, mock-preening. "Now that I'm older and distinguished, I got someone better; for a while, at least."

Paula's face warmed from his compliment and vulnerability. Hayden had withheld his information, in part, because it might have cost him her respect. Were she more forgiving of human failings, he might have come forward, preventing Felix's death. She deserved a share of his blame for that, although she couldn't help being who she was. Could she?

Hayden figured Kenneth had told Callie about his presence at the shooting and seeing him reminded her of the dreadful event. "It still didn't occur to me that Callie had been there. That was probably why she avoided you all summer, so she wouldn't have to deal with me, the ghost from her past, the witness."

The ring of the telephone ripped through the room. Both waited for his voice mail to pick up. This would explain why Callie had chatted so intently with Hayden's nephew the night Paula and Hayden met, at the theater. Callie's avoidance tactic had left Paula alone with Hayden to talk and connect. Strange, how that had worked out.

The shrill rings ended and gave way to the hum of florescent lights. Hayden said Paula's talk of wanting to poke around Felix's house made him worry she would poke too much. Last night, he went to Kenneth's to find out if the old shooting was related to Callie's murder or not. Kenneth agreed to tell him the truth in exchange for his not going to the cops.

"I'm surprised he'd be so forthcoming." She stepped back for a better look at Hayden's face for signs he was lying.

"He views you as an old friend and wants to protect you," Hayden said. "If Kenneth has a driving trait, I'd say it's loyalty."

Kenneth had been loyal to Callie to the end, even though she dumped him for Dimitri.

"You'll be pleased to know that Sam is innocent." Hayden stifled a grimace. "Sam couldn't afford to live away from home with the group. Normally, he and Anne would have been out on a date Saturday night, but he was filling in for someone at his restaurant job. Lucky stiff."

Paula's heart relaxed. She was glad Sam had no part in the shooting. Did this mean she was still judging the others for their involvement? "I gather Callie was threatening to come out with the truth?"

"Kenneth blames Dimitri and his religion for dredging up her guilt. There was her health scare last winter."

"A shadow on her mammogram."

"Her big breakup with Dimitri that sent her career plans down the tube. Kenneth wonders if my sudden reappearance pushed her over an edge."

"Good God."

"It all prompted her to confide her worries to Felix. She remembered the boy's name. Kenneth said none of the others did. That was thoughtful of her." Hayden wiped sweat from his flushed forehead. "Felix did an Internet search and found a website set up by a man looking for his long lost uncle, whose details fit the boy. Callie begged Felix to fly with her to Nova Scotia to meet the family. Felix waffled. Kenneth didn't know any of this before Callie's murder. Felix told him . . ."

". . . when he stopped by Kenneth's house the night before he died."

"Kenneth believed, at first, Callie's murder was random. That's why he didn't come forward with this information."

"So he says."

Hayden picked up the coffee thermos, shook it, and returned it to the bookcase. "Felix and Callie talked to Anne, who said going to the family would be admitting to a crime. The family might contact the police, who would then arrest them all. Callie was confused. Kenneth agrees with you that, at the end, she was coming to you for advice."

"I wonder what I would have said." Paula leaned on the bookcase, toppling Hayden's photographs. She liked to think she would have listened sympathetically and offered to fly to Nova Scotia with Callie, if that's what Callie really wanted. But would she have taken the time from her busy life with Hayden, work, and the move to her new home? She re-set the photographs. "After Callie's death, Felix ultimately decided to do the right thing and come out with the truth in his newspaper column."

"And after Felix's death, Kenneth and Anne met. I think there's a reason Kenneth told me about this tête-à-tête and it explains the type of people you're dealing with." Hayden shuffled back to his desk, shoulder hunched.

Paula followed, her legs tired from standing. She sipped the remnants of her coffee: sweet, cool mud.

Hayden clasped his hands on the manuscript. "At their meeting, Kenneth and Anne agreed on a party line: Felix panicked over the old crime coming out and killed Callie. It's possible."

"I don't believe it."

"You know what? Neither do I. During the tête-à-tête, they discussed the friend who had been the boy's lover."

"Merritt in the story?"

"He became a doctor."

"So that part of Felix's story is true."

"After university, the guy got involved in CUSO and other third world benevolent organizations. Kenneth suggested to Anne that if the doctor had murdered Callie, he would have used a medicine to cause a neater death. An injection in the arm or a few drops in a drink can cause a death that appears so natural it might pass an autopsy exam. Anne agreed that would be a smarter method than guns."

Paula shoved away her mug. Was that sugar in her coffee or had he sweetened it with something else? She picked up Hayden's music box.

"I think he told me all that as a threat: if we pursue this, you and I will be bumped off by a medicine that won't be taken as murder."

"You think Kenneth would do this?"

"Or Anne. Whoever was Callie's and Felix's killer. He or she has a huge motive now to keep the old crime quiet."

"Anne has access to her husband's heart and diabetes medication."

"So does Kenneth. He's Anne's husband's best friend and could easily help himself to something from his medicine cabinet." Hayden glanced at his office door. "The buzz from my colleagues in criminal law is the cops don't have enough evidence to arrest anyone for Callie's murder; they need a confession, which they aren't going to get from Kenneth or Anne. Both are logical, strong, and cool. Why would they confess, when any half-baked lawyer could prove the other one had motive and opportunity for the crime? All the lawyer needs is a reasonable doubt."

"Shouldn't the cops at least try?" A mechanical sound startled her. She had absently turned the music box key. The instrumental played "What a Wonderful World."

"I gave Kenneth my word," Hayden said. "We shook hands. In hindsight, I probably should have walked away and gone to the cops. Kenneth's a shrewd negotiator."

"Is a handshake legally binding?"

"I trust Kenneth if he's on my side, but wouldn't want to be the person who betrayed him. He hinted, if I did, he and Anne would say I assisted with the body disposal. Who's left to argue with that?" His voice was hoarse, his sweaty hair stuck up in spikes.

"You have no alibi for Callie's murder." She returned the music box to his desk. "You were here working alone that morning."

"A good lawyer might imply I hooked up with you to keep tabs on Callie." She stroked the coffee mug handle.

"I knew Callie had phoned you that week. If I was in the loop, I would have guessed the reason. I'd know I had to act before she got to you and brought it into the open. It's a neat scenario."

Too neat. She caught herself sipping from the mug; she clunked it back to the desk. Hayden's story was ringing true and yet she didn't trust him. All she had was his word he hadn't been involved in the crime. For all she knew, he and Kenneth had cooked up that chess-playing story and both participated in the shooting, in accordance with Felix's story. She supposed Sam was off the hook, swimming in ignorance. Hayden wouldn't lie to protect him.

"You mentioned a conspiracy," she said. "Kenneth, Anne, you, but why Dimitri and Sam? Is Dimitri protecting Anne, his mother?"

"Sam and Dimitri are unaware of the old crime and are going along with the Felix murder/suicide verdict so the shit doesn't fall on Dimitri."

"If they knew others have motives as strong as Dimitri's . . . I should tell Sam."

"No. If he runs to the cops—"

"I'll tell him not to mention your involvement."

"Do you have such control over Sam?"

She had no control. She sunk back in her chair. "Sam might not go to the cops. He doesn't care about justice. He proved that by not telling them about Callie's involvement with Dimitri and proved it again by letting his best friend take the rap for her murder. All he wants is assurance his son is innocent."

"If Sam has no faith in his son, that's his problem."

"I honestly believe he will be satisfied with knowing the truth."

"Funny, that's what I thought about you." Hayden swiveled toward the stack of papers and files on his side table. "I'm not getting any more work done tonight. Might as well go home. Can I give you a ride?"

Paula stiffened. "My car is parked out front."

"I'll walk you to it." He passed her the manuscript. "I expect you'll want this back."

She returned it to her briefcase. "I don't suppose Kenneth told you about Felix's novel."

"He may not have known about it." He caught her expression. "And don't you ask him about it either. I repeat: stay away from that group."

Paula drove through the empty downtown streets, thinking it wouldn't be fair to Hayden to give the cops his information. He had put himself at risk by going to Kenneth for her sake. It would also be pointless. Best case scenario: the cops investigate and arrest all three—Kenneth, Anne, and Hayden—who hire sharp lawyers to muddy the waters so much that everyone gets off, after years of stress and career ruin for the two who were innocent of Callie's murder. One of those two was probably Hayden. Did it matter who did it? The public was safe; there would be no more killings unless Anne or Kenneth or, she had to admit, Hayden panicked and killed the others off. Could the innocent two be sure that would never happen? Might a murderer wait until this all blew over and seize the first opportunity to bop off the co-conspirators with a needle poke? Why risk a death-bed confession? Murder got easier each time and this person had killed twice, or three times if you count the accidental shooting of the boy, if that was an accident. Knowing their guns were loaded, one of them might have fired on purpose, out of anger at the boy's taunts. And that person might view outsiders with knowledge as a continuing threat: Hayden, her, and even Isabelle. Eliminate anyone who might one day testify. As long as the killer was out there, Paula would never feel safe. If that killer was Hayden . . .

There was a chance it was, but she didn't believe it. Kenneth, too, had always struck her as, essentially, decent, but who knew what he'd done to make his oil business a success? It was surprising he took charge of the cover-up. Had he sensed, if he threw his lot in with the group, Callie would turn to him? Paula hoped he was happy with his devil's pact. Unless Kenneth was the one who killed Callie.

Paula sped along 9th Avenue. Her lit office suggested Nils was working. Should she stop and chew this over with him? No. It was bad enough that she had involved Isabelle, who would soon be moving in with Erin. Isabelle was sure to blab to Erin about their discovery in Felix's house, which would drag Paula's daughter into the mess. Isabelle would have to go back to Montreal, for Erin's and her own safety. She would be disappointed.

The 8th Street railway barrier lights flashed. Paula could be stuck twiddling her thoughts for ten minutes while the train shrugged past. She floored the accelerator and zoomed across the tracks; the barrier bar skimmed her rear bumper. She signaled a left turn. No. She couldn't go home now. It was wrong to keep this information from Sam. For the rest of his life he would believe his son was a killer. Dimitri would lose his father's love and respect. Paula would explain, she would force Sam to realize it was fruitless to tell the cops, who were as boxed in as they were. Nothing further could be done.

Paula cruised past the Stampede grounds. At the C-train tracks, she skidded to a stop. The light rail cars whipped by.

The one thing she might do is devise a scheme to draw out the killer. As Hayden pointed out, even if he were inclined, he wouldn't kill her knowing the cops had possession of Felix's story. Her death tonight, even by apparently natural means, would alert the cops to take the story seriously and they would investigate to the end. The converse was equally true. If she told Anne and Kenneth she had found the story, but hadn't shown it to anyone yet, one of them might try to bump her off before that situation changed. The attempt would prove guilt. The situation could change as early as tomorrow if the cops got off their tails and started sniffing around. There was an opening between now and then for a fabricated bluff, if she could figure out a way to do it without getting herself killed in the process.

Chapter Thirty

His bare feet resting on the coffee table, Sam read the story without commenting or looking up. Paula held her breath, half-expecting him to shake or turn pale as Hayden had. What if this was a trap? Hayden might have lied or been unaware that Sam was present when the group shot the boy. She glanced at the hall and prepared to bolt at the first bead of sweat on his skin. This was paranoia to the max. She couldn't stand it.

The gas fire crackled, giving off no heat she could detect. Wasn't Sam freezing in his T-shirt? Behind him, a beer bottle stood on the baby grand. Had he been playing the piano when she arrived? She'd assumed the piano was for Callie or possibly Dimitri. Sam turned over another manuscript page; he must be into the meat of the story. No comments, no pallor, no shakes. While she had given him the gist of Hayden's revelations, she would have expected some response to seeing the details in print. She eyed her getaway to the front door. Sam was finishing the last page.

"Wow." His voice and face were strangely calm. "But, in a way, I'm not surprised. I've always had this sense of being outside that clique, that there was some kernel I couldn't crack. I thought it was because I'd been away all those years in the States or was raised working class, but, wow."

"I'm sure this is the reason for the murder," Paula said. "One of them did it to hush up the old crime, to avoid embarrassment and prosecution. Dimitri's innocent."

"I guess."

"You don't look too happy about it."

His hand scrunched the papers on the cushion next to him as he got up. She followed him to the baby grand. Sam faced her, his dark eyes solemn.

"It's a reason for murder," he said. "It doesn't let Dimitri off the hook. This is the first time I've said it aloud. My son could have killed her." His voice wavered.

"Why are you so convinced he did? I know Callie dumped him, he stalked her, has a temper—"

"—had access to my father's gun, knew where Callie would be that morning, had a key to Felix's house, was in town when both Callie and Felix died, with no alibis for either murder. I'd say that looks pretty bad."

"It's all circumstantial evidence. I wish the cops had arrested him."

"Why?" He drew back, hitting the piano. The beer bottle tottered.

"Dimitri's arrest would force Anne to come forward. Killer or not, she wouldn't let her son take the rap. She wouldn't have killed Callie—if she did—had she known he might be charged with the crime. I know that much about Anne. You might know more, since you and she were together once."

They had been lovers, had produced a child. Sam had this strange mix of confidence and confusion that could appeal to single-minded person like Anne—and her.

"That was a long time ago." Sam edged across the hardwood to the sideboard. "We were really only together a few months, until she got pregnant and I callously dumped her, if that's what I did." He ran his hands over the crystal candlesticks, one of which Paula had thrown at him during her last visit. "In his story, Felix speculated that Anne got pregnant on purpose. I think, now, he was right. She was also fat as a child. Her mother put her on diets and told friends she wished Anne was as pretty as her sister. Her father was a macho guy who got daughters instead of the sons he wanted. Anne went hunting and fishing, even to the target range with him, but it was never enough. The result was a coldness I didn't see in her at first. I don't think Anne had much use for me, once she was pregnant."

Paula shivered. "You think Anne is the killer."

Sam picked up a candlestick.

She stepped back. A hiss drew her gaze to the fireplace. "If it was Anne, she inadvertently set up her son. She'd have hoped the murder would be settled as a random crime."

"Plan B in her case would be me," Sam said. "Everyone knows the spouse is the automatic suspect. Anne had seen Callie and me together and would have noticed my indifference. She also knows me well enough to guess that after a couple of years I'd lose interest and might be having an affair that the cops would dredge up as evidence."

"Two years is your shelf-life with women?"

"I'd like to believe I could change." He scanned her from head to toe, looking serious and sincere. "I've been doing a lot of thinking, lately. I think I've been overly attached to Dimitri because he was the only person

I was sure would never dump me. Dimitri's grown up. He doesn't need or want the whole of my love any more . . ."

Her cheeks warmed. He said the love-word more easily than she did. This wasn't the time for romance. She forced her thoughts back to business. "We're assuming both Hayden and Kenneth have told the truth."

"I don't think Kenneth did it."

"Why not?"

"He's been too obvious about his anger and undying love for Callie. A smart killer would have covered up his feelings more. Kenneth's smart and shrewd."

"And depressed since Callie left him for Dimitri, so depressed he might have figured he had nothing to lose and didn't care if he got caught. He was the clean-up guy before and had two motives to get rid of Callie. It might have been a love crime, in part, after all."

Sam moved the candlestick from hand to hand. "About your guy Hayden . . ."

She shuffled her feet on the hardwood floor, which felt cool through her stockings. "I'm almost sure he was telling me the truth."

"What about the doctor, who was involved with the boy? He has the biggest motive of all to keep this quiet. It would ruin his humanitarian image. What if he came back?"

"I thought of that, too. Was he at the funeral?"

Sam shook his head. "I only met him a few times when he lived with the group."

Paula pictured the rows of heads in the church from her seat near the back. "No one's mentioned him being there. You'd think they would. He was an old friend."

Sam returned the candlestick to the sideboard. "I don't want it to be Kenneth or Anne. She's the mother of my son; Kenneth's my squash partner."

"I didn't know that," she said. "The point is, Sam, there's nothing we or the cops can do. This is enough, I think, for you to start believing your son is innocent."

"I'm going to talk to Kenneth," Sam said. "I won't involve the rest of you." He paced between the piano and sideboard. "I'll say I found the story when I was helping Felix's sisters clear out the house."

"What if Kenneth tries to kill you so you won't give the story to the cops?"

"That would prove he did it."

"A bit of a sacrifice on your part."

"I'd be prepared and get out of gun range. He might nick my shoulder or—"

"Hayden thinks the killer won't use a gun next time. Both Kenneth and Anne have access to medication. You'd die by lethal injection."

Sam rubbed his cheek, actually considering this wild plan. Anne had called him a drama queen. "A needle is better," he said. "I mean, easier to defend. I'll pile on layers of clothing. When he pulls out the weapon, you ride to my rescue and catch him in the act."

"I'm the knight in shining armor?"

"At work, we get our vision through by tailoring the pitch to the client."

"Pardon me?" What did this scheme have to do with architecture?

"I'll tell Kenneth a story that fits his perception. I'd say I wanted to get his version before deciding if I'll go to the police, since I don't want to hurt Dimitri and his political career by publicly branding his mother as a criminal."

"What if the killer is Anne?"

He shoved his hands in his jeans pockets, reflecting. "I don't hate Anne. We have a history. Dimitri would find it hard if she went to jail. I'd prefer it was Kenneth."

"It's not who we want it to be, it's who we believe it is, rationally."

"Who is it, then, rationally?"

She scratched her head, willing the answer through her nails. "Supposing it's Kenneth, you could phone him tonight and say you found evidence you want to discuss with him before bringing it to the cops. Make it clear you've told no one else."

Sam glanced at his watch. "It's already ten thirty-five. I'll have to phone right away before he goes to bed. I get where you're going with this. I'll suggest we meet early, before dawn, to play squash . . ."

"This is all hypothetical, by the way," she said.

"Sure." His eyes looked too eager.

"How much time would you need before I rushed to your rescue?"

"We'll iron out those details later. You're staying over?"

"I should go home for some sleep."

"You haven't seen my basement digs yet." He reached for a crystal candlestick. "For atmosphere, how about we light a candle in this thing you tried to kill me with."

Her face burned. "Don't remind me of that. It's embarrassing."

"It kind of turned me on."

She tried to grab the candlestick. He twirled it out of her way.

"It was my fault for egging you on," he said. "I was curious to see how far you'd go."

"You and your drama queen fetish."

"Eh?"

Her fingers slid over the candlestick to his hand. They rested on his rough, warm skin. "If I stay over, I'll call Isabelle to make sure she tells no one about the story. If we do this hypothetical thing, I can't put her at risk."

"Then, I'll phone Kenneth."

"That won't accomplish anything if the murderer is Anne."

"At least, I'll be safe from lethal injection. Kenneth might offer some proof it was her."

"Fat chance. He's too clever and determined to maintain his pact with Anne and too used to playing hardball in business."

"You're right." Sam frowned.

"I could see Anne pointing the finger at him, if she was cornered."

"If nothing works with Kenneth, I'll try her tomorrow night."

"What if he warns her or the cops question her before then?"

"I doubt Anne would fall for it, anyway. She doesn't much trust me or like me."

"She talks positively about you."

"That's a sham. I'm sure now; her plan when Dimitri was born was to raise him alone. I jumped into the parenting and she resents the fact that Dimitri . . ."

". . . liked you better."

"I was the fun parent."

"You were the warm, genuine, feeling one. Dimitri sensed that, even as a child."

He stared at the floor. She loved his modesty. If he weren't so annoying, he might move beyond being merely potential. Since her divorce, she'd been wary of being hurt; Sam had been wary his entire adult life.

"Anne would believe me," she said, "if I approached her with questions before going to the cops. She thinks I trust her. I could say I'd found this story linking you, but not her, to an old crime and wanted to know what was true to see if you and I had potential. She suspects I'm interested in you."

"Are you?"

She had to keep this on track, even though she seemed to be slipping off. "I'd have to go home to get more clothes. I'd need a turtleneck sweater. A thick one. Maybe two."

"You'll find all you need in Callie's closet upstairs. That woman could shop."

"Seriously, Sam, we can't do this sting."

"Why not?"

"There must be hundreds of reasons."

"We've got all night to think them through. If we decide it's too dangerous or won't work, I won't keep my squash date."

"Or I won't keep my fitness center one."

He looked at his watch. "Time's running out for that phone call. Who's the target: Kenneth or Anne?"

Paula closed her eyes to get a better picture of the two. Wiry, muscled Anne lifted weights in her clingy workout gear. Kenneth's long, lean body lunged around a squash court; he slammed a ball. Neither image rushed to the forefront. "You might as well flip a coin."

"Good idea," Sam said.

"I was kidding."

He headed for the hall. What was he up to now?

It was fine for him to risk getting himself killed. He was doing this for his future relationship with his son. Her goal was to secure the safety of Hayden, Isabelle, and herself. If the plan backfired, it could place all of them in further danger.

The candles on the sideboard seemed to taunt: do it for Callie. That relationship was dead. In the last days, the last moments of her life, Callie had turned to Paula for help. Callie might have opened up to her sooner, before she ran out of time, if Paula were a different sort of person, a friend Callie might expect to say, "Hey, you were a kid. We all make mistakes."

Who was Paula to judge anyone's behavior when here she was in Sam's living room hatching this ridiculous plan?

He returned with a penny. "I managed to find a shiny one in the den." He held the coin between his finger and thumb.

"This is too critical to decide with a coin toss," she said.

"You call it: heads or tails." Sam flung the coin to the twelve-foot high ceiling. He hovered underneath, palms upward as the coin came spinning down.

"Heads," she said. "Kenneth was the brain who covered up the old crime. Heads has to be Kenneth."

Sam caught the penny. His head bumped Paula's as they peered at his hand clutching his forearm. She wanted the hand to stay there forever, didn't want to know. Sam's baby finger twitched. He slowly raised his hand. They stared at the image on the coin.

"It's wrong," Paula said. "The killer's the other one."

Chapter Thirty-one

Paula drove into the downtown core. She scratched her throat, which itched from Callie's turtleneck. Callie's running shoes crunched her toes, but no way would she confront a killer in the pumps she had worn to Sam's. In his basement, they had gone through every detail, over and over and over. What if there was a flaw in their premise? A C-train rushed by, only a handful of early-bird workers in its cars. The stars had abandoned the ink sky, although the church spire stretched toward the glowing half moon. *A church.* Dimitri. Her theory that a religious nut was bumping the boy's killer off, one by one. Dimitri was religious. How had they missed that? Sam's headlights shimmered in her rear view mirror. He had been so buoyed by the prospect of his son's innocence.

She crossed the C-train tracks and rifled through her purse for her cell. Was this reasonable concern or last minute panic? At the red light, she called up her saved numbers.

Detective Vincelli answered groggily. She had woken him up. Tough shit. A cop's job was to protect her.

"I'm about to do something stupid," she said.

"What?" Vincelli sounded more alert.

"You can stop me by answering certain questions."

"What stupid thing are you doing?"

A pedestrian stepped onto the street. Her car screeched to a stop. A pickup squealed behind her. She hoped Sam didn't crash into it. The pickup must have cut in.

"Dimitri and Callie were lovers for two years," she said. "Lovers confide, sometimes everything. How do we know she didn't tell him about the killing of the boy?"

"Would you please let this go? We're handling it."

"Dimitri's religious. Could Callie's confession and her dumping him have driven him over the edge, and he started popping the guilty off, first Callie, then Felix . . ."

"Do we need this speculation in the middle of the night?"

"It's early morning," she said.

"Don't approach Dimitri or any of them."

"Any of whom?"

"We'll get on the case tomorrow; today." A toilet flushed at the end of his line. "Where are you? At home? Stay inside. I'll be there in twenty minutes." Running water suggested he was washing his hands.

She stopped for a red light. The pickup was still behind her.

"Sam and I narrowed the suspects to Kenneth and Anne. Should we add Dimitri? I know my theory's wild."

Rustlings on the line might be Vincelli getting dressed. If he was rushing to her home to stop her, he must believe she was on the right track. It took dedication to leave his comfortable bed. This was his first major role in a murder case. He must be ambitious.

"We came up with a plan to draw the murderer out," she said. "It's not too dangerous. If you had to choose a murderer between Dimitri, Anne, and Kenneth, whom would you pick?"

"I'm not answering that."

"I've made my choice and am going ahead unless you give me reason not to."

She slowed for another red light. They were getting them all today, but were ahead of schedule and had plenty of time. If Vincelli didn't fall for her bluff, she was turning around before the bridge. One in two odds, with an educated guess, was good enough. One in three wasn't. If Dimitri did it, their plan was pointless and potentially cruel. The pickup was still sandwiched between her and Sam, who wouldn't welcome her cop-out. She had assured him she would be able to go through with it.

"If I was forced to choose," Vincelli said. "I would probably go with the holdback."

"The what?"

"We always withhold a piece of evidence to screen out crank calls."

"Do you get many?"

"You'd be surprised."

She was stunned he had told her this much. "What was the holdback in this case?"

Vincelli didn't answer. So he didn't want the reward enough to compromise her safety.

"There was a witness." Vincelli's voice was barely audible. "A man saw someone leave the Elbow River trail around the time of Callie's murder.

He described the suspect as a person with bright yellow hair."

Her heart-beat picked up. Bright yellow hair. "The boy . . ."

". . . in Felix's story," Vincelli said.

"You read it?"

"We believe the bad guy wore a yellow wig. Fibers were found at the site."

"A wig. Kenneth is half bald. He'd want to hide his head to not be identified."

"While I was reading the story tonight, something nagged me about the witness's statement." Vincelli's voice was stronger. "I went back to my original notes. He initially said he saw a boy leave the trail, but wasn't sure enough, so we changed it to person."

"A boy." Her heart sank to her stomach. "Dimitri." She didn't want it to be him. Although Dimitri was over thirty and hardly a boy.

"It was dark," Vincelli said. "The witness was standing a block behind the suspect and didn't get a look at the face. Dimitri's quite husky. From that vantage point, you would likely take him as man."

"Would you take Kenneth as a boy? He's thin, but so tall."

"If you're on your way to talk to him, forget it. Kenneth won't cave."

"Dimitri—"

"He doesn't know anything and might screw things up because she's his—"

"I've got to go."

"Paula, wait—"

She hung up. Vincelli had slipped. He agreed with her choice. She drove onto the bridge span, hardly believing she and Sam were right. After her hunch, they had reasoned it out. Kenneth was shrewd. During his tête-à-tête with Anne, Kenneth was the one who suggested lethal injection for future murders. He knew Anne was the killer and was cuing her into a method he felt would work better than guns, the one he would have used from the start. Anne had naturally thought of guns first, given her shooting experience with her father. If Anne was innocent in Callie's and Felix's deaths, wouldn't she have told the police about the old crime when suspicion fell on Dimitri, her son? There was also the timing of Callie's death. During their workout, Paula had mentioned Callie's phone message inviting her to lunch. She may have said things like, "I was surprised to hear from Callie after she's avoided me all summer" and "I can't phone her tonight, since I'm seeing Hayden, but will do it tomorrow night." Anne would have guessed the reason for Callie's call. She had already stolen Sam's father's gun from the shed and planned the murder, but realized she had to act before Paula returned Callie's message.

On the north side of the Bow River, Paula stopped at a light, the pickup still behind her. Or was this a different truck? Rounding the corner, she noted Sam's Acura one vehicle back. He would wait at the next block. Her cell phone rang.

"Watches synchronized?" Sam's tone was ominous. "Ready?"

"More than ever." Now that she had the confidence they were right.

"Good luck."

Small businesses, not yet open for the day, lined the fitness center's street, which seemed amazingly long as she drove past the lanes and sidewalk empty of people. No other cars; no one likely to witness a deed done in the dark. Ahead, the fitness center's church shape was a silhouette against an indigo sky. No lights shone from its windows. Even the Fit for Life sign was dark. As Paula had predicted, Anne had canceled the early morning yoga class, probably with a believable excuse, such as the plumbing was off again. The cops would need more proof than the class cancellation; it could be a coincidence.

Two buildings had a sight-line to the fitness center parking lot: a craft boutique and a coffee shop, both closed. Paula pulled into the lot and stopped in the middle, far from Anne's Honda parked by the back door. Anne trotted down the stairs. Paula gripped the steering wheel to stop her hands from shaking. Her skin burned under three layers of clothes. Anne would question her wearing leather gloves. She grabbed Callie's sports bag, startled by its heaviness. At the last minute, Sam had thrown in a crystal candlestick in case she needed it.

Anne walked briskly toward her. "Why are you parking way out here?"

"Was the yoga class canceled?"

"There was a power surge. I couldn't get the auxiliary to work. I was going to call you, but figured you were on your way. You don't look dressed for working out."

"Neither do you." Anne wore a jacket and jeans. No hug of greeting this time.

"My suit's underneath," she said. "It's damn cold this morning."

Paula hugged her jacket to her sweater, banging the sports bag to her abdomen. Anne's face was a mask in the dark. She also wore gloves, clear ones you wouldn't notice if you weren't looking. Moonlight glanced off the latex, making Anne's hands look unnaturally white. This was impossible, her friend a killer. Anne rubbed her T-shirt exposed by the open jacket. Paula jerked backward. Her sole task was to keep her distance until Sam showed up and they caught Anne with the hypodermic needle. Their word against hers, but they were two against one and had the benefit of the truth and Felix's story, which Vincelli seemed to finally take seriously.

"Did you bring that thing you found in Felix's house?" Anne asked.

"In here." Paula held up the sports bag. "It's too dark for you to read it outside. Mainly I wanted to ask you some questions."

"About Sam?"

Paula's rear grazed the car. Amazing she could feel the metal under the padding. "Like I told you over the phone, Felix's story was about him and some guy friends in university shooting a street kid."

"You said it was fiction."

"But it rang true and the other guys sounded like Kenneth and, in some ways, Sam. He was described as an architecture student. All I want to know is: was Sam involved in that mess?" Her voice trembled. Good effect. "I don't want to squeal to the cops. It was an accident and happened years ago. But I don't know if I could be involved with Sam, knowing he'd done . . . something like this."

"You wouldn't respect him?"

"I don't know. There'd be so much to think about."

"Are you really that hooked on Sam?"

"It's dumb, I know. I can't help it. He's—" The street was deserted. Sam should be appearing about now.

"I don't know anything about some boy being killed," Anne said. "You know the guys don't tell me everything." How could her voice sound so sweet?

"You and Sam were once close. You probably know him better than anyone. He doesn't let himself get close to people."

"That's Sam." Anne's hands hung by her sides. Was the needle in her jacket pocket? Paula leaned back to protect her face, her only exposed skin.

The rest of her was drenched under layers of Callie's clothes. Her heart pounded. Where the fuck was Sam?

"The Sam character in Felix's story had a father who disliked him," she said. "Nothing Sam did was ever good enough. He told me that about his dad."

"It's true." Anne edged forward. "I never liked the old man. He didn't care for me, either."

"He loved Callie."

"Everyone did." There was pain in Anne's voice. "What was so special about her?"

Paula stepped sideways. Her leg hit the rear fender. "Was Sam fat as child?"

Anne's head jerked back and forth. "What do you mean?"

"In the story, Felix said Sam's schoolmates teased him, calling him Porky Pig."

Anne flinched as though she were stabbed. It was horrible to do this. No, it wasn't. This woman had coolly murdered two friends.

"Sam's mother put him on diets," Paula said. "Is that why he exercises so much?"

Anne gazed over Paula's shoulder, at nothing. "He feels if he stops for a minute the fat will roll back on." Under her jacket, Anne was all muscle and bone. Too much muscle.

Paula's calf touched the rear bumper. She had to get around the car and have it between her and Anne when Anne pulled the needle from her pocket.

Anne stumbled toward her. Was she losing her balance? In the circle, the boy had taunted her with these same things as she pointed a gun at him. She and the others knew the guns were loaded.

"Here's what bothers me most," Paula said. "The story implied Sam fired at the boy on purpose. He couldn't stand the hurtful accusations—"

"Can you blame him?"

Anne's hand was under her jacket. Paula swung the sports bag. It hit Anne's shoulder. Anne reeled backward, fumbling with something black and large. Not a needle. Paula raised the bag for a second swing. Anne lunged toward her. The gun dug into Paula's chest. She tottered on her heels. The bag struck Anne's back, pushed Anne into her. If the gun went off, if Paula fell, she was finished. She dropped the bag and grabbed for the gun. Her hand slipped over latex. Gulping in Anne's coffee-soaked breath, she forced the muzzle to the sky.

"Don't, Anne," she said. "The cops will catch you."

"They won't know it was me." Anne twisted the muzzle toward Paula.

"They'll identify your gun."

"Felix's gun."

The muzzle pressed the rough turtleneck wool into Paula's skin. In a minute, she would be dead, shot in the neck. "They'll think Dimitri did it. He's the one they suspect."

"They'll blame Sam, thanks to Felix's story in your bag."

"I lied. The story's not there."

"What?"

Paula shoved. She staggered to the back of her car. Anne regained her balance first. She aimed the gun. The bullet noise blasted Paula's ears. She hit the pavement, clutched her calf. She tried to move. Pain burned her leg. Damp warmth seeped through her glove. Blood? She would die here like this. Leah and Erin, her daughters. Never see them again.

Anne's shaking legs were a foot away from the sports bag. She gripped the gun with both hands, to steady it. A car rumbled down the street. Sam? At last. No, an SUV cruised by. Even if Sam had missed a light, he should be here. Anne stepped closer. She planted her legs astride, knocking the sports bag. The candlestick rolled out. Paula reached for it. The crystal slithered past her fingers. Fuck. Shit. Anne was adjusting the gun to get the position right. Could Paula throw her off balance mentally again?

She stared past the muzzle to Anne's face, its features shrouded by darkness. "I lied about the story, Anne. There was no Sam character. He was working that night. You were there. I gave the story to the cops. When they find me, they'll know right away you did it."

Anne's whole body shook.

From the corner of her eye, Paula glimpsed a flash of crystal, a few feet behind her. She could grab it and whack Anne's ankles. She edged toward the candlestick, on the pavement, wincing in pain.

Anne steadied her legs. "Nice try."

"There's no story in the sports bag. Look for yourself."

"I'm not stupid enough to fall for that."

"You're not stupid, Anne, that's why I don't understand how you could do this. We're friends."

"No, we're not."

"We are."

Anne tightened her double-handed grip on the gun. "You preferred Callie. Why? You and I are more alike."

"I'm not a . . ."

"Callie got everything, even my son."

Her gaze fixed on the gun, Paula inched back. "Think of your business, Anne. You worked so hard to build it up. Don't throw it away."

"Sam stole Dimitri, too. I'm getting my son back."

"You'll lose him if you go to jail." Her fingertips brushed glass.

"I'll lose everything when you squeal to the cops."

"I won't."

"Liar. You always think you're so right."

"Not this time."

"You think you're above all of this."

"I don't."

"You think you're better than me."

Brakes squealed on the street. A car roared into the lot. Headlights zoomed straight for Paula.

Chapter Thirty-two

Through the fog, a man's words, "You killed her."

Female laughter.

Sam's voice. "You're a fucking murderer."

On the opposite side of the car, Paula's hand rested on the candlestick. Was she alive? There was no pain in her leg.

"What the fuck are you doing?" Sam said. "You're an idiot if you think you can stick this on me."

"I don't need to," Anne said. "You ran over her with your car. You killed her."

Blood oozed from Paula's calf. That meant life. One gloved hand clutched the candlestick; the other pressed the bleeding wound. Sam's car had crashed into her rear bumper. If she'd been an inch closer to Anne, he would have jammed her between the cars. She shivered. Anne must have jumped out the way. The cars concealed her from Anne and Sam. Should she let them know she was here?

"I saw you pointing the gun at her," Sam said. "She was a crumpled heap."

"Wrong, as always, Sam. I hadn't fired yet. That is, you fired a wild shot at her and jumped in your car to finish the deed. That's what the cops will deduce."

"You won't get away with that lie."

"They'll find the evidence to support it."

Paula flexed her leg. It felt normal.

Across the car, Anne laughed. "What will your son think of you now? My only regret is that having a jailbird father might wreck Dimitri's career. He and I will work on damage control."

Paula rolled onto her knees to hoist herself up. She dropped to the pavement, her head woozy. Was that a light on the street? Another vehicle?

"Get your fucking hands off of me, Sam," Anne said. "I'll say I witnessed it all. You thought you were setting me up by arranging to meet Paula here."

A car screeched into the lot. Paula curled into a ball. Not again. Footsteps on the pavement. Male voices: Sam and another man.

"No," Anne screamed. "You've got the wrong . . ."

More footsteps pounded toward Paula. A silhouette halted. She looked up at Sam.

"Paula." He tumbled on top of her, hugging, kissing, knocking the candlestick from her hand. "I can't believe it. You're alive." His warm arms enclosed her; his lips drank in her hair.

"What's happening with Anne?"

"Never mind her."

"Are the police—?"

Sam squeezed her hard to his chest. They fell to the pavement. More footsteps were rounding the rear of his car. A woman and man hovered behind Sam.

"They followed us here," he said.

Pre-dawn light lit up Isabelle's and Walter's faces.

"They were what made me late getting here," Sam said. "Almost too late. When I saw . . . I thought you were dead. All I thought of was ramming down Anne."

"I knew something was up when you called last night," Isabelle said. "I got Walter to drive to Sam's. We staked out the house."

"Why?" Paula looked at Walter. "Was that your pickup following me?"

"We were arguing about if we should cut you off," Isabelle said.

"Then you got too far ahead," Walter added.

"So, instead, they cut me off," Sam said.

Voices mumbled on the other side of Sam's car. A man's and a woman's. Angry tones. The female voice was Anne's. The man sounded like Detective Vincelli.

Sam helped Paula up to her wobbly leg. He rested his hand on the small of her back. "Walter blocked me from turning onto this street," he said. "I tried to go around the truck and almost ran down Isabelle, who'd got out to flag me down. I argued with her to let me pass and finally told them to get in and crouch in the back seat."

"We didn't want to miss the action," Isabelle said.

"I don't think the murderer-lady knew we was there," Walter said.

"She threw the gun in the front seat," Isabelle said.

"To implicate me," Sam said. "At least with Walter and Isabelle, we've plenty of witnesses against Anne."

A siren blared down the street.

"That must be the cop car Vincelli called," Sam said.

Across Sam's car, the large detective gripped Anne's upper arm. Her face was turned away.

"Vincelli phoned my cell looking for you," Sam said. "At that point, I figured we could use some backup."

Its red light whirling, the police car sped into the parking lot and stopped behind Vincelli's sedan. Two officers leapt out. Vincelli dragged Anne toward them. As he handed her over, Anne turned toward the group standing next to Sam's car. Her gaze settled on Paula. The first rays of dawn flashed across her face filled with hatred.

Paula's skin went clammy. Her vision blurred. She clung to Sam's arm.

"Paula?" Sam said through the fog. "Are you all right?"

Three hours later Paula sat in the coffee shop across the parking lot, her leg propped on a chair, a warm mug in her hand. The police had cordoned off the fitness center property to the end of the lane. Officers guarded the perimeter; the crime scene unit scoured the scene. The bullet that had grazed Paula's leg was found at the site, Vincelli told her. The paramedics said her injury was merely a flesh wound, but everyone insisted she go to hospital Emergency.

"It's a bloody shooting wound," Vincelli said. "It has to be reported through proper channels."

Vincelli had ordered Sam, Isabelle, and Walter to the station for questioning. He conceded to Paula's request that she be returned to the crime scene to watch the wrap-up of the attempt on her life. He took her statement and spent the rest of the time moving back and forth between the crime scene and coffee shop, giving her updates.

The gun Anne shot her with was registered to Felix. Presumably, Anne had taken it from his house after she murdered him, in case she had a future need.

It bugged Paula that she and Sam hadn't thought of that. Why had they assumed Anne would take Kenneth's advice to switch tactics and use a needle?

"We must have been too tired to think totally clearly," she told Vincelli.

"Obviously," he said. "Or you wouldn't have done any of it."

Two officers had gone to the hospital to relay the news to Anne's husband. Others were hauling in Kenneth and Hayden. A computer search had located an old record of an unknown body washed up from the Bow River. The details fit those known about the boy. Vincelli believed Kenneth's and Hayden's versions of the old crime were essentially true. He couldn't see Hayden being charged and suspected Kenneth would plead guilty to a lesser charge in exchange for his testimony.

"That seems fair," Paula said. "While Anne was trying to kill me, she all but admitted she shot the boy on purpose."

"Kenneth told us Felix suggested that to him a number of years ago. Kenneth dismissed it as speculation. Now he's starting to wonder if Anne manipulated them all into the original cover-up. She's a piece of work."

Now that Paula wasn't facing the muzzle of a gun, she felt sorry for Anne. She must have felt desperate, thinking her life would be ruined by that old crime. Even if Anne didn't go to jail for it, the damage to her reputation and legal fees might cost her the business and, for certain, Dimitri's respect. She was always competing with Sam about him. Part of her motive for Callie's murder seemed to be the prospect of nailing Sam for the crime and, in a weird way, getting rid of a rival for Paula's friendship. It made Paula feel responsible.

For thirty years Anne had nurtured her jealousy of Callie's charmed life. Men adored Callie. Money and successes arrived with no apparent effort on her part. Anne had worked hard to achieve less. *You and I are more alike.* What was Anne's envy of Callie but a heightened version of Paula's?

Paula brightened at the sight of Vincelli entering the coffee shop, tall, broad, dressed in a dark suit. The crowd seemed to part as he made his way toward her. He took his seat across the table.

She shifted her bandaged leg on the chair to make it more comfortable. There had been something she wanted to ask. She should have been jotting notes.

"Oh yeah," she said. "Callie wanted to make amends to the family of the boy they shot. Can your forensics guy find the nephew's website Felix located in his Internet search?"

"If he can't, we'll get the boy's name from his long ago doctor friend. Kenneth supplied the doctor's name. He's in Africa now. I have a hunch he'll speak to the relatives, as Callie wanted."

Vincelli set his large hands on the table, fingers splayed. "I owe you an apology. It was unprofessional to give you confidential details, especially ones you would use to confront Anne."

"You didn't know what I was up to."

"I had a general idea. I also knew we'd never solve this if I didn't send you in. Greed got the better of me."

"Between the lot of us, we're racking up the Seven Deadlies today."

"My superiors will be giving me a well-deserved knuckle rap."

"I'm not sure you have any superiors." She liked watching the color rise up his face.

After Vincelli left, Hayden showed up. She hoisted herself from the chair to greet him. From the circles under his eyes, she guessed he hadn't slept much more than she did last night.

"I told the cops everything," he said. "I botched it by not telling them before."

"We've all botched something in this case."

"My non-action almost got you killed."

"My action was more to blame."

"I sent you running to Sam, who got to play the hero."

"Kind of a bumbling one." She shifted her weight to her uninjured leg.

"So, this is good-bye." His eyes looked resigned, almost serene. "We may run into each other on occasion. Calgary's still, in many ways, a small town."

"I'm sure we can handle it," she said. "We're mature adults. At least, you are."

"Don't be in a hurry to grow up. It's not all it's cracked up to be."

Hayden flashed his self-deprecating smile and hugged her with his big strong warm arms. She missed him already.

He left her alone with her coffee. Vincelli returned to say he was ready to drive her home. Outside, the crime scene unit was packing up. Officers were taking down the yellow tape.

She hobbled to the coffee shop entrance and stopped. "I forgot all about calling work."

"Already done." Vincelli opened the door for her. "Your boss didn't sound happy about your taking off the rest of the week. He said he might call Isabelle to start work earlier than planned. He seems to think she'll be a help."

"She may turn out to be sharper than we think." Paula blinked in the sunlight. A stout man limped toward them. Detective Novak, Vincelli's partner she hadn't seen since that day they interviewed her. She shook his hand. "I thought you were on sick leave."

"I couldn't miss the endgame," he said.

"Is this really the end?"

"For you it is. We've got to collect the evidence for the trial. That's a massive job. You should stop by the station, some time. We'll show you the ropes."

"I'd like that."

Novak looked at her cut-off pants and bandaged calf. He patted his thigh. "You and I have something in common, except my injury was caused by a skittish horse; yours was in the line of duty."

"Do I get a medal or commendation?"

"We're working on it."

Novak went to speak with the officers at the site. Vincelli led her to his sedan. They drove to the bridge and crossed the river to downtown. Vincelli sped through the light mid-morning traffic. With his dark hair growing in and rough stubble shaved, he was a handsome young man. Too bad she wasn't twenty years younger, not for him but for an organization like the cops. Grueling and frustrating as it was, it must feel like meaningful work. Fifty-two was too old to join the force. At Vincelli's age, she wouldn't have dreamed of it. If she could go back . . . well, she couldn't go back and ought to be grateful she came through this experience alive.

High-rise towers merged into the gray zone. Vincelli steered onto 9th Avenue. They passed her office building, where Nils would be slogging through claim files.

"It will be hard to return to my dull insurance job," she said.

"What I've seen of insurance isn't dull," he said. "Arson. Break and enter. I investigated a hit-and-run that turned out to be homicide in disguise. That's what inspired me to apply to Major Crimes."

"I've got a hit-and-run to tackle tomorrow. I doubt it will turn out to be as exciting as yours."

"The adjuster in that homicide-hit-and-run wasn't too swift off the mark. A brighter light on the insurance investigation side would have helped."

They crossed the Elbow River Bridge, turned onto 8th Street and stopped behind the line of cars waiting for the train to pass.

Vincelli turned toward her. "The next insurance-related case that comes up in Major Crimes, I'll get the company to transfer the adjusting to you."

"They won't do that for a case that's already assigned."

"They will when I explain your help would boost our chance of proving crime or fraud that saves them from paying a million bucks. One thing I know about insurance firms: they think with their wallets."

"A few claims like that might boost my spirit for the job." Once word got around that she had expertly settled a few, intriguing work might pour into Nils's little adjusting firm. A niche like this would give them a chance against giants.

"Besides," Vincelli said. "How could your work be boring with Isabelle around?"

The train chugged to a stop and began to reverse.

Vincelli drummed the steering wheel. "Do you realize your neighborhood is almost surrounded by railroad tracks?"

"That's how we like it," she said. "Keeps out the riff-raff." For all she knew, one of the homeless men she saw regularly on this street had been the person who witnessed Anne leaving the murder site. She would rather live here than in an enclave protected from city life.

The barriers lifted. They bumped over the tracks to the Elbow pathway entrance bathed in sun. Would she ever pass this spot without thinking of Callie's death? They turned onto her street and parked in front of Walter's now infamous pickup truck. He waved from his front porch.

"I'll walk you to your door," Vincelli said.

"Now that the bad guy's in jail, I can walk there alone."

"I thought you might like protection from your neighbor."

Walter was making his way down the stairs. She said good-bye to Vincelli, whom she should really start thinking of as Mike, and joined Walter on the sidewalk.

"Was that the cop in the car?" he said. "What happened after they dragged me to the station? They took my fingerprints." He held up his boney hands.

He just wanted a little excitement, like her. From Anne's and Vincelli's perspectives, Paula had been as meddling as Walter. She would probably find him an irritation tomorrow, but why not go with the mellow mood?

"It's supposed to stay warm this afternoon," she said. "I need a nap first, but how about around three o'clock, we break open some cold ones on the porch and I'll tell you all about it."

"Sure thing." He winked at her. "Which of the fellows are you going with? Your old boyfriend or Sam?"

Irritation might return before tomorrow. She opened her gate and crunched over leaves up the stairs. The newspaper lodged between her front doors forecast arctic air moving in. Inside, she pulled off Callie's running shoes. Something felt missing. She sniffed. No fresh paint smell. Her next moving-in task would be to shop for paintings that would turn this place into her home. Also missing were Isabelle's clothes and CDs scattered throughout her house. Sam must have already brought her by to collect them on their way to Erin's house. Well, he did have a motive to get that done, since Paula had asked him to spend the night.

While the coffee brewed, she slumped in her kitchen chair. The sun was passing to the front of the house, but remnants of light shone on her crabapple tree, naked aside from the bitter fruit the birds and squirrels would peck on during the winter. The phone rang. She jumped to answer, wincing from the pressure on her leg.

It was wonderful to hear her daughter Leah's voice. "Isabelle, Erin, and I were thinking of taking you out to dinner tonight."

"That's really thoughtful of you all."

"We want to get the whole dirt."

Paula suggested they arrive at six o'clock to watch the news, giving them plenty of time for dinner before Sam arrived.

He was waiting when Leah pulled the car to a stop at the Elbow pathway entrance now shadowed by dark gray sky. Paula introduced Sam to her daughters and left them to chat while she opened the trunk. She took out the cheese plate she had got from the restaurant and the box of Callie's ashes.

"Can't I go with you to scatter them?" Isabelle said.

"You're doing your scattering with Dimitri on the mountain top. One per person is enough." Kenneth would bury his share of the cremains in the ground. Callie's daughter would toss her fifth to the sky. Callie's son would sculpt his into art. It was a bit weird, but Paula thought Callie would like it.

Sam, Leah, and Erin were laughing.

"What's so funny?" she asked.

"Nothing," they said.

She hugged her three girls good-bye. "I love you," she told each one.

"Even me?" Isabelle beamed.

"Even you."

Isabelle and Erin hopped into the car. Leah halted at the driver's door, glanced at Sam and gave Paula a thumbs-up.

"What was the joke?" Paula asked Sam as they entered the trail.

"I'm not telling," he said. "No way am I getting in the middle of three women."

"Did you bring everything?"

He held up his shopping bag.

The trees on the pathway still held onto their leaves. Their silhouettes swayed above the gorge. Twenty feet below the river rushed over rocks. Paula and Sam stopped by the slope where Callie's body was found.

"It's flat at the top," Sam said.

They walked up the hill and smoothed the blanket he had brought on the grass beside the trail. Paula set the cheese plate and wine glasses on it.

Sam took out the crystal candlestick. "Why did you want this?"

"Its mate saved my life. If I hadn't been crawling back to reach it you'd have driven right into me."

"I remembered a candle." He wedged it into the candlestick.

In the dark, the box containing Callie's ashes looked like it was painted shades of gray, not green and blue. Paula carried it to the ledge. "Should we say something?"

"Your call." Sam echoed his words from the coin toss.

Their scheme had worked out, just not exactly as planned. She hadn't planned for this moment, either. A gust cooled her arms. In the morning, frost would coat the grass, but this evening was balmy enough for their little wake.

Staring at the box, she cleared her throat. "Callie, I hope you're at rest. I hope I did right by you in the end. I hope—" Her voice cracked.

Sam's shoulder brushed against hers. Candle light flickered across his face. He was far away, immersed in his own thoughts. The box squeaked as she opened the lid. A warm breeze caressed her cheek. Strange, changing weather they were having this night.

Paula held the box out to the gorge. She turned it upside down. Callie's ashes swirled into a cloud falling into the river. A breeze blew some particles back. The candle flame sucked them in. They shimmered pink, gold, red, mauve. Colors danced in the flame. They faded and were gone.

Acknowledgements

Twenty years ago I took up writing. Many people contributed to this journey to publication. I thank you all. I especially thank:

Jean Humphreys, Stephen Humphreys, Shaun Hunter, Marilyn Letts, Steven Owad, and Bernice Pyke, who read drafts of the manuscript and provided thoughtful comments and encouragement for the book.

Lawrence Hill and the Booming Ground online mentorship program, for taking the story to another level.

My writing communities at the Alexandra Writers' Centre Society, Mystery Writers INK, and the Writers Guild of Alberta; AWCS instructors Eileen Coughlan and Fred Stenson; Steven Galloway and the Sage Hill Writing Experience.

The Calgary Police Service Citizens' Police Academy and RCMP Sergeant Patrick Webb, for advice on crime and police procedure. Any errors are mine.

Ruth Linka and TouchWood Editions, for giving me this chance.

My editor, Frances Thorsen, owner of Chronicles of Crime bookstore in Victoria, BC, and a great person to work with. My copy editor Lenore Hietkamp. Promotion experts Tara Saracuse at TouchWood and Susan Toy in Alberta.

Leslie Gavel, Pamela McDowell, and Lianne DesBrisay, for helping me through the lean writing times, with laughs.

My parents, Murray and Emilie Calder. I wish you were still here. My siblings Moira, Lorna, Lynn, and Bruce.

Deborah Donnelly, for youthful adventures shared.

Finally, my three men: my husband, Will Arnold, and our sons, Dan and Matt, who lived with the quirks of a writer wife/mom and managed to thrive. Much love. You made the journey worthwhile.

SUSAN CALDER is a member of Mystery Writers INK and the Writers Guild of Alberta. She has a degree in Urban Studies from Concordia University. Susan's poems and short stories have been published in *The Prairie Journal*, *Alberta Views*, *Other Voices*, and the *Silver Boomers Anthology*. She teaches writing at the Alexandra Writers' Centre in Calgary. *Deadly Fall* is her first novel.